'*Far from here in the la... of Narnia there lives an aged king. He has no heir because his only son was stolen from him many years ago and no one in Narnia knows where that prince went or whether he is alive. But he is. I lay on you this command, that you seek this lost prince until either you have found him and brought him to his father's house, or else died in the attempt, or else gone back into your own world.*'

Thus Aslan sends Jill Pole and Eustace Scrubb, unhappy pupils at a school called Experiment House, off on a journey which takes them out of Narnia into the ruined city of the ancient giants. Their companion is a charmingly doleful Marsh-wiggle called Puddleglum and their enemies include the Green Witch and the giants of Harfang, whose cook has a book with a recipe beginning: '*MAN. This elegant little biped has long been valued as a delicacy.*'

Several times, through laziness or tiredness or magic enchantments, they forget Aslan's instructions and nearly muff the whole business, but in the end they find their Prince, cut him loose from the silver chair, and together fight their way back to Narnia, and then back to the school, where they find they've gained the strength and confidence to defeat an entire army of bullies.

A MAP OF THE
WILD LANDS
OF THE NORTH

LANTERN
WASTE

GREAT RIVER

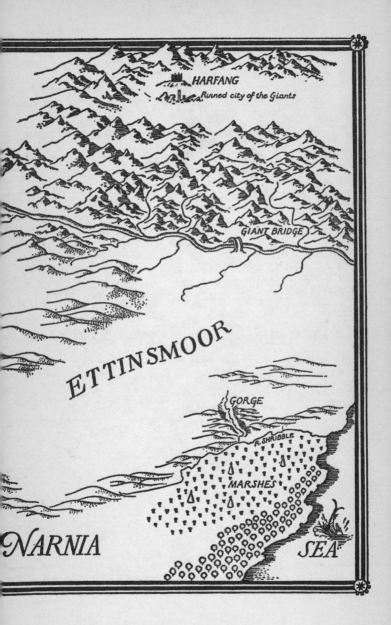

THE SILVER CHAIR

A Story for Children

BY

C. S. LEWIS

ILLUSTRATED BY PAULINE BAYNES

PENGUIN BOOKS

Penguin Books Ltd, Harmondsworth, Middlesex, England
Penguin Books Australia Ltd, Ringwood, Victoria, Australia

—

First published by Geoffrey Bles 1953
Published in Puffin Books 1965
Reprinted 1966, 1967, 1968, 1970 (twice), 1971, 1972

—

Copyright © the Estate of C. S. Lewis, 1953

—

Made and printed in Great Britain
by Richard Clay (The Chaucer Press) Ltd,
Bungay, Suffolk
Set in Monotype Garamond

TO
NICHOLAS HARDIE

CONTENTS

1	*Behind the Gym*	11
2	*Jill is Given a Task*	24
3	*The Sailing of the King*	35
4	*A Parliament of Owls*	48
5	*Puddleglum*	60
6	*The Wild Waste Lands of the North*	72
7	*The Hill of the Strange Trenches*	86
8	*The House of Harfang*	98
9	*How They Discovered Something Worth Knowing*	111
10	*Travels Without the Sun*	123
11	*In the Dark Castle*	136
12	*The Queen of Underland*	148
13	*Underland Without the Queen*	160
14	*The Bottom of the World*	172
15	*The Disappearance of Jill*	183
16	*The Healing of Harms*	194

CHAPTER I

BEHIND THE GYM

IT was a dull autumn day and Jill Pole was crying behind the gym.

She was crying because they had been bullying her. This is not going to be a school story, so I shall say as little as possible about Jill's school, which is not a pleasant subject. It was 'Co-educational,' a school for both boys and girls, what used to be called a 'mixed' school; some said it was not nearly so mixed as the minds of the people who ran it. These people had the idea that boys and girls should be allowed to do what they liked. And unfortunately what ten or fifteen of the biggest boys and girls liked best was bullying the others. All sorts of things, horrid things, went on which at an ordinary school would have been found out and stopped in half a term; but at this school they weren't. Or even if they were, the people who did them were not expelled or punished. The Head said they were interesting psychological cases and sent for them and talked to them for hours. And if you knew the right sort of things to say to the Head, the main result was that you became rather a favourite than otherwise.

That was why Jill Pole was crying on that dull autumn day on the damp little path which runs between the back of the gym and the shrubbery. And she hadn't nearly finished her cry when a boy came round the corner of the gym whistling, with his hands in his pockets. He nearly ran into her.

'Can't you look where you're going?' said Jill Pole.

'All *right*,' said the boy, 'you needn't start –' and then he noticed her face. 'I say, Pole,' he said, 'what's up?'

Jill only made faces; the sort you make when you're trying to say something but find that if you speak you'll start crying again.

'It's *Them*, I suppose – as usual,' said the boy grimly, digging his hands farther into his pockets.

Jill nodded. There was no need for her to say anything, even if she could have said it. They both knew.

'Now, look here,' said the boy, 'there's no good us all –'

He meant well, but he *did* talk rather like someone beginning a lecture. Jill suddenly flew into a temper (which is quite a likely thing to happen if you have been interrupted in a cry).

'Oh, go away and mind your own business,' she said. 'Nobody asked you to come barging in, did they? And you're a nice person to start telling us what we all ought to do, aren't you? I suppose you mean we ought to spend all our time sucking up to Them, and currying favour, and dancing attendance on Them like you do.'

'Oh, Lor!' said the boy, sitting down on the grassy bank at the edge of the shrubbery and very quickly getting up again because the grass was soaking wet. His name unfortunately was Eustace Scrubb, but he wasn't a bad sort.

'Pole!' he said. 'Is that fair? Have I been doing anything of the sort this term? Didn't I stand up to Carter about the rabbit? And didn't I keep the secret about Spivvins – under torture too? And didn't I –'

'I d-don't know and I don't care,' sobbed Jill.

Scrubb saw that she wasn't quite herself yet and very

sensibly offered her a peppermint. He had one too.
Presently Jill began to see things in a clearer light.

'I'm sorry, Scrubb,' she said presently. 'I wasn't fair.
You have done all that – this term.'

'Then wash out last term if you can,' said Eustace.
'I was a different chap then. I was – gosh! what a little
tick I was.'

'Well, honestly, you were,' said Jill.

'You think there has been a change, then?' said
Eustace.

'It's not only me,' said Jill. 'Everyone's been saying
so. *They*'ve noticed it. Eleanor Blakiston heard Adela
Pennyfather talking about it in our changing room yesterday. She said, "Someone's got hold of that Scrubb kid.
He's quite unmanageable this term. We shall have to
attend to *him* next."'

Eustace gave a shudder. Everyone at Experiment
House knew what it was like being 'attended to' by
Them.

Both children were quiet for a moment. The drops
dripped off the laurel leaves.

'Why were you so different last term?' said Jill
presently.

'A lot of queer things happened to me in the hols,'
said Eustace mysteriously.

'What sort of things?' asked Jill.

Eustace didn't say anything for quite a long time.
Then he said:

'Look here, Pole, you and I hate this place about as
much as anybody can hate anything, don't we?'

'I know I do,' said Jill.

'Then I really think I can trust you.'

'Dam' good of you,' said Jill.

'Yes, but this is a really terrific secret. Pole, I say, are you good at believing things? I mean things that everyone here would laugh at?'

'I've never had the chance,' said Jill, 'but I think I would be.'

'Could you believe me if I said I'd been right out of the world – outside this world – last hols?'

'I wouldn't know what you meant.'

'Well, don't let's bother about worlds then. Supposing I told you I'd been in a place where animals can talk and where there are – er – enchantments and dragons – and – well, all the sorts of things you have in fairy-tales.' Scrubb felt terribly awkward as he said this and got red in the face.

'How did you get there?' said Jill. She also felt curiously shy.

'The only way you can – by Magic,' said Eustace almost in a whisper. 'I was with two cousins of mine. We were just – whisked away. They'd been there before.'

Now that they were talking in whispers Jill somehow felt it easier to believe. Then suddenly a horrible suspicion came over her and she said (so fiercely that for the moment she looked like a tigress):

'If I find you've been pulling my leg I'll never speak to you again; never, never, never.'

'I'm not,' said Eustace. 'I swear I'm not. I swear by – by everything.'

(When I was at school one would have said, 'I swear by the Bible.' But Bibles were not encouraged at Experiment House.)

'All right,' said Jill, 'I'll believe you.'

'And tell nobody?'

'What do you take me for?'

They were very excited as they said this. But when they had said it and Jill looked round and saw the dull autumn sky and heard the drip off the leaves and thought of all the hopelessness of Experiment House (it was a thirteen-week term and there were still eleven weeks to come) she said:

'But after all, what's the good? We're not there: we're here. And we jolly well can't get *there*. Or can we?'

'That's what I've been wondering,' said Eustace. 'When we came back from That Place, Someone said that the two Pevensie kids (that's my two cousins) could never go there again. It was their third time, you see. I suppose they've had their share. But he never said I couldn't. Surely he would have said so, unless he meant that I was to get back? And I can't help wondering, can we – could we –?'

'Do you mean, do something to make it happen?'

Eustace nodded.

'You mean we might draw a circle on the ground – and write things in queer letters in it – and stand inside it – and recite charms and spells?'

'Well,' said Eustace after he had thought hard for a bit. 'I believe that was the sort of thing I was thinking of, though I never did it. But now that it comes to the point, I've an idea that all those circles and things are rather rot. I don't think he'd like them. It would look as if we thought we could make him do things. But really, we can only ask him.'

'Who is this person you keep on talking about?'

'They call him Aslan in That Place,' said Eustace.

'What a curious name!'

'Not half so curious as himself,' said Eustace solemnly. 'But let's get on. It can't do any harm, just asking. Let's stand side by side, like this. And we'll hold out our arms in front of us with the palms down: like they did in Ramandu's island –'

'Whose island?'

'I'll tell you about that another time. And he might like us to face the east. Let's see, where is the east?'

'I don't know,' said Jill.

'It's an extraordinary thing about girls that they never know the points of the compass,' said Eustace.

'You don't know either,' said Jill indignantly.

'Yes I do, if only you didn't keep on interrupting. I've got it now. That's the east, facing up into the laurels. Now, will you say the words after me?'

'What words?' asked Jill.

'The words I'm going to say, of course,' answered Eustace. 'Now –'

And he began, 'Aslan, Aslan, Aslan!'

'Aslan, Aslan, Aslan,' repeated Jill.

'Please let us two go into –'

At that moment a voice from the other side of the gym was heard shouting out, 'Pole? Yes. I know where she is. She's blubbing behind the gym. Shall I fetch her out?'

Jill and Eustace gave one glance at each other, dived under the laurels, and began scrambling up the steep, earthy slope of the shrubbery at a speed which did them great credit. (Owing to the curious methods of teaching at Experiment House, one did not learn much French or Maths or Latin or things of that sort; but one did learn a lot about getting away quickly and quietly when They were looking for one.)

After about a minute's scramble they stopped to listen, and knew by the noises they heard that they were being followed.

'If only the door was open again!' said Scrubb as they went on, and Jill nodded. For at the top of the shrubbery was a high stone wall and in that wall a door by which you could get out on to open moor. This door was nearly always locked. But there had been times when people had found it open; or perhaps there had been only one time. But you may imagine how the memory of even one time kept people hoping, and trying the door; for if it should happen to be unlocked it would be a splendid way of getting outside the school grounds without being seen.

Jill and Eustace, now both very hot and very grubby from going along bent almost double under the laurels, panted up to the wall. And there was the door, shut as usual.

'It's sure to be no good,' said Eustace with his hand on the handle; and then, 'O-o-oh. By Gum!!' For the handle turned and the door opened.

A moment before, both of them had meant to get through that doorway in double quick time, if by any chance the door was not locked. But when the door

actually opened, they both stood stock still. For what they saw was quite different from what they had expected.

They had expected to see the grey, heathery slope of the moor going up and up to join the dull autumn sky. Instead, a blaze of sunshine met them. It poured through the doorway as the light of a June day pours into a garage when you open the door. It made the drops of water on the grass glitter like beads and showed up the dirtiness of Jill's tear-stained face. And the sunlight was coming from what certainly did look like a different world – what they could see of it. They saw smooth turf, smoother and brighter than Jill had ever seen before, and blue sky, and, darting to and fro, things so bright that they might have been jewels or huge butterflies.

Although she had been longing for something like this, Jill felt frightened. She looked at Scrubb's face and saw that he was frightened too.

'Come on, Pole,' he said in a breathless voice.

'Can we get back? Is it safe?' asked Jill.

At that moment a voice shouted from behind, a mean, spiteful little voice. 'Now then, Pole,' it squeaked. 'Everyone knows you're there. Down you come.' It was the voice of Edith Jackle, not one of Them herself but one of their hangers-on and tale-bearers.

'Quick!' said Scrubb. 'Here. Hold hands. We mustn't get separated.' And before she quite knew what was happening, he had grabbed her hand and pulled her through the door, out of the school grounds, out of England, out of our whole world into That Place.

The sound of Edith Jackle's voice stopped as suddenly as the voice on the radio when it is switched off. Instantly there was a quite different sound all about them. It came from those bright things overhead, which now turned out to be birds. They were making a riotous noise, but it was much more like music – rather advanced music which you don't quite take in at the first hearing – than birds' songs ever are in our world. Yet, in spite of the singing, there was a sort of background of immense silence. That silence, combined with the freshness of the air, made Jill think they must be on the top of a very high mountain.

Scrubb still had her by the hand and they were walking forward, staring about them on every side. Jill saw that huge trees, rather like cedars but bigger, grew in every direction. But as they did not grow close together, and as there was no undergrowth, this did not prevent one from seeing a long way into the forest to left and right. And as far as Jill's eye could reach, it was all the same – level turf, darting birds with yellow, or dragonfly

blue, or rainbow plumage, blue shadows, and emptiness. There was not a breath of wind in that cool, bright air. It was a very lonely forest.

Right ahead there were no trees: only blue sky. They went straight on without speaking till suddenly Jill heard Scrubb say, 'Look out!' and felt herself jerked back. They were at the very edge of a cliff.

Jill was one of those lucky people who have a good head for heights. She didn't mind in the least standing on the edge of a precipice. She was rather annoyed with Scrubb for pulling her back – 'just as if I was a kid', she said – and she wrenched her hand out of his. When she saw how very white he had turned, she despised him.

'What's the matter?' she said. And to show that she was not afraid, she stood very near the edge indeed; in fact, a good deal nearer than even she liked. Then she looked down.

She now realized that Scrubb had some excuse for looking white, for no cliff in our world is to be compared with this. Imagine yourself at the top of the very highest cliff you know. And imagine yourself looking down to the very bottom. And then imagine that the precipice goes on below that, as far again, ten times as far, twenty times as far. And when you've looked down all that distance imagine little white things that might, at first glance, be mistaken for sheep, but presently you realize that they are clouds – not little wreaths of mist but the enormous white, puffy clouds which are themselves as big as most mountains. And at last, in between those clouds, you get your first glimpse of the real bottom, so far away that you can't make out whether it's field or wood, or land or water: farther below those clouds than you are above them.

Jill stared at it. Then she thought that perhaps, after all, she would step back a foot or so from the edge; but she didn't like to for fear of what Scrubb would think. Then she suddenly decided that she didn't care what he thought, and that she would jolly well get away from that horrible edge and never laugh at anyone for not liking heights again. But when she tried to move, she found she couldn't. Her legs seemed to have turned into putty. Everything was swimming before her eyes.

'What are you doing, Pole? Come back - blithering little idiot!' shouted Scrubb. But his voice seemed to be coming from a long way off. She felt him grabbing at her. But by now she had no control over her own arms and legs. There was a moment's struggling on the cliff edge. Jill was too frightened and dizzy to know quite what she was doing, but two things she remembered as long as she lived (they often came back to her in dreams). One was that she had wrenched herself free of Scrubb's clutches; the other was that, at the same moment, Scrubb himself, with a terrified scream, had lost his balance and gone hurtling to the depths.

Fortunately, she was given no time to think over what she had done. Some huge, brightly coloured animal had rushed to the edge of the cliff. It was lying down, leaning over, and (this was the odd thing) blowing. Not roaring or snorting, but just blowing from its wide-opened mouth; blowing out as steadily as a vacuum cleaner sucks in. Jill was lying so close to the creature that she could feel the breath vibrating steadily through its body. She was lying still because she couldn't get up. She was nearly fainting: indeed, she wished she could really faint, but faints don't come for the asking. At last she saw, far away below her, a tiny black speck floating away from the cliff and slightly upwards. As it rose, it also got farther away. By the time it was nearly on a level with the cliff-top it was so far off that she lost sight of it. It was obviously moving away from them at a great speed. Jill couldn't help thinking that the creature at her side was blowing it away.

So she turned and looked at the creature. It was a lion.

CHAPTER 2

JILL IS GIVEN A TASK

Without a glance at Jill the lion rose to its feet and gave one last blow. Then, as if satisfied with its work, it turned and stalked slowly away, back into the forest.

'It must be a dream, it must, it must,' said Jill to herself. 'I'll wake up in a moment.' But it wasn't, and she didn't.

'I do wish we'd never come to this dreadful place,' said Jill. 'I don't believe Scrubb knew any more about it than I do. Or if he did, he had no business to bring me here without warning me what it was like. It's not my fault he fell over that cliff. If he'd left me alone we should both be all right.' Then she remembered again the scream that Scrubb had given when he fell, and burst into tears.

Crying is all right in its way while it lasts. But you have to stop sooner or later, and then you still have to decide what to do. When Jill stopped, she found she was dreadfully thirsty. She had been lying face downward, and now she sat up. The birds had ceased singing and there was perfect silence except for one small, persistent sound, which seemed to come a good distance away. She listened carefully, and felt almost sure it was the sound of running water.

Jill got up and looked round her very carefully. There was no sign of the lion; but there were so many trees about that it might easily be quite close without her seeing it. For all she knew, there might be several lions. But her thirst was very bad now, and she plucked up her courage

to go and look for that running water. She went on tip-
toes, stealing cautiously from tree to tree, and stopping to
peer round her at every step.

The wood was so still that it was not difficult to
decide where the sound was coming from. It grew clearer
every moment and, sooner than she expected, she came
to an open glade and saw the stream, bright as glass,
running across the turf a stone's throw away from her.
But although the sight of the water made her feel ten
times thirstier than before, she didn't rush forward and

drink. She stood as still as if she had been turned into
stone, with her mouth wide open. And she had a very
good reason; just on this side of the stream lay the lion.

It lay with its head raised and its two fore-paws out
in front of it, like the lions in Trafalgar Square. She
knew at once that it had seen her, for its eyes looked
straight into hers for a moment and then turned away – as
if it knew her quite well and didn't think much of her.

'If I run away, it'll be after me in a moment,' thought
Jill. 'And if I go on, I shall run straight into its mouth.'
Anyway, she couldn't have moved if she had tried, and

she couldn't take her eyes off it. How long this lasted, she could not be sure; it seemed like hours. And the thirst became so bad that she almost felt she would not mind being eaten by the lion if only she could be sure of getting a mouthful of water first.

'If you're thirsty, you may drink.'

They were the first words she had heard since Scrubb had spoken to her on the edge of the cliff. For a second she stared here and there, wondering who had spoken. Then the voice said again, 'If you are thirsty, come and drink,' and of course she remembered what Scrubb had said about animals talking in that other world, and realized that it was the lion speaking. Anyway, she had seen its lips move this time, and the voice was not like a man's. It was deeper, wilder, and stronger; a sort of heavy, golden voice. It did not make her any less frightened than she had been before, but it made her frightened in rather a different way.

'Are you not thirsty?' said the Lion.

'I'm *dying* of thirst,' said Jill.

'Then drink,' said the Lion.

'May I – could I – would you mind going away while I do?' said Jill.

The Lion answered this only by a look and a very low growl. And as Jill gazed at its motionless bulk, she realized that she might as well have asked the whole mountain to move aside for her convenience.

The delicious rippling noise of the stream was driving her nearly frantic.

'Will you promise not to – do anything to me, if I do come?' said Jill.

'I make no promise,' said the Lion.

Jill was so thirsty now that, without noticing it, she had come a step nearer.

'*Do* you eat girls?' she said.

'I have swallowed up girls and boys, women and men, kings and emperors, cities and realms,' said the Lion. It didn't say this as if it were boasting, nor as if it were sorry, nor as if it were angry. It just said it.

'I daren't come and drink,' said Jill.

'Then you will die of thirst,' said the Lion.

'Oh dear!' said Jill, coming another step nearer. 'I suppose I must go and look for another stream then.'

'There is no other stream,' said the Lion.

It never occurred to Jill to disbelieve the Lion – no one who had seen his stern face could do that – and her mind suddenly made itself up. It was the worst thing she had ever had to do, but she went forward to the stream, knelt down, and began scooping up water in her hand. It was the coldest, most refreshing water she had ever tasted. You didn't need to drink much of it, for it quenched your thirst at once. Before she tasted it she had been intending to make a dash away from the Lion the moment she had finished. Now, she realized that this would be on the whole the most dangerous thing of all. She got up and stood there with her lips still wet from drinking.

'Come here,' said the Lion. And she had to. She was almost between its front paws now, looking straight into its face. But she couldn't stand that for long; she dropped her eyes.

'Human Child,' said the Lion. 'Where is the Boy?'

'He fell over the cliff,' said Jill, and added, 'Sir.'

She didn't know what else to call him, and it sounded cheek to call him nothing.

'How did he come to do that, Human Child?'

'He was trying to stop me from falling, Sir.'

'Why were you so near the edge, Human Child?'

'I was showing off, Sir.'

'That is a very good answer, Human Child. Do so no more. And now' (here for the first time the Lion's face became a little less stern) 'the Boy is safe. I have blown him to Narnia. But your task will be the harder because of what you have done.'

'Please, what task, Sir?' said Jill.

'The task for which I called you and him here out of your own world.'

This puzzled Jill very much. 'It's mistaking me for someone else,' she thought. She didn't dare to tell the Lion this, though she felt things would get into a dreadful muddle unless she did.

'Speak your thought, Human Child,' said the Lion.

'I was wondering – I mean – could there be some mistake? Because nobody called me and Scrubb, you know. It was we who asked to come here. Scrubb said we were to call to – to Somebody – it was a name I wouldn't know – and perhaps the Somebody would let us in. And we did, and then we found the door open.'

'You would not have called to me unless I had been calling to you,' said the Lion.

'Then you are Somebody, Sir?' said Jill.

'I am. And now hear your task. Far from here in the land of Narnia there lives an aged king who is sad because he has no prince of his blood to be king after him. He has no heir because his only son was stolen from him many years ago, and no one in Narnia knows where that prince went or whether he is still alive. But he is. I lay on you this command, that you seek this lost prince until either you have found him and brought him to his father's house, or else died in the attempt, or else gone back into your own world.'

'How, please?' said Jill.

'I will tell you, Child,' said the Lion. 'These are the signs by which I will guide you in your quest. First; as soon as the Boy Eustace sets foot in Narnia, he will meet an old and dear friend. He must greet that friend at once; if he does, you will both have good help. Second; you must journey out of Narnia to the north till you come to the ruined city of the ancient giants. Third; you shall find a writing on a stone in that ruined city, and you must do what the writing tells you. Fourth; you will know the lost prince (if you find him) by this, that he will be the first person you have met in your travels who will ask you to do something in my name, in the name of Aslan.'

As the Lion seemed to have finished, Jill thought she should say something. So she said, 'Thank you very much. I see.'

'Child,' said Aslan, in a gentler voice than he had yet used, 'perhaps you do not see quite as well as you think. But the first step is to remember. Repeat to me, in order, the four signs.'

Jill tried, and didn't get them quite right. So the Lion corrected her, and made her repeat them again and again till she could say them perfectly. He was very patient over this, so that, when it was done, Jill plucked up courage to ask:

'Please, how am I to get to Narnia?'

'On my breath,' said the Lion. 'I will blow you into the west of the world as I blew Eustace.'

'Shall I catch him in time to tell him the first sign? But I suppose it won't matter. If he sees an old friend, he's sure to go and speak to him, isn't he?'

'You will have no time to spare,' said the Lion. 'That is why I must send you at once. Come. Walk before me to the edge of the cliff.'

Jill remembered very well that if there was no time to spare, that was her own fault. 'If I hadn't made such a fool of myself, Scrubb and I would have been going together. And he'd have heard all the instructions as well as me,' she thought. So she did as she was told. It was very alarming walking back to the edge of the cliff, especially as the Lion did not walk with her but behind her – making no noise on his soft paws.

But long before she had got anywhere near the edge, the voice behind her said, 'Stand still. In a moment I will blow. But, first, remember, remember, remember the signs. Say them to yourself when you wake in the morning and when you lie down at night, and when you wake in the middle of the night. And whatever strange things may happen to you, let nothing turn your mind from following the signs. And secondly, I give you a warning. Here on the mountain I have spoken to you clearly: I will not often do so down in Narnia. Here on the mountain, the air is clear and your mind is clear; as you drop down into Narnia, the air will thicken. Take great care that it does not confuse your mind. And the signs which you have learned here will not look at all as you expect them to look, when you meet them there. That is why it is so

important to know them by heart and pay no attention
to appearances. Remember the signs and believe the
signs. Nothing else matters. And now, daughter of Eve,
farewell –'

The voice had been growing softer towards the end
of this speech and now it faded away altogether. Jill
looked behind her. To her astonishment she saw the
cliff already more than a hundred yards behind her,
and the Lion himself a speck of bright gold on the edge
of it. She had been setting her teeth and clenching her
fists for a terrible blast of lion's breath; but the breath
had really been so gentle that she had not even noticed
the moment at which she left the earth. And now,
there was nothing but air for thousands upon thousands
of feet below her.

She felt frightened only for a second. For one thing,
the world beneath her was so very far away that it
seemed to have nothing to do with her. For another,
floating on the breath of the Lion was so extremely
comfortable. She found she could lie on her back or on
her face and twist any way she pleased, just as you can
in water (if you've learned to float really well). And
because she was moving at the same pace as the breath,
there was no wind, and the air seemed beautifully warm.
It was not in the least like being in an aeroplane, because
there was no noise and no vibration. If Jill had ever
been in a balloon she might have thought it more like
that; only better.

When she looked back now she could take in for the
first time the real size of the mountain she was leaving.
She wondered why a mountain so huge as that was not
covered with snow and ice – 'but I suppose all that sort

of thing is different in this world', thought Jill. Then she looked below her; but she was so high that she couldn't make out whether she was floating over land or sea, nor what speed she was going at.

'By Jove! The signs!' said Jill suddenly. 'I'd better repeat them.' She was in a panic for a second or two, but she found she could still say them all correctly. 'So that's all right,' she said, and lay back on the air as if it was a sofa, with a sigh of contentment.

'Well, I do declare,' said Jill to herself some hours later, 'I've been asleep. Fancy sleeping on air. I wonder if anyone's done it before. I don't suppose they have. Oh bother – Scrubb probably has! On this same journey, a little bit before me. Let's see what it looks like down below.'

What it looked like was an enormous, very dark blue plain. There were no hills to be seen, but there were biggish white things moving slowly across it. 'Those must be clouds,' she thought. 'But far bigger than the ones we saw from the cliff. I suppose they're bigger because they're nearer. I must be getting lower. Bother this sun.'

The sun which had been high overhead when she began her journey was now getting in her eyes. This meant that it was getting lower, ahead of her. Scrubb was quite right in saying that Jill (I don't know about girls in general) didn't think much about points of the compass. Otherwise she would have known, when the sun began getting in her eyes, that she was travelling pretty nearly due west.

Staring at the blue plain below her, she presently noticed that there were little dots of brighter, paler

colour in it here and there. 'It's the sea!' thought Jill.
'I do believe those are islands.' And so they were. She
might have felt rather jealous if she had known that some
of them were islands which Scrubb had seen from a
ship's deck and even landed on; but she didn't know this.
Then, later on, she began to see that there were little
wrinkles on the blue flatness: little wrinkles which must
be quite big ocean waves if you were down among them.
And now, all along the horizon there was a thick dark
line which grew thicker and darker so quickly that you
could see it growing. That was the first sign she had had
of the great speed at which she was travelling. And she
knew that the thickening line must be land.

Suddenly from her left (for the wind was in the south)
a great white cloud came rushing towards her, this time
on the same level as herself. And before she knew where
she was, she had shot right into the middle of its cold,
wet fogginess. That took her breath away, but she was
in it only for a moment. She came out blinking in the
sunlight and found her clothes wet. (She had on a blazer
and sweater and shorts and stockings and pretty thick
shoes; it had been a muddy sort of day in England.)
She came out lower than she had gone in; and as soon
as she did so she noticed something which, I suppose,
she ought to have been expecting, but which came as a
surprise and a shock. It was Noises. Up till then she had
travelled in total silence. Now, for the first time, she
heard the noise of waves and the crying of seagulls.
And now, too, she smelled the smell of the sea. There was
no mistake about her speed now. She saw two waves
meet with a smack and a spout of foam go up between
them; but she had hardly seen it before it was a hundred

yards behind her. The land was getting nearer at a great
pace. She could see mountains far inland, and other
nearer mountains on her left. She could see bays and
headlands, woods and fields, stretches of sandy beach.
The sound of waves breaking on the shore was growing
louder every second and drowning the other sea noises.

Suddenly the land opened right ahead of her. She
was coming to the mouth of a river. She was very low
now, only a few feet above the water. A wave-top came
against her toe and a great splash of foam spurted up,
drenching her nearly to the waist. Now she was losing
speed. Instead of being carried up the river she was
gliding in to the river bank on her left. There were so
many things to notice that she could hardly take them
all in; a smooth, green lawn, a ship so brightly coloured
that it looked like an enormous piece of jewellery, towers
and battlements, banners fluttering in the air, a crowd,
gay clothes, armour, gold, swords, a sound of music.
But this was all jumbled. The first thing that she knew
clearly was that she had alighted and was standing
under a thicket of trees close by the river side, and there,
only a few feet away from her, was Scrubb.

The first thing she thought was how very grubby and
untidy and generally unimpressive he looked. And the
second was 'How wet I am!'

CHAPTER 3

THE SAILING OF THE KING

WHAT made Scrubb look so dingy (and Jill too, if she could only have seen herself) was the splendour of their surroundings. I had better describe them at once.

Through a cleft in those mountains which Jill had seen far inland as she approached the land, the sunset light was pouring over a level lawn. On the far side of the lawn, its weather-vanes glittering in the light, rose a many-towered and many-turreted castle; the most beautiful castle Jill had ever seen. On the near side was a quay of white marble and, moored to this, the ship: a tall ship with high forecastle and high poop, gilded and crimson, with a great flag at the mast-head, and many banners waving from the decks, and a row of shields, bright as silver, along the bulwarks. The gang-plank was laid to her, and at the foot of it, just ready to go on board, stood an old, old man. He wore a rich mantle of scarlet which opened in front to show his silver mail shirt. There was a thin circlet of gold on his head. His beard, white as wool, fell nearly to his waist. He stood straight enough, leaning one hand on the shoulder of a richly dressed lord who seemed younger than himself: but you could see he was very old and frail. He looked as if a puff of wind could blow him away, and his eyes were watery.

Immediately in front of the King – who had turned round to speak to his people before going on board the ship – there was a little chair on wheels, and, harnessed to it, a little donkey: not much bigger than a big retriever.

In this chair sat a fat little dwarf. He was as richly dressed as the King, but because of his fatness and because he was sitting hunched up among cushions, the effect was quite different: it made him look like a shapeless little bundle of fur and silk and velvet. He was as old as the King, but more hale and hearty, with very keen

eyes. His bare head, which was bald and extremely large, shone like a gigantic billiard ball in the sunset light.

Farther back, in a half-circle, stood what Jill at once knew to be the courtiers. They were well worth looking at for their clothes and armour alone. As far as that went, they looked more like a flower-bed than a crowd. But what really made Jill open her eyes and mouth as wide as they would go, was the people themselves. If 'people' was the right word. For only about one in every five was human. The rest were things you never see in our world. Fauns, satyrs, centaurs: Jill could give a name to these, for she had seen pictures of them. Dwarfs too. And there were a lot of animals she knew as well; bears, badgers, moles, leopards, mice, and various birds. But then they were so very different from the animals which one called by the same names in England. Some of them were much bigger – the mice, for instance, stood on their hind legs and were over two feet high. But quite apart from that, they all looked different. You could see by the expression in their faces that they could talk and think just as well as you could.

'Golly!' thought Jill. 'So it's true after all.' But next moment she added, 'I wonder are they friendly?' For she had just noticed, on the outskirts of the crowd, one or two giants and some people whom she couldn't give a name to at all.

At that moment Aslan and the signs rushed back into her mind. She had forgotten all about them for the last half-hour.

'Scrubb!' she whispered, grabbing his arm. 'Scrubb, quick! Do you see anyone you know?'

'So *you've* turned up again, have you?' said Scrubb disagreeably (for which he had some reason). 'Well, keep quiet, can't you? I want to listen.'

'Don't be a fool,' said Jill. 'There isn't a moment to lose. Don't you see some old friend here? Because you've got to go and speak to him at once.'

'What are you talking about?' said Scrubb.

'It's Aslan – the Lion -- says you've got to,' said Jill despairingly. 'I've seen him.'

'Oh, you have, have you? What did he say?'

'He said the very first person you saw in Narnia would be an old friend, and you'd got to speak to him at once.'

'Well, there's nobody here I've ever seen in my life before; and anyway, I don't know whether this is Narnia.'

'Thought you said you'd been here before,' said Jill.

'Well, you thought wrong then.'

'Well, I like that! You told me –'

'For heaven's sake dry up and let's hear what they're saying.'

The King was speaking to the Dwarf, but Jill couldn't hear what he said. And, as far as she could make out, the Dwarf made no answer, though he nodded and wagged his head a great deal. Then the King raised his voice and addressed the whole court: but his voice was so old and cracked that she could understand very little of his speech – especially since it was all about people and places she had never heard of. When the speech was over, the King stooped down and kissed the Dwarf on both cheeks, straightened himself, raised his right hand as if in blessing, and went, slowly and with feeble steps, up the gangway and on board the ship. The courtiers appeared to be greatly moved by his departure. Handkerchiefs were got out, sounds of sobbing were heard in every direction. The gangway was cast off, trumpets sounded from the poop, and the ship moved away from the quay. (It was being towed by a rowing-boat, but Jill didn't see that.)

'Now –' said Scrubb, but he didn't get any farther, because at that moment a large white object – Jill thought for a second that it was a kite – came gliding through the air and alighted at his feet. It was a white owl, but so big that it stood as high as a good-sized dwarf.

It blinked and peered as if it were short-sighted, and put its head a little on one side, and said in a soft, hooting kind of voice.

'Tu-whoo, tu-whoo! Who are you two?'

'My name's Scrubb, and this is Pole,' said Eustace. 'Would you mind telling us where we are?'

'In the land of Narnia, at the King's castle of Cair Paravel.'

'Is that the King who's just taken ship?'

'Too true, too true,' said the Owl sadly, shaking its big head. 'But who are you? There's something magic about you two. I saw you arrive: you *flew*. Everyone else was so busy seeing the King off that nobody knew. Except me. I happened to notice you, you flew.'

'We were sent here by Aslan,' said Eustace in a low voice.

'Tu-whoo, tu-whoo!' said the Owl, ruffling out its feathers. 'This is almost too much for me, so early in the evening. I'm not quite myself till the sun's down.'

'And we've been sent to find the lost Prince,' said Jill, who had been anxiously waiting to get into the conversation.

'It's the first I've heard about it,' said Eustace. 'What prince?'

'You had better come and speak to the Lord Regent at once,' it said. 'That's him, over there in the donkey carriage; Trumpkin the Dwarf.' The bird turned and began leading the way, muttering to itself, 'Whoo! Tu-whoo! What a to-do! I can't think clearly yet. It's too early.'

'What is the King's name?' asked Eustace.

'Caspian the Tenth,' said the Owl. And Jill wondered why Scrubb had suddenly pulled up short in his walk and turned an extraordinary colour. She thought she had never seen him look so sick about anything. But before she had time to ask any questions they had reached the

Dwarf, who was just gathering up the reins of his donkey and preparing to drive back to the castle. The crowd of courtiers had broken up and were going in the same direction, by ones and twos and little knots, like people coming away from watching a game or a race.

'Tu-whoo! Ahem! Lord Regent,' said the Owl, stooping down a little and holding its beak near the Dwarf's ear.

'Heh? What's that?' said the Dwarf.

'Two strangers, my lord,' said the Owl.

'Rangers! What d'ye mean?' said the Dwarf. 'I see two uncommonly grubby man-cubs. What do they want?'

'My name's Jill,' said Jill, pressing forward. She was very eager to explain the important business on which they had come.

'The girl's called Jill,' said the Owl, as loud as it could.

'What's that?' said the Dwarf. 'The girls are all killed! I don't believe a word of it. What girls? Who killed 'em?'

'Only one girl, my lord,' said the Owl. 'Her name is Jill.'

'Speak up, speak up,' said the Dwarf. 'Don't stand there buzzing and twittering in my ear. Who's been killed?'

'Nobody's been killed,' hooted the Owl.

'Who?'

'NOBODY.'

'All right, all right. You needn't shout. I'm not so deaf as all that. What do you mean by coming here to tell me that nobody's been killed? Why should anyone have been killed?'

'Better tell him I'm Eustace,' said Scrubb.

'The boy's Eustace, my lord,' hooted the Owl as loud as it could.

'Useless?' said the Dwarf irritably. 'I dare say he is. Is that any reason for bringing him to court? Hey?'

'Not useless,' said the Owl. 'EUSTACE.'

'Used to it, is he? I don't know what you're talking about, I'm sure. I tell you what it is, Master Glimfeather; when I was a young Dwarf there used to be *talking* beasts and birds in this country who really could talk. There wasn't all this mumbling and muttering and whispering. It wouldn't have been tolerated for a moment. Not for a moment, Sir. Urnus, my trumpet please –'

A little Faun who had been standing quietly beside the Dwarf's elbow all this time now handed him a silver ear-trumpet. It was made like the musical instrument called a serpent, so that the tube curled right round the Dwarf's neck. While he was getting it settled the Owl, Glimfeather, suddenly said to the children in a whisper:

'My brain's a bit clearer now. Don't say anything about the lost Prince. I'll explain later. It wouldn't do, wouldn't do, Tu-Whoo! Oh *what* a to-do!'

'Now,' said the Dwarf, 'if you *have* anything sensible to say, Master Glimfeather, try and say it. Take a deep breath and don't attempt to speak too quickly.'

With help from the children, and in spite of a fit of coughing on the part of the Dwarf, Glimfeather explained that the strangers had been sent by Aslan to visit the court of Narnia. The Dwarf glanced quickly up at them with a new expression in his eyes.

'Sent by the Lion Himself, hey?' he said. 'And from – m'm – from that other Place – beyond the world's end, hey?'

'Yes, my lord,' bawled Eustace into the trumpet.

'Son of Adam and daughter of Eve, hey?' said the Dwarf. But people at Experiment House haven't heard of Adam and Eve, so Jill and Eustace couldn't answer this. But the Dwarf didn't seem to notice.

'Well, my dears,' he said, taking first one and then the other by the hand and bowing his head a little. 'You are very heartily welcome. If the good King, my poor Master, had not this very hour set sail for Seven Isles, he would have been glad of your coming. It would have brought back his youth to him for a moment – for a moment. And now, it is high time for supper. You shall tell me your business in full council tomorrow morning. Master Glimfeather, see that bedchambers and suitable clothes and all else are provided for these guests in the most honourable fashion. And – Glimfeather – in your ear –'

Here the Dwarf put his mouth close to the Owl's head

and, no doubt, intended to whisper: but, like other deaf people, he wasn't a very good judge of his own voice, and both children heard him say, 'See that they're properly washed.'

After that, the Dwarf touched up his donkey and it set off towards the castle at something between a trot and a waddle (it was a very fat little beast), while the Faun, the Owl, and the children followed at a rather slower pace. The sun had set and the air was growing cool.

They went across the lawn and then through an orchard and so to the North Gate of Cair Paravel, which stood wide open. Inside, they found a grassy courtyard. Lights were already showing from the windows of the great hall on their right and from a more complicated mass of buildings straight ahead. Into these the Owl led them, and there a most delightful person was called to look after Jill. She was not much taller than Jill herself, and a good deal slenderer, but obviously full grown, graceful as a willow, and her hair was willowy too, and there seemed to be moss in it. She brought Jill to a round room in one of the turrets, where there was a little bath sunk in the floor and a fire of sweet-smelling woods burning on the flat hearth and a lamp hanging by a silver chain from the vaulted roof. The window looked west into the strange land of Narnia, and Jill saw the red remains of the sunset still glowing behind distant mountains. It made her long for more adventures and feel sure that this was only the beginning.

When she had had her bath, and brushed her hair, and put on the clothes that had been laid out for her – they were the kind that not only felt nice, but looked nice and smelled nice and made nice sounds when you moved as well – she would have gone back to gaze out of that exciting window, but she was interrupted by a bang on the door.

'Come in,' said Jill. And in came Scrubb, also bathed and splendidly dressed in Narnian clothes. But his face didn't look as if he were enjoying it.

'Oh, here you are at last,' he said crossly, flinging himself into a chair. 'I've been trying to find you for ever so long.'

'Well, now you have,' said Jill. 'I say, Scrubb, isn't it all simply too exciting and scrumptious for words.' She had forgotten all about the signs and the lost Prince for the moment.

'Oh! That's what you think, is it?' said Scrubb: and then, after a pause, 'I wish to goodness we'd never come.'

'Why on earth?'

'I can't bear it,' said Scrubb. 'Seeing the King – Caspian – a doddering old man like that. It's – it's frightful.'

'Why, what harm does it do you?'

'Oh, you don't understand. Now that I come to think of it, you couldn't. I didn't tell you that this world has a different time from ours.'

'How do you mean?'

'The time you spend here doesn't take up any of our time. Do you see? I mean, however long we spend here, we shall still get back to Experiment House at the moment we left it –'

'That won't be much fun –'

'Oh, dry up! Don't keep interrupting. And when you're back in England – in our world – you can't tell how time is going here. It might be any number of years in Narnia while we're having one year at home. The Pevensies explained it all to me, but, like a fool, I forgot about it. And now apparently it's been about seventy years – Narnian years – since I was here last. Do you see now? And I come back and find Caspian an old, old man.'

'Then the King *was* an old friend of yours!' said Jill. A horrid thought had struck her.

'I should jolly well think he was,' said Scrubb miserably. 'About as good a friend as a chap could have. And last time he was only a few years older than me. And to see that old man with a white beard, and to remember Caspian as he was the morning we captured the Lone Islands, or in the fight with the Sea Serpent – oh, it's frightful. It's worse than coming back and finding him dead.'

'Oh, shut up,' said Jill impatiently. 'It's far worse than you think. We've muffed the first Sign.' Of course Scrubb did not understand this. Then Jill told him about her conversation with Aslan and the four signs and the task of finding the lost prince which had been laid upon them.

'So you see,' she wound up, 'you did see an old friend, just as Aslan said, and you ought to have gone and spoken to him at once. And now you haven't, and everything is going wrong from the very beginning.'

'But how was I to know?' said Scrubb.

'If you'd only listened to me when I tried to tell you, we'd be all right,' said Jill.

'Yes, and if you hadn't played the fool on the edge of that cliff and jolly nearly murdered me – all right, I said *murder*, and I'll say it again as often as I like, so keep your hair on – we'd have come together and both known what to do.'

'I suppose he *was* the very first person you saw?' said Jill. 'You must have been here hours before me. Are you sure you didn't see anyone else first?'

'I was only here about a minute before you,' said Scrubb. 'He must have blown you quicker than me. Making up for lost time: the time *you* lost.'

'Don't be a perfect beast, Scrubb,' said Jill. 'Hallo! What's that?'

It was the castle bell ringing for supper, and thus what looked like turning into a first-rate quarrel was happily cut short. Both had a good appetite by this time.

Supper in the great hall of the castle was the most splendid thing either of them had ever seen; for though Eustace had been in that world before, he had spent his whole visit at sea and knew nothing of the glory and courtesy of the Narnians at home in their own land. The banners hung from the roof, and each course came in with trumpeters and kettledrums. There were soups that would make your mouth water to think of, and the lovely fishes called pavenders, and venison and peacock and pies, and ices and jellies and fruit and nuts, and all manner of wines and fruit drinks. Even Eustace cheered up and admitted that it was 'something like'. And when all the serious eating and drinking was over, a blind poet came forward and struck up the grand old tale of Prince Cor and Aravis and the horse Bree, which is called *The Horse and his Boy* and tells of an adventure that happened in Narnia and Calormen and the lands between, in the Golden Age when Peter was High King in Cair Paravel. (I haven't time to tell it now, though it is well worth hearing.)

When they were dragging themselves upstairs to bed, yawning their heads off, Jill said, 'I bet we sleep well, tonight'; for it had been a full day. Which just shows how little anyone knows what is going to happen to them next.

CHAPTER 4

A PARLIAMENT OF OWLS

IT is a very funny thing that the sleepier you are, the longer you take about getting to bed; especially if you are lucky enough to have a fire in your room. Jill felt she couldn't even start undressing unless she sat down in front of the fire for a bit first. And once she had sat down, she didn't want to get up again. She had already said to herself about five times, 'I must go to bed', when she was startled by a tap on the window.

She got up, pulled the curtain, and at first saw nothing but darkness. Then she jumped and started backwards, for something very large had dashed itself against the window, giving a sharp tap on the glass as it did so. A very unpleasant idea came into her head – 'Suppose they have giant moths in this country! Ugh!' But then the thing came back, and this time she was almost sure she saw a beak, and that the beak had made the tapping noise. 'It's some huge bird,' thought Jill. 'Could it be an eagle?' She didn't very much want a visit even from an eagle, but she opened the window and looked out. Instantly, with a great whirring noise, the creature alighted on the window-sill and stood there filling up the whole window, so that Jill had to step back to make room for it. It was the Owl.

'Hush, hush! Tu-whoo, tu-whoo,' said the Owl. 'Don't make a noise. Now, are you two really in earnest about what you've got to do?'

'About the lost Prince, you mean?' said Jill. 'Yes, we've got to be.' For now she remembered the Lion's voice and face, which she had nearly forgotten during the feasting and story-telling in the hall.

'Good!' said the Owl. 'Then there's no time to waste. You must get away from here at once. I'll go and wake the other human. Then I'll come back for you. You'd better change those court clothes and put on something you can travel in. I'll be back in two twos. Tu-whoo!' And without waiting for an answer, he was gone.

If Jill had been more used to adventures, she might have doubted the Owl's word, but this never occurred to her: and in the exciting idea of a midnight escape she forgot her sleepiness. She changed back into sweater and shorts – there was a guide's knife on the belt of the shorts which might come in useful – and added a few of the things that had been left in the room for her by the girl with the willowy hair. She chose a short cloak that came down to her knees and had a hood ('just the thing, if it rains,' she thought), a few handkerchiefs and a comb. Then she sat down and waited.

She was getting sleepy again when the Owl returned.

'Now we're ready,' it said.

'You'd better lead the way,' said Jill. 'I don't know all these passages yet.'

'Tu-whoo!' said the Owl. 'We're not going through the castle. That would never do. You must ride on me. We shall fly.'

'Oh!' said Jill, and stood with her mouth open, not much liking the idea. 'Shan't I be far too heavy for you?'

'Tu-whoo, tu-whoo! Don't you be a fool. I've already carried the other one. Now. But we'll put out that lamp first.'

As soon as the lamp was out, the bit of the night which you saw through the window looked less dark – no longer black, but grey. The Owl stood on the window-sill with his back to the room and raised his wings. Jill had to

climb on to his short fat body and get her knees under the wings and grip tight. The feathers felt beautifully warm and soft but there was nothing to hold on by. 'I wonder how Scrubb liked *his* ride!' thought Jill. And just as she was thinking this, with a horrid plunge they had left the window-sill, and the wings were making a flurry round her ears, and the night air, rather cool and damp, was flying in her face.

It was much lighter than she expected, and though the sky was overcast, one patch of watery silver showed where the moon was hiding above the clouds. The fields beneath her looked grey, and the trees black. There was a certain amount of wind – a hushing, ruffling sort of wind which meant that rain was coming soon.

The Owl wheeled round so that the castle was now ahead of them. Very few of the windows showed lights. They flew right over it, northwards, crossing the river: the air grew colder, and Jill thought she could see the white reflection of the Owl in the water beneath her. But soon they were on the north bank of the river, flying above wooded country.

The Owl snapped at something which Jill couldn't see.

'Oh, don't, please!' said Jill. 'Don't jerk like that. You nearly threw me off.'

'I beg your pardon,' said the Owl. 'I was just nabbing a bat. There's nothing so sustaining, in a small way, as a nice plump little bat. Shall I catch you one?'

'No, thanks,' said Jill with a shudder.

He was flying a little lower now and a large, black-looking object was looming up towards them. Jill had just time to see that it was a tower – a partly ruinous tower, with a lot of ivy on it, she thought – when she found herself ducking to avoid the archway of a window, as the Owl squeezed with her through the ivied and cobwebby opening, out of the fresh, grey night into a dark place inside the top of the tower. It was rather fusty inside and, the moment she slipped off the Owl's back, she knew (as one usually does somehow) that it was quite crowded. And when voices began saying out of the darkness from every direction 'Tu-whoo! Tu-whoo!' she knew it was crowded with owls. She was rather relieved when a very different voice said:

'Is that you, Pole?'

'Is that you, Scrubb?' said Jill.

'Now,' said Glimfeather, 'I think we're all here. Let us hold a parliament of owls.'

'Tu-whoo, tu-whoo. True for you. That's the right thing to do,' said several voices.

'Half a moment,' said Scrubb's voice. 'There's something I want to say first.'

'Do, do, do,' said the owls; and Jill said, 'Fire ahead.'

'I suppose all you chaps – owls, I mean,' said Scrubb, 'I suppose you all know that King Caspian the Tenth, in his young days, sailed to the eastern end of the world. Well, I was with him on that journey: with him and Reepicheep the Mouse, and the Lord Drinian and all of them. I know it sounds hard to believe, but people don't grow older in our world at the same speed as they do in yours. And what I want to say is this, that I'm the King's man; and if this parliament of owls is any sort of plot against the King, I'm having nothing to do with it.'

'Tu-whoo, tu-whoo, we're all the King's owls too,' said the owls.

'What's it all about then?' said Scrubb.

'It's only this,' said Glimfeather. 'That if the Lord Regent, the Dwarf Trumpkin, hears you are going to look for the lost Prince, he won't let you start. He'd keep you under lock and key sooner.'

'Great Scott!' said Scrubb. 'You don't mean that Trumpkin is a traitor? I used to hear a lot about him in the old days, at sea. Caspian – the King, I mean – trusted him absolutely.'

'Oh no,' said a voice. 'Trumpkin's no traitor. But more than thirty champions (knights, centaurs, good giants, and all sorts) have at one time or another set out to look for the lost Prince, and none of them have ever come back. And at last the King said he was not going to have all the bravest Narnians destroyed in the search for his son. And now nobody is allowed to go.'

'But surely he'd let *us* go,' said Scrubb. 'When he knew who I was and who had sent me.'

('Sent both of us,' put in Jill.)

'Yes,' said Glimfeather, 'I think, very likely, he would. But the King's away. And Trumpkin will stick to the rules. He's as true as steel, but he's deaf as a post and very peppery. You could never make him see that this might be the time for making an exception to the rule.'

'You might think he'd take some notice of *us*, because we're owls and everyone knows how wise owls are,' said someone else. 'But he's so old now he'd only say, "You're a mere chick. I remember you when you were an egg. Don't come trying to teach *me*, Sir. Crabs and crumpets!"'

This owl imitated Trumpkin's voice rather well, and there were sounds of owlish laughter all round. The children began to see that the Narnians all felt about Trumpkin as people feel at school about some crusty teacher, whom everyone is a little afraid of and everyone makes fun of and nobody really dislikes.

'How long is the King going to be away?' asked Scrubb.

'If only we knew!' said Glimfeather. 'You see, there has been a rumour lately that Aslan himself has been seen in the islands – in Terebinthia, I think it was. And the King said he would make one more attempt before he died to see Aslan face to face again, and ask his advice about who is to be King after him. But we're all afraid that, if he doesn't meet Aslan in Terebinthia, he'll go on east, to Seven Isles and Lone Islands – and on and on. He never talks about it, but we all know he has never forgotten that voyage to the world's end. I'm sure in his heart of hearts he wants to go there again.'

'Then there's no good waiting for him to come back?' said Jill.

'No, no good,' said the Owl. 'Oh, what a to-do! If only you two had known and spoken to him at once! He'd have arranged everything – probably given you an army to go with you in search of the Prince.'

Jill kept quiet at this and hoped Scrubb would be sporting enough not to tell all the owls why this hadn't happened. He was, or very nearly. That is, he only muttered under his breath, 'Well, it wasn't *my* fault,' before saying out loud:

'Very well. We'll have to manage without it. But there's just one thing more I want to know. If this owls' parliament, as you call it, is all fair and above board and means no mischief, why does it have to be so jolly secret – meeting in a ruin in dead of night, and all that?'

'Tu-whoo! Tu-whoo!' hooted several owls. 'Where should we meet? When would anyone meet except at night?'

'You see,' explained Glimfeather, 'most of the creatures in Narnia have such unnatural habits. They do things by day, in broad blazing sunlight (ugh!) when everyone ought to be asleep. And, as a result, at night they're so blind and stupid that you can't get a word out of them. So we owls have got into the habit of meeting at sensible hours, on our own, when we want to talk about things.'

'I see,' said Scrubb. 'Well now, let's get on. Tell us all about the lost Prince.' Then an old owl, not Glimfeather, related the story.

About ten years ago, it appeared, when Rilian, the son of Caspian, was a very young knight, he rode with the Queen his mother on a May morning in the north parts of Narnia. They had many squires and ladies with them and all wore garlands of fresh leaves on their heads, and horns at their sides; but they had no hounds with them, for they were maying, not hunting. In the warm part of the day they came to a pleasant glade where a fountain flowed freshly out of the earth, and there they dismounted and ate and drank and were merry. After a time the Queen felt sleepy, and they spread cloaks for her on the grassy bank, and Prince Rilian with the rest of the party went a little way from her, that their tales and laughter might not wake her. And so, presently, a great serpent came out of the thick wood and stung the Queen in her hand. All heard her cry out and rushed towards her, and Rilian was first at her side. He saw the worm gliding away from her and made after it with his sword drawn. It was great, shining, and as green as poison, so that he could see it well: but it glided away into thick bushes and he could not come at it. So he returned to his mother, and found them all busy about her. But they were busy in vain, for at the first glance of her face Rilian knew that no physic in the world would do her good. As long as the life was in her she seemed to be trying hard to tell him something. But she could not speak clearly and, whatever her message was, she died without delivering it. It was then hardly ten minutes since they had first heard her cry.

They carried the dead Queen back to Cair Paravel, and she was bitterly mourned by Rilian and by the King, and by all Narnia. She had been a great lady, wise and

gracious and happy, King Caspian's bride whom he had brought home from the eastern end of the world. And men said that the blood of the stars flowed in her veins. The Prince took his mother's death very hardly, as well he might. After that, he was always riding on the northern marches of Narnia, hunting for that venomous worm, to kill it and be avenged. No one remarked much on this, though the Prince came home from these wanderings looking tired and distraught. But about a month after the Queen's death, some said they could see a change in him. There was a look in his eyes as of a man who has seen visions, and though he would be out all day, his horse did not bear the signs of hard riding. His chief friend among the older courtiers was the Lord Drinian, he who had been his father's captain on that great voyage to the east parts of earth.

One evening Drinian said to the Prince, 'Your Highness must soon give over seeking the worm. There is no true vengeance on a witless brute as there might be on a man. You weary yourself in vain.' The Prince answered him, 'My lord, I have almost forgotten the worm this seven days.' Drinian asked him why, if that were so, he rode so continually in the northern woods. 'My lord,' said the Prince, 'I have seen there the most beautiful thing that was ever made.' 'Fair Prince,' said Drinian, 'of your courtesy let me ride with you tomorrow, that I also may see this fair thing.' 'With a good will,' said Rilian.

Then in good time on the next day they saddled their horses and rode a great gallop into the northern woods and alighted at that same fountain where the Queen got her death. Drinian thought it strange that the Prince should choose that place of all places, to linger in. And there they rested till it came to high noon: and at noon Drinian looked up and saw the most beautiful lady he had ever seen; and she stood at the north side of the fountain and said no word but beckoned to the Prince with her hand as if she bade him come to her. And she was tall and great, shining, and wrapped in a thin garment as green as poison. And the Prince stared at her like a man out of his wits. But suddenly the lady was gone, Drinian knew not where; and they two returned to Cair Paravel. It stuck in Drinian's mind that this shining green woman was evil.

Drinian doubted very much whether he ought not to tell this adventure to the King, but he had little wish to be a blab and a tale-bearer and so he held his tongue. But afterwards he wished he had spoken. For next day Prince Rilian rode out alone. That night he came not back, and from that hour no trace of him was ever found in Narnia nor any neighbouring land, and neither his horse nor his hat nor his cloak nor anything else was ever found. Then Drinian in the bitterness of his heart went to Caspian and said, 'Lord King, slay me speedily as a great traitor: for by my silence I have destroyed your son.' And he told him the story. Then Caspian caught up a battle-axe and rushed upon the Lord Drinian to kill him, and Drinian stood still as a stock for the death blow. But when the axe was raised, Caspian suddenly threw it away and cried out, 'I have lost my queen and my son: shall I lose my friend also?' And he fell upon the Lord Drinian's neck and embraced him and both wept, and their friendship was not broken.

Such was the story of Rilian. And when it was over, Jill said, 'I bet that serpent and that woman were the same person.'

'True, true, we think the same as you,' hooted the owls.

'But we don't think she killed the Prince,' said Glimfeather, 'because no bones –'

'We know she didn't,' said Scrubb. 'Aslan told Pole he was still alive somewhere.'

'That almost makes it worse,' said the oldest owl. 'It means she has some use for him, and some deep scheme against Narnia. Long, long ago, at the very beginning, a White Witch came out of the North and bound our land in snow and ice for a hundred years. And we think this may be one of the same crew.'

'Very well, then,' said Scrubb. 'Pole and I have got to find this Prince. Can you help us?'

'Have you any clue, you two?' asked Glimfeather.

'Yes,' said Scrubb. 'We know we've got to go north. And we know we've got to reach the ruins of a giant city.'

At this there was a greater tu-whooing than ever, and noises of birds shifting their feet and ruffling their feathers, and then all the owls started speaking at once. They all explained how very sorry they were that they themselves could not go with the children on their search for the lost Prince. 'You'd want to travel by day, and we'd want to travel by night,' they said. 'It wouldn't do, wouldn't do.' One or two owls added that even here in the ruined tower it wasn't nearly so dark as it had been when they began, and that the parliament had been going on quite long enough. In fact, the mere mention of a journey to the ruined city of giants seemed to have damped the spirits of those birds. But Glimfeather said:

'If they want to go that way – into Ettinsmoor – we must take them to one of the Marsh-wiggles. They're the only people who can help them much.'

'True, true. Do,' said the owls.

'Come on, then,' said Glimfeather. 'I'll take one. Who'll take the other? It must be done tonight.'

'I will: as far as the Marsh-wiggles,' said another owl.

'Are you ready?' said Glimfeather to Jill.

'I think Pole's asleep,' said Scrubb.

CHAPTER 5

PUDDLEGLUM

JILL was asleep. Ever since the owls' parliament began she had been yawning terribly and now she had dropped off. She was not at all pleased at being waked again, and at finding herself lying on bare boards in a dusty belfry sort of place, completely dark, and almost completely full of owls. She was even less pleased when she heard that they had to set off for somewhere else – and not, apparently, for bed – on the Owl's back.

'Oh, come on, Pole, buck up,' said Scrubb's voice. 'After all, it *is* an adventure.'

'I'm sick of adventures,' said Jill crossly.

She did, however, consent to climb on to Glimfeather's back, and was thoroughly waked up (for a while) by the unexpected coldness of the air when he flew out with her into the night. The moon had disappeared and there were no stars. Far behind her she could see a single lighted window well above the ground; doubtless, in one of the towers of Cair Paravel. It made her long to be back in that delightful bedroom, snug in bed, watching the firelight on the walls. She put her hands under her cloak and wrapped it tightly round her. It was uncanny to hear two voices in the dark air a little distance away; Scrubb and his owl were talking to one another. '*He* doesn't sound tired,' thought Jill. She did not realize that he had been on great adventures in that world before and that the Narnian air was bringing back to him a strength he had won when he sailed the Eastern Seas with King Caspian.

Jill had to pinch herself to keep awake, for she knew
that if she dozed on Glimfeather's back she would probably fall off. When at last the two owls ended their flight,
she climbed stiffly off Glimfeather and found herself on
flat ground. A chilly wind was blowing and they appeared to be in a place without trees. 'Tu-whoo, tu-
whoo!' Glimfeather was calling. 'Wake up, Puddleglum.
Wake up. It is on the Lion's business.'

For a long time there was no reply. Then, a long way
off, a dim light appeared and began to come nearer.
With it came a voice.

'Owls ahoy!' it said. 'What is it? Is the King dead?
Has an enemy landed in Narnia? Is it a flood? Or
dragons?'

When the light reached them, it turned out to be that
of a large lantern. She could see very little of the person
who held it. He seemed to be all legs and arms. The owls
were talking to him, explaining everything, but she was
too tired to listen. She tried to wake herself up a bit when
she realized that they were saying good-bye to her. But
she could never afterwards remember much except that,
sooner or later, she and Scrubb were stooping to enter
a low doorway and then (oh, thank heavens) were lying
down on something soft and warm, and a voice was
saying:

'There you are. Best we can do. You'll lie cold and
hard. Damp too, I shouldn't wonder. Won't sleep a
wink, most likely; even if there isn't a thunderstorm or a
flood or the wigwam doesn't fall down on top of us all,
as I've known them do. Must make the best of it –' But
she was fast asleep before the voice had ended.

When the children woke late next morning they found

that they were lying, very dry and warm, on beds of straw in a dark place. A triangular opening let in the daylight.

'Where on earth are we?' asked Jill.

'In the wigwam of a Marsh-wiggle,' said Eustace.

'A what?'

'A Marsh-wiggle. Don't ask me what it is. I couldn't see it last night. I'm getting up. Let's go and look for it.'

'How beastly one feels after sleeping in one's clothes,' said Jill, sitting up.

'I was just thinking how nice it was not to have to dress,' said Eustace.

'Or wash either, I suppose,' said Jill scornfully. But Scrubb had already got up, yawned, shaken himself, and crawled out of the wigwam. Jill did the same.

What they found outside was quite unlike the bit of Narnia they had seen on the day before. They were on a great flat plain which was cut into countless little islands

by countless channels of water. The islands were covered
with coarse grass and bordered with reeds and rushes.
Sometimes there were beds of rushes about an acre in
extent. Clouds of birds were constantly alighting in them
and rising from them again – duck, snipe, bitterns, herons.
Many wigwams like that in which they had passed the
night could be seen dotted about, but all at a good distance from one another; for Marsh-wiggles are people
who like privacy. Except for the fringe of the forest
several miles to the south and west of them, there was
not a tree in sight. Eastward the flat marsh stretched
to low sand-hills on the horizon, and you could tell by
the salt tang in the wind which blew from that direction
that the sea lay over there. To the North there were low
pale-coloured hills, in places bastioned with rock. The
rest was all flat marsh. It would have been a depressing
place on a wet evening. Seen under a morning sun,
with a fresh wind blowing, and the air filled with the
crying of birds, there was something fine and fresh and
clean about its loneliness. The children felt their spirits
rise.

'Where has the thingummy got to, I wonder?' said
Jill.

'The Marsh-wiggle,' said Scrubb, as if he were rather
proud of knowing the word. 'I expect – hullo, that must
be him.' And then they both saw him, sitting with his
back to them, fishing, about fifty yards away. He had
been hard to see at first because he was nearly the same
colour as the marsh and because he sat so still.

'I suppose we'd better go and speak to him,' said Jill.
Scrubb nodded. They both felt a little nervous.

As they drew nearer, the figure turned its head and

showed them a long thin face with rather sunken cheeks, a tightly shut mouth, a sharp nose, and no beard. He was wearing a high, pointed hat like a steeple, with an enormously wide flat brim. The hair, if it could be called hair, which hung over his large ears was greeny-grey,

and each lock was flat rather than round, so that they were like tiny reeds. His expression was solemn, his complexion muddy, and you could see at once that he took a serious view of life.

'Good morning, Guests,' he said. 'Though when I say *good* I don't mean it won't probably turn to rain or it might be snow, or fog, or thunder. You didn't get any sleep, I dare say.'

'Yes we did, though,' said Jill. 'We had a lovely night.'

'Ah,' said the Marsh-wiggle, shaking his head. 'I see you're making the best of a bad job. That's right. You've been well brought up, you have. You've learned to put a good face on things.'

'Please, we don't know your name,' said Scrubb.

'Puddleglum's my name. But it doesn't matter if you forget it. I can always tell you again.'

The children sat down on each side of him. They now saw that he had very long legs and arms, so that although his body was not much bigger than a dwarf's, he would be taller than most men when he stood up. The fingers of his hands were webbed like a frog's, and so were his bare feet which dangled in the muddy water. He was dressed in earth-coloured clothes that hung loose about him.

'I'm trying to catch a few eels to make an eel stew for our dinner,' said Puddleglum. 'Though I shouldn't wonder if I didn't get any. And you won't like them much if I do.'

'Why not?' asked Scrubb.

'Why, it's not in reason that you should like our sort of victuals, though I've no doubt you'll put a bold face on it. All the same, while I am a catching of them, if you two could try to light the fire – no harm trying –! The wood's behind the wigwam. It may be wet. You could light it inside the wigwam, and then we'd get all the smoke in our eyes. Or you could light it outside, and then the rain would come and put it out. Here's my tinder-box. You won't know how to use it, I expect.'

But Scrubb had learned that sort of thing on his last adventure. The children ran back together to the wigwam, found the wood (which was perfectly dry) and succeeded in lighting a fire with rather less than the usual difficulty. Then Scrubb sat and took care of it while Jill went and had some sort of wash – not a very nice one – in the nearest channel. After that she saw to the fire and he had a wash. Both felt a good deal fresher, but very hungry.

Presently the Marsh-wiggle joined them. In spite of his expectation of catching no eels, he had a dozen or so, which he had already skinned and cleaned. He put a big pot on, mended the fire, and lit his pipe. Marsh-wiggles smoke a very strange, heavy sort of tobacco (some people say they mix it with mud) and the children noticed the smoke from Puddleglum's pipe hardly rose in the air at all. It trickled out of the bowl and downwards and drifted along the ground like a mist. It was very black and set Scrubb coughing.

'Now,' said Puddleglum. 'Those eels will take a mortal long time to cook, and either of you might faint with hunger before they're done. I knew a little girl – but I'd better not tell you that story. It might lower your

spirits, and that's a thing I never do. So, to keep your minds off your hunger, we may as well talk about our plans.'

'Yes, do let's,' said Jill. 'Can you help us to find Prince Rilian?'

The Marsh-wiggle sucked in his cheeks till they were hollower than you would have thought possible. 'Well, I don't know that you'd call it *help*,' he said. 'I don't know that anyone can exactly *help*. It stands to reason we're not likely to get very far on a journey to the North, not at this time of the year, with the winter coming on soon and all. And an early winter too, by the look of things. But you mustn't let that make you down-hearted. Very likely, what with enemies, and mountains, and rivers to cross, and losing our way, and next to nothing to eat, and sore feet, we'll hardly notice the weather. And if we don't get far enough to do any good, we may get far enough not to get back in a hurry.'

Both children noticed that he said 'we', not 'you', and both exclaimed at the same moment. 'Are you coming with us?'

'Oh yes, I'm coming of course. Might as well, you see. I don't suppose we shall ever see the King back in Narnia, now that he's once set off for foreign parts; and he had a nasty cough when he left. Then there's Trumpkin. He's failing fast. And you'll find there'll have been a bad harvest after this terrible dry summer. And I shouldn't wonder if some enemy attacked us. Mark my words.'

'And how shall we start?' said Scrubb.

'Well,' said the Marsh-wiggle very slowly, 'all the others who ever went looking for Prince Rilian started from that same fountain where the Lord Drinian saw the lady. They went north, mostly. And as none of them ever came back, we can't exactly say how they got on.'

'We've got to start by finding a ruined city of giants,' said Jill. 'Aslan said so.'

'Got to start by *finding* it, have we?' answered Puddle-glum. 'Not allowed to start by *looking* for it, I suppose?'

'That's what I meant, of course,' said Jill. 'And then, when we've found it –'

'Yes, when!' said Puddleglum very drily.

'Doesn't anyone know where it is?' asked Scrubb.

'I don't know about Anyone,' said Puddleglum. 'And I won't say I haven't heard of that Ruined City. You wouldn't start from the fountain, though. You'd have to go across Ettinsmoor. That's where the Ruined City is, if it's anywhere. But I've been as far in that direction as most people and I never got to any ruins, so I won't deceive you.'

'Where's Ettinsmoor?' said Scrubb.

'Look over there northward,' said Puddleglum, point-ing with his pipe. 'See those hills and bits of cliff? That's the beginning of Ettinsmoor. But there's a river between it and us; the river Shribble. No bridges, of course.'

'I suppose we can ford it, though,' said Scrubb.

'Well, it *has* been forded,' admitted the Marsh-wiggle.

'Perhaps we shall meet people on Ettinsmoor who can tell us the way,' said Jill.

'You're right about meeting people,' said Puddleglum.

'What sort of people live there?' she asked.

'It's not for me to say they aren't all right in their own way,' answered Puddleglum. 'If you like their way.'

'Yes, but what *are* they?' pressed Jill. 'There are so many queer creatures in this country. I mean, are they animals, or birds, or dwarfs, or what?'

The Marsh-wiggle gave a long whistle. 'Phew!' he said. 'Don't you know? I thought the owls had told you. They're giants.'

Jill winced. She had never liked giants even in books, and she had once met one in a nightmare. Then she saw Scrubb's face, which had turned rather green, and thought to herself, 'I bet he's in a worse funk than I am.' That made her feel braver.

'The King told me long ago,' said Scrubb – 'that time when I was with him at sea – that he'd jolly well beaten those giants in war and made them pay him tribute.'

'That's true enough,' said Puddleglum. 'They're at peace with us all right. As long as we stay on our own side of the Shribble, they won't do us any harm. Over on their side, on the Moor – Still, there's always a chance. If we don't get near any of them, and if none of them forget themselves, and if we're not seen, it's just possible we might get a long way.'

'Look here!' said Scrubb, suddenly losing his temper, as people so easily do when they have been frightened. 'I don't believe the whole thing can be half as bad as you're making out; any more than the beds in the wigwam were hard or the wood was wet. I don't think Aslan would ever have sent us if there was so little chance as all that.'

He quite expected the Marsh-wiggle to give him an angry reply, but he only said, 'That's the spirit, Scrubb. That's the way to talk. Put a good face on it. But we all need to be very careful about our tempers, seeing all the hard times we shall have to go through together. Won't do to quarrel, you know. At any rate, don't begin it too soon. I know these expeditions usually *end* that way: knifing one another, I shouldn't wonder, before all's done. But the longer we can keep off it –'

'Well, if you feel it's so hopeless,' interrupted Scrubb, 'I think you'd better stay behind. Pole and I can go on alone, can't we, Pole?'

'Shut up and don't be an ass, Scrubb,' said Jill hastily, terrified lest the Marsh-wiggle should take him at his word.

'Don't you lose heart, Pole,' said Puddleglum. 'I'm coming, sure and certain. I'm not going to lose an opportunity like this. It will do me good. They all say – I mean, the other wiggles all say – that I'm too flighty; don't take life seriously enough. If they've said it once, they've said it a thousand times. "Puddleglum," they've said, "you're altogether too full of bobance and bounce and high spirits. You've got to learn that life isn't all fricasseed frogs and eel pie. You want something to sober you down a bit. We're only saying it for your own good, Puddleglum." That's what they say. Now a job like this – a journey up north just as winter's beginning, looking for a Prince that probably isn't there, by way of a ruined city that no one has ever seen – will be just the thing. If that doesn't steady a chap, I don't know what will.' And he rubbed his big frog-like hands together as if he were talking of going to a party or a pantomime. 'And now,' he added, 'let's see how those eels are getting on.'

When the meal came it was delicious and the children had two large helpings each. At first the Marsh-wiggle wouldn't believe that they really liked it, and when they had eaten so much that he had to believe them, he fell back on saying that it would probably disagree with them horribly. 'What's food for wiggles may be poison for humans, I shouldn't wonder,' he said. After the meal they had tea, in tins (as you've seen men having it who are working on the road), and Puddleglum had a good many sips out of a square black bottle. He offered the children some of it, but they thought it very nasty.

The rest of the day was spent in preparations for an early start tomorrow morning. Puddleglum, being far the biggest, said he would carry three blankets, with a large bit of bacon rolled up inside them. Jill was to carry the remains of the eels, some biscuit, and the tinder-box. Scrubb was to carry both his own cloak and Jill's when they didn't want to wear them. Scrubb (who had learned some shooting when he sailed to the East under Caspian) had Puddleglum's second-best bow, and Puddleglum had his best one; though he said that what with winds, and damp bowstrings, and bad light, and cold fingers, it was a hundred to one against either of them hitting anything. He and Scrubb both had swords – Scrubb had brought the one which had been left out for him in his room at Cair Paravel, but Jill had to be content with her knife. There would have been a quarrel about this, but as soon as they started sparring the wiggle rubbed his hands and said, 'Ah, there you are. I thought as much. That's what usually happens on adventures.' This made them both shut up.

All three went to bed early in the wigwam. This time the children really had a rather bad night. That was because Puddleglum, after saying, 'You'd better try for some sleep, you two; not that I suppose any of us will close an eye tonight,' instantly went off into such a loud, continuous snore that, when Jill at last got to sleep, she dreamed all night about road-drills and waterfalls and being in express trains in tunnels.

CHAPTER 6

THE WILD WASTE LANDS OF THE NORTH

AT about nine o'clock next morning three lonely figures might have been seen picking their way across the Shribble by the shoals and stepping-stones. It was a shallow, noisy stream, and even Jill was not wet above her knees when they reached the northern bank. About fifty yards ahead, the land rose up to the beginning of the moor, everywhere steeply, and often in cliffs.

'I suppose *that's* our way!' said Scrubb, pointing left and west to where a stream flowed down from the moor through a shallow gorge. But the Marsh-wiggle shook his head.

'The giants mainly live along the side of that gorge,' he said. 'You might say the gorge was like a street to them. We'll do better straight ahead, even though it's a bit steep.'

They found a place where they could scramble up, and in about ten minutes stood panting at the top. They cast a longing look back at the valley-land of Narnia and then turned their faces to the North. The vast, lonely moor stretched on and up as far as they could see. On their left was rockier ground. Jill thought that must be the edge of the giants' gorge and did not much care about looking in that direction. They set out.

It was good, springy ground for walking, and a day of pale winter sunlight. As they got deeper into the moor, the loneliness increased: one could hear peewits and see an occasional hawk. When they halted in the middle of the morning for a rest and a drink in a little hollow by a stream, Jill was beginning to feel that she might enjoy adventures after all, and said so.

'We haven't had any yet,' said the Marsh-wiggle.

Walks after the first halt – like school mornings after break or railway journeys after changing trains – never go on as they were before. When they set out again, Jill noticed that the rocky edge of the gorge had drawn nearer. And the rocks were less flat, more upright, than they had been. In fact they were like little towers of rock. And what funny shapes they were!

'I do believe,' thought Jill, 'that all the stories about giants might have come from those funny rocks. If you were coming along here when it was half dark, you could easily think those piles of rock were giants. Look at that one, now! You could almost imagine that the lump on top was a head. It would be rather too big for the body, but it would do well enough for an ugly giant. And all that bushy stuff – I suppose it's heather and birds' nests, really – would do quite well for hair and beard. And the things sticking out on each side are quite like ears. They'd be horribly big, but then I dare say giants would have big ears, like elephants. And – o-o-o-h! –'

Her blood froze. The thing moved. It was a real giant. There was no mistaking it; she had seen it turn its head. She had caught a glimpse of the great, stupid, puff-cheeked face. All the things were giants, not rocks. There were forty or fifty of them, all in a row; obviously standing with their feet on the bottom of the gorge and their elbows resting on the edge of the gorge, just as men might stand leaning on a wall – lazy men, on a fine morning after breakfast.

'Keep straight on,' whispered Puddleglum, who had

noticed them too. 'Don't look at them. And whatever you do, don't *run*. They'd all be after us in a moment.'

So they kept on, pretending not to have seen the giants. It was like walking past the gate of a house where

there is a fierce dog, only far worse. There were dozens and dozens of these giants. They didn't look angry – or kind – or interested at all. There was no sign that they had seen the travellers.

Then – whizz-whizz-whizz – some heavy object came hurtling through the air, and with a crash a big boulder fell about twenty paces ahead of them. And then – thud! – another fell twenty feet behind.

'Are they aiming at us?' asked Scrubb.

'No,' said Puddleglum. 'We'd be a good deal safer if they were. They're trying to hit *that* – that cairn over there to the right. They won't hit *it*, you know. *It's* safe enough; they're such very bad shots. They play cock-shies most fine mornings. About the only game they're clever enough to understand.'

It was a horrible time. There seemed no end to the line of giants, and they never ceased hurling stones, some of which fell extremely close. Quite apart from the real danger, the very sight and sound of their faces and voices were enough to scare anyone. Jill tried not to look at them.

After about twenty-five minutes the giants apparently had a quarrel. This put an end to the cock-shies, but it is not pleasant to be within a mile of quarrelling giants. They stormed and jeered at one another in long, meaningless words of about twenty syllables each. They foamed and jibbered and jumped in their rage, and each jump shook the earth like a bomb. They lammed each other on the head with great, clumsy stone hammers; but their skulls were so hard that the hammers bounced off again, and then the monster who had given the blow would drop his hammer and howl with pain because it had stung his fingers. But he was so stupid that he would do exactly the same thing a minute later. This was a good thing in the long run, for by the end of an hour all the giants were so hurt that they sat down and began to cry. When they sat down, their heads were below the edge of the gorge, so that you saw them no more; but Jill could hear them howling and blubbering and boo-hooing like great babies even after the place was a mile behind.

That night they bivouacked on the bare moor, and Puddleglum showed the children how to make the best of their blankets by sleeping back to back. (The backs keep each other warm and you can then have both blankets on top.) But it was chilly even so, and the ground was hard and lumpy. The Marsh-wiggle told them they would feel more comfortable if only they thought how very much colder it would be later on and farther north; but this didn't cheer them up at all.

They travelled across Ettinsmoor for many days, saving the bacon and living chiefly on the moor-fowl (they were not, of course, *talking* birds) which Eustace and the wiggle shot. Jill rather envied Eustace for being able to shoot; he had learned it on his voyage with King Caspian. As there were countless streams on the moor, they were never short of water. Jill thought that when, in books, people live on what they shoot, it never tells you what a long, smelly, messy job it is plucking and cleaning dead birds, and how cold it makes your fingers. But the great thing was that they met hardly any giants. One giant saw them, but he only roared with laughter and stumped away about his own business.

About the tenth day, they reached a place where the country changed. They came to the northern edge of the moor and looked down a long, steep slope into a different, and grimmer, land. At the bottom of the slope were cliffs: beyond these, a country of high mountains, dark precipices, stony valleys, ravines so deep and narrow that one could not see far into them, and rivers that poured out of echoing gorges to plunge sullenly into black depths. Needless to say, it was Puddleglum who pointed out a sprinkling of snow on the more distant slopes.

'But there'll be more on the north side of them, I shouldn't wonder,' he added.

It took them some time to reach the foot of the slope and, when they did, they looked down from the top of the cliffs at a river running below them from west to east. It was walled in by precipices on the far side as well as on their own, and it was green and sunless, full of rapids and waterfalls. The roar of it shook the earth even where they stood.

'The bright side of it is,' said Puddleglum, 'that if we break our necks getting down the cliff, then we're safe from being drowned in the river.'

'What about *that*?' said Scrubb suddenly, pointing upstream to their left. Then they all looked and saw the last thing they were expecting – a bridge. And what a bridge, too! It was a huge, single arch that spanned the gorge from cliff-top to cliff-top; and the crown of that arch was as high above the cliff-tops as the dome of St Paul's is above the street.

'Why, it must be a giants' bridge!' said Jill.

'Or a sorcerer's, more likely,' said Puddleglum. 'We've got to look out for enchantments in a place like this. I think it's a trap. I think it'll turn into mist and melt away just when we're out on the middle of it.'

'Oh, for goodness' sake, don't be such a wet blanket,' said Scrubb. 'Why on earth shouldn't it be a proper bridge?'

'Do you think any of the giants we've seen would have sense to build a thing like that?' said Puddleglum.

'But mightn't it have been built by other giants?' said Jill. 'I mean, by giants who lived hundreds of years ago, and were far cleverer than the modern kind. It might have been built by the same ones who built the giant city we're looking for. And that would mean we were on the right track – the old bridge leading to the old city!'

'That's a real brain-wave, Pole,' said Scrubb. 'It must be that. Come on.'

So they turned and went to the bridge. And when they reached it, it certainly seemed solid enough. The single stones were as big as those at Stonehenge and must have been squared by good masons once, though now they were cracked and crumbled. The balustrade had apparently been covered with rich carvings, of which some traces remained; mouldering faces and forms of

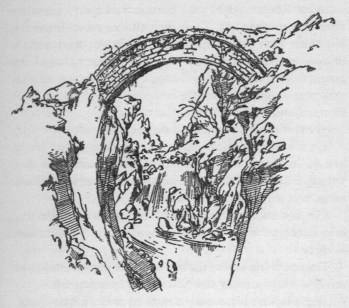

giants, minotaurs, squids, centipedes, and dreadful gods. Puddleglum still didn't trust it, but he consented to cross it with the children.

The climb up to the crown of the arch was long and heavy. In many places the great stones had dropped out, leaving horrible gaps through which you looked down on the river foaming thousands of feet below. They saw an eagle fly through under their feet. And the higher they went, the colder it grew, and the wind blew so that they could hardly keep their footing. It seemed to shake the bridge.

When they reached the top and could look down the farther slope of the bridge, they saw what looked like the remains of an ancient giant road stretching away before them into the heart of the mountains. Many stones of its pavement were missing and there were wide patches of grass between those that remained. And riding towards them on that ancient road were two people of normal grown-up human size.

'Keep on. Move towards them,' said Puddleglum. 'Anyone you meet in a place like this is as likely as not to be an enemy, but we mustn't let them think we're afraid.'

By the time they had stepped off the end of the bridge on to the grass, the two strangers were quite close. One was a knight in complete armour with his visor down. His armour and his horse were black; there was no device on his shield and no banneret on his spear. The other was a lady on a white horse, a horse so lovely that you wanted to kiss its nose and give it a lump of sugar at once. But the lady, who rode side-saddle and wore a long, fluttering dress of dazzling green, was lovelier still.

'Good day, t-r-r-avellers,' she cried out in a voice as sweet as the sweetest bird's song, trilling her R's delightfully. 'Some of you are young pilgrims to walk this rough waste.'

'That's as may be, Ma'am,' said Puddleglum very stiffly and on his guard.

'We're looking for the ruined city of the giants,' said Jill.

'The r-r-ruined city?' said the Lady. 'That is a strange place to be seeking. What will you do if you find it?'

'We've got to –' began Jill, but Puddleglum interrupted.

'Begging your pardon, Ma'am. But we don't know you or your friend – a silent chap, isn't he? – and you

don't know us. And we'd as soon not talk to strangers about our business, if you don't mind. Shall we have a little rain soon, do you think?'

The Lady laughed: the richest, most musical laugh you can imagine. 'Well, children,' she said, 'you have a wise, solemn old guide with you. I think none the worse of him for keeping his own counsel, but I'll be free with mine. I have often heard the name of the giantish City Ruinous, but never met any who would tell me the way thither. This road leads to the burgh and castle of Harfang, where dwell the gentle giants. They are as mild, civil, prudent, and courteous as those of Ettinsmoor are foolish, fierce, savage, and given to all beastliness. And in Harfang you may or may not hear tidings of the City Ruinous, but certainly you shall find good lodgings and merry hosts. You would be wise to winter there, or, at the least, to tarry certain days for your ease and refreshment. There you shall have steaming baths, soft beds, and bright hearths; and the roast and the baked and the sweet and the strong will be on the table four times in a day.'

'I say!' exclaimed Scrubb. 'That's something like! Think of sleeping in a bed again.'

'Yes, and having a hot bath,' said Jill. 'Do you think they'll ask us to stay? We don't know them, you see.'

'Only tell them,' answered the Lady, 'that She of the Green Kirtle salutes them by you, and has sent them two fair Southern children for the Autumn Feast.'

'Oh, thank you, thank you ever so much,' said Jill and Scrubb.

'But have a care,' said the Lady. 'On whatever day you reach Harfang, that you come not to the door too late. For they shut their gates a few hours after noon, and it is the custom of the castle that they open to none when once they have drawn bolt, how hard so ever he knock.'

The children thanked her again, with shining eyes, and the Lady waved to them. The Marsh-wiggle took off his steeple-hat and bowed very stiffly. Then the silent Knight and the Lady started walking their horses up the slope of the bridge with a great clatter of hoofs.

'Well!' said Puddleglum. 'I'd give a good deal to know where *she's* coming from and where she's going. Not the sort you expect to meet in the wilds of Giant-land, is she? Up to no good, I'll be bound.'

'Oh rot!' said Scrubb. 'I thought she was simply super. And think of hot meals and warm rooms. I do hope Harfang isn't a long way off.'

'Same here,' said Jill. 'And hadn't she a scrumptious dress. And the horse!'

'All the same,' said Puddleglum, 'I wish we knew a bit more about her.'

'I *was* going to ask her all about herself,' said Jill. 'But how could I when you wouldn't tell her anything about us?'

'Yes,' said Scrubb. 'And why were you so stiff and unpleasant. Didn't you like them?'

'Them?' said the wiggle. 'Who's *them*? I only saw one.'

'Didn't you see the Knight?' asked Jill.

'I saw a suit of armour,' said Puddleglum. 'Why didn't he speak?'

'I expect he was shy,' said Jill. 'Or perhaps he just wants to look at her and listen to her lovely voice. I'm sure I would if I was him.'

'I was wondering,' remarked Puddleglum, 'what you'd really see if you lifted up the visor of that helmet and looked inside.'

'Hang it all,' said Scrubb. 'Think of the shape of the armour! What *could* be inside it except a man?'

'How about a skeleton?' asked the Marsh-wiggle with ghastly cheerfulness. 'Or perhaps,' he added as an after-thought, 'nothing at all. I mean, nothing you could see. Someone invisible.'

'Really, Puddleglum,' said Jill with a shudder, 'you do have the most horrible ideas. How do you think of them all?'

'Oh, bother his ideas!' said Scrubb. 'He's always expecting the worst, and he's always wrong. Let's think about those Gentle Giants and get on to Harfang as quickly as we can. I wish I knew how far it is.'

And now they nearly had the first of those quarrels which Puddleglum had foretold: not that Jill and Scrubb hadn't been sparring and snapping at each other a good deal before, but this was the first really serious disagreement. Puddleglum didn't want them to go to Harfang at all. He said that he didn't know what a giant's idea of being 'gentle' might be, and that, anyway, Aslan's signs had said nothing about staying with giants, gentle or otherwise. The children, on the other hand, who were sick of wind and rain, and skinny fowl roasted over camp-fires, and hard, cold earth to sleep on, were absolutely dead set to visit the Gentle Giants. In the end, Puddleglum agreed to do so, but only on one condition. The others must give an absolute promise that, unless he gave them leave, they would not tell the Gentle Giants that they came from Narnia or that they were looking for Prince Rilian. And they gave him this promise, and went on.

After that talk with the Lady things got worse in two different ways. In the first place the country was much harder. The road led through endless, narrow valleys down which a cruel north wind was always blowing in their faces. There was nothing that could be used for fire-wood, and there were no nice little hollows to camp in, as there had been on the moor. And the ground was all stony, and made your feet sore by day and every bit of you sore by night.

In the second place, whatever the Lady had intended

by telling them about Harfang, the actual effect on the children was a bad one. They could think about nothing but beds and baths and hot meals and how lovely it would be to get indoors. They never talked about Aslan, or even about the lost prince, now. And Jill gave up her habit of repeating the signs over to herself every night and morning. She said to herself, at first, that she was too tired, but she soon forgot all about it. And though you might have expected that the idea of having a good time at Harfang would have made them more cheerful, it really made them more sorry for themselves and more grumpy and snappy with each other and with Puddle-glum.

At last they came one afternoon to a place where the gorge in which they were travelling widened out and dark fir woods rose on either side. They looked ahead and saw that they had come through the mountains. Before them lay a desolate, rocky plain: beyond it, further mountains capped with snow. But between them and those further mountains rose a low hill with an irregular, flattish top.

'Look! Look!' cried Jill, and pointed across the plain; and there, through the gathering dusk, from beyond the flat hill, everyone saw lights. Lights! Not moonlight, nor fires, but a homely cheering row of lighted windows. If you have never been in the wild wilderness, day and night, for weeks, you will hardly understand how they felt.

'Harfang!' cried Scrubb and Jill in glad, excited voices; and 'Harfang,' repeated Puddleglum in a dull, gloomy voice. But he added, 'Hullo! Wild geese!' and had the bow off his shoulder in a second. He brought down a good fat goose. It was far too late to think of reaching Harfang that day. But they had a hot meal and a fire, and started the night warmer than they had been for over a week. After the fire had gone out, the night grew bitterly cold, and when they woke next morning, their blankets were stiff with frost.

'Never mind!' said Jill, stamping her feet. 'Hot baths tonight!'

CHAPTER 7

THE HILL OF THE STRANGE TRENCHES

THERE is no denying it was a beast of a day. Overhead was a sunless sky, muffled in clouds that were heavy with snow; underfoot, a black frost; blowing over it, a wind that felt as if it would take your skin off. When they got down into the plain they found that this part of the ancient road was much more ruinous than any they had yet seen. They had to pick their way over great broken stones and between boulders and across rubble: hard going for sore feet. And, however tired they got, it was far too cold for a halt.

At about ten o'clock the first tiny snow flakes came loitering down and settled on Jill's arm. Ten minutes later they were falling quite thickly. In twenty minutes the ground was noticeably white. And by the end of half an hour a good steady snowstorm, which looked as if it meant to last all day, was driving in their faces so that they could hardly see.

In order to understand what followed, you must keep on remembering how little they could see. As they drew near the low hill which separated them from the place where the lighted windows had appeared, they had no general view of it at all. It was a question of seeing the next few paces ahead, and, even for that, you had to screw up your eyes. Needless to say, they were not talking.

When they reached the foot of the hill they caught a glimpse of what might be rocks on each side – squarish rocks, if you looked at them carefully, but no one did. All were more concerned with the ledge right in front of them which barred their way. It was about four feet high. The Marsh-wiggle, with his long legs, had no difficulty in jumping on to the top of it, and he then helped the others up. It was a nasty wet business for them, though not for him, because the snow now lay quite deep on the ledge. They then had a stiff climb – Jill fell once – up very rough ground for about a hundred yards, and came to a second ledge. There were four of these ledges altogether, at quite irregular intervals.

As they struggled on to the fourth ledge, there was no mistaking the fact that they were now at the top of the flat hill. Up till now the slope had given them some shelter; here, they got the full fury of the wind. For the hill, oddly enough, was quite as flat on top as it had looked from a distance: a great level tableland which the storm tore across without resistance. In most places the snow was still hardly lying at all, for the wind kept catching it up off the ground in sheets and clouds, and hurling it in their faces. And round their feet little eddies of snow ran about as you sometimes see them doing over ice. And, indeed, in many places, the surface was almost as smooth as ice. But to make matters worse it was crossed and criss-crossed with curious banks or dykes, which sometimes divided it up into squares and oblongs. All these of course had to be climbed; they varied from two to five feet in height and were about a couple of yards thick. On the north side of each bank the snow already lay in deep drifts; and after each climb you came down into drift and got wet.

Fighting her way forward with hood up and head down and numb hands inside her cloak, Jill had glimpses of other odd things on that horrible tableland – things on her right that looked vaguely like factory chimneys, and, on her left, a huge cliff, straighter than any cliff ought to be. But she wasn't at all interested and didn't give them a thought. The only things she thought about were her cold hands (and nose and chin and ears) and hot baths and beds at Harfang.

Suddenly she skidded, slid about five feet, and found herself to her horror sliding down into a dark, narrow chasm which seemed that moment to have appeared in front of her. Half a second later she had reached the bottom. She appeared to be in a kind of trench or groove, only about three feet wide. And though she was shaken by the fall, almost the first thing she noticed was the relief of being out of the wind; for the walls of the trench rose high above her. The next thing she noticed was, naturally, the anxious faces of Scrubb and Puddleglum looking down at her from the edge.

'Are you hurt, Pole?' shouted Scrubb.

'*Both* legs broken, I shouldn't wonder,' shouted Puddleglum.

Jill stood up and explained that she was all right, but they'd have to help her out.

'What is it you've fallen into?' asked Scrubb.

'It's a kind of trench, or it might be a kind of sunken lane or something,' said Jill. 'It runs quite straight.'

'Yes, by Jove,' said Scrubb. 'And it runs due north! I wonder is it a sort of road? If it was, we'd be out of this infernal wind down there. Is there a lot of snow at the bottom?'

'Hardly any. It all blows over the top, I suppose.'

'What happens farther on?'

'Half a sec. I'll go and see,' said Jill. She got up and walked along the trench; but before she had gone far, it turned sharply to the right. She shouted this information back to the others.

'What's round the corner?' asked Scrubb.

Now it happened that Jill had the same feeling about twisty passages and dark places underground, or even nearly underground, that Scrubb had about the edges of cliffs. She had no intention of going round that corner alone; especially when she heard Puddleglum bawling out from behind her:

'Be careful, Pole. It's just the sort of place that might lead to a dragon's cave. And in a giant country, there might be giant earth-worms or giant beetles.'

'I don't think it goes anywhere much,' said Jill, coming hastily back.

'I'm jolly well going to have a look,' said Scrubb. 'What do you mean by *anywhere much*, I should like to know?' So he sat down on the edge of the trench (everyone was too wet by now to bother about being a bit wetter) and then dropped in. He pushed past Jill and, though he didn't say anything, she felt sure that he knew she had funked it. So she followed him close, but took care not to get in front of him.

It proved, however, a disappointing exploration. They went round the right-hand turn and straight on for a few paces. Here there was a choice of ways: straight on again, or sharp to the right. 'That's no good,' said Scrubb, glancing down the right-hand turn, 'that would be taking us back – south.' He went straight on, but once more, in a few steps, they found a second turn to the right. But this time there was no choice of ways, for the trench they had been following here came to a dead end.

'No good,' grunted Scrubb. Jill lost no time in turning and leading the way back. When they returned to the place where Jill had first fallen in, the Marsh-wiggle with his long arms had no difficulty in pulling them out.

But it was dreadful to be out on top again. Down in those narrow slits of trenches, their ears had almost begun to thaw. They had been able to see clearly and breathe easily and hear each other speak without shouting. It was absolute misery to come back into the withering coldness. And it did seem hard when Puddle-glum chose that moment for saying:

'Are you still sure of those signs, Pole? What's the one we ought to be after, now?'

'Oh, come *on*! Bother the signs,' said Pole. 'Something about someone mentioning Aslan's name, I think. But I'm jolly well not going to give a recitation here.'

As you see, she had got the order wrong. That was because she had given up saying the signs over every night. She still really knew them, if she troubled to think: but she was no longer so 'pat' in her lesson as to be sure of reeling them off in the right order at a moment's notice and without thinking. Puddleglum's question annoyed her because, deep down inside her, she was already annoyed with herself for not knowing the Lion's lesson quite so well as she felt she ought to have known it. This annoyance, added to the misery of being very cold and tired, made her say, 'Bother the signs.' She didn't perhaps quite mean it.

'Oh, that was next, was it?' said Puddleglum. 'Now I wonder, are you right? Got 'em mixed, I shouldn't wonder. It seems to me, this hill, this flat place we're on, is worth stopping to have a look at. Have you noticed –'

'Oh Lor!' said Scrubb, 'is this a time for stopping to admire the view? For goodness' sake let's get on.'

'Oh, look, look, look,' cried Jill and pointed. Everyone turned, and everyone saw. Some way off to the north, and a good deal higher up than the tableland on which they stood, a line of lights had appeared. This time, even more obviously than when the travellers had seen them the night before, they were windows: smaller windows that made one think deliciously of bedrooms, and larger windows that made one think of great halls with fires roaring on the hearth and hot soup or juicy sirloins smoking on the table.

'Harfang!' exclaimed Scrubb.

'That's all very well,' said Puddleglum. 'But what I was saying was –'

'Oh, shut up,' said Jill crossly. 'We haven't a moment to lose. Don't you remember what the Lady said about their locking up so early? We must get there in time, we must, we must. We'll *die* if we're shut out on a night like this.'

'Well, it isn't exactly a night, not yet,' began Puddle-glum; but the two children both said, 'Come on,' and began stumbling forward on the slippery tableland as quickly as their legs would carry them. The Marsh-wiggle followed them: still talking, but now that they were forcing their way into the wind again, they could not have heard him even if they had wanted to. And they didn't want. They were thinking of baths and beds and hot drinks; and the idea of coming to Harfang too late and being shut out was almost unbearable.

In spite of their haste, it took them a long time to cross the flat top of that hill. And even when they had crossed it, there were still several ledges to climb down on the far side. But at last they reached the bottom and could see what Harfang was like.

It stood on a high crag, and in spite of its many towers was more a huge house than a castle. Obviously, the Gentle Giants feared no attack. There were windows in the outside wall quite close to the ground – a thing no one would have in a serious fortress. There were even odd little doors here and there, so that it would be quite easy to get in and out of the castle without going through the courtyard. This raised the spirits of Jill and Scrubb. It made the whole place look more friendly and less forbidding.

At first the height and steepness of the crag frightened them, but presently they noticed that there was an easier way up on the left and that the road wound up towards it. It was a terrible climb, after the journey they had already had, and Jill nearly gave up. Scrubb and Puddleglum had to help her for the last hundred yards. But in the end they stood before the castle gate. The portcullis was up and the gate open.

However tired you are, it takes some nerve to walk up to a giant's front door. In spite of all his previous warnings against Harfang, it was Puddleglum who showed most courage.

'Steady pace, now,' he said. 'Don't look frightened, whatever you do. We've done the silliest thing in the world by coming at all: but now that we *are* here, we'd best put a bold face on it.'

With these words he strode forward into the gateway, stood still under the arch where the echo would help his voice, and called out as loud as he could.

'Ho! Porter! Guests who seek lodging.'

And while he was waiting for something to happen, he took off his hat and knocked off the heavy mass of snow which had gathered on its wide brim.

'I say,' whispered Scrubb to Jill. 'He may be a wet blanket, but he has plenty of pluck – and cheek.'

A door opened, letting out a delicious glow of fire-light, and the Porter appeared. Jill bit her lips for fear she should scream. He was not a perfectly enormous giant; that is to say, he was rather taller than an apple tree but nothing like so tall as a telegraph pole. He had bristly red hair, a leather jerkin with metal plates fastened all over it so as to make a kind of mail shirt, bare knees (very hairy indeed) and things like puttees on his legs. He stooped down and goggled at Puddleglum.

'And what sort of a creature do you call yourself,' he said.

Jill took her courage in both hands. 'Please,' she said, shouting up at the giant. 'The Lady of the Green Kirtle salutes the King of the Gentle Giants, and has sent us two Southern children and this Marsh-wiggle (his name's Puddleglum) to your Autumn Feast. – If it's quite con-venient, of course,' she added.

'O-ho!' said the Porter. 'That's quite a different story. Come in, little people, come in. You'd best come into the lodge while I'm sending word to his Majesty.' He looked at the children with curiosity. 'Blue faces,' he said. 'I didn't know they were that colour. Don't care about it myself. But I dare say you look quite nice to one another. Beetles fancy other beetles, they do say.'

'Our faces are only blue with cold,' said Jill. 'We're not this colour *really*.'

'Then come in and get warm. Come in, little shrimps,' said the Porter. They followed him into the lodge. And though it was rather terrible to hear such a big door clang shut behind them, they forgot about it as soon as they saw the thing they had been longing for ever since supper time last night – a fire. And such a fire! It looked as if four or five whole trees were blazing on it, and it was so hot they couldn't go within yards of it. But they all flopped down on the brick floor, as near as they could bear the heat, and heaved great sighs of relief.

'Now, youngster,' said the Porter to another giant who had been sitting in the back of the room, staring at the visitors till it looked as if his eyes would start out of his head, 'run across with this message to the House.' And he repeated what Jill had said to him. The younger giant, after a final stare, and a great guffaw, left the room.

'Now, Froggy,' said the Porter to Puddleglum, 'you look as if you wanted some cheering up.' He produced a black bottle very like Puddleglum's own, but about twenty times larger. 'Let me see, let me see,' said the Porter. 'I can't give you a cup or you'll drown yourself. Let me scc. This salt-cellar will be just the thing. You needn't mention it over at the House. The silver *will* keep on getting over here, and it's not my fault.'

The salt-cellar was not very like one of ours, being narrower and more upright, and made quite a good cup for Puddleglum, when the giant set it down on the floor beside him. The children expected Puddleglum to refuse it, distrusting the Gentle Giants as he did. But he muttered, 'It's rather late to be thinking of precautions now that we're inside and the door shut behind us.' Then he sniffed at the liquor. 'Smells all right,' he said. 'But that's nothing to go by. Better make sure,' and took a sip. 'Tastes all right too,' he said. 'But it might do that at the *first* sip. How does it go on?' He took a larger sip. 'Ah!' he said. 'But is it the same all the way down?' and took another. 'There'll be something nasty at the bottom, I shouldn't wonder,' he said, and finished the drink. He licked his lips and remarked to the children, 'This'll be a test, you see. If I curl up, or burst, or turn into a lizard, or something, then you'll know not to take anything they offer you.' But the giant, who was too far up to hear the things Puddleglum had been saying under his breath, roared with laughter and said, 'Why, Froggy, you're a man. See him put it away!'

'Not a man . . . Marsh-wiggle,' replied Puddleglum in a somewhat indistinct voice. 'Not frog either: Marsh-wiggle.'

At that moment the door opened behind them and the younger giant came in saying, 'They're to go to the throne-room at once.'

The children stood up but Puddleglum remained sitting and said, 'Marsh-wiggle. Marsh-wiggle. Very respectable Marsh-wiggle. Respectowiggle.'

'Show them the way, young 'un,' said the giant Porter. 'You'd better carry Froggy. He's had a drop more than's good for him.'

'Nothing wrong with me,' said Puddleglum. 'Not a frog. Nothing frog with me. I'm a respectabiggle.'

But the young giant caught him up by the waist and signed to the children to follow. In this undignified way they crossed the courtyard. Puddleglum, held in the giant's fist, and vaguely kicking the air, did certainly look very like a frog. But they had little time to notice this, for they soon entered the great doorway of the main castle – both their hearts were beating faster than usual – and, after pattering along several corridors at a trot to keep up with the giant's paces, found themselves blinking in the light of an enormous room, where lamps glowed

and a fire roared on the hearth and both were reflected
from the gilding of roof and cornice. More giants than
they could count stood on their left and right, all in
magnificent robes; and on two thrones at the far end, sat
two huge shapes that appeared to be the King and Queen.

About twenty feet from the thrones, they stopped.
Scrubb and Jill made an awkward attempt at a bow
(girls are not taught how to curtsey at Experiment
House) and the young giant carefully put Puddleglum
down on the floor, where he collapsed into a sort of
sitting position. With his long limbs he looked, to tell the
truth, uncommonly like a large spider.

CHAPTER 8

THE HOUSE OF HARFANG

'Go on, Pole, do your stuff,' whispered Scrubb.

Jill found that her mouth was so dry that she couldn't speak a word. She nodded savagely at Scrubb.

Thinking to himself that he would never forgive her (or Puddleglum either), Scrubb licked his lips and shouted up to the King giant.

'If you please, Sire, the Lady of the Green Kirtle salutes you by us and said you'd like to have us for your Autumn Feast.'

The giant King and Queen looked at each other, nodded to each other, and smiled in a way that Jill didn't exactly like. She liked the King better than the Queen. He had a fine, curled beard and a straight eagle-like nose, and was really rather good-looking as giants go. The Queen was dreadfully fat and had a double chin and a fat, powdered face – which isn't a very nice thing at the best of times, and of course looks much worse when it is ten times too big. Then the King put out his tongue and licked his lips. Anyone might do that: but his tongue was so very large and red, and came out so unexpectedly, that it gave Jill quite a shock.

'Oh, what *good* children!' said the Queen. ('Perhaps she's the nice one after all,' thought Jill.)

'Yes indeed,' said the King. 'Quite excellent children. We welcome you to our court. Give me your hands.'

He stretched down his great right hand – very clean and with any number of rings on the fingers, but also with terrible pointed nails. He was much too big to shake the hands which the children, in turn, held up to him; but he shook the arms.

'And what's *that*?' asked the King, pointing to Puddleglum.

'Reshpeckobiggle,' said Puddleglum.

'Oh!' screamed the Queen, gathering her skirts close about her ankles. 'The horrid thing! It's alive.'

'He's quite all right, your Majesty, really, he is,' said Scrubb hastily. 'You'll like him much better when you get to know him. I'm sure you will.'

I hope you won't lose all interest in Jill for the rest of the book if I tell you that at this moment she began to cry. There was a good deal of excuse for her. Her feet and hands and ears and nose were still only just beginning to thaw; melted snow was trickling off her clothes; she had had hardly anything to eat or drink that day; and her legs were aching so that she felt she could not go on standing much longer. Anyway, it did more good at the moment than anything else would have done, for the Queen said:

'Ah, the poor child! My lord, we do wrong to keep our guests standing. Quick, some of you! Take them away. Give them food and wine and baths. Comfort the little girl. Give her lollipops, give her dolls, give her physics, give her all you can think of – possets and comfits and caraways and lullabies and toys. Don't cry, little girl, or you won't be good for anything when the feast comes.'

Jill was just as indignant as you and I would have been at the mention of toys and dolls; and, though lollipops and comfits might be all very well in their way, she very much hoped that something more solid would be

provided. The Queen's foolish speech, however, produced excellent results, for Puddleglum and Scrubb were at once picked up by gigantic gentlemen-in-waiting, and Jill by a gigantic maid of honour, and carried off to their rooms.

Jill's room was about the size of a church, and would have been rather grim if it had not had a roaring fire on the hearth and a very thick crimson carpet on the floor. And here delightful things began to happen to her. She was handed over to the Queen's old Nurse, who was, from the giants' point of view, a little old woman almost bent double with age, and, from the human point of view, a giantess small enough to go about an ordinary room without knocking her head on the ceiling. She was very capable, though Jill did wish she wouldn't keep on clicking her tongue and saying things like 'Oh la, la! Ups-a-daisy' and 'There's a duck' and 'Now we'll be all right, my poppet'. She filled a giant foot-bath with hot water and helped Jill into it. If you can swim (as Jill could) a giant bath is a lovely thing. And giant towels, though a bit rough and coarse, are lovely too, because there are acres of them. In fact you don't need to dry at all, you just roll about on them in front of the fire and enjoy yourself. And when that was over, clean, fresh, warmed clothes were put on Jill: very splendid clothes and a little too big for her, but clearly made for humans not giantesses. 'I suppose if that woman in the green kirtle comes here, they must be used to guests of our size,' thought Jill.

She soon saw that she was right about this, for a table and chair of the right height for an ordinary grown-up human were placed for her, and the knives and forks and spoons were the proper size too. It was delightful to sit down, feeling warm and clean at last. Her feet were still bare and it was lovely to tread on the giant carpet. She sank in it well over her ankles and it was just the thing for sore feet. The meal – which I suppose we must call dinner, though it was nearer tea time – was cock-a-leekie soup, and hot roast turkey, and a steamed pudding, and roast chestnuts, and as much fruit as you could eat.

The only annoying thing was that the Nurse kept coming in and out, and every time she came in, she brought a gigantic toy with her – a huge doll, bigger than Jill herself, a wooden horse on wheels, about the size of an elephant, a drum that looked like a young gasometer, and a woolly lamb. They were crude, badly

made things, painted in very bright colours, and Jill hated the sight of them. She kept on telling the Nurse she didn't want them, but the Nurse said:

'Tut-tut-tut-tut. You'll want 'em all right when you've had a bit of a rest, I know! Te-he-he! Beddy bye, now. A precious poppet!'

The bed was not a giant bed but only a big four-poster, like what you might see in an old-fashioned hotel; and very small it looked in that enormous room. She was very glad to tumble into it.

'Is it still snowing, Nurse?' she asked sleepily.

'No. Raining now, ducky!' said the giantess. 'Rain'll wash away all the nasty snow. Precious poppet will be able to go out and play tomorrow!' And she tucked Jill up and said good night.

I know nothing so disagreeable as being kissed by a giantess. Jill thought the same, but was asleep in five minutes.

The rain fell steadily all the evening and all the night, dashing against the windows of the castle, and Jill never heard it but slept deeply, past supper time and past midnight. And then came the deadest hour of the night and nothing stirred but mice in the house of the giants. At that hour there came to Jill a dream. It seemed to her that she awoke in the same room and saw the fire, sunk low and red, and in the firelight the great wooden horse. And the horse came of its own will, rolling on its wheels across the carpet, and stood at her head. And now it was no longer a horse, but a lion as big as the horse. And then it was not a toy lion, but a real lion, The Real Lion, just as she had seen him on the mountain beyond the world's end. And a smell of all sweet-smelling things there are filled the room. But there was some trouble in Jill's mind, though she could not think what it was, and the tears streamed down her face and wet the pillow. The Lion told her to repeat the signs, and she found that she had forgotten them all. At that, a great horror came over her. And Aslan took her up in his jaws (she could feel his lips and his breath but not his teeth) and carried her to the window and made her look out. The moon shone bright; and written in great letters across the world or the sky (she did not know which) were the words UNDER ME. After that, the dream faded away, and when she woke, very late next morning, she did not remember that she had dreamed at all.

She was up and dressed and had finished breakfast in front of the fire when the Nurse opened the door and said: 'Here's pretty poppet's little friends come to play with her.'

In came Scrubb and the Marsh-wiggle.

'Hullo! Good morning,' said Jill. 'Isn't this fun? I've slept about fifteen hours, I believe. I do feel better, don't you?'

'*I* do,' said Scrubb, 'but Puddleglum says he has a headache. Hullo! – your window has a window seat. If we got up on that, we could see out.' And at once they all did so: and at the first glance Jill said, 'Oh, how perfectly dreadful!'

The sun was shining and, except for a few drifts, the snow had been almost completely washed away by the rain. Down below them, spread out like a map, lay the flat hill-top which they had struggled over yesterday afternoon; seen from the castle, it could not be mistaken for anything but the ruins of a gigantic city. It had been flat, as Jill now saw, because it was still, on the whole, paved, though in places the pavement was broken. The criss-cross banks were what was left of the walls of huge buildings which might once have been giants' palaces and temples. One bit of wall, about five hundred feet high, was still standing; it was that which she had thought was a cliff. The things that had looked like factory chimneys were enormous pillars, broken off at unequal heights; their fragments lay at their bases like felled trees of monstrous stone. The ledges which they had climbed down on the north side of the hill – and also, no doubt the other ledges which they had climbed up on the south side – were the remaining steps of giant stairs. To crown all, in large, dark lettering across the centre of the pavement, ran the words UNDER ME.

The three travellers looked at each other in dismay, and, after a short whistle, Scrubb said what they were all thinking, 'The second and third signs muffed.' And at that moment Jill's dream rushed back into her mind.

'It's my fault,' she said in despairing tones. 'I – I'd given up repeating the signs every night. If I'd been thinking about them I could have seen it was the city, even *in* all that snow.'

'I'm worse,' said Puddleglum. 'I *did* see, or nearly. I thought it looked uncommonly like a ruined city.'

'You're the only one who isn't to blame,' said Scrubb. 'You *did* try to make us stop.'

'Didn't try hard enough, though,' said the Marshwiggle. 'And I'd no call to be trying. I ought to have done it. As if I couldn't have stopped you two with one hand each!'

'The truth is,' said Scrubb, 'we were so jolly keen on getting to this place that we weren't bothering about anything else. At least I know I was. Ever since we met that woman with the knight who didn't talk, we've been thinking of nothing else. We'd nearly forgotten about Prince Rilian.'

'I shouldn't wonder,' said Puddleglum, 'if that wasn't exactly what she intended.'

'What I don't quite understand,' said Jill, 'is how we didn't see the lettering? Or could it have come there since last night. Could he – Aslan – have put it there in the night? I had such a queer dream.' And she told them all about it.

'Why, you chump!' said Scrubb. 'We did see it. We got into the lettering. Don't you see? We got into the letter E in ME. That was your sunk lane. We walked along the bottom stroke of the E, due north – turned to our right along the upright – came to another turn to the right – that's the middle stroke – and then went on to the top left-hand corner, or (if you like) the north-eastern corner of the letter, and came back. Like the bally idiots we are.' He kicked the window seat savagely, and went on, 'So it's no good, Pole. I know what you were thinking because I was thinking the same. You were thinking how nice it would have been if Aslan hadn't put the instructions on the stones of the ruined city till after we'd passed it. And then it would have been his fault, not ours. So likely, isn't it? No. We must just own up. We've only four signs to go by, and we've muffed the first three.'

'You mean I have,' said Jill. 'It's quite true. I've spoiled everything ever since you brought me here. All the same – I'm frightfully sorry and all that – all the same, what *are* the instructions? UNDER ME doesn't seem to make much sense.'

'Yes it does, though,' said Puddleglum. 'It means we've got to look for the Prince under that city.'

'But how can we?' asked Jill.

'That's the question,' said Puddleglum, rubbing his big, frog-like hands together. 'How can we *now*? No doubt, if we'd had our minds on our job when we were at the Ruinous City, we'd have been shown how – found a little door, or a cave, or a tunnel, met someone to help us. Might have been (you never know) Aslan himself. We'd have got down under those paving-stones somehow or other. Aslan's instructions always work: there are no exceptions. But how to do it *now* – that's another matter.'

'Well, we shall just have to go back, I suppose,' said Jill.

'Easy, isn't it?' said Puddleglum. 'We might try opening that door to begin with.' And they all looked at the door and saw that none of them could reach the handle, and that almost certainly no one could turn it if they did.

'Do you think they won't let us out if we ask?' said Jill. And nobody said, but everyone thought, 'Supposing they don't.'

It was not a pleasant idea. Puddleglum was dead against any idea of telling the giants their real business and simply asking to be let out; and of course the children couldn't tell without his permission, because they had promised. And all three felt pretty sure that there would be no chance of escaping from the castle by night. Once they were in their rooms with the doors shut, they would be prisoners till morning. They might, of course, ask to have their doors left open, but that would rouse suspicions.

'Our only chance,' said Scrubb, 'is to try to sneak away by daylight. Mightn't there be an hour in the after-noon when most of the giants are asleep? – and if we could steal down into the kitchen, mightn't there be a back door open?'

'It's hardly what I call a Chance,' said the Marshwiggle. 'But it's all the chance we're likely to get.' As a matter of fact, Scrubb's plan was not quite so hopeless as you might think. If you want to get out of a house without being seen, the middle of the afternoon is in some ways a better time to try it than the middle of the night. Doors and windows are more likely to be open; and if you *are* caught, you can always pretend you weren't meaning to go far and had no particular plans. (It is very hard to make either giants or grown-ups believe this if you're found climbing out of a bedroom window at one o'clock in the morning.)

'We must put them off their guard, though,' said Scrubb. 'We must pretend we love being here and are longing for this Autumn Feast.'

'That's tomorrow night,' said Puddleglum. 'I heard one of them say so.'

'I see,' said Jill. 'We must pretend to be awfully excited about it, and keep on asking questions. They think we're absolute infants anyway, which will make it easier.'

'Gay,' said Puddleglum with a deep sigh. 'That's what we've got to be, Gay. As if we hadn't a care in the world. Frolicsome. You two youngsters haven't always got very high spirits, I've noticed. You must watch me, and do as I do. I'll be gay. Like this' – and he assumed a ghastly grin. 'And frolicsome' – here he cut a most mournful caper. 'You'll soon get into it, if you keep your eyes on me. They think I'm a funny fellow already, you see. I dare say you two thought I was a trifle tipsy last

night, but I do assure you it was – well, most of it was –
put on. I had an idea it would come in useful, somehow.'

The children, when they talked over their adventures
afterwards, could never feel sure whether this last statement was quite strictly true; but they were sure that
Puddleglum thought it was true when he made it.

'All right. Gay's the word,' said Scrubb. 'Now, if we
could only get someone to open this door. While we're
fooling about and being gay, we've got to find out all
we can about this castle.'

Luckily, at that very moment the door opened, and
the giant Nurse bustled in saying, 'Now, my poppets.
Like to come and see the King and all the court setting
out on the hunting? Such a pretty sight!'

They lost no time in rushing out past her and climbing
down the first staircase they came to. The noise of hounds
and horns and giant voices guided them, so that in a few
minutes they reached the courtyard. The giants were all
on foot, for there are no giant horses in that part of the
world, and the giants' hunting is done on foot; like
beagling in England. The hounds also were of normal
size. When Jill saw that there were no horses she was at
first dreadfully disappointed, for she felt sure that the
great fat Queen would never go after hounds on foot;
and it would never do to have her about the house all
day. But then she saw the Queen in a kind of litter
supported on the shoulders of six young giants. The
silly old creature was all got up in green and had a horn
at her side. Twenty or thirty giants, including the King,
were assembled, ready for the sport, all talking and
laughing fit to deafen you: and down below, nearer Jill's
level, there were wagging tails, and barking, and loose,

slobbery mouths and noses of dogs thrust into your hand.
Puddleglum was just beginning to strike what he thought
a gay and gamesome attitude (which might have spoiled

everything if it had been noticed) when Jill put on her
most attractively childish smile, rushed across to the
Queen's litter and shouted up to the Queen.

'Oh, please! You're not going *away*, are you? You will
come back?'

'Yes, my dear,' said the Queen. 'I'll be back tonight.'

'Oh, *good*. How lovely!' said Jill. 'And we *may* come
to the feast tomorrow night, mayn't we? We're so longing
for tomorrow night! And we do love being here. And
while you're out, we may run over the whole castle and
see everything, mayn't we? Do say yes.'

The Queen did say yes, but the laughter of all the
courtiers nearly drowned her voice.

CHAPTER 9

HOW THEY DISCOVERED SOMETHING
WORTH KNOWING

THE others admitted afterwards that Jill had been wonderful that day. As soon as the King and the rest of the hunting party had set off, she began making a tour of the whole castle and asking questions, but all in such an innocent, babyish way that no one could suspect her of any secret design. Though her tongue was never still, you could hardly say she talked: she *prattled* and giggled. She made love to everyone – the grooms, the porters, the housemaids, the ladies-in-waiting, and the elderly giant lords whose hunting days were past. She submitted to being kissed and pawed about by any number of giantesses, many of whom seemed sorry for her and called her 'a poor little thing' though none of them explained why. She made especial friends with the cook and discovered the all-important fact there was a scullery door which let you out through the outer wall, so that you did not have to cross the courtyard or pass the great gatehouse. In the kitchen she pretended to be greedy, and ate all sorts of scraps which the cook and scullions delighted to give her. But upstairs among the ladies she asked questions about how she would be dressed for the great feast, and how long she would be allowed to sit up, and whether she would dance with some very, very small giant. And then (it made her hot all over when she remembered it afterwards) she would put her head on one side in an idiotic fashion which grown-ups, giant and otherwise, thought very fetching, and shake her curls, and fidget, and say, 'Oh, I do wish it was tomorrow night, don't you? Do you think the time will go quickly till then?' And all the giantesses said she was a perfect little darling; and some of them dabbed their eyes with enormous handkerchiefs as if they were going to cry.

'They're dear little things at that age,' said one giantess to another. 'It seems almost a pity . . .'

Scrubb and Puddleglum both did their best, but girls do that kind of thing better than boys. Even boys do it better than Marsh-wiggles.

At lunchtime something happened which made all three of them more anxious than ever to leave the castle of the Gentle Giants. They had lunch in the great hall at a little table of their own, near the fireplace. At a bigger table, about twenty yards away, half a dozen old giants were lunching. Their conversation was so noisy, and so high up in the air, that the children soon took no more notice of it than you would of hooters outside the window or traffic noises in the street. They were eating cold venison, a kind of food which Jill had never tasted before, and she was liking it.

Suddenly Puddleglum turned to them, and his face had gone so pale that you could see the paleness under the natural muddiness of his complexion. He said:

'Don't eat another bite.'

'What's wrong?' asked the other two in a whisper.

'Didn't you hear what those giants were saying? "That's a nice tender haunch of venison," said one of them. "Then that stag was a liar," said another. "Why?" said the first one. "Oh," said the other. "They say that when he was caught he said, Don't kill me, I'm tough. You won't like me."'

For a moment Jill did not realize the full meaning of this. But she did when Scrubb's eyes opened wide with horror and he said:

'So we've been eating a *Talking* stag.'

This discovery didn't have exactly the same effect on all of them. Jill, who was new to that world, was sorry for the poor stag and thought it rotten of the giants to have killed him. Scrubb, who had been in that world before and had at least one Talking beast as his dear friend, felt horrified; as you might feel about a murder. But Puddleglum, who was Narnian born, was sick and faint, and felt as you would feel if you found you had eaten a baby.

'We've brought the anger of Aslan on us,' he said. 'That's what comes of not attending to the signs. We're under a curse, I expect. If it was allowed, it would be the best thing we could do, to take these knives and drive them into our own hearts.'

And gradually even Jill came to see it from his point of view. At any rate, none of them wanted any more lunch. And as soon as they thought it safe they crept quietly out of the hall.

It was now drawing near to that time of the day on which their hopes of escape depended, and all became nervous. They hung about in passages and waited for things to become quiet. The giants in the hall sat on a dreadfully long time after the meal was over. The bald one was telling a story. When that was over, the three travellers dawdled down to the kitchen. But there were still plenty of giants there, or at least in the scullery, washing up and putting things away. It was agonizing, waiting till these finished their jobs and, one by one, wiped their hands and went away. At last only one old giantess was left in the room. She pottered about, and pottered about, and at last the three travellers realized with horror that she did not intend to go away at all.

'Well, dearies,' she said to them. 'That job's about through. Let's put the kettle there. That'll make a nice cup of tea presently. Now I can have a little bit of a rest. Just look into the scullery, like good poppets, and tell me if the back door is open.'

'Yes, it is,' said Scrubb.

'That's right. I always leave it open so as Puss can get in and out, the poor thing.'

Then she sat down on one chair and put her feet up on another.

'I don't know as I mightn't have forty winks,' said the giantess. 'If only that blamey hunting party doesn't come back too soon.'

All their spirits leaped up when she mentioned forty winks, and flopped down again when she mentioned the return of the hunting party.

'When do they usually come back?' asked Jill.

'You never can tell,' said the giantess. 'But there; go and be quiet for a bit, my dearies.'

They retreated to the far end of the kitchen, and would have slipped out into the scullery there and then if the giantess had not sat up, opened her eyes, and brushed away a fly. 'Don't try it till we're sure she's really asleep,' whispered Scrubb. 'Or it'll spoil everything.' So they all huddled at the kitchen end, waiting and watching. The thought that the hunters might come back at any moment was terrible. And the giantess was fidgety.

Whenever they thought she had really gone to sleep, she moved.

'I can't bear this,' thought Jill. To distract her mind, she began looking about her. Just in front of her was a clean wide table with two clean pie-dishes on it, and an open book. They were giant pie-dishes of course. Jill thought that she could lie down just comfortably in one of them. Then she climbed up on the bench beside the table to look at the book. She read:

MALLARD. This delicious bird can be cooked in a variety of ways.

'It's a cookery book,' thought Jill without much interest, and glanced over her shoulder. The giantess's eyes were shut but she didn't look as if she were properly asleep. Jill glanced back at the book. It was arranged alphabetically: and at the very next entry her heart seemed to stop beating. It ran –

MAN. This elegant little biped has long been valued as a delicacy. It forms a traditional part of the Autumn Feast, and is served between the fish and the joint. Each Man –

but she could not bear to read any more. She turned round. The giantess had waked up and was having a fit of coughing. Jill nudged the other two and pointed to the book. They also mounted the bench and bent over the huge pages. Scrubb was still reading about how to cook Men when Puddleglum pointed to the next entry below it. It was like this:

MARSH-WIGGLE. Some authorities reject this animal altogether as unfit for giants' consumption because of its stringy consistency and muddy flavour. The flavour can, however, be greatly reduced if –

Jill touched his feet, and Scrubb's, gently. All three looked back at the giantess. Her mouth was slightly open and from her nose there came a sound which at that moment was more welcome to them than any music; she snored. And now it was a question of tip-toe work, not daring to go too fast, hardly daring to breathe, out through the scullery (giant sculleries smell horrid), out at last into the pale sunlight of a winter afternoon.

They were at the top of a rough little path which ran steeply down. And, thank heavens, on the right side of the castle; the City Ruinous was in sight. In a few minutes they were back on the broad, steep road which led down from the main gate of the castle. They were also in full view from every single window on that side. If it had been one, or two, or five windows there'd be a reasonable chance that no one might be looking out. But there were nearer fifty than five. They now realized, too, that the road on which they were, and indeed all the ground between them and the City Ruinous, didn't offer as much cover as would hide a fox; it was all coarse grass and pebbles and flat stones. To make matters worse, they were now in the clothes that the giants had provided for them last night: except Puddleglum, whom nothing would fit. Jill wore a vivid green robe, rather too long for her, and over that a scarlet mantle fringed with white fur. Scrubb had scarlet stockings, blue tunic and cloak, a gold-hilted sword, and a feathered bonnet.

'Nice bits of colour, you two are,' muttered Puddleglum. 'Show up very prettily on a winter day. The worst archer in the world couldn't miss either of you if you were in range. And talking of archers, we'll be sorry not to have our own bows before long, I shouldn't wonder. Bit thin, too, those clothes of yours, are they?'

'Yes, I'm freezing already,' said Jill.

A few minutes ago when they had been in the kitchen, she had thought that if only they could once get out of the castle, their escape would be almost complete. She now realized that the most dangerous part of it was still to come.

'Steady, steady,' said Puddleglum. 'Don't look back. Don't walk too quickly. Whatever you do, don't run. Look as if we were just taking a stroll, and then, if anyone sees us, he might, just possibly, not bother. The moment we look like people running away, we're done.'

The distance to the City Ruinous seemed longer than Jill would have believed possible. But bit by bit they were covering it. Then came a noise. The other two gasped. Jill, who didn't know what it was, said, 'What's that?'

'Hunting horn,' whispered Scrubb.

'But don't run even now,' said Puddleglum. 'Not till I give the word.'

This time Jill couldn't help glancing over her shoulder. There, about half a mile away, was the hunt returning from behind them on the left.

They walked on. Suddenly a great clamour of giant voices arose: then shouts and hollas.

'They've seen us. Run,' said Puddleglum.

Jill gathered up her long skirts – horrible things for running in – and ran. There was no mistaking the danger now. She could hear the music of the hounds. She could hear the King's voice roaring out, 'After them, after them, or we'll have no man-pies tomorrow.'

She was last of the three now, cumbered with her dress, slipping on loose stones, her hair getting in her mouth, running-pains across her chest. The hounds were much nearer. Now she had to run uphill, up the stony slope which led to the lowest step of the giant stairway. She had no idea what they would do when they got there, or how they would be any better off even if they reached the top. But she didn't think about that. She was like a hunted animal now; as long as the pack was after her, she must run till she dropped.

The Marsh-wiggle was ahead. As he came to the lowest step he stopped, looked a little to his right, and all of a sudden darted into a little hole or crevice at the bottom of it. His long legs, disappearing into it, looked very like those of a spider. Scrubb hesitated and then vanished after him. Jill, breathless and reeling, came to the place about a minute later. It was an unattractive hole – a crack between the earth and the stone about three feet long and hardly more than a foot high. You had to fling yourself flat on your face and crawl in. You couldn't do it so very quickly either. She felt sure that a dog's

teeth would close on her heel before she had got inside.

'Quick, quick. Stones. Fill up the opening,' came
Puddleglum's voice in the darkness beside her. It was

pitch black in there, except for the grey light in the opening by which they had crawled in. The other two were
working hard. She could see Scrubb's small hands and
the Marsh-wiggle's big, frog-like hands black against the
light, working desperately to pile up stones. Then she
realized how important this was and began groping for
large stones herself, and handing them to the others.
Before the dogs were baying and yelping at the cave
mouth, they had it pretty well filled; and now, of course,
there was no light at all.

'Farther in, quick,' said Puddleglum's voice.

'Let's all hold hands,' said Jill.

'Good idea,' said Scrubb. But it took them quite a
long time to find one another's hands in the darkness.
The dogs were sniffing at the other side of the barrier
now.

'Try if we can stand up,' suggested Scrubb. They did and found that they could. Then, Puddleglum holding out a hand behind him to Scrubb, and Scrubb holding a hand out behind him to Jill (who wished very much that she was the middle one of the party and not the last), they began groping with their feet and stumbling forwards into the blackness. It was all loose stones under-foot. Then Puddleglum came up to a wall of rock. They turned a little to their right and went on. There were a good many more twists and turns. Jill had now no sense of direction at all, and no idea where the mouth of the cave lay.

'The question is,' came Puddleglum's voice out of the darkness ahead, 'whether, taking one thing with another, it wouldn't be better to go back (if we *can*) and give the giants a treat at that feast of theirs, instead of losing our way in the guts of a hill where, ten to one, there's dragons and deep holes and gases and water and – Ow! Let go! Save yourselves. I'm –'

After that all happened quickly. There was a wild cry, a swishing, dusty, gravelly noise, a rattle of stones, and Jill found herself sliding, sliding, hopelessly sliding, and sliding quicker every moment down a slope that grew steeper every moment. It was not a smooth, firm slope, but a slope of small stones and rubbish. Even if you could have stood up, it would have been no use. Any bit of that slope you had put your foot on would have slid away from under you and carried you down with it. But Jill was more lying than standing. And the farther they all slid, the more they disturbed all the stones and earth, so that the general downward rush of everything (including themselves) got faster and louder and dustier and dirtier.

From the sharp cries and swearing of the other two, Jill got the idea that many of the stones which she was dislodging were hitting Scrubb and Puddleglum pretty hard. And now she was going at a furious rate and felt sure she would be broken to bits at the bottom.

Yet somehow they weren't. They were a mass of bruises, and the wet sticky stuff on her face appeared to be blood. And such a mass of loose earth, shingle, and larger stones was piled up round her (and partly over her) that she couldn't get up. The darkness was so complete that it made no difference at all whether you had your eyes open or shut. There was no noise. And that was the very worst moment Jill had ever known in her life. Supposing she was alone: supposing the others . . . Then she heard movements around her. And presently all three, in shaken voices, were explaining that none of them seemed to have any broken bones.

'We can never get up that again,' said Scrubb's voice.

'And have you noticed how warm it is?' said the voice of Puddleglum. 'That means we're a long way down. Might be nearly a mile.'

No one said anything. Some time later Puddleglum added:

'My tinder-box has gone.'

After another long pause Jill said, 'I'm terribly thirsty.'

No one suggested doing anything. There was so obviously nothing to be done. For the moment, they did not feel it quite so badly as one might have expected; that was because they were so tired.

Long, long afterwards, without the slightest warning, an utterly strange voice spoke. They knew at once that it was not the one voice in the whole world for which each had secretly been hoping; the voice of Aslan. It was a dark, flat voice – almost, if you know what that means, a pitch-black voice. It said:

'What make you here, creatures of the Overworld?'

CHAPTER 10

TRAVELS WITHOUT THE SUN

'Who's there?' shouted the three travellers.

'I am the Warden of the Marches of Underland, and with me stand a hundred Earthmen in arms,' came the reply. 'Tell me quickly who you are and what is your errand in the Deep Realm?'

'We fell down by accident,' said Puddleglum, truthfully enough.

'Many fall down, and few return to the sunlit lands,' said the voice. 'Make ready now to come with me to the Queen of the Deep Realm.'

'What does she want with us?' asked Scrubb cautiously.

'I do not know,' said the voice. 'Her will is not to be questioned but obeyed.'

While he said these words there was a noise like a soft explosion and immediately a cold light, grey with a little blue in it, flooded the cavern. All hope that the speaker had been idly boasting when he spoke of his hundred armed followers died at once. Jill found herself blinking and staring at a dense crowd. They were of all sizes, from little gnomes barely a foot high to stately figures taller than men. All carried three-pronged spears in their hands, and all were dreadfully pale, and all stood as still as statues. Apart from that, they were very different; some had tails and others not, some wore great beards and others had very round, smooth faces, big as pumpkins. There were long, pointed noses, and long, soft noses like small trunks, and great blobby noses. Several had single horns in the middle of their foreheads. But in one respect they were all alike: every face in the whole hundred was as sad as a face could be. They were so sad that, after the first glance, Jill almost forgot to be afraid of them. She felt she would like to cheer them up.

'Well!' said Puddleglum, rubbing his hands. 'This is just what I needed. If these chaps don't teach me to take a serious view of life, I don't know what will. Look at that fellow with the walrus moustache – or that one with the –'

'Get up,' said the leader of the Earthmen.

There was nothing else to be done. The three travellers scrambled to their feet and joined hands. One wanted the touch of a friend's hand at a moment like that. And the Earthmen came all round them, padding on large, soft feet, on which some had ten toes, some twelve, and others none.

'March,' said the Warden: and march they did.

The cold light came from a large ball on the top of a long pole, and the tallest of the gnomes carried this at the head of the procession. By its cheerless rays they could see that they were in a natural cavern; the walls and roof were knobbed, twisted, and gashed into a thousand fan tastic shapes, and the stony floor sloped downward as they proceeded. It was worse for Jill than for the others, because she hated dark, underground places. And when, as they went on, the cave got lower and narrower, and when, at last, the light-bearer stood aside, and the gnomes, one by one, stooped down (all except the very smallest ones) and stepped into a little dark crack and disappeared, she felt she could bear it no longer.

'I can't go in there, I can't! I can't! I won't,' she panted. The Earthmen said nothing but they all lowered their spears and pointed them at her.

'Steady, Pole,' said Puddleglum. 'Those big fellows wouldn't be crawling in there if it didn't get wider later on. And there's one thing about this underground work, we shan't get any rain.'

'Oh, you don't understand. I can't,' wailed Jill.

'Think how *I* felt on that cliff, Pole,' said Scrubb. 'You go first, Puddleglum, and I'll come after her.'

'That's right,' said the Marsh-wiggle, getting down on his hands and knees. 'You keep a grip of my heels, Pole, and Scrubb will hold on to yours. Then we'll all be comfortable.'

'Comfortable!' said Jill. But she got down and they crawled in on their elbows. It was a nasty place. You had to go flat on your face for what seemed like half an hour, though it may really have been only five minutes. It was hot. Jill felt she was being smothered. But at last a dim light showed ahead, the tunnel grew wider and higher, and they came out, hot, dirty, and shaken, into a cave so large that it scarcely seemed like a cave at all.

It was full of a dim, drowsy radiance, so that here they had no need of the Earthmen's strange lantern. The floor

was soft with some kind of moss and out of this grew
many strange shapes, branched and tall like trees, but
flabby like mushrooms. They stood too far apart to make
a forest; it was more like a park. The light (a greenish
grey) seemed to come both from them and from the moss,
and it was not strong enough to reach the roof of the cave,
which must have been a long way overhead. Across the
mild, soft, sleepy place they were now made to march.
It was very sad, but with a quiet sort of sadness like soft
music.

Here they passed dozens of strange animals lying on
the turf, either dead or asleep, Jill could not tell which.
These were mostly of a dragonish or bat-like sort; Puddleglum did not know what any of them were.

'Do they grow here?' Scrubb asked the Warden. He
seemed very surprised at being spoken to, but replied,
'No. They are all beasts that have found their way down
by chasms and caves, out of Overland into the Deep
Realm. Many come down, and few return to the sunlit
lands. It is said that they will all wake at the end of the
world.'

His mouth shut like a box when he had said this, and
in the great silence of that cave the children felt that they
would not dare to speak again. The bare feet of the
gnomes, padding on the deep moss, made no sound.
There was no wind, there were no birds, there was no
sound of water. There was no sound of breathing from
the strange beasts.

When they had walked for several miles, they came to
a wall of rock, and in it a low archway leading into
another cavern. It was not, however, so bad as the last
entrance and Jill could go through it without bending

her head. It brought them into a smaller cave, long and narrow, about the shape and size of a cathedral. And here, filling almost the whole length of it, lay an enormous man fast asleep. He was far bigger than any of the giants, and his face was not like a giant's, but noble and beautiful. His breast rose and fell gently under the snowy beard which covered him to the waist. A pure, silver light (no one saw where it came from) rested upon him.

'Who's that?' asked Puddleglum. And it was so long since anyone had spoken, that Jill wondered how he had the nerve.

'That is old Father Time, who once was a King in Overland,' said the Warden. 'And now he has sunk down into the Deep Realm and lies dreaming of all the things that are done in the upper world. Many sink down, and few return to the sunlit lands. They say he will wake at the end of the world.'

And out of that cave they passed into another, and then into another and another, and so on till Jill lost count, but always they were going downhill and each cave was lower than the last, till the very thought of the weight and depth of earth above you was suffocating. At last they came to a place where the Warden commanded his cheerless lantern to be lit again. Then they passed into a cave so wide and dark that they could see nothing of it except that right in front of them a strip of pale sand ran down into still water. And there, beside a little jetty, lay a ship without mast or sail but with many oars. They were made to go on board her and led forward to the bows where there was a clear space in front of the rowers' benches and a seat running round inside the bulwarks.

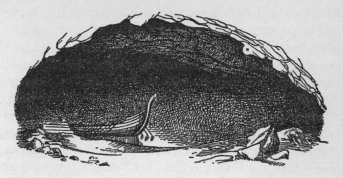

'One thing I'd like to know,' said Puddleglum, 'is whether anyone from our world – from up-a-top, I mean – has ever done this trip before?'

'Many have taken ship at the pale beaches,' replied the Warden, 'and –'

'Yes, I know,' interrupted Puddleglum. '*And few return to the sunlit lands.* You needn't say it again. You *are* a chap of one idea, aren't you?'

The children huddled close together on each side of Puddleglum. They had thought him a wet blanket while they were still above ground, but down here he seemed the only comforting thing they had. Then the pale lantern was hung up amidships, the Earthmen sat to the oars, and the ship began to move. The lantern cast its light only a very short way. Looking ahead, they could see nothing but smooth, dark water, fading into absolute blackness.

'Oh, whatever will become of us?' said Jill despairingly.

'Now don't you let your spirits down, Pole,' said the Marsh-wiggle. 'There's one thing you've got to remember. We're back on the right lines. We were to go under the Ruined City, and we *are* under it. We're following the instructions again.'

Presently they were given food – flat, flabby cakes of some sort which had hardly any taste. And after that, they gradually fell asleep. But when they woke, everything was just the same; the gnomes still rowing, the ship still gliding on, still dead blackness ahead. How often they woke and slept and ate and slept again, none of them could ever remember. And the worst thing about it was that you began to feel as if you had always lived on that ship, in that darkness, and to wonder whether sun and blue skies and wind and birds had not been only a dream.

They had almost given up hoping or being afraid about anything when at last they saw lights ahead: dreary lights, like that of their own lantern. Then, quite suddenly, one of these lights came close and they saw that they were passing another ship. After that they met several ships. Then, staring till their eyes hurt, they saw that some of the lights ahead were shining on what looked like wharfs, walls, towers, and moving crowds. But still there was hardly any noise.

'By Jove,' said Scrubb. 'A city!' and soon they all saw that he was right.

But it was a queer city. The lights were so few and far apart that they would hardly have done for scattered cottages in our world. But the little bits of the place which you could see by the lights were like glimpses of a great sea-port. You could make out in one place a whole crowd of ships loading or unloading; in another, bales of stuff and warehouses; in a third, walls and pillars that suggested great palaces or temples; and always, wherever the light fell, endless crowds – hundreds of Earthmen, jostling one another as they padded softly about their business in narrow streets, broad squares, or up great flights of steps. Their continued movement made a sort of soft, murmuring noise as the ship drew nearer and nearer; but there was not a song or a shout or a bell or the rattle of a wheel anywhere. The City was as quiet, and nearly as dark, as the inside of an ant-hill.

At last their ship was brought alongside a quay and made fast. The three travellers were taken ashore and marched up into the City. Crowds of Earthmen, no two alike, rubbed shoulders with them in the crowded streets, and the sad light fell on many sad and grotesque faces. But no one showed any interest in the strangers. Every gnome seemed to be as busy as it was sad, though Jill never found what they were so busy about. But the endless moving, shoving, hurrying, and the soft pad-pad-pad went on.

At last they came to what appeared to be a great castle, though few of the windows in it were lighted. Here they were taken in and made to cross a courtyard, and to climb many staircases. This brought them in the end to a great murkily lit room. But in one corner of it – oh joy! – there was an archway filled with a quite different sort of light; the honest, yellowish, warm light of such a lamp as humans use. What showed by this light inside the archway was the foot of a staircase which wound upward between walls of stone. The light seemed to come from the top. Two Earthmen stood one on each side of the arch like sentries, or footmen.

The Warden went up to these two, and said, as if it were a password:

'Many sink down to the Underworld.'

'And few return to the sunlit lands,' they answered, as if it were the countersign. Then all three put their heads together and talked. At last one of the two gnomes-in-waiting said, 'I tell you the Queen's grace is gone from hence on her great affair. We had best keep these top dwellers in strait prison till her homecoming. Few return to the sunlit lands.'

At that moment the conversation was interrupted by what seemed to Jill the most delightful noise in the world. It came from above, from the top of the staircase; and it was a clear, ringing, perfectly human voice, the voice of a young man.

'What coil are you keeping down there, Mullu-gutherum?' it shouted. 'Overworlders, ha! Bring them up to me, and that presently.'

'Please it your Highness to remember,' began Mullu-gutherum, but the voice cut him short.

'It pleases my Highness principally to be obeyed, old mutterer. Bring them up,' it called.

Mullugutherum shook his head, motioned to the travellers to follow and began going up the staircase. At every step the light increased. There were rich tapestries hanging on the walls. The lamplight shone golden through thin curtains at the staircase-head. The Earthmen parted the curtains and stood aside. The three passed in. They were in a beautiful room, richly tapes-tried, with a bright fire on a clean hearth, and red wine and cut glass sparkling on the table. A young man with fair hair rose to greet them. He was handsome and looked both bold and kind, though there was some-thing about his face that didn't seem quite right. He was dressed in black and altogether looked a little bit like Hamlet.

'Welcome, Overworlders,' he cried. 'But stay a moment! I cry you mercy! I have seen you two fair children, and this, your strange governor, before. Was it not you three that met me by the bridge on the borders of Ettinsmoor when I rode there by my Lady's side?'

'Oh . . . you were the black knight who never spoke?' exclaimed Jill.

'And was that lady the Queen of Underland?' asked Puddleglum, in no very friendly voice. And Scrubb, who was thinking the same, burst out, 'Because if it was, I think she was jolly mean to send us off to a castle of giants who intended to eat us. What harm had we ever done her, I should like to know?'

'How?' said the Black Knight with a frown. 'If you were not so young a warrior, Boy, you and I must have fought to the death on this quarrel. I can hear no words against my Lady's honour. But of this you may be assured, that whatever she said to you, she said of a good intent. You do not know her. She is a nosegay of all virtues, as truth, mercy, constancy, gentleness, courage, and the rest. I say what I know. Her kindness to me alone, who can in no way reward her, would make an admirable history. But you shall know and love her hereafter. Meanwhile, what is your errand in the Deep Lands?'

And before Puddleglum could stop her, Jill blurted out, 'Please we are trying to find Prince Rilian of Narnia.' And then she realized what a frightful risk she had taken; these people might be enemies. But the Knight showed no interest.

'Rilian? Narnia?' he said carelessly. 'Narnia? What land is that? I have never heard the name. It must be a thousand leagues from those parts of the Overworld that I know. But it was a strange fantasy that brought you seeking this – how do you call him? – Billian? Trillian? in my Lady's realm. Indeed, to my certain knowledge, there is no such man here.' He laughed very loudly at this, and Jill thought to herself, 'I wonder is *that* what's wrong with his face? Is he a bit silly?'

'We had been told to look for a message on the stones of the City Ruinous,' said Scrubb. 'And we saw the words UNDER ME.'

The Knight laughed even more heartily than before. 'You were the more deceived,' he said. 'Those words meant nothing to your purpose. Had you but asked my Lady, she could have given you better counsel. For those words are all that is left of a longer script, which in ancient times, as she well remembers, expressed this verse:

> Though under Earth and throneless now I be,
> Yet, while I lived, all Earth was under me.

From which it is plain that some great king of the ancient giants, who lies buried there, caused this boast to be cut in the stone over his sepulchre; though the breaking up of some stones, and the carrying away of others for new buildings, and the filling up of the cuts with rubble, has left only two words that can still be read. Is it not the merriest jest in the world that you should have thought they were written to you?'

This was like cold water down the back to Scrubb and Jill; for it seemed to them very likely that the words had

nothing to do with their quest at all, and that they had
been taken in by a mere accident.

'Don't you mind him,' said Puddleglum. 'There *are*
no accidents. Our guide is Aslan; and he was there when
the giant King caused the letters to be cut, and he knew
already all things that would come of them; including
this.'

'This guide of yours must be a long liver, friend,' said
the Knight with another of his laughs.

Jill began to find them a little irritating.

'And it seems to me, Sir,' answered Puddleglum,
'that this Lady of yours must be a long liver too, if she
remembers the verse as it was when they first cut it.'

'Very shrewd, Frog-face,' said the Knight, clapping
Puddleglum on the shoulder and laughing again. 'And
you have hit the truth. She is of divine race, and knows
neither age nor death. I am the more thankful to her for
all her infinite bounty to such a poor mortal wretch as I.
For you must know, Sirs, I am a man under most strange
afflictions, and none but the Queen's grace would have
had patience with me. Patience, said I? But it goes far
beyond that. She has promised me a great kingdom in
Overland, and, when I am king, her own most gracious
hand in marriage. But the tale is too long for you to hear
fasting and standing. Hi there, some of you! Bring wine
and Updwellers' food for my guests. Please you, be
seated, gentlemen. Little maiden, sit in this chair. You
shall hear it all.'

CHAPTER II

IN THE DARK CASTLE

WHEN the meal (which was pigeon pie, cold ham, salad, and cakes) had been brought, and all had drawn their chairs up to the table and begun, the Knight continued:

'You must understand, friends, that I know nothing of who I was and whence I came into this Dark World. I remember no time when I was not dwelling, as now, at the court of this all but heavenly Queen; but my thought is that she saved me from some evil enchantment and brought me hither of her exceeding bounty. (Honest Frog-foot, your cup is empty. Suffer me to refill it.) And this seems to me the likelier because even now I am bound by a spell, from which my Lady alone can free me. Every night there comes an hour when my mind is most horribly changed, and, after my mind, my body. For first I become furious and wild and would rush upon my dearest friends to kill them, if I were not bound. And soon after that, I turn into the likeness of a great serpent, hungry, fierce, and deadly. (Sir, be pleased to take another breast of pigeon, I entreat you.) So they tell me, and they certainly speak truth, for my Lady says the same. I myself know nothing of it, for when my hour is past I awake forgetful of all that vile fit and in my proper shape and sound mind – saving that I am somewhat wearied. (Little lady, eat one of these honey cakes, which are brought for me from some barbarous land in the far south of the world.) Now the Queen's majesty knows by her art that I shall be freed from this enchantment when once she has made me king of a land in the Overworld and set its crown upon my head. The land is already chosen and the very place of our breaking out. Her Earthmen have worked day and night digging a way beneath it, and have now gone so far and so high that they tunnel not a score of feet beneath the very grass on which the Updwellers of that country walk. It will be very soon now that those Uplanders' fate will come upon them. She herself is at the diggings tonight, and I expect a message to go to her. Then the thin roof of earth which still keeps me from my kingdom will be broken through, and with her to guide me and a thousand Earthmen at my back, I shall ride forth in arms, fall suddenly on our enemies, slay their chief men, cast down their strong places, and doubtless be their crowned king within four and twenty hours.'

'It's a bit rough luck on *them*, isn't it?' said Scrubb.

'Thou art a lad of a wondrous, quick-working wit!' exclaimed the Knight. 'For, on my honour, I had never thought of it so before. I see your meaning.' He looked slightly, very slightly troubled for a moment or two; but his face soon cleared and he broke out, with another of his loud laughs, 'But fie on gravity! Is it not the most comical and ridiculous thing in the world to think of them all going about their business and never dreaming that under their peaceful fields and floors, only a fathom down, there is a great army ready to break out upon them like a fountain! And they never to have suspected! Why, they themselves, when once the first smart of their defeat is over, can hardly choose but laugh at the thought!'

'I don't think it's funny at all,' said Jill. 'I think you'll be a wicked tyrant.'

'What?' said the Knight, still laughing and patting

her head in a quite infuriating fashion. 'Is our little maid a deep politician? But never fear, sweetheart. In ruling that land, I shall do all by the counsel of my Lady, who will then be my Queen too. Her word shall be my law, even as my word will be law to the people we have conquered.'

'Where I come from,' said Jill, who was disliking him more every minute, 'they don't think much of men who are bossed about by their wives.'

'Shalt think otherwise when thou hast a man of thine own, I warrant you,' said the Knight, apparently thinking this very funny. 'But with my Lady, it is another matter. I am well content to live by her word, who has already saved me from a thousand dangers. No mother has taken pains more tenderly for her child, than the Queen's grace has for me. Why, look you, amid all her cares and business, she rideth out with me in the Overworld many a time and oft to accustom my eyes to the sunlight. And then I must go fully armed and with visor down, so that no man may see my face, and I must speak to no one. For she has found out by art magical that this would hinder my deliverance from the grievous enchantment I lie under. Is not that a lady worthy of a man's whole worship?'

'Sounds a very nice lady indeed,' said Puddleglum in a voice which meant exactly the opposite.

They were thoroughly tired of the Knight's talk before they had finished supper. Puddleglum was thinking, 'I wonder what game that witch is really playing with this young fool.' Scrubb was thinking, 'He's a great baby, really: tied to that woman's apron strings; he's a sap.' And Jill was thinking, 'He's the silliest, most conceited,

selfish pig I've met for a long time.' But when the meal
was over, the Knight's mood had changed. There was no
more laughter about him.

'Friends,' he said, 'my hour is now very near. I am
ashamed that you should see me yet I dread being left
alone. They will come in presently and bind me hand
and foot to yonder chair. Alas, so it must be: for in my
fury, they tell me, I would destroy all that I could reach.'

'I say,' said Scrubb, 'I'm awfully sorry about your
enchantment of course, but what will those fellows do
to *us* when they come to bind you? They talked of putting
us in prison. And we don't like all those dark places very
much. We'd much rather stay here till you're ... better ...
if we may.'

'It is well thought of,' said the Knight. 'By custom
none but the Queen herself remains with me in my evil
hour. Such is her tender care for my honour that she
would not willingly suffer any ears but her own to hear
the words I utter in that frenzy. But I could not easily
persuade my attendant gnomes that you should be left

with me. And I think I hear their soft feet even now upon the stairs. Go through yonder door: it leads into my other apartments. And there, either await my coming when they have unbound me; or, if you will, return and sit with me in my ravings.'

They followed his directions and passed out of the room by a door which they had not yet seen opened. It brought them, they were pleased to see, not into darkness but into a lighted corridor. They tried various doors and found (what they very badly needed) water for washing and even a looking glass. 'He never offered us a wash before supper,' said Jill, drying her face. 'Selfish, self-centred pig.'

'Are we going back to watch the enchantment, or shall we stay here?' said Scrubb.

'Stay here, I vote,' said Jill. 'I'd much rather not see it.' But she felt a little inquisitive all the same.

'No, go back,' said Puddleglum. 'We may pick up some information, and we need all we can get. I am sure that Queen is a witch and an enemy. And those Earthmen would knock us on the head as soon as look at us. There's a stronger smell of danger and lies and magic and treason about this land than I've ever smelled before. We need to keep our eyes and ears open.'

They went back down the corridor and gently pushed the door open. 'It's all right,' said Scrubb, meaning that there were no Earthmen about. Then they all came back into the room where they had supped.

The main door was now shut, concealing the curtain between which they had first entered. The Knight was seated in a curious silver chair, to which he was bound by his ankles, his knees, his elbows, his wrists, and his waist. There was sweat on his forehead and his face was filled with anguish.

'Come in, friends,' he said, glancing quickly up. 'The fit is not yet upon me. Make no noise, for I told that prying chamberlain that you were in bed. Now . . . I can feel it coming. Quick! Listen while I am master of myself. When the fit is upon me, it well may be that I shall beg and implore you, with entreaties and threatenings, to loosen my bonds. They say I do. I shall call upon you by all that is most dear and most dreadful. But do not listen to me. Harden your hearts and stop your ears. For while I am bound you are safe. But if once I were up and out of this chair, then first would come my fury, and after that' – he shuddered – 'the change into a loathsome serpent.'

'There's no fear of our loosing you,' said Puddleglum. 'We've no wish to meet wild men; or serpents either.'

'I should think not,' said Scrubb and Jill together.

'All the same,' added Puddleglum in a whisper. 'Don't let's be too sure. Let's be on our guard. We've muffed everything else, you know. He'll be cunning, I shouldn't wonder, once he gets started. Can we trust one another? Do we all promise that whatever he says we don't touch those cords? *Whatever* he says, mind you?'

'Rather!' said Scrubb.

'There's nothing in the world he can say or do that'll make me change my mind,' said Jill.

'Hush! Something's happening,' said Puddleglum.

The Knight was moaning. His face was as pale as putty, and he writhed in his bonds. And whether because she was sorry for him, or for some other reason, Jill thought that he looked a nicer sort of man than he had looked before.

'Ah,' he groaned. 'Enchantments, enchantments . . . the heavy, tangled, cold, clammy web of evil magic. Buried alive. Dragged down under the earth, down into the sooty blackness . . . how many years is it? . . . Have I lived ten years, or a thousand years, in the pit? Maggot-men all around me. Oh, have mercy. Let me out, let me go back. Let me feel the wind and see the sky . . . There used to be a little pool. When you looked down into it you could see all the trees growing upside-down in the water, all green, and below them, deep, very deep, the blue sky.'

He had been speaking in a low voice; now he looked up, fixed his eyes upon them, and said loud and clear:

'Quick! I am sane now. Every night I am sane. If only I could get out of this enchanted chair, it would last. I should be a man again. But every night they bind me, and so every night my chance is gone. But you are not enemies. I am not *your* prisoner. Quick! Cut these cords.'

'Stand fast! Steady,' said Puddleglum to the two children.

'I beseech you to hear me,' said the Knight, forcing himself to speak calmly. 'Have they told you that if I am released from this chair I shall kill you and become a serpent? I see by your faces that they have. It is a lie. It is at this hour that I am in my right mind: it is all the rest of the day that I am enchanted. You are not Earthmen nor witches. Why should you be on their side? Of your courtesy, cut my bonds.'

'Steady! Steady! Steady!' said the three travellers to one another.

'Oh, you have hearts of stone,' said the Knight. 'Believe me, you look upon a wretch who has suffered almost more than any mortal heart can bear. What wrong have I ever done you, that you should side with my enemies to keep me in such miseries? And the minutes are slipping past. *Now* you can save me; when this hour has passed, I shall be witless again – the toy and lap-dog, nay, more likely the pawn and tool, of the most devilish sorceress that ever planned the woe of men. And this night, of all nights, when she is away! You take from me a chance that may never come again.'

'This is dreadful. I do wish we'd stayed away till it was over,' said Jill.

'Steady!' said Puddleglum.

The prisoner's voice was now rising into a shriek. 'Let me go, I say. Give me my sword. My sword! Once I am free I shall take such revenge on Earthmen that Underland will talk of it for a thousand years!'

'Now the frenzy is beginning,' said Scrubb. 'I hope those knots are all right.'

'Yes,' said Puddleglum. 'He'd have twice his natural strength if he got free now. And I'm not clever with my sword. He'd get us both, I shouldn't wonder; and then Pole on her own would be left to tackle the snake.'

The prisoner was now so straining at his bonds that they cut into his wrists and ankles. 'Beware,' he said. 'Beware. One night I *did* break them. But the witch was there that time. You will not have her to help you to-night. Free me now, and I am your friend. I'm your mortal enemy else.'

'Cunning, isn't he?' said Puddleglum.

'Once and for all,' said the prisoner, 'I adjure you to set me free. By all fears and all loves, by the bright skies of Overland, by the great Lion, by Aslan himself, I charge you –'

'Oh!' cried the three travellers as though they had been hurt. 'It's the sign,' said Puddleglum. 'It was the *words* of the sign,' said Scrubb more cautiously. 'Oh, what *are* we to do?' said Jill.

It was a dreadful question. What had been the use of promising one another that they would not on any account set the Knight free, if they were now to do so the first time he happened to call upon a name they really

cared about? On the other hand, what had been the use of learning the signs if they weren't going to obey them? Yet could Aslan have really meant them to unbind anyone – even a lunatic – who asked it in his name? Could it be a mere accident? Or how if the Queen of the Underworld knew all about the signs and had made the Knight learn this name simply in order to entrap them? But then, supposing this was the real sign? . . . They had muffed three already; they daren't muff the fourth.

'Oh, if only we knew!' said Jill.

'I think we do know,' said Puddleglum.

'Do you mean you think everything will come right if we do untie him?' said Scrubb.

'I don't know about that,' said Puddleglum. 'You see, Aslan didn't tell Pole what would happen. He only told her what to do. That fellow will be the death of us once he's up, I shouldn't wonder. But that doesn't let us off following the sign.'

They all stood looking at one another with bright eyes. It was a sickening moment. 'All right!' said Jill suddenly. 'Let's get it over. Good-bye, everyone . . .!' They all shook hands. The Knight was screaming by now; there was foam on his cheeks.

'Come on, Scrubb,' said Puddleglum. He and Scrubb drew their swords and went over to the captive.

'In the name of Aslan,' they said and began methodically cutting the cords. The instant the prisoner was free, he crossed the room in a single bound, seized his own sword (which had been taken from him and laid on the table), and drew it.

'You first!' he cried and fell upon the silver chair. That must have been a good sword. The silver gave way before its edge like string, and in a moment a few twisted fragments, shining on the floor, were all that was left. But as the chair broke, there came from it a bright flash, a sound like small thunder, and (for one moment) a loathsome smell.

'Lie there, vile engine of sorcery,' he said, 'lest your mistress should ever use you for another victim.' Then he turned and surveyed his rescuers; and the something wrong, whatever it was, had vanished from his face.

'What?' he cried, turning to Puddleglum. 'Do I see before me a Marsh-wiggle – a real, live, honest, Narnian Marsh-wiggle?'

'Oh, so you *have* heard of Narnia after all?' said Jill.

'Had I forgotten it when I was under the spell?' asked the Knight. 'Well, that and all other bedevilments are now over. You may well believe that I know Narnia, for I am Rilian, Prince of Narnia, and Caspian the great King is my father.'

'Your Royal Highness,' said Puddleglum, sinking on one knee (and the children did the same), 'we have come hither for no other end than to seek you.'

'And who are you, my other deliverers?' said the Prince to Scrubb and Jill.

'We were sent by Aslan himself from beyond the world's end to seek your Highness,' said Scrubb. 'I am Eustace who sailed with him to the island of Ramandu.'

'I owe all three of you a greater debt than I can ever pay,' said Prince Rilian. 'But my father? Is he yet alive?'

'He sailed east again before we left Narnia, my lord,' said Puddleglum. 'But your Highness must consider that the King is very old. It is ten to one his Majesty must die on the voyage.'

'He is old, you say. How long then have I been in the power of the witch?'

'It is more than ten years since your Highness was lost in the woods at the north side of Narnia.'

'Ten years!' said the Prince, drawing his hand across his face as if to rub away the past. 'Yes, I believe you. For now that I am myself I can remember that enchanted life, though while I was enchanted I could not remember my true self. And now, fair friends – but wait! I hear their feet (does it not sicken a man, that padding woolly tread! faugh!) on the stairs. Lock the door, boy. Or stay. I have a better thought than that. I will fool these Earthmen, if Aslan gives me the wit. Take your cue from me.'

He walked resolutely to the door and flung it wide open.

CHAPTER 12

THE QUEEN OF UNDERLAND

Two Earthmen entered, but instead of advancing into the room, they placed themselves one on each side of the door, and bowed deeply. They were followed immediately by the last person whom anyone had expected or wished to see: the Lady of the Green Kirtle, the Queen of Underland. She stood dead still in the doorway, and they could see her eyes moving as she took in the whole situation – the three strangers, the silver chair destroyed, and the Prince free, with his sword in his hand.

She turned very white; but Jill thought it was the sort of whiteness that comes over some people's faces not when they are frightened but when they are angry. For a moment the Witch fixed her eyes on the Prince, and there was murder in them. Then she seemed to change her mind.

'Leave us,' she said to the two Earthmen. 'And let none disturb us till I call, on pain of death.' The gnomes padded away obediently, and the Witch-queen shut and locked the door.

'How now, my lord Prince,' she said. 'Has your nightly fit not yet come upon you, or is it over so soon? Why stand you here unbound? Who are these aliens? And is it they who have destroyed the chair which was your only safety?'

Prince Rilian shivered as she spoke to him. And no wonder: it is not easy to throw off in half an hour an enchantment which has made one a slave for ten years. Then, speaking with a great effort, he said:

'Madam, there will be no more need of that chair. And you, who have told me a hundred times how deeply you pitied me for the sorceries by which I was bound, will doubtless hear with joy that they are now ended for ever. There was, it seems, some small error in your Ladyship's way of treating them. These, my true friends, have delivered me. I am now in my right mind, and there are two things I will say to you. First – as for your Ladyship's design of putting me at the head of an army of Earthmen so that I may break out into the Overworld and there, by main force, make myself king over some nation that never did me wrong – murdering their natural lords and holding their throne as a bloody and foreign tyrant – now that I know myself, I do utterly abhor and renounce it as plain villainy. And second: I am the King's son of Narnia, Rilian, the only child of Caspian, Tenth of that name, whom some call Caspian the Seafarer. Therefore, Madam, it is my purpose, as it is also my duty, to depart suddenly from your Highness's court into my own country. Please it you to grant me and my friends safe conduct and a guide through your dark realm.'

Now the Witch said nothing at all, but moved gently across the room, always keeping her face and eyes very steadily towards the Prince. When she had come to a little ark set in the wall not far from the fireplace, she opened it, and took out first a handful of a green powder. This she threw on the fire. It did not blaze much, but a very sweet and drowsy smell came from it. And all through the conversation which followed, that smell grew stronger, and filled the room, and made it harder to think. Secondly, she took out a musical instrument rather like a mandolin. She began to play it with her fingers –

a steady, monotonous thrumming that you didn't notice after a few minutes. But the less you noticed it, the more it got into your brain and your blood. This also made it hard to think. After she had thrummed for a time (and the sweet smell was now strong) she began speaking in a sweet, quiet voice.

'Narnia?' she said. 'Narnia? I have often heard your Lordship utter that name in your ravings. Dear Prince, you are very sick. There is no land called Narnia.'

'Yes there is, though, Ma'am,' said Puddleglum. 'You see, I happen to have lived there all my life.'

'Indeed,' said the Witch. 'Tell me, I pray you, where that country is?'

'Up there,' said Puddleglum, stoutly, pointing overhead. 'I – I don't know exactly where.'

'How?' said the Queen, with a kind, soft, musical laugh. 'Is there a country up among the stones and mortar of the roof?'

'No,' said Puddleglum, struggling a little to get his breath. 'It's in Overworld.'

'And what, or where, pray is this . . . how do you call it . . . *Overworld?*'

'Oh, don't be so silly,' said Scrubb, who was fighting hard against the enchantment of the sweet smell and the thrumming. 'As if you didn't know! It's up above, up where you can see the sky and the sun and the stars. Why, you've been there yourself. We met you there.'

'I cry you mercy, little brother,' laughed the Witch (you couldn't have heard a lovelier laugh). 'I have no memory of that meeting. But we often meet our friends in strange places when we dream. And unless all dreamed alike, you must not ask them to remember it.'

'Madam,' said the Prince sternly, 'I have already told your Grace that I am the King's son of Narnia.'

'And shalt be, dear friend,' said the Witch in a soothing voice, as if she was humouring a child, 'shalt be king of many imagined lands in thy fancies.'

'We've been there, too,' snapped Jill. She was very angry because she could feel enchantment getting hold of her every moment. But of course the very fact that she could still feel it, showed that it had not yet fully worked.

'And thou art Queen of Narnia too, I doubt not, pretty one,' said the Witch in the same coaxing, half-mocking tone.

'I'm nothing of the sort,' said Jill, stamping her foot. '*We* come from another world.'

'Why, this is a prettier game than the other,' said the Witch. 'Tell us, little maid, where is this other world? What ships and chariots go between it and ours?'

Of course a lot of things darted into Jill's head at once: Experiment House, Adela Pennyfather, her own home, radio-sets, cinemas, cars, aeroplanes, ration-books, queues. But they seemed dim and far away. (*Thrum - thrum - thrum* - went the strings of the Witch's instrument.) Jill couldn't remember the names of the things in our world. And this time it didn't come into her head that she was being enchanted, for now the magic was in its full strength; and of course, the more enchanted you get, the more certain you feel that you are not enchanted at all. She found herself saying (and at the moment it was a relief to say):

'No. I suppose that other world must be all a dream.'

'Yes. It *is* all a dream,' said the Witch, always thrumming.

'Yes, all a dream,' said Jill.

'There never was such a world,' said the Witch.

'No,' said Jill and Scrubb, 'never was such a world.'

'There never was any world but mine,' said the Witch.

'There never was any world but yours,' said they.

Puddleglum was still fighting hard. 'I don't know
rightly what you all mean by a world,' he said, talking
like a man who hasn't enough air. 'But you can play
that fiddle till your fingers drop off, and still you won't
make me forget Narnia; and the whole Overworld too.
We'll never see it *again*, I shouldn't wonder. You may
have blotted it out and turned it dark like this, for all I
know. Nothing more likely. But I know I was there once.
I've seen the sky full of stars. I've seen the sun coming up
out of the sea of a morning and sinking behind the
mountains at night. And I've seen him up in the midday
sky when I couldn't look at him for brightness.'

Puddleglum's words had a very rousing effect. The
other three all breathed again and looked at one another
like people newly awaked.

'Why, there it is!' cried the Prince. 'Of course! The
blessing of Aslan upon this honest Marsh-wiggle. We
have all been dreaming, these last few minutes. How
could we have forgotten it? Of course we've all seen the
sun.'

'By Jove, so we have!' said Scrubb. 'Good for you,
Puddleglum! You're the only one of us with any sense,
I do believe.'

Then came the Witch's voice, cooing softly like the
voice of a wood-pigeon from the high elms in an old

garden at three o'clock in the middle of a sleepy, summer afternoon; and it said:

'What is this *sun* that you all speak of? Do you mean anything by the word?'

'Yes, we jolly well do,' said Scrubb.

'Can you tell me what it's like?' asked the Witch (*thrum, thrum, thrum*, went the strings).

'Please it your Grace,' said the Prince, very coldly and politely. 'You see that lamp. It is round and yellow and gives light to the whole room; and hangeth moreover from the roof. Now that thing which we call the sun is like the lamp, only far greater and brighter. It giveth light to the whole Overworld and hangeth in the sky.'

'Hangeth from what, my lord?' asked the Witch; and then, while they were all still thinking how to answer her, she added, with another of her soft, silver laughs: 'You see? When you try to think out clearly what this *sun* must be, you cannot tell me. You can only tell me it is like the lamp. Your *sun* is a dream; and there is nothing in that dream that was not copied from the lamp. The lamp is the real thing; the *sun* is but a tale, a children's story.'

'Yes, I see now,' said Jill in a heavy, hopeless tone. 'It must be so.' And while she said this, it seemed to her to be very good sense.

Slowly and gravely the Witch repeated, 'There is no *sun*.' And they all said nothing. She repeated, in a softer and deeper voice. 'There is no *sun*.' After a pause, and after a struggle in their minds, all four of them said together. 'You are right. There is no sun.' It was such a relief to give in and say it.

'There never was a *sun*,' said the Witch.

'No. There never was a sun,' said the Prince, and the Marsh-wiggle, and the children.

For the last few minutes Jill had been feeling that there was something she must remember at all costs. And now she did. But it was dreadfully hard to say it. She felt as if huge weights were laid on her lips. At last, with an effort that seemed to take all the good out of her, she said:

'There's Aslan.'

'Aslan?' said the Witch, quickening ever so slightly the pace of her thrumming. 'What a pretty name! What does it mean?'

'He is the great Lion who called us out of our own world,' said Scrubb, 'and sent us into this to find Prince Rilian.'

'What is a *lion*?' asked the Witch.

'Oh, hang it all!' said Scrubb. 'Don't you know? How can we describe it to her? Have you ever seen a cat?'

'Surely,' said the Queen. 'I love cats.'

'Well, a lion is a little bit - only a little bit, mind you – like a huge cat – with a mane. At least, it's not like a horse's mane, you know, it's more like a judge's wig. And it's yellow. And terrifically strong.'

The Witch shook her head. 'I see,' she said, 'that we should do no better with your *lion*, as you call it, than we did with your *sun*. You have seen lamps, and so you imagined a bigger and better lamp and called it the *sun*. You've seen cats, and now you want a bigger and better cat, and it's to be called a *lion*. Well, 'tis a pretty make-believe, though, to say truth, it would suit you all better if you were younger. And look how you can put nothing into your make-believe without copying it from the real world, this world of mine, which is the only world. But even you children are too old for such play. As for you, my lord Prince, that art a man full grown, fie upon you! Are you not ashamed of such toys? Come, all of you. Put away these childish tricks. I have work for you all in the real world. There is no Narnia, no Overworld, no sky, no sun, no Aslan. And now, to bed all. And let us begin a wiser life tomorrow. But, first, to bed; to sleep; deep sleep, soft pillows, sleep without foolish dreams.'

The Prince and the two children were standing with their heads hung down, their cheeks flushed, their eyes half closed; the strength all gone from them; the enchantment almost complete. But Puddleglum, desperately gathering all his strength, walked over to the fire. Then he did a very brave thing. He knew it wouldn't hurt him quite as much as it would hurt a human; for his feet (which were bare) were webbed and hard and cold-blooded like a duck's. But he knew it would hurt him badly enough; and so it did. With his bare foot he stamped on the fire, grinding a large part of it into ashes on the flat hearth. And three things happened at once.

First, the sweet heavy smell grew very much less. For though the whole fire had not been put out, a good bit of it had, and what remained smelled very largely of burnt Marsh-wiggle, which is not at all an enchanting smell. This instantly made everyone's brain far clearer. The Prince and the children held up their heads again and opened their eyes.

Secondly, the Witch, in a loud, terrible voice, utterly different from all the sweet tones she had been using up till now, called out, 'What are you doing? Dare to touch my fire again, mud-filth, and I'll turn the blood to fire inside your veins.'

Thirdly, the pain itself made Puddleglum's head for a moment perfectly clear and he knew exactly what he really thought. There is nothing like a good shock of pain for dissolving certain kinds of magic.

'One word, Ma'am,' he said, coming back from the fire; limping, because of the pain. 'One word. All you've been saying is quite right, I shouldn't wonder. I'm a chap who always liked to know the worst and then put the best face I can on it. So I won't deny any of what you said. But there's one thing more to be said, even so. Suppose we *have* only dreamed, or made up, all those things – trees and grass and sun and moon and stars and Aslan himself. Suppose we have. Then all I can say is that, in that case, the made-up things seem a good deal more important than the real ones. Suppose this black pit of a kingdom of yours *is* the only world. Well, it strikes me as a pretty poor one. And that's a funny thing, when you come to think of it. We're just babies making up a game, if you're right. But four babies playing a game can make a play-world which licks your real world hollow. That's why I'm going to stand by the play-world. I'm on Aslan's side even if there isn't any Aslan to lead it. I'm going to live as like a Narnian as I can even if there isn't any Narnia. So, thanking you kindly for our supper, if these two gentlemen and the young lady are ready, we're leaving your court at once and setting out in the dark to spend our lives looking for Overland. Not that our lives will be very long, I should think; but that's small loss if the world's as dull a place as you say.'

'Oh, hurrah! Good old Puddleglum!' cried Scrubb and Jill. But the Prince shouted suddenly, 'Ware! Look to the Witch.'

When they did look their hair nearly stood on end.

The instrument dropped from her hands. Her arms appeared to be fastened to her sides. Her legs were intertwined with each other, and her feet had disappeared. The long green train of her skirt thickened and grew solid, and seemed to be all one piece with the writhing green pillar of her interlocked legs. And that writhing green pillar was curving and swaying as if it had no joints, or else were all joints. Her head was thrown far back and while her nose grew longer and longer, every other part of her face seemed to disappear, except her eyes. Huge flaming eyes they were now, without brows or lashes. All this takes time to write down; it happened so quickly that there was only just time to see it. Long before there was time to do anything, the change was complete, and the great serpent which the Witch had become, green as poison, thick as Jill's waist, had flung two or three coils of its loathsome body round the Prince's legs. Quick as lightning another great loop darted round, intending to pinion his sword-arm to his side. But the Prince was just in time. He raised his arms and got them clear: the living knot closed only round his chest – ready to crack his ribs like firewood when it drew tight.

The Prince caught the creature's neck in his left hand, trying to squeeze it till it choked. This held its face (if you could call it a face) about five inches from his own. The forked tongue flickered horribly in and out, but could not reach him. With his right hand he drew back his sword for the strongest blow he could give. Meanwhile Scrubb and Puddleglum had drawn their weapons and rushed to his aid. All three blows fell at once: Scrubb's (which did not even pierce the scales and did no good) on the body of the snake below the Prince's hand, but the Prince's own blow and Puddleglum's both on its neck. Even that did not quite kill it, though it began to loosen its hold on Rilian's legs and chest. With repeated blows they hacked off its head. The horrible thing went on coiling and moving like a bit of wire long after it had died; and the floor, as you may imagine, was a nasty mess.

The Prince, when he had breath, said, 'Gentlemen, I thank you.' Then the three conquerors stood staring at one another and panting, without another word, for a long time. Jill had very wisely sat down and was keeping quiet; she was saying to herself, 'I do hope I don't faint – or blub – or do anything idiotic.'

'My royal mother is avenged,' said Rilian presently. 'This is undoubtedly the same worm that I pursued in vain by the fountain in the forest of Narnia, so many years ago. All these years I have been the slave of my mother's slayer. Yet I am glad, gentlemen, that the foul Witch took to her serpent form at the last. It would not have suited well either with my heart or with my honour to have slain a woman. But look to the lady.' He meant Jill.

'I'm all right, thanks,' said she.

'Damsel,' said the Prince, bowing to her. 'You are of a high courage, and therefore, I doubt not, you come of a noble blood in your own world. But come, friends. Here is some wine left. Let us refresh ourselves and each pledge his fellows. After that, to our plans.'

'A jolly good idea, Sir,' said Scrubb.

CHAPTER 13

UNDERLAND WITHOUT THE QUEEN

ALL felt that they had earned what Scrubb called a 'breather'. The Witch had locked the door and told the Earthmen not to disturb her, so there was no danger of interruption for the present. Their first business was, of course, Puddleglum's burnt foot. A couple of clean shirts from the Prince's bedroom, torn into strips, and well greased on the inside with butter and salad oil off the supper table, made a fairly good dressing. When this had been applied, they all sat down and had a little refreshment, and discussed plans for escaping from the Underworld.

Rilian explained that there were quite a lot of outlets by which one could get to the surface; he had been taken out through most of them at one time or another. But he had never gone out alone, only with the Witch; and he had always reached these outlets by going in a ship across the Sunless Sea. What the Earthmen would say if he went down to the harbour without the Witch, and with four strangers, and simply ordered a ship, no one could guess. But most likely they would ask awkward questions. On the other hand the new outlet, the one for the invasion of Overworld, was on this side of the sea, and only a few miles away. The Prince knew that it was nearly finished; only a few feet of earth divided the diggings from the outer air. It was even possible that it had now been quite finished. Perhaps the Witch had come back to tell him this and to start the attack. Even if it was not, they could probably dig themselves out by that route in a few hours – if they could only get there without being stopped, and if only they found the diggings unguarded. But those were the difficulties.

'If you ask me –' began Puddleglum, when Scrubb interrupted.

'I say,' he asked, 'what's that noise?'

'I've been wondering that for some time!' said Jill.

They had all, in fact, been hearing the noise but it had begun and increased so gradually that they did not know when they had first noticed it. For a time it had been only a vague disquiet like gentle winds, or traffic very far away. Then it swelled to a murmur like the sea. Then came rumblings and rushings. Now there seemed to be voices as well and also a steady roaring that was not voices.

'By the Lion,' said Prince Rilian, 'it seems this silent land has found a tongue at last.' He rose, walked to the window, and drew aside the curtains. The others crowded round him to look out.

The very first thing they noticed was a great red glow. Its reflection made a red patch on the roof of the Underworld thousands of feet above them, so that they could see a rocky ceiling which had perhaps been hidden in darkness ever since the world was made. The glow itself came from the far side of the city so that many buildings, grim and great, stood up blackly against it. But it also cast its light down many streets that ran from it towards the castle. And in those streets something very strange was going on. The closely-packed, silent crowds of Earthmen had vanished. Instead, there were figures darting about by ones, or twos, or threes. They behaved like people who do not want to be seen: lurking in shadow behind buttresses or in doorways, and then moving quickly across the open into fresh places of hiding. But the strangest thing of all, to anyone who knew the gnomes, was the noise. Shouts and cries came from all directions. But from the harbour there came a low, rumbling roar which grew steadily louder and was already shaking the whole city.

'What's happened to the Earthmen?' said Scrubb. 'Is it *them* shouting?'

''Tis hardly possible,' said the Prince. 'I never heard one of the rascals so much as speak with a loud voice in all the weary years of my bondage. Some new devilry, I don't doubt.'

'And what is that red light over there?' asked Jill. 'Is something on fire?'

'If you ask me,' said Puddleglum, 'I should say that was the central fires of the Earth breaking out to make a new volcano. We'll be in the middle of it, I shouldn't wonder.'

'Look at that ship!' said Scrubb. 'Why's it coming on so quickly? No one's rowing it.'

'Look, look!' said the Prince. 'The ship is already far this side of the harbour – it is in the street. Look! All the ships are driving into the city! By my head, the sea's rising. The flood is upon us. Aslan be praised, this castle stands on high ground. But the water comes on grimly fast.'

'Oh, what *can* be happening?' cried Jill. 'Fire and water and all those people dodging about the streets.'

'I'll tell you what it is,' said Puddleglum. 'That Witch has laid a train of magic spells so that whenever she was killed, at that same moment her whole kingdom would fall to pieces. She's the sort that wouldn't so much mind dying herself if she knew that the chap who killed her was going to be burned, or buried, or drowned five minutes later.'

'Hast hit it, friend wiggle,' said the Prince. 'When our swords hacked off the Witch's head, that stroke ended all her magic works, and now the Deep Lands are falling to pieces. We are looking on the end of Underworld.'

'That's it, Sir,' said Puddleglum. 'Unless it should happen to be the end of the whole world.'

'But are we just going to stay here and – wait?' gasped Jill.

'Not by my counsel,' said the Prince. 'I would save my horse, Coalblack, and the Witch's Snowflake (a noble beast and worthy of a better mistress) which are both stabled in the courtyard. After that, let us make shift to get out to high ground and pray that we shall find an outlet. The horses can carry two each at need, and if we put them to it they may outstrip the flood.'

'Will your Highness not put on armour?' asked Puddleglum. 'I don't like the look of *those*' – and he pointed down to the street. Everyone looked down. Dozens of creatures (and now that they were close, they obviously were Earthmen) were coming up from the direction of the harbour. But they were not moving like an aimless crowd. They behaved like modern soldiers in an attack, making rushes and taking cover, anxious not to be seen from the castle windows.

'I dare not see the inside of that armour again,' said the Prince. 'I rode in it as in a movable dungeon, and it stinks of magic and slavery. But I will take the shield.'

He left the room and returned with a strange light in his eyes a moment later.

'Look, friends,' he said, holding out the shield towards them. 'An hour ago it was black and without device; and now, this.' The shield had turned bright as silver, and on it, redder than blood or cherries, was the figure of the Lion.

'Doubtless,' said the Prince, 'this signifies that Aslan will be our good lord, whether he means us to live or die. And all's one, for that. Now, by my counsel, we shall all kneel and kiss his likeness, and then all shake hands one with another, as true friends that may shortly be parted. And then, let us descend into the city and take the adventure that is sent us.'

And they all did as the Prince had said. But when Scrubb shook hands with Jill, he said, 'So long, Jill. Sorry I've been a funk and so ratty. I hope you get safe home,' and Jill said, 'So long, Eustace. And I'm sorry I've been such a pig.' And this was the first time they had ever used Christian names, because one didn't do it at school.

The Prince unlocked the door and they all went down the stairs: three of them with drawn swords, and Jill with drawn knife. The attendants had vanished and the great room at the foot of the Prince's stairs was empty. The grey, doleful lamps were still burning and by their light they had no difficulty in passing gallery after gallery and descending stairway after stairway. The noises from outside the castle were not so easily heard here as they had been in the room above. Inside the house all was still as death, and deserted. It was as they turned a corner into the great hall on the ground floor that they met their first Earthman – a fat, whitish creature with a very pig-like face who was gobbling up all the remains of food on the tables. It squealed (the squeal also was very like a pig's) and darted under a bench, whisking its long tail out of Puddleglum's reach in the nick of time. Then it rushed away through the far door too quickly to be followed.

From the hall they came out into the courtyard. Jill, who went to a riding school in the holidays, had just noticed the smell of a stable (a very nice, honest, homely smell it is to meet in a place like Underland) when Eustace said, 'Great Scott! Look at that!' A magnificent rocket had risen from somewhere beyond the castle walls and broken into green stars.

'Fireworks!' said Jill in a puzzled voice.

'Yes,' said Eustace, 'but you can't imagine those Earth people letting them off for fun! It must be a signal.'

'And means no good to us, I'll be bound,' said Puddle-glum.

'Friends,' said the Prince, 'when once a man is launched on such an adventure as this, he must bid farewell to hopes and fears, otherwise death or deliverance will both come too late to save his honour and his reason. Ho, my beauties' (he was now opening the stable door). 'Hey cousins! Steady, Coalblack! Softly now, Snowflake! You are not forgotten.'

The horses were both frightened by the strange lights and the noises. Jill, who had been so cowardly about going through a black hole between one cave and another, went in without fear between the stamping and snorting beasts, and she and the Prince had them saddled and bridled in a few minutes. Very fine they looked as they came out into the courtyard, tossing their heads. Jill mounted Snowflake, and Puddleglum got up behind her. Eustace got up behind the Prince on Coalblack. Then with a great echo of hoofs, they rode out of the main gateway into the street.

'Not much danger of being burnt. That's the bright side of it,' observed Puddleglum, pointing to their right. There, hardly a hundred yards away, lapping against the walls of the houses, was water.

'Courage!' said the Prince. 'The road there goes down steeply. That water has climbed only half up the greatest hill in the city. It might come so near in the first half-hour and come no nearer in the next two. My fear is more of that –' and he pointed with his sword to a great tall Earthman with boar's tusks, followed by six others of assorted shapes and sizes who had just dashed out of a side street and stepped into the shadow of the houses where no one could see them.

The Prince led them, aiming always in the direction of the glowing red light but a little to the left of it. His plan was to get round the fire (if it was a fire) on to high ground, in hope that they might find their way to the new diggings. Unlike the other three, he seemed to be almost enjoying himself. He whistled as he rode, and sang snatches of an old song about Corin Thunder-fist of Archenland. The truth is, he was so glad at being free from his long enchantment that all dangers seemed a game in comparison. But the rest found it an eerie journey.

Behind them was the sound of clashing and entangled ships, and the rumble of collapsing buildings. Overhead

was the great patch of lurid light on the roof of the
Underworld. Ahead was the mysterious glow, which did
not seem to grow any bigger. From the same direction
came a continual hubbub of shouts, screams, cat-calls,
laughter, squeals, and bellowings; and fireworks of all
sorts rose in the dark air. No one could guess what they
meant. Nearer to them, the city was partly lit up by the
red glow, and partly by the very different light of the
dreary Gnome lamps. But there were many places where
neither of these lights fell, and those places were jet-
black. And in and out of those places the shapes of
Earthmen were darting and slipping all the time, always
with their eyes fixed on the travellers, always trying to
keep out of sight themselves. There were big faces and
little faces, huge eyes like fishes' eyes and little eyes like
bears'. There were feathers and bristles, horns and tusks,
noses like whipcord, and chins so long that they looked
like beards. Every now and then a group of them would
get too big or come too near. Then the Prince would
brandish his sword and make a show of charging them.
And the creatures, with all manner of hootings, squeak-
ings, and cluckings, would dive away into the darkness.

But when they had climbed many steep streets and
were far away from the flood, and almost out of the town
on the inland side, it began to be more serious. They
were now close to the red glow and nearly on a level with
it, though they still could not see what it really was. But
by its light they could see their enemies more clearly.
Hundreds – perhaps a few thousands – of gnomes were
all moving towards it. But they were doing so in short
rushes, and whenever they stopped, they turned and
faced the travellers.

'If your Highness asked me,' said Puddleglum, 'I'd say those fellows were meaning to cut us off in front.'

'That was my thought too, Puddleglum,' said the Prince. 'And we can never fight our way through so many. Hark you! Let us ride forth close by the edge of yonder house. And even as we reach it, do you slip off into its shadow. The Lady and I will go forward a few paces. Some of these devils will follow us, I doubt not; they are thick behind us. Do you, who have long arms, take one alive if you may, as it passes your ambush. We may get a true tale of it or learn what is their quarrel against us.'

'But won't the others all come rushing at us to rescue the one we catch,' said Jill in a voice not so steady as she tried to make it.

'Then, Madam,' said the Prince, 'you shall see us die fighting around you, and you must commend yourself to the Lion. Now, good Puddleglum.'

The Marsh-wiggle slipped off into the shadow as quickly as a cat. The others, for a sickening minute or so, went forward at a walk. Then suddenly from behind them there broke out a series of blood-curdling screams, mixed with the familiar voice of Puddleglum, saying, 'Now then! Don't cry out before you're hurt, or you *will* be hurt, see? Anyone would think it was a pig being killed.'

'That was good hunting,' exclaimed the Prince, immediately turning Coalblack and coming back to the corner of the house. 'Eustace,' he said, 'of your courtesy, take Coalblack's head.' Then he dismounted, and all three gazed in silence while Puddleglum pulled his catch out into the light. It was a most miserable little gnome, only about three feet long. It had a sort of ridge, like a cock's comb (only hard), on the top of its head, little pink eyes, and a mouth and chin so large and round that its face looked like that of a pigmy hippopotamus. If they had not been in such a tight place, they would have burst into laughter at the sight of it.

'Now, Earthman,' said the Prince, standing over it and holding his sword point very near the prisoner's neck, 'speak, up, like an honest gnome, and you shall go free. Play the knave with us, and you are but a dead Earthman. Good Puddleglum, how can it speak while you hold its mouth tight shut?'

'No, and it can't bite either,' said Puddleglum. 'If I had the silly soft hands that you humans have (saving your Highness's reverence) I'd have been all over blood by now. Yet even a Marsh-wiggle gets tired of being chewed.'

'Sirrah,' said the Prince to the gnome, 'one bite and you die. Let its mouth open, Puddleglum.'

'Oo-ee-ee,' squealed the Earthman, 'let me go, let me go. It isn't me. I didn't do it.'

'Didn't do what?' asked Puddleglum.

'Whatever your Honours say I *did* do,' answered the creature.

'Tell me your name,' said the Prince, 'and what you Earthmen are all about today.'

'Oh please, your Honours, please, kind gentlemen,' whimpered the gnome. 'Promise you will not tell the Queen's grace anything I say.'

'The Queen's grace, as you call her,' said the Prince sternly, 'is dead. I killed her myself.'

'What!' cried the gnome, opening its ridiculous

mouth wider and wider in astonishment. 'Dead? The
Witch dead? And by your Honour's hand?' It gave a
huge sigh of relief and added, 'Why then your Honour
is a friend!'

The Prince withdrew his sword an inch or so. Puddleglum let the creature sit up. It looked round on the four
travellers with its twinkling, red eyes, chuckled once or
twice, and began.

CHAPTER 14

THE BOTTOM OF THE WORLD

'My name is Golg,' said the gnome. 'And I'll tell your Honours all I know. About an hour ago we were all going about our work – *her* work, I should say – sad and silent, same as we've done any other day for years and years. Then there came a great crash and bang. As soon as they heard it, everyone says to himself, I haven't had a song or a dance or let off a squib for a long time; why's that? And everyone thinks to himself, Why, I must have been enchanted. And then everyone says to himself, I'm blessed if I know why I'm carrying this load, and I'm not going to carry it any farther: that's that. And down we all throw our sacks and bundles and tools. Then everyone turns and sees the great red glow over yonder. And everyone says to himself, What's that? And everyone answers himself and says, There's a crack or chasm split open and a nice warm glow coming up through it from the Really Deep Land, a thousand fathom under us.'

'Great Scott,' exclaimed Eustace, 'are there other lands still lower down?'

'Oh yes, your Honour,' said Golg. 'Lovely places; what we call the Land of Bism. This country where we are now, the Witch's country, is what *we* call the Shallow Lands. It's a good deal too near the surface to suit us. Ugh! You might almost as well be living outside, on the surface itself. You see, we're all poor gnomes from Bism whom the Witch has called up here by magic to work for her. But we'd forgotten all about it till that crash came and the spell broke. We didn't know who we were or where we belonged. We couldn't do anything, or think anything, except what she put into our heads. And it was glum and gloomy things she put there all those years. I've nearly forgotten how to make a joke or dance a jig. But the moment the bang came and the chasm opened and the sea began rising, it all came back. And of course we all set off as quick as we could to get down the crack and home to our own place. And you can see them over there all letting off rockets and standing on their heads for joy. And I'll be very obliged to your Honours if you'll soon let me go and join in.'

'I think this is simply splendid,' said Jill. 'I'm so glad we freed the gnomes as well as ourselves when we cut off the Witch's head! And I'm so glad they aren't really horrid and gloomy any more than the Prince really was – well, what he seemed like.'

'That's all very well, Pole,' said Puddleglum cautiously. 'But those gnomes didn't look to me like chaps who were just running away. It looked more like military formations, if you ask me. Do you look me in the face, Mr Golg, and tell me you weren't preparing for battle?'

'Of course we were, your Honour,' said Golg. 'You see, we didn't know the Witch was dead. We thought she'd be watching from the castle. We were trying to slip away without being seen. And then when you four came out with swords and horses, of course everyone says to himself, Here it comes: not knowing that his Honour wasn't on the Witch's side. And we were determined to fight like anything rather than give up the hope of going back to Bism.'

'I'll be sworn 'tis an honest gnome,' said the Prince.

'Let go of it, friend Puddleglum. As for me, good Golg, I have been enchanted like you and your fellows, and have but newly remembered myself. And now, one question more. Do you know the way to those new diggings, by which the sorceress meant to lead out an army against Overland?'

'Ee-ee-ee!' squeaked Golg. 'Yes, I know that terrible road. I will show you where it begins. But it is no manner of use your Honour asking me to go with you on it. I'll die rather.'

'Why?' asked Eustace anxiously. 'What's so dreadful about it?'

'Too near the top, the outside,' said Golg, shuddering. 'That was the worst thing the Witch did to us. We were going to be led out into the open – on to the outside of the world. They say there's no roof at all there; only a horrible great emptiness called the sky. And the diggings have gone so far that a few strokes of the pick would bring you out to it. I wouldn't dare go near them.'

'Hurrah! Now you're talking!' cried Eustace, and Jill said, 'But it's not horrid at all up there. We like it. We live there.'

'I know you Overlanders live there,' said Golg. 'But I thought it was because you couldn't find your way down inside. You can't really *like* it – crawling about like flies on the top of the world!'

'What about showing us the road at once?' said Puddleglum.

'In a good hour,' cried the Prince. The whole party set out. The Prince remounted his charger, Puddleglum climbed up behind Jill, and Golg led the way. As he went, he kept shouting out the good news that the Witch was dead and that the four Overlanders were not dangerous. And those who heard him shouted it on to others, so that in a few minutes the whole of Underland was ringing with shouts and cheers, and gnomes by hundreds and

thousands, leaping, turning cart-wheels, standing on their heads, playing leap-frog, and letting off huge crackers, came pressing round Coalblack and Snowflake. And the Prince had to tell the story of his own enchantment and deliverance at least ten times.

In this way they came to the edge of the chasm. It was about a thousand feet long and perhaps two hundred wide. They dismounted from their horses and came to the edge, and looked down into it. A strong heat smote up into their faces, mixed with a smell which was quite unlike any they had ever smelled. It was rich, sharp, exciting, and made you sneeze. The depth of the chasm was so bright that at first it dazzled their eyes and they could see nothing. When they got used to it they thought they could make out a river of fire, and, on the banks of that river, what seemed to be fields and groves of an unbearable, hot brilliance – though they were dim compared with the river. There were blues, reds, greens, and whites all jumbled together: a very good stained-glass window with the tropical sun staring straight through it at midday might have something the same effect. Down the rugged sides of the chasm, looking black like flies against all that fiery light, hundreds of Earthmen were climbing.

'Your honours,' said Golg (and when they turned to look at him they could see nothing but blackness for a few minutes, their eyes were so dazzled). 'Your honours, why don't you come down to Bism? You'd be happier there than in that cold, unprotected, naked country out on top. Or at least come down for a short visit.'

Jill took it for granted that none of the others would listen to such an idea for a moment. To her horror she heard the Prince saying:

'Truly, friend Golg, I have half a mind to come down with you. For this is a marvellous adventure, and it may be no mortal man has ever looked into Bism before or will ever have the chance again. And I know not how, as the years pass, I shall bear to remember that it was once in my power to have probed the uttermost pit of Earth and that I forbore. But could a man live there? You do not swim in the fire-river itself?'

'Oh no, your Honour. Not we. It's only salamanders live in the fire itself.'

'What kind of beast is your salamander?' asked the Prince.

'It is hard to tell their kind, your Honour,' said Golg. 'For they are too white-hot to look at. But they are most like small dragons. They speak to us out of the fire. They are wonderfully clever with their tongues: very witty and eloquent.'

Jill glanced hastily at Eustace. She had felt sure that he would like the idea of climbing down that chasm even less than she did. Her heart sank as she saw that his face was quite changed. He looked much more like the Prince than like the old Scrubb at Experiment House. For all his adventures, and the days when he had sailed with King Caspian, were coming back to him.

'Your Highness,' he said. 'If my old friend Reepicheep the Mouse were here, he would say we could not now refuse the adventures of Bism without a great impeachment to our honour.'

'Down there,' said Golg, 'I could show you real gold, real silver, real diamonds.'

'Bosh!' said Jill rudely. 'As if we didn't know that we're below the deepest mines even here.'

'Yes,' said Golg. 'I have heard of those little scratches in the crust that you Topdwellers call mines. But that's where you get dead gold, dead silver, dead gems. Down in Bism we have them alive and growing. There I'll pick you bunches of rubies that you can eat and squeeze you a cup full of diamond-juice. You won't care much about fingering the cold, dead treasures of your shallow mines after you have tasted the live ones of Bism.'

'My father went to the world's end,' said Rilian thoughtfully. 'It would be a marvellous thing if his son went to the bottom of the world.'

'If your Highness wants to see your father while he's still alive, which I think he'd prefer,' said Puddleglum, 'it's about time we were getting on to that road to the diggings.'

'And I won't go down that hole, whatever anyone says,' added Jill.

'Why, if your Honours are really set to go back to Overworld,' said Golg, 'there *is* one bit of the road that's rather lower than this. And perhaps, if that flood's still rising –'

'Oh, do, do, do come *on*!' begged Jill.

'I fear it must be so,' said the Prince with a deep sigh. 'But I have left half of my heart in the land of Bism.'

'Please!' begged Jill.

'Where is the road?' asked Puddleglum.

'There are lamps all the way,' said Golg. 'Your Honour can see the beginning of the road on the far side of the chasm.'

'How long will the lamps burn for?' asked Puddleglum.

At that moment a hissing, scorching voice like the voice of Fire itself (they wondered afterwards if it could have been a salamander's) came whistling up out of the very depths of Bism.

'Quick! Quick! Quick! To the cliffs, to the cliffs, to the cliffs!' it said. 'The rift closes. It closes. It closes. Quick! Quick!' And at the same time, with ear-shattering cracks and creaks, the rocks moved. Already, while they looked, the chasm was narrower. From every side belated gnomes were rushing into it. They would not wait to climb down the rocks. They flung themselves headlong and, either because so strong a blast of hot air was beating up from the bottom, or for some other reason, they could be seen floating downwards like leaves. Thicker and thicker they floated, till their blackness almost blotted out the fiery river and the groves of live gems. 'Good-bye to your Honours. I'm off,' shouted Golg, and dived. Only a few were left to follow him. The chasm was now no broader than a stream. Now it was narrow as the slit in a pillar-box. Now it was only an intensely bright thread. Then, with a shock like a thousand goods trains crashing into a thousand pairs of buffers, the lips of rock closed. The hot, maddening smell vanished. The travellers were alone in an Underworld which now looked far blacker than before. Pale, dim, and dreary, the lamps marked the direction of the road.

'Now,' said Puddleglum, 'it's ten to one we've already stayed too long, but we may as well make a try. Those lamps will give out in five minutes, I shouldn't wonder.'

They urged the horses to a canter and thundered along the dusky road in fine style. But almost at once it began going downhill. They would have thought Golg had sent

them the wrong way if they had not seen, on the other side of the valley, the lamps going on and upwards as far as the eye could reach. But at the bottom of the valley the lamps shone on moving water.

'Haste,' cried the Prince. They galloped down the

slope. It would have been nasty enough at the bottom even five minutes later for the tide was running up the valley like a mill-race, and if it had come to swimming, the horses could hardly have won over. But it was still only a foot or two deep, and though it swished terribly round the horses' legs, they reached the far side in safety.

Then began the slow, weary march uphill with nothing ahead to look at but the pale lamps which went up and up as far as the eye could reach. When they looked back they could see the water spreading. All the hills of Underland were now islands, and it was only on those islands that the lamps remained. Every moment some distant light vanished. Soon there would be total darkness everywhere except on the road they were following; and even on the lower part of it behind them, though no lamps had yet gone out, the lamplight shone on water.

Although they had good reason for hurrying, the horses could not go on for ever without a rest. They halted: and in silence they could hear the lapping of water.

'I wonder is what's his name – Father Time – flooded out now,' said Jill. 'And all those queer sleeping animals.'

'I don't think we're as high as that,' said Eustace. 'Don't you remember how we had to go downhill to reach the sunless sea? I shouldn't think the water has reached Father Time's cave yet.'

'That's as may be,' said Puddleglum. 'I'm more interested in the lamps on this road. Look a bit sickly, don't they?'

'They always did,' said Jill.

'Ah,' said Puddleglum. 'But they're greener now.'

'You don't mean to say you think they're going out?' cried Eustace.

'Well, however they work, you can't expect them to last for ever, you know,' replied the Marsh-wiggle. 'But don't let your spirits down, Scrubb. I've got my eye on the water too, and I don't think it's rising so fast as it did.'

'Small comfort, friend,' said the Prince. 'If we cannot find our way out. I cry you mercy, all. I am to blame for my pride and fantasy which delayed us by the mouth of the land of Bism. Now, let us ride on.'

During the hour or so that followed Jill sometimes thought that Puddleglum was right about the lamps, and sometimes thought it was only her imagination. Meanwhile the land was changing. The roof of Underland was so near that even by that dull light they could now see it quite distinctly. And the great, rugged walls of Underland could be seen drawing closer on each side. The road, in fact, was leading them up into a steep tunnel. They began to pass picks and shovels and barrows and other signs that the diggers had recently been at work. If only one could be sure of getting out, all this was very cheering. But the thought of going on into a hole that would get narrower and narrower, and harder to turn back in, was very unpleasant.

At last the roof was so low that Puddleglum and the Prince knocked their heads against it. The party dismounted and led the horses. The road was uneven here and one had to pick one's steps with some care. That was how Jill noticed the growing darkness. There was no doubt about it now. The faces of the others looked strange and ghastly in the green glow. Then all at once (she couldn't help it) Jill gave a little scream. One light, the next one ahead, went out altogether. The one behind them did the same. Then they were in absolute darkness.

'Courage, friends,' came Prince Rilian's voice. 'Whether we live or die Aslan will be our good lord.'

'That's right, Sir,' said Puddleglum's voice. 'And you must always remember there's one good thing about being trapped down here: it'll save funeral expenses.'

Jill held her tongue. (If you don't want other people to know how frightened you are, this is always a wise thing to do; it's your voice that gives you away.)

'We might as well go on as stand here,' said Eustace; and when she heard the tremble in *his* voice, Jill knew how wise she'd been not to trust her own.

Puddleglum and Eustace went first with their arms stretched out in front of them, for fear of blundering into anything; Jill and the Prince followed, leading the horses.

'I say,' came Eustace's voice much later, 'are my eyes going queer or is there a patch of light up there?'

Before anyone could answer him, Puddleglum called out: 'Stop. I'm up against a dead end. And it's earth, not rock. What were you saying, Scrubb?'

'By the Lion,' said the Prince, 'Eustace is right. There is a sort of –'

'But it's not daylight,' said Jill. 'It's only a cold blue sort of light.'

'Better than nothing, though,' said Eustace. 'Can we get up to it?'

'It's not right overhead,' said Puddleglum. 'It's above us, but it's in this wall that I've run into. How would it be, Pole, if you got on my shoulders and saw whether you could get up to it?'

CHAPTER 15

THE DISAPPEARANCE OF JILL

THE patch of light did not show up anything down in the darkness where they were standing. The others could only hear, not see, Jill's efforts to get on to the Marsh-wiggle's back. That is, they heard him saying, 'You needn't put your finger in my eye,' and, 'Nor your foot in my mouth either,' and, 'That's more like it,' and, 'Now, I'll hold on to your legs. That'll leave your arms free to steady yourself against the earth.'

Then they looked up and soon they saw the black shape of Jill's head against the patch of light.

'Well?' they all shouted up anxiously.

'It's a hole,' called Jill's voice. 'I could get through it if I was a little bit higher.'

'What do you see through it?' asked Eustace.

'Nothing much yet,' said Jill. 'I say, Puddleglum, let go my legs so that I can stand on your shoulders instead of sitting on them. I can steady myself all right against the edge.'

They could hear her moving and then much more of her came into sight against the greyness of the opening; in fact all of her down to the waist.

'I say –' began Jill, but suddenly broke off with a cry: not a sharp cry. It sounded more as if her mouth had been muffled up or had something pushed into it. After that she found her voice and seemed to be shouting out as loud as she could, but they couldn't hear the words. Two things then happened at the same moment. The patch of light was completely blocked up for a second or so; and they heard both a scuffling, struggling sound and the voice of the Marsh-wiggle gasping: 'Quick! Help! Hold on to her legs. Someone's pulling her. There! No, here. Too late!'

The opening, and the cold light which filled it, were now perfectly clear again. Jill had vanished.

'Jill! Jill!' they shouted frantically, but there was no answer.

'Why the dickens couldn't you have held her feet?' said Eustace.

'I don't know, Scrubb,' groaned Puddleglum. 'Born to be a misfit, I shouldn't wonder. Fated. Fated to be Pole's death, just as I was fated to eat Talking Stag at Harfang. Not that it isn't my own fault as well, of course.'

'This is the greatest shame and sorrow that could have fallen on us,' said the Prince. 'We have sent a brave lady into the hands of enemies and stayed behind in safety.'

'Don't paint it *too* black, Sir,' said Puddleglum. 'We're not very safe except for death by starvation in this hole.'

'I wonder am *I* small enough to get through where Jill did?' said Eustace.

What had really happened to Jill was this. As soon as she got her head out of the hole she found that she was looking down as if from an upstairs window, not up as if through a trap-door. She had been so long in the dark that her eyes couldn't at first take in what they were seeing: except that she was not looking at the daylit, sunny world which she so wanted to see. The air seemed to be deadly cold, and the light was pale and blue. There was also a good deal of noise going on and a lot of white objects flying about in the air. It was at that moment that she had shouted down to Puddleglum to let her stand up on his shoulders.

When she had done this, she could see and hear a good deal better. The noises she had been hearing turned out to be of two kinds: the rhythmical thump of several feet, and the music of four fiddles, three flutes, and a drum. She also got her own position clear. She was looking out of a hole in a steep bank which sloped down and reached the level about fourteen feet below her. Everything was very white. A lot of people were moving about. Then she gasped! The people were trim little Fauns, and Dryads with leaf-crowned hair floating behind them. For a second they looked as if they were moving anyhow; then she saw that they were really doing a dance – a dance with so many complicated steps and figures that it took you some time to understand it. Then it came over her like a thunderclap that the pale, blue light was really moon-light, and the white stuff on the ground was really snow. And of course! There were the stars staring in a black frosty sky overhead. And the tall black things behind the dancers were trees. They had not only got out into the upper world at last, but had come out in the heart of Narnia. Jill felt she could have fainted with delight; and the music – the wild music, intensely sweet and yet just the least bit eerie too, and full of good magic as the Witch's thrumming had been full of bad magic – made her feel it all the more.

All this takes a long time to tell, but of course it took a very short time to see. Jill turned almost at once to shout down to the others, 'I say! It's all right. We're out, and we're home.' But the reason she never got further than 'I say' was this. Circling round and round the dancers was a ring of Dwarfs, all dressed in their finest clothes; mostly scarlet with fur-lined hoods and golden tassels and big furry top-boots. As they circled round they were all diligently throwing snowballs. (Those were the white things that Jill had seen flying through the air.) They weren't throwing them *at* the dancers as silly boys might have been doing in England. They were throwing them through the dance in such perfect time with the music and with such perfect aim that if all the dancers were in exactly the right places at exactly the right moments, no one would be hit. This is called the Great Snow Dance and it is done every year in Narnia on the first moonlit night when there is snow on the ground. Of course it is a kind of game as well as a dance, because every now and then some dancer will be the least little bit wrong and get a snowball in the face, and then everyone laughs. But a good team of dancers, Dwarfs, and musicians will keep it up for hours without a single hit. On fine nights when the cold and the drum-taps, and the hooting of the owls, and the moonlight, have got into their wild, woodland blood and made it even wilder, they will dance till daybreak. I wish you could see it for yourselves.

What had stopped Jill when she got as far as the *say* of 'I say' was of course simply a fine big snowball that came sailing through the dance from a Dwarf on the far side and got her fair and square in the mouth. She didn't in the least mind; twenty snowballs would not have damped her spirits at that moment. But however happy you are feeling, you can't talk with your mouth full of snow. And when, after considerable spluttering, she could speak again, she quite forgot in her excitement that the others, down in the dark, behind her, still didn't know the good news. She simply leaned as far out of the hole as she could, and yelled to the dancers.

'Help! Help! We're buried in the hill. Come and dig us out.'

The Narnians, who had not even noticed the little hole in the hillside, were of course very surprised, and looked about in several wrong directions before they found out where the voice was coming from. But when they caught sight of Jill they all came running towards her, and as many as could scrambled up the bank, and a dozen or more hands were stretched up to help her. And Jill caught hold of them and thus got out of the hole and came slithering down the bank head first, and then picked herself up and said:

'Oh, do go and dig the others out. There are three others, besides the horses. And one of them is Prince Rilian.'

She was already in the middle of a crowd when she said this, for besides the dancers all sorts of people who had been watching the dance, and whom she had not seen at first, came running up. Squirrels came out of the trees in showers, and so did Owls. Hedgehogs came waddling as fast as their short legs would carry them. Bears and Badgers followed at a slower pace. A great Panther, twitching its tail with excitement, was the last to join the party.

But as soon as they understood what Jill was saying, they all became active. 'Pick and shovel, boys, pick and shovel. Off for our tools!' said the Dwarfs, and dashed away into the woods at top speed. 'Wake up some Moles,

they're the chaps for digging. They're quite as good as
Dwarfs,' said a voice. 'What was that she said about
Prince Rilian?' said another. 'Hush!' said the Panther.
'The poor child's crazed, and no wonder after being lost
inside the hill. She doesn't know what she's saying.'
'That's right,' said an old Bear. 'Why, she said Prince
Rilian was a horse!' – 'No, she didn't,' said a Squirrel,
very pert. 'Yes, she did,' said another Squirrel, even
perter.

'It's quite t-t-t-true. D-d-don't be so silly,' said Jill.
She spoke like that because her teeth were now chattering
with the cold.

Immediately one of the Dryads flung round her a furry
cloak which some Dwarf had dropped when he rushed to
fetch his mining tools, and an obliging Faun trotted off
among the trees to a place where Jill could see firelight
in the mouth of a cave, to get her a hot drink. But before
it came, all the Dwarfs reappeared with spades and pickaxes and charged at the hillside. Then Jill heard cries of
'Hi! What are you doing? Put that sword down,' and
'Now, young 'un: none of that,' and, 'He's a vicious
one, now, isn't he?' Jill hurried to the spot and didn't
know whether to laugh or cry when she saw Eustace's
face, very pale and dirty, projecting from the blackness
of the hole, and Eustace's right hand brandishing a sword
with which he made lunges at anyone who came near
him.

For of course Eustace had been having a very different
time from Jill during the last few minutes. He had heard
Jill cry out and seen her disappear into the unknown.
Like the Prince and Puddleglum, he thought that some
enemies had caught her. And from down below he didn't

see that the pale, blueish light was moonlight. He thought the hole would lead only into some other cave, lit by some ghostly phosphorescence and filled with goodness-knows-what evil creatures of the Underworld. So that when he had persuaded Puddleglum to give him a back, and drawn his sword, and poked out his head, he had really been doing a very brave thing. The others would have done it first if they could, but the hole was too small for them to climb through. Eustace was a little bigger, and a lot clumsier, than Jill, so that when he looked out he bumped his head against the top of the hole and brought a small avalanche of snow down on his face. And so, when he could see again, and saw dozens of figures coming at him as hard as they could run, it is not surprising that he tried to ward them off.

'Stop, Eustace, stop,' cried Jill. 'They're all friends. Can't you see? We've come up in Narnia. Everything's all right.'

Then Eustace did see, and apologized to the Dwarfs (and the Dwarfs said not to mention it), and dozens of thick, hairy, dwarfish hands helped him out just as they had helped Jill out a few minutes before. Then Jill scrambled up the bank and put her head in at the dark opening and shouted the good news in to the prisoners. As she turned away she heard Puddleglum mutter. 'Ah, poor Pole. It's been too much for her, this last bit. Turned her head, I shouldn't wonder. She's beginning to see things.'

Jill rejoined Eustace and they shook one another by both hands and took in great deep breaths of the free midnight air. And a warm cloak was brought for Eustace and hot drinks, for both. While they were sipping it, the

Dwarfs had already got all the snow and all the sods off a large strip of the hillside round the original hole, and the pickaxes and spades were now going as merrily as the feet of Fauns and Dryads had been going in the dance ten minutes before. Only ten minutes! Yet already it felt to Jill and Eustace as if all their dangers in the dark and heat and general smotheriness of the earth must have been only a dream. Out here, in the cold, with the moon and the huge stars overhead (Narnian stars are nearer than stars in our world) and with kind, merry faces all round them, one couldn't quite believe in Underland.

Before they had finished their hot drinks, a dozen or so Moles, newly waked and still very sleepy, and not well pleased, had arrived. But as soon as they understood what it was all about, they joined in with a will. Even the Fauns made themselves useful by carting away the earth in little barrows, and the Squirrels danced and leaped to and fro in great excitement, though Jill never found out exactly what they thought they were doing. The Bears and Owls contented themselves with giving advice, and kept on asking the children if they wouldn't like to come into the cave (that was where Jill had seen the firelight) and get warm and have supper. But the children couldn't bear to go without seeing their friends set free.

No one in our world can work at a job of that sort as Dwarfs and Talking Moles work in Narnia; but then, of course, Moles and Dwarfs don't look on it as work. They like digging. It was therefore not really long before they had opened a great black chasm in the hillside. And out from the blackness into the moonlight – this would have been rather dreadful if one hadn't known who they were –

came, first, the long, leggy, steeple-hatted figure of the Marsh-wiggle, and then, leading two great horses, Rilian the Prince himself.

As Puddleglum appeared shouts broke out on every side: 'Why, it's a Wiggle – why, it's old Puddleglum – old Puddleglum from the Eastern Marshes – what ever have you been doing, Puddleglum? – there've been search-parties out for you – the Lord Trumpkin has been putting up notices – there's a reward offered!' But all this died away, all in one moment, into dead silence, as quickly as the noise dies away in a rowdy dormitory if the Headmaster opens the door. For now they saw the Prince.

No one doubted for a moment who he was. There were plenty of Beasts and Dryads and Dwarfs and Fauns who remembered him from the days before his enchanting. There were some old ones who could just remember how his father, King Caspian, had looked when he was a young man, and saw the likeness. But I think they would have known him anyway. Pale though he was from long imprisonment in the Deep Lands, dressed in black, dusty, dishevelled, and weary, there was something in his face and air which no one could mistake. That look is in the face of all true kings of Narnia, who rule by the will of

Aslan and sit at Cair Paravel on the throne of Peter the
High King. Instantly every head was bared and every
knee was bent; a moment later such cheering and shouting, such jumps and reels of joy, such hand-shakings and
kissings and embracings of everybody by everybody else
broke out that the tears came into Jill's eyes. Their quest
had been worth all the pains it cost.

'Please it your Highness,' said the oldest of the Dwarfs,
'there is some attempt at a supper in the cave yonder,
prepared against the ending of the snow-dance –'

'With a good will, Father,' said the Prince. 'For never
had any Prince, Knight, Gentleman, or Bear so good a
stomach to his victuals as we four wanderers have
tonight.'

The whole crowd began to move away through the
trees towards the cave. Jill heard Puddleglum saying to
those who pressed round him. 'No, no, my story can
wait. Nothing worth talking about has happened to me.
I want to hear the news. Don't try breaking it to me
gently, for I'd rather have it all at once. Has the King
been shipwrecked? Any forest fires? No wars on the
Calormen border? Or a few dragons, I shouldn't won-

der?' And all the creatures laughed aloud and said, 'Isn't that just like a Marsh-wiggle?'

The two children were nearly dropping with tiredness and hunger, but the warmth of the cave, and the very sight of it, with the firelight dancing on the walls and dressers and cups and saucers and plates and on the smooth stone floor, just as it does in a farmhouse kitchen, revived them a little. All the same they went fast asleep while supper was being got ready. And while they slept Prince Rilian was talking over the whole adventure with the older and wiser Beasts and Dwarfs. And now they all saw what it meant; how a wicked Witch (doubtless the same kind as that White Witch who had brought the Great Winter on Narnia long ago) had contrived the whole thing, first killing Rilian's mother and enchanting Rilian himself. And they saw how she had dug right under Narnia and was going to break out and rule it through Rilian: and how he had never dreamed that the country of which she would make him king (king in name, but really her slave) was his own country. And from the children's part of the story they saw how she was in league and friendship with the dangerous giants of Harfang. 'And the lesson of it all is, your Highness,' said the oldest Dwarf, 'that those Northern Witches always mean the same thing, but in every age they have a different plan for getting it.'

CHAPTER 16

THE HEALING OF HARMS

WHEN Jill woke next morning and found herself in a cave, she thought for one horrid moment that she was back in the Underworld. But when she noticed that she was lying on a bed of heather with a furry mantle over her, and saw a cheery fire crackling (as if newly lit) on a stone hearth and, farther off, morning sunlight coming in through the cave's mouth, she remembered all the happy truth. They had had a delightful supper, all crowded into that cave, in spite of being so sleepy before it was properly over. She had a vague impression of Dwarfs crowding round the fire with frying-pans rather bigger than themselves, and the hissing, and delicious smell of sausages, and more, and more, and more sausages. And not wretched sausages half full of bread and soya bean either, but real meaty, spicy ones, fat and piping hot and burst and just the tiniest bit burnt. And great mugs of frothy chocolate, and roast potatoes and roast chestnuts, and baked apples with raisins stuck in where the cores had been, and then ices just to freshen you up after all the hot things.

Jill sat up and looked around. Puddleglum and Eustace were lying not far away, both fast asleep.

'Hi, you two!' shouted Jill in a loud voice. 'Aren't you ever going to get up?'

'Shoo, shoo!' said a sleepy voice somewhere above her. 'Time to be settling down. Have a good snooze, do, do. Don't make a to-do. Tu-whoo!'

'Why, I do believe,' said Jill, glancing up at a white

bundle of fluffy feathers which was perched on top of a grandfather clock in one corner of the cave, 'I do believe it's Glimfeather!'

'True, true,' whirred the Owl, lifting its head out from under its wing and opening one eye. 'I came up with a message for the Prince at about two. The squirrels brought us the good news. Message for the Prince. He's gone. You're to follow too. Good-day –' and the head disappeared again.

As there seemed no further hope of getting any information from the Owl, Jill got up and began looking round for any chance of a wash and some breakfast. But almost at once a little Faun came trotting into the cave with a sharp click-clack of his goaty hoofs on the stone floor.

'Ah! You've woken up at last, Daughter of Eve,' he said. 'Perhaps you'd better wake the Son of Adam. You've got to be off in a few minutes and two Centaurs have very kindly offered to let you ride on their backs down to Cair Paravel.' He added in a lower voice. 'Of course, you realize it is a most special and unheard-of honour to be allowed to ride a Centaur. I don't know that I ever heard of anyone doing it before. It wouldn't do to keep them waiting.'

'Where's the Prince?' was the first question of Eustace and Puddleglum as soon as they had been waked.

'He's gone down to meet the King, his father, at Cair Paravel,' answered the Faun, whose name was Orruns. 'His Majesty's ship is expected in harbour any moment. It seems that the King met Aslan – I don't know whether it was in a vision or face to face – before he had sailed far, and Aslan turned him back and told him he would find his long-lost son awaiting him when he reached Narnia.'

Eustace was now up and he and Jill set about helping Orruns to get the breakfast. Puddleglum was told to stay in bed. A Centaur called Cloudbirth, a famous healer, or (as Orruns called it) a 'leach', was coming to see to his burnt foot.

'Ah!' said Puddleglum in a tone almost of contentment, 'he'll want to have the leg off at the knee, I shouldn't wonder. You see if he doesn't.' But he was quite glad to stay in bed.

Breakfast was scrambled eggs and toast and Eustace tackled it just as if he had not had a very large supper in the middle of the night.

'I say, Son of Adam,' said the Faun, looking with a certain awe at Eustace's mouthfuls. 'There's no need to hurry *quite* so dreadfully as that. I don't think the Centaurs have quite finished *their* breakfasts yet.'

'Then they must have got up very late,' said Eustace. 'I bet it's after ten o'clock.'

'Oh no,' said Orruns. 'They got up before it was light.'

'Then they must have waited the dickens of a time for breakfast,' said Eustace.

'No, they didn't,' said Orruns. 'They began eating the minute they woke.'

'Golly!' said Eustace. 'Do they eat a very big breakfast?'

'Why, Son of Adam, don't you understand? A Centaur has a man-stomach and a horse-stomach. And of course both want breakfast. So first of all he has porridge and pavenders and kidneys and bacon and omelette and cold ham and toast and marmalade and coffee and beer. And after that he attends to the horse part of himself by grazing for an hour or so and finishing up with a hot mash, some oats, and a bag of sugar. That's why it's such a serious thing to ask a Centaur to stay for the week-end. A very serious thing indeed.'

At that moment there was a sound of horse-hoofs tapping on rock from the mouth of the cave, and the children looked up. The two Centaurs, one with a black and one with a golden beard flowing over their magnificent bare chests, stood waiting for them, bending their heads a little so as to look into the cave. Then the children became very polite and finished their breakfast very quickly. No one thinks a Centaur funny when he sees it. They are solemn, majestic people, full of ancient wisdom which they learn from the stars, not easily made either merry or angry; but their anger is terrible as a tidal wave when it comes.

'Good-bye, dear Puddleglum,' said Jill, going over to the Marsh-wiggle's bed. 'I'm sorry we called you a wet blanket.'

'So'm I,' said Eustace. 'You've been the best friend in the world.'

'And I do hope we'll meet again,' added Jill.

'Not much chance of that, I should say,' replied Puddleglum. 'I don't reckon I'm very likely to see my old wigwam again either. And that Prince – he's a nice chap – but do you think he's very strong? Constitution ruined with living underground, I shouldn't wonder. Looks the sort that might go off any day.'

'Puddleglum!' said Jill. 'You're a regular old humbug. You sound as doleful as a funeral and I believe you're perfectly happy. And you talk as if you were afraid of everything, when you're really as brave as – as a lion.'

'Now, speaking of funerals,' began Puddleglum, but Jill, who heard the Centaurs tapping with their hoofs behind her, surprised him very much by flinging her arms round his thin neck and kissing his muddy-looking face, while Eustace wrung his hand. Then they both rushed away to the Centaurs, and the Marsh-wiggle, sinking back on his bed, remarked to himself, 'Well, I wouldn't have dreamt of her doing that. Even though I *am* a good-looking chap.'

To ride on a Centaur is, no doubt, a great honour (and except Jill and Eustace there is probably no one alive in the world today who has had it) but it is very uncomfortable. For no one who valued his life would suggest putting a saddle on a Centaur, and riding bare-back is no fun; especially if, like Eustace, you have never learned to ride at all. The Centaurs were very polite in a grave, gracious, grown-up kind of way, and as they cantered through the Narnian woods they spoke, without turning their heads, telling the children about the properties of herbs and roots, the influences of the planets, the nine names of Aslan with their meanings, and things of that sort. But however sore and jolted the two humans were, they would now give anything to have that journey over again: to see those glades and slopes sparkling with last night's snow, to be met by rabbits and squirrels and birds that wished you good morning, to breathe again the air of Narnia and hear the voices of the Narnian trees.

They came down to the river, flowing bright and blue in winter sunshine, far below the last bridge (which is at the snug, red-roofed little town of Beruna) and were

ferried across in a flat barge by the ferryman; or rather,
by the ferry-wiggle, for it is Marsh-wiggles who do most
of the watery and fishy kinds of work in Narnia. And
when they had crossed they rode along the south bank
of the river and presently came to Cair Paravel itself.
And at the very moment of their arrival they saw that
same bright ship which they had seen when they first set
foot in Narnia, gliding up the river like a huge bird. All
the court were once more assembled on the green between
the castle and the quay to welcome King Caspian home
again. Rilian, who had changed his black clothes and
was now dressed in a scarlet cloak over silver mail, stood
close to the water's edge, bare-headed, to receive his
father; and the Dwarf Trumpkin sat beside him in his
little donkey-chair. The children saw there would be no
chance of reaching the Prince through all that crowd,
and, anyway, they now felt rather shy. So they asked the
Centaurs if they might go on sitting on their backs a little
longer and thus see everything over the heads of the
courtiers. And the Centaurs said they might.

A flourish of silver trumpets came over the water from
the ship's deck: the sailors threw a rope; rats (Talking
Rats, of course) and Marsh-wiggles made it fast ashore;
and the ship was warped in. Musicians, hidden somewhere in the crowd, began to play solemn, triumphal
music. And soon the King's galleon was alongside and
the Rats ran the gangway on board her.

Jill expected to see the old King come down it. But
there appeared to be some hitch. A Lord with a pale face
came ashore and knelt to the Prince and to Trumpkin.
The three were talking with their heads close together
for a few minutes, but no one could hear what they said.

The music played on, but you could feel that everyone was becoming uneasy. Then four Knights, carrying something and going very slowly, appeared on deck. When they started to come down the gangway you could see what they were carrying: it was the old King on a bed, very pale and still. They set him down. The Prince knelt beside him and embraced him. They could see King Caspian raising his hand to bless his son. And everyone cheered, but it was a half-hearted cheer, for they all felt that something was going wrong. Then suddenly the King's head fell back upon his pillows, the musicians stopped and there was a dead silence. The Prince, kneeling by the King's bed, laid down his head upon it and wept.

There were whisperings and goings to and fro. Then Jill noticed that all who wore hats, bonnets, helmets, or hoods were taking them off – Eustace included. Then she heard a rustling and flapping noise up above the castle; when she looked she saw that the great banner with the golden Lion on it was being brought down to half-mast. And after that, slowly, mercilessly, with wailing strings and disconsolate blowing of horns, the music began again: this time, a tune to break your heart.

They both slipped off their Centaurs (who took no notice of them).

'I wish I was at home,' said Jill.

Eustace nodded, saying nothing, and bit his lip.

'I have come,' said a deep voice behind them. They turned and saw the Lion himself, so bright and real and strong that everything else began at once to look pale and shadowy compared with him. And in less time than it takes to breathe Jill forgot about the dead King of Narnia and remembered only how she had made Eustace fall over the cliff, and how she had helped to muff nearly all the signs, and about all the snappings and quarrellings. And she wanted to say 'I'm sorry' but she could not speak. Then the Lion drew them towards him with his eyes, and bent down and touched their pale faces with his tongue, and said:

'Think of that no more. I will not always be scolding. You have done the work for which I sent you into Narnia.'

'Please, Aslan,' said Jill, 'may we go home now?'

'Yes. I have come to bring you Home,' said Aslan. Then he opened his mouth wide and blew. But this time they had no sense of flying through the air: instead, it seemed that they remained still, and the wild breath of Aslan blew away the ship and the dead King and the castle and the snow and the winter sky. For all these things floated off into the air like wreaths of smoke, and suddenly they were standing in a great brightness of mid-summer sunshine, on smooth turf, among mighty trees, and beside a fair, fresh stream. They they saw that they were once more on the Mountain of Aslan, high up above and beyond the end of that world in which Narnia lies. But the strange thing was that the funeral music for King Caspian still went on, though no one could tell where it came from. They were walking beside the stream and the Lion went before them: and he became so beautiful, and the music so despairing, that Jill did not know which of them it was that filled her eyes with tears.

Then Aslan stopped, and the children looked into the stream. And there, on the golden gravel of the bed of the stream, lay King Caspian, dead, with the water flowing over him like liquid glass. His long white beard swayed in it like water-weed. And all three stood and wept. Even the Lion wept: great Lion-tears, each tear more precious than the Earth would be if it was a single solid diamond. And Jill noticed that Eustace looked neither like a child crying, nor like a boy crying and wanting to hide it, but like a grown-up crying. At least, that is the nearest she could get to it; but really, as she said, people don't seem to have any particular ages on that mountain.

'Son of Adam,' said Aslan, 'go into that thicket and pluck the thorn that you will find there, and bring it to me.'

Eustace obeyed. The thorn was a foot long and sharp as a rapier.

'Drive it into my paw, son of Adam,' said Aslan, holding up his right fore-paw and spreading out the great pad towards Eustace.

'Must I?' said Eustace.

'Yes,' said Aslan.

Then Eustace set his teeth and drove the thorn into the Lion's pad. And there came out a great drop of blood, redder than all redness that you have ever seen or imagined. And it splashed into the stream over the dead body of the King. At the same moment the doleful music stopped. And the dead King began to be changed. His white beard turned to grey, and from grey to yellow, and got shorter and vanished altogether; and his sunken cheeks grew round and fresh, and the wrinkles were smoothed, and his eyes opened, and his eyes and lips both laughed, and suddenly he leaped up and stood before them – a very young man, or a boy. (But Jill couldn't say which, because of people having no particular ages in Aslan's country. Even in this world, of course, it is the

stupidest children who are most childish and the stupidest
grown-ups who are most grown-up.) And he rushed
to Aslan and flung his arms as far as they would go round
the huge neck; and he gave Aslan the strong kisses of a
King, and Aslan gave him the wild kisses of a Lion.

At last Caspian turned to the others. He gave a great
laugh of astonished joy.

'Why! Eustace!' he said. 'Eustace! So you did reach
the end of the world after all. What about my second-best
sword that you broke on the sea-serpent?'

Eustace made a step towards him with both hands held
out, but then drew back with a somewhat startled
expression.

'Look here! I say,' he stammered. 'It's all very well.
But aren't you? – I mean didn't you –?'

'Oh, don't be such an ass,' said Caspian.

'But,' said Eustace, looking at Aslan. 'Hasn't he – er –
died?'

'Yes,' said the Lion in a very quiet voice, almost (Jill
thought) as if he were laughing. 'He has died. Most
people have, you know. Even I have. There are very few
who haven't.'

'Oh,' said Caspian. 'I see what's bothering you. You
think I'm a ghost, or some nonsense. But don't you see?
I would be that if I appeared in Narnia now: because I
don't belong there any more. But one can't be a ghost in
one's own country. I might be a ghost if I got into your
world. I don't know. But I suppose it isn't yours either,
now you're here.'

A great hope rose in the children's hearts. But Aslan
shook his shaggy head. 'No, my dears,' he said. 'When
you meet me here again, you will have come to stay.

But not now. You must go back to your own world for a while.'

'Sir,' said Caspian, 'I've always wanted to have just one glimpse of *their* world. Is that wrong?'

'You cannot want wrong things any more, now that you have died, my son,' said Aslan. 'And you shall see their world – for five minutes of *their* time. It will take no longer for you to set things right there.' Then Aslan explained to Caspian what Jill and Eustace were going back to and all about Experiment House: he seemed to know it quite as well as they did.

'Daughter,' said Aslan to Jill, 'pluck a switch off that bush.' She did; and as soon as it was in her hand it turned into a fine new riding crop.

'Now, sons of Adam, draw your swords,' said Aslan. 'But use only the flat, for it is cowards and children, not warriors, against whom I send you.'

'Are you coming with us, Aslan?' said Jill.

'They shall see only my back,' said Aslan.

He led them rapidly through the wood, and before they had gone many paces, the wall of Experiment House appeared before them. Then Aslan roared so that the sun shook in the sky and thirty feet of the wall fell down before them. They looked through the gap, down into the school shrubbery and on to the roof of the gym, all under the same dull autumn sky which they had seen before their adventures began. Aslan turned to Jill and Eustace and breathed upon them and touched their foreheads with his tongue. Then he lay down amid the gap he had made in the wall and turned his golden back to England, and his lordly face towards his own lands. At the same moment Jill saw figures whom she knew only

too well running up through the laurels towards them.
Most of the gang were there – Adela Pennyfather and
Cholmondely Major, Edith Winterblott, 'Spotty' Sorner,
big Bannister, and the two loathsome Garrett twins. But
suddenly they stopped. Their faces changed, and all the
meanness, conceit, cruelty, and sneakishness almost disappeared in one single expression of terror. For they saw
the wall fallen down, and a lion as large as a young
elephant lying in the gap, and three figures in glittering
clothes with weapons in their hands rushing down upon
them. For, with the strength of Aslan in them, Jill plied
her crop on the girls and Caspian and Eustace plied the
flats of their swords on the boys so well that in two
minutes all the bullies were running like mad, crying out,
'Murder! Fascists! Lions! It isn't *fair*.' And then the
Head (who was, by the way, a woman) came running
out to see what was happening. And when she saw the
lion and the broken wall and Caspian and Jill and Eustace
(whom she quite failed to recognize) she had hysterics
and went back to the house and began ringing up the
police with stories about a lion escaped from a circus,
and escaped convicts who broke down walls and carried
drawn swords. In the midst of all this fuss Jill and Eustace
slipped quietly indoors and changed out of their bright
clothes into ordinary things, and Caspian went back into
his own world. And the wall, at Aslan's word, was made
whole again. When the police arrived and found no lion,
no broken wall, and no convicts, and the Head behaving
like a lunatic, there was an inquiry into the whole thing.
And in the inquiry all sorts of things about Experiment
House came out, and about ten people got expelled.
After that, the Head's friends saw that the Head was no

use as a Head, so they got her made an Inspector to interfere with other Heads. And when they found she wasn't much good even at that, they got her into Parliament where she lived happily ever after.

Eustace buried his fine clothes secretly one night in the school grounds, but Jill smuggled hers home and wore them at a fancy-dress ball next holidays. And from that day forth things changed for the better at Experiment House, and it became quite a good school. And Jill and Eustace were always friends.

But far off in Narnia, King Rilian buried his father, Caspian the Navigator, Tenth of that name, and mourned for him. He himself ruled Narnia well and the land was happy in his days, though Puddleglum (whose foot was as good as new in three weeks) often pointed out that bright mornings brought on wet afternoons, and that you couldn't expect good times to last. The opening into the hillside was left open, and often in hot summer days the Narnians go in there with ships and lanterns and down to the water and sail to and fro, singing, on the cool, dark underground sea, telling each other stories of the cities that lie fathoms deep below. If ever you have the luck to go to Narnia yourself, do not forget to have a look at those caves.

ABOUT THE AUTHOR

CLIVE STAPLES LEWIS was born on 29 November 1898 at Belfast. His father was a solicitor, and his mother (who died when he was a child) was a clergyman's daughter. He had one brother a few years older than himself, and when both were at home they spent much of their time together inventing imaginary lands and writing about them – though not at all in the romantic way we would expect of the future creator of Narnia.

But much of Lewis's time as a boy was spent alone – or in the world of books. 'I am the product of long corridors, empty sunlit rooms, upstair indoor silences, attics explored in solitude, distant noises of gurgling cisterns and pipes, and the noise of wind under the tiles. Also, of endless books,' he wrote. 'There were books in the study, books in the drawing-room, books in the cloakroom, books (two deep) in the great bookcase on the landing, books in a bedroom, books piled as high as my shoulder in the cistern attic, books of all kinds reflecting every transient stage of my parents' interests, books readable and unreadable, books suitable for a child and books most emphatically not. Nothing was forbidden me. In the seemingly endless rainy afternoons I took volume after volume from the shelves. . . .'

At first his favourites were E. Nesbit and *Gulliver's Travels*; but as he grew older the Norse myths and sagas became his dearest literary loves, only to be rivalled later by Homer and the wonderful world of Greek legend and literature as soon as he was able to read it in the original.

Meanwhile, he was not enjoying school, calling the first one to which he went 'Belsen' and disliking Malvern College intensely. However, between Malvern and Oxford he spent three years with a private 'coach' who taught him to love learning and to read Greek for pleasure, with the result that he took a Classical Scholarship to University College, Oxford, in 1917. His education was interrupted by a year of active service in the First World War, in which he was seriously wounded; but on returning he took a Classical 'Double

First' and then a First in English, becoming English Tutor at Magdalen for thirty years and earning great distinction by several works of scholarship, before becoming a Professor at Cambridge for ten years.

The seven Chronicles of Narnia, which were published annually from 1950 to 1956, have already taken their place among the great children's classics. But like the other great books which are enjoyed by all ages, the Narnian stories were really written to please himself. 'I wrote the books I should have liked to read,' Lewis said. 'That's always been my reason for writing. People won't write the books I want, so I have to do it for myself,' and he believed that the proper reason for writing a children's story is 'because a children's story is the best art form for something you have to say'.

Besides his works of literary scholarship, Lewis is best known for various books on Theology, the most famous being *The Screwtape Letters* – from an old devil to a younger one on the best means of tempting mankind, which of course was intended to help his readers to be on their guard against the more cunningly hidden temptations by which we are beset. And also for his two romances of other worlds, *Out of the Silent Planet* and *Perelandra*, perhaps the finest and most poetical stories of visits to Mars and Venus ever written.

C. S. Lewis died in 1963.

GREEK
REVIVAL

GREEK REVIVAL

FIRTH HARING

A Critic's Choice paperback
from Lorevan Publishing, Inc.
New York, New York

To Carl, with love

Reprinted by arrangement with E. P. Dutton

ISBN: 1-55547-137-4

First Critic's Choice edition: 1987

From LOREVAN PUBLISHING, INC.

Critic's Choice Paperbacks
31 E. 28th St.
New York, New York 10016

Manufactured in the United States of America

1

Point of no return now, Jack Troy thought, as he drove onto the bridge and into the lanes of traffic streaming west over the river.

The same thing he'd thought going to his own wedding. But too late for a U-turn now. Or then. Though he'd been good at executing them all his life. He swallowed his stomach back to where it belonged.

It was as bright as day under the bridge lights. He wanted darkness, black, silent night, no illumination at all. He shielded his eyes from the oncoming headlights with his left hand, drove with his right, and once he was off the bridge and traveling north on the wooded parkway, he turned his headlights down to low beam, as if he could slip unseen back into the town where he had spent all the important summers of his life. See it at night, before it saw him, and leave if he didn't like what he saw.

He was returning, for the first time in twenty years, to attend the wedding of a young man he had never met, a cousin of the woman he had been living with for a year. But Beryl was not with him. Gone was Beryl. Gone three weeks ago, on a day's notice, to marry some old flame she'd met on an airplane. A woman of thirty-two could move like greased lightning when she wanted to reproduce. It had struck Beryl one day during the winter that if she never had children she would never have grandchildren.

He already had enough children. Testy, tearful twin boys of nearly twelve. Wanting him. Wanting him back with their mother. Denise plugging for it, too. Please, Jack. Please, Dad. Please, please come home. He sighed a sigh that ended in a groan and lit a cigarette, although he had been trying to quit smoking for a month. Beryl's unexpected and final departure had caused both some short- and some long-term problems for him: having to return to Brewerton alone tonight; having to look for another woman eventually. He would never go back to Denise, no matter what Denise thought he'd do. He dragged a couple of times on the cigarette and threw it out the window.

The digital clock on the dashboard flashed another passing minute. 12:12. It was late. He had put off starting. Almost picked up the phone to call and say he wasn't coming. But call who? The mother of the bride? Tina?

Late for a small-town motel to stay open. If it had closed by the time he got there, then what? Find Tina's house and park in her driveway till morning? Climb up the drainpipe and lie on the roof outside her room, listening to Hugh Gardiner snore?

Right, Jack. He turned up his high beams and looked for a place to make a U-turn. But the road was one way, divided by thick woods. He accelerated. If the motel office was dark, let that settle it. Drive back to the city. Send a telegram. Urgent business.

Beryl had handed him the invitation a month ago. He had glanced at it, then read it again. Brewerton was where he had gone in the summers! Where his grandmother was buried. And then it had dawned on him as he read it a third time that the bride-to-be's mother and father were Connie Sanders and John Breene. But I knew these people, he said. Let's go, then, shall we? Beryl said.

He looked at her stupidly. Roots, she said, as if he were retarded. You know. Your old stomping grounds. We'll take in the locals and reunite you with your storied past. I will get to meet the girls in all the stories, and we'll have a good laugh at how burbed out and boojy they are.

What's burbed out and boojy? he said. Suburban and bourgeois, Beryl said.

But what if she wasn't?

He had seen her twice in the twenty years. Once by chance on Fifth Avenue. Then not by chance, in 1963, for a few weeks, after he was married. Let's? Beryl wheedled.

Brewerton, on a rare day in June. All right, he said. But call first. About me.

So Beryl, cousin of the groom, called Connie, mother of the bride, and asked if she could bring a friend, and told Connie who the friend was, and Connie said, according to Beryl, Jack Troy? Is he still alive? Beryl thought that was hilarious.

He had called Connie, too, the next day, to make sure she

knew he was still alive and to make sure he was welcome, and to find out, which was the reason for calling, of course, if anybody had any idea what had ever happened to Tina Penney. He struck, he thought, just the note of detached interest, that note of friendly curiosity after twenty years. He had practiced it in his head for hours.

Somebody named Hugh Gardiner happened to her, Connie said, in the merry way people took when they were sticking something to you. They live right here on Stephen Street. Stephen Street? he had stammered. In Brewerton? The same Stephen Street? . . .

The very same, Connie said gleefully. Surprised?

I never did much care for weddings, he said. Connie, nice talking to you. Bye now. But you have to come, Connie cried. We'll be crushed if you don't come. Now that we know you're alive and well.

He wouldn't vouch for well. Alive, he said glumly. What made her keep suggesting he might not be alive?

Besides, she said. I'm sure all is forgiven. We all made our little mistakes.

And Jack certainly did remember a few of Connie's.

And then he'd been possessed by a need to rectify a few of his mistakes. Besides, he felt obscurely disputed, and he didn't like the feeling. It reminded him of the time he'd learned that a favorite painting he had once owned was hanging in a certain man's house. He had gone to see it, sure that that particular man could not have hung it as well as he had. And he'd been right, and he had bought it back again from the man and hung it in his own house again.

At the exit, he turned off the parkway onto the wooded

road leading down into Brewerton. The first traffic light on the outskirts of town was green, but the second one by the railroad siding was red. As he waited for it to change, he noticed the rundown old ice and coal company building, now with a faded sign on it he could just read by the streetlight: Kolyrion Bros.

Mickey Kolyrion had trashed him his first day in Brewerton in 1948, for wearing shorts and riding a girl's bike (Tina Penney's), and for introducing himself with his southern military-school manners: Hi, y'all, I'm Jack Troy. I'm visitin' up here for the summer. Whomp! Take that, you little fruit. Whomp! Whomp!

Mickey Kolyrion was supposed to have drowned Clarice Heard in 1956, but he must have gotten away with it. Kolyrion Bros. Business as usual. Around the back of the building, by the light of a naked bulb above the loading platform, two men loaded or unloaded a panel truck. One of his more visceral desires as a youth had been to reduce MK to a bit of pulverized bone. Mickey chanting beneath his window: *Jack Troy | Bastard boy*. And worse. He winced.

The light changed. As he moved on, under maples arching over the broad street, past lawns and houses whose silhouettes he half-remembered, he felt as if he were seeing a movie a second time, having forgotten what it was about in the interim. And then, through the open window, the night, fragrant with wet grass and honeysuckle, brought back to him summer nights twenty years gone. And suddenly he didn't want to stay.

He accelerated; without looking down it, drove past Stephen Street. And yet because he had come, after all, and because there was no one but him to know it, and because he had learned to forgive his own indulgences, he U-turned and drove back to the corner and down the street. He and Tina had been at a party in that house one New Year's Eve, he recalled with a stab of regret.

The first-floor rooms were lighted. Through the sheer curtains in the long front windows, he could see pieces of things, corners of paintings, tops of mantels, long fronds in a tall vase, the pediment of a chest on chest, lampshades, the upper shelves of bookcases, decanters in a glass-fronted highboy, fragments of the orderly arrangements of the things she lived with that made him think of the disorder his own life had fallen into.

The porch Bug-Away light was on and a light on the back porch, and a light on the second floor in the back. The garage was open, no cars in view. They were out. The rehearsal dinner maybe. Did people still have rehearsal dinners? He remembered his own, with a pang of guilt. Made love to one of the bridesmaids the afternoon of.

He turned in the driveway, backed around, a stranger in a strange land, and drove back up the hill to Front Street. Behind him, a dog barked. He turned toward town and up to the top of Main Street, his loneliness upon him like a pall.

But a light was on in the motel office, so he checked in.

2

The river surged its tide northward in the last hour of darkness, dashing loud waves against the shore of the sleeping town. Wind moved in the willows along the riverbanks, and in the oaks lining the still streets. As the hour passed, houses, like photographic images emerging in a black bath, began to appear out of the night under the deep-leafed trees.

He left the motel on Gansevoort Street and walked a mile down Main Street in the early gray dawn. He wanted to see the town again (before it saw him), and remember all that had happened to him, and try to figure out why.

A mile south of Main Street, on Stephen Street, light through dim windows illuminated the attic of the large old-fashioned shingle-style house. Then, descending through lowered shades and drawn curtains, it lighted the second story, where four people slept in three rooms, and three rooms were unslept in. Tina Gardiner slept beside Hugh Gardiner. In their private dream worlds, their bodies curved away from each other's in the bed, like the sides of an ornate letter H, though one lacking a connection, as if they did not share a single destiny. Quickly dropping, light next fell on the first story, through long, unshaded windows onto patterns in old rugs. And finally, in the cellar of the house, a sliver of light pierced even the long-unused coal bin.

In that quarter-minute that it took the morning to travel from attic to cellar of the house on Stephen Street, light touched Tina Gardiner's face, and she dreamed something that distorted her facial muscles and woke her, as a loud report would have. She opened her eyes and listened, to determine if what she had heard had been part of her dream, if what she had dreamed she had called out in her sleep. Her throat ached, as if with the effort of a shout too loud for it, but Hugh slept on. She woke with a throat ache from time to time, when she dreamed of him, this man Jack Troy she was going to see again in the middle of a life of which he no longer knew anything, and in which he had once been everything.

She turned onto her back and lay thinking why this should have been, why in anyone's life anyone else could acquire power of possession, until the sun crowded around the edges of the window shades. Then, because to that question there were too many answers, all of them pretty good, she got out of bed and let her nightgown fall off her body into a blue circle on the carpet and went into the bathroom.

Her nightgown on the floor was the first thing Hugh saw when he opened his eyes a few minutes later. He turned in the bed to look for her. She stood naked with her back to him in front of the mirror, slowly brushing out her long hair, the color of a split-open muskmelon. When she raised her arms, her breasts showed from behind at the sides, round and weighty. A strip of white, untanned skin was drawn like a chalk mark across her back.

Hugh Gardiner had had every advantage in life that America could offer. And in his long, advantaged youth, he had imagined the wife he would bring his advantages to. When he met Tina in 1963, at a cocktail party at the Brewerton Boat Club, he knew she was it, marrying her the logical, fitting, right thing to do. And he persisted until he did it.

He leaned over the side of his bed to see the time. "Where are you going so early?" She turned, brushing her long hair, the dark palm at her thighs waking him for sure, even after thirteen years. He raised his head on his arm to see her better. She smiled at him, went on brushing her hair slowly, rhythmically, stark naked and flagrant—a minister's daughter with a bit of a wenchy streak; he rather loved it.

"For a jog."

"It's 5:30," he said.

"I know."

"Coming back?"

She smiled.

He lay his head down again on the pillow. "Come back," he commanded tenderly.

She put on her underwear, cotton no-nonsense panties and a large sturdy bra that seemed to organize her body, supervise her breasts into orderly, modest areas. She stepped into gym shorts and pulled on a dark cotton T-shirt and sat on the edge of the bed to put her socks on and tie her running shoes, garish turquoise and chartreuse. She pinned her hair up with their daughter's barrettes and stood to look at herself in the mirror, smoothing her shirt over her flat stomach, criticizing her outline as if she were going to submit it to someone. She put a sun visor on her head and stooped over the bed to kiss him swiftly on the mouth. "Hurry back," he called after her, softly.

"Today is Jenny's wedding day," she called back, also softly, so as not to wake Amy and Bo.

"That is a non sequitur," she heard him say, as she went down the hall.

But for her there was a logical connection between Jenny's wedding day and why she might not hurry back to bed with Hugh. Hugh had forgotten that Jack Troy was coming, and she hadn't reminded him.

She walked down to the end of the street and stood on the seawall and stared out at the wide river sparkling in the sun.

They had swum in it too many times to count, Jack Troy and she, a minor seduction every time he persuaded her to; no-swimming-in-the-river had been a Penney household decree as firm as a Mosaic commandment. But he had the force of the river himself, could make her go with any tide he liked. They had swum in it once, late at night, in spite of everything that warned her not to, at high tide in a full moon with an August hurricane on its way up the coast. The cold briny black water was deep right off the rocks, alive and mobile: out it sucked her, under it dashed her. Storm swollen, driven by a chain of low silent barges plying upriver in the night, far out in the channel, over her unremittingly it washed its heavy oily waves. Laughing, Jack swam away from her in the dark; she struggled toward shore, her arms and legs ineffectual as weeds in the swells. A rough wave caught her and cast her within reach of the boulders that littered the riverbank. She crawled out, lay on a slab of rock the size of a bed, panting, grateful to be alive, not even caring that a bruise was already rising on her thigh. You put me in danger, she said, when he climbed up beside her. You're a big girl, he said in the dark, lying down beside her, trying to get her to warm him, kiss him, curl her body around his. You can take care of yourself, can't you? She pushed him away from her, turned her head away. See, he said, how you turn your back on me. And you say you love me. You say the same, she said. And look how you treat me. When are we ever going to be good to each other? he cried.

She stooped and lowered herself from the seawall onto the damp rocks and sand. From Stephen Street she could walk, before the tide covered the beach, to the Breenes' property to see the caterer's striped marquee where she would meet Jack Troy again.

The last time she had seen him in Brewerton was in April of 1956, the day after the night Clarice Heard drowned, though nobody knew that then.

Clarice swimming in April in the quarry. Because a freak heat wave had struck the Northeast. Temperatures in the 90s for a week. And Jack's grandmother dying in her house next door. The nurses on twenty-four-hour duty. Her mother had given her an electric fan to take over to them, sweating in the sickroom. Cora.

Clarice's body wasn't found till later in the week, floating facedown, skull smashed. Dead for days. Died on April 18, she read, in the coroner's faded report over Hugh's shoulder twenty years later. Multiple fractures. And only in her mind would April 18, 1956, have rung a bell after two decades. We saw him, Hugh, she said. He was there the night of April 18, 1956. Who saw who? Hugh said. I saw Mickey Kolyrion, she said. Jack Troy and I saw him at the quarry that night. Where is Jack Troy these days? Hugh said, thinking fast. (He always said the name, whenever he said it, which wasn't very often—she herself hadn't said it aloud in years—with a sneer, as if it were the alias of an infamous bounder.) In Dallas, the last she knew. If I find the diary, Hugh mused, I'll look for him. The diary, you and he as witnesses, Frank Kolyrion's changed testimony, the tire tread, and Mickey Kolyrion goes bye-bye. But I don't want to testify, she said. Hugh laughed. Then I'll subpoena you, my darling. And your old flame, too.

It was a month ago, out of the blue, that he had called, almost as if something had told him to. This is Jack Troy, he said. He might as well have added, I've decided I want to come back into your life now, but he didn't.

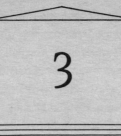

3

He had arrived in her life the first time in 1948, on a rare day in June. That June, when every morning the wisteria on Brewerton's front porches climbed higher up the columns, and blue and purple morning glories on the back porches flew like birds up their green twine, Congress voted to build a monument to Francis Scott Key, Harry Truman spoke to a nearly empty auditorium in Omaha, Nebraska (everyone knew Dewey would win), and a steamer trunk arrived via Railway Express on the front porch of old Mrs. Thile's, who lived behind the parsonage on North Front Street.

On the river, at the foot of Main Street, a half-submerged log pitched toward shore. He stared at it, remembering the Brewerton summers. Three days after his trunk had arrived, he arrived. He had boarded the train the day before in Chattanooga, and he was glad to get off it, even though Colonel Howe, the head of the school he went to, had told him that the train part of the trip would be the easy part. The hard part would be to make his way out of the largest train shed in the entire world, the colonel said, through the enormous edifice that was the New York City station to 42nd Street, and from there by bus, ferry, and another train, to the house of his grandmother, whom he had never met, in Brewerton, New York.

The colonel had made the boy agree not to dally at any stage of his journey, especially in the terminal, but to keep putting one foot in front of the other, until he arrived at his grandmother's house. But the boy had other plans. He only agreed not to dally; he didn't promise not to.

He knew that there were lockers in the terminal where he could deposit his khaki canvas valise and do what it was he wanted to do while he had the chance. He found the lockers just where his friend had told him they would be, and he left his valise in one of them, and joined the thousands of people who surged like the eddying crosscurrents of a turbulent river through the vast terminal to destinations he could not begin to fathom. He knew from his friend that the terminal would be big. But he was not at all prepared for its dimensions, its height and breadth, its scope, its distances, its hurrying throngs, its commerce. There were a hundred shops inside the station; it gave the impression of being a city in itself, inside a city. When he finally got the attention of one of the harried men encircled by a high mahogany counter at which scores of people demanded information, all at the same time, the man pointed wearily in answer to the boy's question, as if he had been asked it too many times to count, to a far-off area under the high ceiling. And there Jack Troy discovered the phone books he had been told would be there for every city in America and most of the counties.

New York City had five books to itself, but none of them had yellow pages. Finally he found a whole book of yellow pages, all for Manhattan, and he looked up what he wanted to know. He had heard that New York City had at least one of everything, and he found that it had one dealer in military miniatures. He wrote down the address of this place, which he planned to visit on another day, on the back of the colonel's directions to Brewerton.

He also looked up his mother's name (Troy, Mona), in the Chattanooga book. It was there, even though she had married and already moved to Panama City. He looked up some of her friends and his friends in Chattanooga, and the father of a boy he knew in Cincinnati, and then he set out to find the restaurant he had heard was somewhere downstairs in the station, where you could get a plate of fresh oysters for sixty-five cents.

The floor of the station, Colonel Howe had told him, was of Tennessee marble, and he admired the pink-veined squares quarried out of the Smoky Mountains as he walked over them. The idea of their being of Tennessee marble even made him feel a little homesick, although he had never really cared for Tennessee, or ever thought of it as his real home. He found the Oyster Bar with its grand tiled ceiling arching over its exotic foyer, and its palm trees and its Oriental rugs, but he was too awed by it to go in. Anyway, he thought, it seemed more like a place where you would find desert food, figs and dates and olives and

[17]

coconut cakes, not oysters. He went upstairs again and had a hot dog and a cup of coffee instead, at a restaurant with no doors and no chairs. A no-account place, he thought to himself. Whoever heard of having to pay to stand up to eat? It would never go over in the South.

When he had seen enough, he got his valise out of the locker and made his way back through the vast terminal to the street, where he waited for the bus with the number on it that Colonel Howe had promised him would appear from the east.

He sat at the front of the bus to watch for the Hudson River to appear on the horizon. And on the ferry, he stood in the stern and, passing west over the roiling river with the sun behind him and the city distancing before him, he had the sense that he was passing in the churnings of the wake from one life into another, and that he was going to meet a destiny that had already been prepared for him. He tried to shake off this feeling. He liked to think that he, and not unmet forces, was in charge of his destiny.

From time to time he drew the slip of paper out of his pocket and read it and read the address he had written on the back of it and returned the slip to his pocket. Colonel Howe, who had never been to New York City, had elicited his instructions from a guidebook and two maps, and they were very fine and precise, as might be expected from a man who taught geography, topography, and cartography as well as military history.

At Weehawken, he poured with a thousand others through another terminal, and the sound of thousands of feet hurrying homeward over wooden platforms and the smells of impatient fired engines and cindery steam made him know he was truly on his way to where he was going. Among the trains that panted to be off, he found the one to Brewerton. The conductor smiled at him as he boarded, and he took a seat by a window on the right side of the corridor. The train was not crowded, but almost every window seat was taken by the time it started, and just as it did start a woman, slim and about the age of his mother and wearing a blue dress patterned in white seagulls, appeared next to his seat and smiled down at him.

Ma'am! he murmured, jumping up. Why, thank you, she said. He remained standing until she had arranged her packages on the rack above and settled herself beside him. She smiled at him. She was pretty and clean, like the nurse in the infirmary at his school, and he learned that she was a nurse, on her day off. On the town, she said happily. All on my own, in the big city. She seemed very pleased with herself. She asked him where he was going. Brewerton is the stop after mine, she said contentedly, when he told her. It's a good place to spend the summer. Nice and shady and right on the river.

He looked out the window at the passing greenery and wondered if his steamer trunk had arrived safely at his grandmother's house. In it was his collection of miniature lead soldiers, given to him on his tenth birthday by Mona, who had been saving them for him from his father. His father, much older than Mona, had died before he was born. It was his intention to have the collection appraised while he was in the North, to see if it was worth what Mona said it was worth.

The train was an ancient one, extremely filthy and hot. There were holes in the roof. When it rains, the woman said confidingly, they have to use umbrellas. He laughed, and she laughed, too, at the picture. I'm glad I don't have to commute, she said. Aren't you? He had never heard the word used before, but he knew what it meant. He laughed again, and he thought that he would like it, that that was what he would do someday, commute to New York City from a large white house on the river in cool, shady Brewerton. He told her that there were trains with holes in their roofs in the South, too, but that he had expected the North to be more advanced. The poor old South, she said. The poor old North.

For twenty cents, they bought ham sandwiches in wax-paper bags from the Dining Service cart and for fifteen cents half-pint bottles of orange juice, which they drank with straws. Her name was Cora, and she was talkative. She was lonely, he surmised. Her husband, she told him, had not come home from France.

He knew what this phrase might mean. Is that to say he was killed in action? he asked.

Yes, she said. In the Ardennes. She looked at him to see if he understood.

Where?

Châlons-sur-Marne.

June of 1944, he said wonderingly.

Yes, she said. Exactly four years ago this week. How did you know?

I studied it, he said. I go to a military school.

Oh, do you? she said.

He was a fine, healthy-looking boy, tall for his age, with dusky skin and dark blue eyes. She studied him. Her nurse's eye judged him to have just passed the edge, to have just gone over the brink between boyhood and adolescence. His upper lip showed a trace of dark at the corners. The man he would be in five or six years was evident already in the structure of his forehead, the cut of his temples and the beginning fullness of his shoulders and chest inside his white, short-sleeved shirt. He had a well-cut mouth and straight white teeth, and his abundant eyelashes protected eyes that she assumed were innocent of expressing anything but curiosity and wonder at the death of a man in a war. But, in fact, the boy felt almost inexpressibly sad at the thought of a young man dying for his country in another country and leaving a young wife all by herself. Did you have children? he asked her. She shook her head. He turned his face away from her to stare out the window. He did not really want to be going to Brewerton-on-Hudson any more than her husband had wanted to go to Châlons-sur-Marne to fight the enemy. But there was no other place for him to go.

Beside him, on the prickly plush seat, without her wanting or expecting it, when he turned his face away from her the roots of Cora's hair grew hot, and her scalp began to exude sweat. Sweat broke out around her waist and on her abdomen and under her arms, and her body, beyond all propriety or any command to desist that she might consider making, stirred unmistakably in the ways that sexual desire makes itself known. She felt faint and wonderfully amorous, and she sighed and lay her head back against the odorous plush of the seat, luxuriating in her unexpected state of eroticism, and imagining for a moment the mouth of this young boy upon her mouth. She smiled gently to herself and closed her eyes and gave herself up to the throes of forbidden pleasures, the kiss leading in her imagination by natural extension to a fully developed act of love, and she gave thanks in a tiny unoccupied corner of her mind that minds could not be read.

Are you warm? he asked.

Her eyes fluttered open. Yes, she murmured.

He rose and opened the window and sat back down beside her. The air rushed in, cooling her. That's better, she said, smiling.

A cinder flew into his eye. He cried out in pain. It was the eye on his far side, next to the window, where she had to lean over him to hold his lids apart with her thumb and middle finger, and with the hemmed edge of a clean handkerchief smelling faintly of lavender attempt to touch the cinder and bring it forth.

Her face was just above his; he could smell her skin and her breath, which smelled like white bread, and see clearly the fine powdered texture of the skin across her nose and cheeks, and her eyes, which were dark and intent. He flinched, and his eye teared. I think we better do this standing up, she said. In the lavatory.

They went into the lavatory. Firmly, she closed the steel door behind them. Stand against the door, she said calmly, to steady yourself. She wet the hanky in the tap water and approached him again in the very close quarters of the lavatory. He kept his arms rigidly at his sides. His face was flushed, and his blue eyes had darkened. She held his head steady with her hand, two fingers of which peeled back the lid of his right eye. With the hanky in her other hand, she approached the cinder very carefully, with a firm and professional nurselike angle to her arm. Be still, she whispered. Don't move. She touched tip of corner of hanky to black smut. There, she said, and showed it to him. He looked at it, the tiny speck on the corner of her white hanky, and he looked at her face, still very close to his face. And at this moment, to his horror, within his clothing, his body, all of its own accord, began to direct itself toward her body.

In his eyes and in his quickened breath and in the guilty flush that deepened on his face, she read this information, and she smiled and looked at his mouth and then into his eyes and then at his mouth again, and she bent toward him and kissed him on the mouth with her eyes open and her lips closed. Then, of their own accord, too, his lips parted, and the tip of her warm tongue strolled against the tip of his. You are going to be simply wonderful some day, she said breathlessly. You have the gift. This is my stop. Goodbye. And she fled.

The log pitched toward him in the oily waves like a drowned man. He turned to go. Down the beach, he saw a woman in jogging shorts walking in the other direction under the shadows of the deep-hanging willow trees. Her legs reminded him of Tina Penney's legs. If it hadn't been for Cora, . . . he thought.

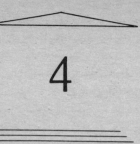

4

The Hudson River was never dull. It had its surprises every day, any day. Anything might bob up on it. Even a body now and then. On a day like this in June, a rare day in June, even sturgeon. Believe it or not, hundreds, even thousands, of sturgeon, some six feet long, had been seen schooling right out there in the Hudson River even as late in the era as 1976.

Still, it had taken her breath away to come upon him at six in the morning, on a rock jetty at the foot of Main Street, not very far ahead of her up the beach, gazing out over the river, smoking. Just there, the way he always arrived in June. *Veni vidi vici.*

There were three central images, three stages it had all always fallen into: Arrival, Connection, Departure. Appearance,

[24]

Presence, Disappearance. Beginning Middle End. Meeting Seduction Betrayal. Innumerable repeated variations, innumerable meetings and new starts, innumerable seductions and betrayals. It was careless of me to have stopped hating him, she thought, staring at the back of him.

She had practiced hating him, until practice made perfect. Had hated at last with a hatred born out of perfect justification. But the hate, one day, had given way to something else, as if it had reached a certain temperature and consumed itself, a fire dying for lack of oxygen. In a kind of spontaneous remission, she had one day been cured of him. The perfection of what she had practiced converged, without her intending it to, or even expecting it to, or imagining it was possible for it to, with its opposite—love being capable of a similar intensity, after all—and produced a certain forgetfulness, benignity, even. So that one day, or one unsuspecting year in the mellowing of middle life, in the calm of a comradely marriage, in the solid American stupefaction of life as wife, mother, daughter, worker, friend, citizen, she realized that she had forgiven him, without even trying. Instead of hate she felt a distant, detached sympathy for his frailty, a sympathy that even resembled her former love for him. How had life treated him after all?

It was still early when she let herself back into the house, not yet seven o'clock. She closed the front door behind her and stood in the hall listening, as if she could hear something not previously audible, sense around her an alteration of an undefinable kind. In her mind's eye, he was caught, hands in his pockets, staring into the river, a certain resignation in his back, an unmistakable ache she unmistakably wanted to hear about in the slope of his shoulders. Forty going on forty-one, and the game plan askew. She shivered, shook the sight of him out of her head, but the impression of a change in something persisted. The house was too quiet, as if it had been abandoned in her short absence, invisible dust cloths draped over the furniture, the past waiting for her in some corner like a mystery to be solved or a puzzle to be assembled.

And she remembered the summer she had found him waiting for her in a corner of her bedroom in the parsonage to tell her what his grandmother had somehow come to the conclusion it was time that he should know: Captain Price, who had married Mona Troy in 1947, was Mona's first husband. No further details were supplied. It was all poor Mrs. Thile could rise to: the one bald fact. It wasn't cruelty on her part to separate her grandson from his illusions of his deceased father the colonel, but rather a well-intentioned attempt to warn him of the terrible consequences of love, which she had begun to notice was warming up his heart for Tina Penney.

She had felt that day, joined with him in his knowledge, as if they were Siamese twins, linked from the womb, each other's from some dim beginning they could not recall, one in adult knowledge till death did them part. And they *were* one in some inscrutable, but unalterable way, from that moment on. She was his, his mirror. They were struck mute by the news; all she could do was look at him and reflect, like his mirror, his own profound sadness, shame, indignation, and at last his defiance and his defense: It didn't matter.

It *doesn't* matter, she had said. Nevertheless, he avoided her for days afterward. Left on his bike alone in the morning, stayed away all day. She half-looked for him on her own bike, in places she wouldn't ordinarily have gone alone. But she never found him. He didn't want her to find him, or to see him. The emotions on her face too closely resembled those on his own. He might have cracked, looking at her. It really doesn't matter, she said, one night in the back garden, where she caught up with him. I know that, he said. Don't talk about it.

She shivered again and went quickly up the stairs, tossing her sun visor on a table on the landing, taking the stairs two at a time, unpinning her hair, stripping off her shirt in the upstairs hall. She stepped out of her shorts beside the bed, untied her shoes and kicked them into the closet, got naked fast, for safety's sake. Got next to Hugh. "Warm me," she whispered, her mouth on his ear. He turned in his second sleep. "Don't ever leave me," she whispered.

"Why would I do a dumb thing like that?" he whispered back, turning to her.

In her house on Second Street, Sybil Dye opened her eyes at seven o'clock, and her waking thought was of the wedding in the afternoon, and of Jack Troy's coming to it, which she had learned only the night before at Erica Bowen's party on Smith's Point in honor of the bride and groom. Even though Tina had known it for a month!

On Mendham Place, Erica Bowen stirred, too, with a hangover that experience told her would be monumental. She groaned, rued ouzo and red wine, cursed her Greek bacchanal to celebrate the bride- and groom-to-be and the signing of the contract to buy the Greek Revival house she no doubt shouldn't be buying, staggered out of bed for aspirin, and staggered back again, swearing never again, never, never.

And on Cliff Avenue, Mickey Kolyrion also woke, after a restless night, to remember with a sickening start the two unrelated problems that had recently emerged to threaten his life, and perhaps even to eliminate it.

Sweating, he threw the covers off, as if he could throw off with them the net he felt subtly settling over him, its strings pulled on one side by Fulgencio, to whom he owed $3.5 million, and on the other side by Hugh Gardiner, running for district attorney next year and needing just the right case to give him just the right publicity. Murderous little hate balls popped in Mickey's head (kill! kill!) as always when he was in danger of being cornered, hate balls exploding in his head like corn in a popper.

He got out of bed, glancing once at Jeanne. Jeanne, who had not spoken to him nicely in some years, except in public, slumbered on; she would not wake until noon, in time to get ready to go to the wedding.

He put on a silk robe and wandered over the thick carpets through his immaculate house, sorting the facts as he had learned them at Erica Bowen's party, and discarding them or storing them for future reference, as they seemed to require. The one most unpleasant new fact was that Jack Troy was alive and well and coming back to Brewerton this very day. But why? After twenty years, why just now? Unless Hugh had already found Clarice's diary and in the diary a motive and with a motive the grounds to call a grand jury together, summon witnesses from far-off places?

He wandered into the kitchen and stood at the window looking out onto the flagstone terrace and the pool beyond and the two new flocks of Brown Jordan furniture Jeanne had just bought. (If Jeanne didn't use her American Express card every day, she felt unpatriotic.)

Witnesses—but all they had witnessed was him leaving in a hurry. Evidence—but only one piece of it, a twenty-year-old tire tread. They didn't find her body for two days, and by then he'd disposed of the clothes in her suitcase and the suitcase as well. (Just drove to Newton early one morning and deposited it on somebody's trash that was set out for the town to pick up. Her family didn't report it missing, or the clothes missing till weeks later.) He was questioned, of course. He was the prime suspect. But there was no weapon, and best of all no motive: The autopsy showed she wasn't pregnant, after all.

Unless the diary supplied an explanation. (Such as: If I tell him, will he? I'll tell him so he will. I told him! He's going to! So happy! So happy!) Rising from the grave twenty years later to nail him. Jesus!

He felt lightheaded and sick. Just when he had made up his mind to get out of the business. He had meant to make a few more runs, pay off his debts, stash the rest, and get out. Three years was pushing your luck.

His stomach churned. He stepped into the marble-walled powder room and vomited.

In the house on Stephen Street, Hugh Gardiner sang in the shower. " 'Lift up your head and shout. It's gonna be a great day.' " He dried himself vigorously. Even if he had remembered about Jack Troy coming to the wedding, he would have sung. He was not one to whom the possibility of a thirty-year romance made any sense.

It already was a great day. He had made love to his wife

first thing in the morning, whomped Bill Tyler 6–4, 6–2, second thing in the morning, and third thing in the morning, he was on his way to make the Saturday rounds of his little empire. First, to drop in on law office in the Mews to make sure painters were painting, then crosstown to condos on Grove financed by a consortium he was part of, then back downtown to marine-supply store he owned a share in on Main Street, then cruise up Main past wife-owned TG Interiors, then check out their jointly owned multifamily house on Oakwood, and finally, take Amy's collie, Fanny, for a romp in a pasture he was thinking of buying on the other side of the quarry.

He liked having his fingers in lots of little local pies. Liked being a big frog in a little puddle. How many times he'd been glad he'd left the big New York law firm to join a small one in Brewerton, he thought, carefully combing his straight dark hair in the bathroom mirror. He liked small-town life with all its dramas and traumas. It made things interesting to pass clients on the street or meet up with them at a party and know what special terror lurked in their hearts, what sordid romance they'd been involved in, what tacky undertaking, what unspeakable family mess. " 'It's gonna be a great day,' " he sang again. And to top it off, a party in the afternoon.

The Breenes could be counted on to give the kind of wedding party he liked the best: outdoors on a rare day in June under a gay-striped tent, with a lively band playing tunes you could dance to, lots of bonny bridesmaids and friends of the bride to ogle, good old boys to gab with, waitresses passing lots of damn-the-expense hors d'oeuvres and champagne. Dom Perignon 1973 had been ordered. Cases and cases of it. Weddings! Lovely!

He looked out of the bedroom window. Tina sat on the deck below, enjoying the morning, too, he thought. " 'What is so rare as a day in June?' " he called down.

She looked up and smiled.

"I'm going to read it," he said.

"It sounds like a threat," she said.

He laughed. He found the anthology the poem was in and took it down to read to her. His grandfather had known the whole long thing by heart and recited it every year on the first best day of June.

" 'Then, if ever, come perfect days,' " he read. " 'Then Heaven tries the earth if it be in tune. And over it softly her warm ear lays.' "

He read on and on, lulling her with the singsong verses. She liked, she said, when he was finished, heaven being a her and having a warm ear.

"Why not heaven she is a woman? A woman she is heaven."

"What woman is heaven?"

"Some women." He reached for her bare foot.

She extended it to him. He lifted it to his mouth. "Tasty. Wish I could stay for more, love."

" 'More happy love?' " she said, quoting the poem that had echoed through her head all morning.

" 'More happy, happy love,' " he said, remembering the same one.

"Stay, while I read it," she said, leafing through his anthology for it.

Last night, Erica had hired three brothers away from a souvlaka and falafel stand on 33rd Street to tend a side of beef

[31]

over an open wood fire. A case of ouzo had been consumed, and a cask of red wine. Two antique wooden washtubs of salad studded with feta and black olives were emptied. And a heifer (rented from a farm out in the country and decorated by Erica's daughters with garlands of beach roses) wandered about in the woods of Smith's Point among the bemused guests, most of whom had never seen a lowering heifer up close, garlanded or otherwise, or heard of Grecian urns or odes thereon.

Hugh looked at his watch. He did have to go.

" 'Thou still unravish'd bride of quietness, . . .' " Tina read, despite him.

Greek music had blared from loudspeakers in the trees, and the guests, all more or less drunk, all more or less in togas and tinsel wreaths, considered the three lithesome daughters of Erica, togaed and bewreathed between the crumbling Ionic pillars of the porch of the Greek Revival house, acting out the Ode while Erica read:

> *Heard melodies are sweet, but those unheard*
> *Are sweeter; . . .*
> *Fair youth, beneath the trees, thou canst not leave*
> *Thy song, nor ever can those trees be bare;*
> *Bold Lover, never, never canst thou kiss,*
> *Though winning near the goal—yet, do not grieve;*
> *She cannot fade, though thou has not thy bliss,*
> *For ever wilt thou love, and she be fair!*

"What's it all about anyway?" he said.

"The grass is greener?"

"The love you imagine is better than the love you experience?"

"Yes."

"It's not," he said.

She laughed, but she shivered, too, and closed her eyes against the beauty of the day, or against his innocence. Lost! she thought. Gone. Lost, the one moment of contentment in the day's beauty she had felt earlier, the fleeting perception she had caught almost even of beauty's source.

She shivered again. The morning had altered in some obscure way, its perfection just off, as if the earth had moved six sidereal feet from June toward December.

He looked at his watch again. He had to leave. He crunched down the driveway in his station wagon, honked, flashed a thumb at her out of the sunroof. "I'll be back," he called. "For more happy, happy love!" And he was gone.

And though phrases from other poems rose in her mind to describe the lost perfection of the day, all she could capture was a line from something she couldn't place: "In a day/ Blossom and June and rapture pass away."

Remember that, she thought. Remember it all day.

5

He wandered, in the morning air, up Main Street, where America since 1956 presented itself like an historic document all around him. Changed. Altered. Brewerton had transformed itself, while he, it seemed to him, had merely turned his back on it for a minute. Whole blocks had disappeared, replaced with stark, sharp-cornered bright red brick buildings not even common ivy associated with.

He remembered the old blocks, familiar as the ones he had roamed in with the maid's son Willie in Chattanooga. Remembered the greasy, smoky smells, urine, sweat, ham-bone cooking, greens boiling, dogs. He had felt at home in Brewerton in 1948 because of the colored section. He had been sent to military school in the seventh grade, but before that he had been free to play innumerable complicated day-long, week-long, spring-, summer-, and fall-long games with Willie in the dirt streets and dirt yards of Willie's neighborhood, while his mother bathed or napped or took a bus to have her hair done, or played cards, or shopped or languidly gave herself manicures in the breeze on the upstairs porches of the various houses where they lived. Here, like there, the doors to the dark, greasy, smoky, weathered shacks were never closed in the summer, even at night. Now to find them gone, those pungent streets where he had found another friend, Roy-boy, and shot aggies in his dirt yard, smoked cigarettes, and known that behind the blanket hung across the dark back of Roy-boy's house like a theater curtain a man and woman sometimes tusseled quietly on a low bed: to find them gone dislocated him.

On the side street where Mickey Kolyrion had lived, the houses seemed to have moved closer together, as if to huddle for protection from the now full-grown trees that dwarfed them. He had never been inside the house of the Kolyrions. Mickey Kolyrion's father had once come out on the porch in his undershirt, and taken a long look at him as he waited on his bike for Mickey to come out and go to the park to fight. He had had the same turkey-breasted shape as Mickey.

They had a ritual fight every summer. He lost the first few. June meant blood and mud in his mouth. Then Colonel Howe gave him a few boxing lessons. He got in one smart punch, and Mickey lost interest in physical contact and took up poetry. *Mama didn't bother / To marry your father.* Under his window late one night, two or three of them, chanting.

The movie house was gone, the ice-cream parlor, the landmarks of his boyhood summers removed. He stood across the street from the church where he was supposed to have gotten married. But for Cora, he thought. Cora, one chance moment on a train and the course of his life was altered forever. Is that what you think? Tina had said. You think it was *Cora?*

To find out that she still lived in Brewerton, married to a man he had never met, and living in a house where he and Tina had once almost made love on the third floor, still knocked him out. What did you imagine, Beryl said. That she was pining for you all these years? Not exactly; but he hadn't imagined that one past for her would be as usable as another, that she could coolly substitute somebody else for him and go on living in the town that had been their town. Check out, he thought in despair. Send a telegram. Or not even that. Just disappear for another couple of decades. He threw his cigarette into the gutter. He smoked too much. Start over, he decided. Quit now. Don't call her. Do call her. See her, damn it. Don't see her.

He kept remembering the two times he had seen her in those twenty years. In 1959 on the street in New York. And then for a few weeks in 1963. At the end of which, the last time they had spoken until a month ago, she had been so very cold on the phone he couldn't imagine her ever melting for anyone.

He was with Denise, in front of Cartier's in 1959, and he had seen Tina walking toward him from half a block away, heading straight toward him without even recognizing him. He had had to reach out and touch her arm as she passed him, say her name, and from the look that came over her face when she saw him, he had known she would have gone with him that day if he had wanted her to. If he had blurted out to her that he did want her to. This is Denise, he had said instead, still holding onto her arm, while Denise had hold of his other arm. She glanced carelessly at Denise, as if Denise were an inconsequential stranger he had just met himself. How are you? she had asked, meaning it. They stood gazing into each other's familiar faces. Fine, he'd said wonderingly. How are you? She nodded, dumb. He was getting married in a month, he said. Married? she said, as if it were a new word in her vocabulary.

And you? She was just finishing design school, she told him, bleakly, searching his face. Denise turned her back on them, watched their reflections in Cartier's window. Are you married? Of course not, she said.

Tina!

Too late now, she said. I wish you luck.

I don't even want to, he said.

Then why do it? her voice low and fierce.

I don't know.

You never know what's good for you, she said.

All because of Cora? he said.

Don't be so dense, she said. Good-bye.

My God! Denise said. What is this? She still loves you?

Of course not, he said, staring after her disappearing up Fifth Avenue in the jostling noontime crowds.

Do you, Denise demanded, love her?

Of course not, he said. But watching her go was like watching his chances, his hope for himself ebb away from him. He started walking.

This way, Denise said, putting her hand on his arm again. We were going downtown.

He had turned and walked with Denise in the other direction, down Fifth Avenue, stiffly, as if someone had drawn a straitjacket down over his breast.

He found her name in the phone book that night and called and called her for days and nights. But no one answered the phone, and so he married Denise, as planned. The invitations had already been engraved. The presents were rolling in. The parties had begun. The last fittings of the dresses had been arranged. The plane tickets to Bermuda had arrived from the travel agent. At the end, he made drunken love to a bridesmaid in a room at the Biltmore and married Denise the next day.

He crossed the street and walked around the back of the church to see his grandmother's house. It was a little white clapboard house with gingerbread trim and a steep roof and a wisteria vine smothering the front porch, the house where his Granny had tried to educate him, but where he instead educated her and wore her out in the process. She died a few months after he got engaged to Tina, as if glad at last to relinquish to someone else her responsibilities for him. But not before he had educated Tina in it, too, that innocent little white house.

Forgiveness was supposed to be second nature for ministers, but the Reverend Mr. Penney hadn't been notably charitable to him in the end. And he hadn't been generous to Mr. Penney either. Especially not with explanations. How do you explain unlove to your fiancée's father? You had to explain it to yourself first. And was it really unlove, or was it something else, a resistance to love, an acquired immunity to it, as to a disease that could be fatal?

It was for him the archetypal house that, when he dreamed at night of houses, he wandered in, looking for something he couldn't find, something he had misplaced, though he knew it was right in front of him all the time. The floor plan was so clear in his mind, the doors opened into rooms so familiar! But the thing, whatever it was, was never there, never anywhere. He had sold the house, not long after he inherited it, and used the money to start his own brokerage firm.

Some things never changed. Behind the picket fence, his grandmother's perennial garden was still going strong. He no longer knew a hollyhock from a delphinium, but floral names flooded through his mind now—lilac, mock orange, phlox, strawberry bush, lupines. She had tried every summer to make him learn which one was which, the way she had tried to make him learn all the other correct connections he had assured her there was plenty of time to learn later on in life. Heliotrope and hyacinths and gardenias. But, no, gardenias were from florists, for dances. And hyacinths bloomed out of clay pots, in April, as he remembered only too well. Tina forced a huge clay pot of them the winter they were engaged, to bloom in April. And smashed the pot against the kitchen wall on her way out the last day. And who was that Cora anyway? He had seen her only twice. Yet he regarded her, when he tried to understand his life, as the element of random chance in it, the unsought, unwanted goddess in the machine who had somehow intervened in his affairs and separated him from what he had wanted his life to have in it. All wrong, Tina shouted at him. You've got it all wrong! *You* have, he shouted back. What do you know about it?

He walked around the corner to see the back of the house, his old room. He remembered the back stairs from the kitchen to the hall outside his bedroom, and the girls he had smuggled in from the time he was sixteen. And the two married women. Those two had teased him they would come one night, and one dark night they did, appearing under his window and then at the door to his room like two bad pale angels only a few years older than he was, but teaching him things at eighteen he hadn't yet discovered for himself. Collector, she had said bitterly, that time or some other. You collect women. That's your calling in life.

He walked back down Front Street to Main Street. Herd's Dry Goods was still on the corner next to what he had once been inspired to call Burd's Wet Goods. The liquor store was never after called anything else. A dusty little jewelry store that had always been there was still there, and a men's clothing store still calling itself Brewerton Haberdashery, and the drugstore where she had worked in the summer, though now with a slick, streamlined new look to its windows and aisles. A grocery store and a five-and-ten were familiar; a kitchen boutique and a health-food store were not. The hardware store was unaccountably missing. Miss Helene, the milliner, was not unaccountably missing. It was his grandmother's patronage that had undoubtedly kept Miss Helene in business. His grandmother's hats: dozens of hats, in the attic, in their lavender Miss Helene boxes. He had thrown them all out after she died and sold the house to a young couple who didn't even comment on how eerily hatless the attic was.

The stationery store was still in place. And the tobacconist's where he used to buy his Pall Malls, no questions asked. But the storefront rented by SANE was new, and the audio shop and the adult bookstore, and a blue aluminum-sided bank advertising a full four percent on deposits.

He caught a glimpse of himself in the bank window. Twenty pounds in twenty years. At that rate. . . . He dropped his half-full pack of Pall Malls into a wooden trash receptacle and sucked in his stomach.

He shouldn't have come. Especially alone. He should have abandoned the whole idea when Beryl split. He stopped in front of a red, white, and blue Bicentennial storefront to look at a group of mannequins wigged and dressed as signers of the Constitution. Why had he? To find life, liberty, and happiness? He was going! Send a cable. What was there to say to her when they did meet? I made a mess of things. How about you?

So: execute the famous Troy turn while you still can. The idea that he could go, send a telegram, let the past lie, lightened him. He would make a quick visit to the cemetery, and then, the Jack Troy Vanishing Act.

And then, across the street, at the top of the block, he saw it, just below where he would turn the corner to the motel and make his getaway, under a blue awning in the front window of a little frame house: a shingle, blowing in the wind: Tina Gardiner Interiors. He stood staring at it, at the name he had heard only a month ago, only just begun to believe. Tina *Gardiner?*

He crossed the street and stepped onto the porch of the little house to look in the windows of the showroom. The mix of styles bewildered him at first. A Recamier couch covered in raspberry silk, a mahogany Empire table, a Queen Anne wing chair, a Pennsylvania Dutch dower chest. But she was her own bewildering mix of styles, too, as he remembered all too well. Private, but she had made him make love to her one winter's night in the park under a full moon. Now, she said fiercely. Right here. In a park that anyone might have crossed to get from one side of Brewerton to the other at ten o'clock at night.

A hand-lettered sign on the door (her hand) read, "Closed Saturdays June July and August"—with no commas, as if she had been in a hurry to close on Saturdays. He broke a leaf off a geranium plant by the door and smelled it, its pungence bringing back to him his grandmother's garden again, and he looked up at the morning sky, as clean as a slate that wanted to be written on.

6

In the end, he was late for the wedding, because he drove around too long looking for houses he remembered and coming upon some he didn't. He stopped in front of the twin mansions of Mickey and Frank Kolyrion, side by side on Cliff Avenue, identified by small, discreet nameplates at the end of the driveways. Tudor palaces immodestly on the order of Hampton Court, they were set in green lawns behind bloom-studded terraces and shaded by well-maintained trees. He wondered what it could be they loaded and unloaded at the former ice and coal company building to be able to afford such a show.

He had run down the stairs and out onto the front porch that night, where they threw the rhyme wrapped around a rock at his feet and ran. *Jack Troy so fine so swell/ Hear the tales he's got to tell./ A pack of lies by a nigger maid/ While Mama went out to carry on her trade.* He went back up to his room and lay on his bed till morning, stunned into a state of apathy. The day after, apathy seemed fitting, and so he acted as if nothing had happened, as if he didn't care one way or the other what anyone said about his mother. But it altered him. He was different after that, and for years he hated Mickey Kolyrion so much it almost made him retch.

On a second-floor balcony of Mickey's house, in striped robe, a man appeared, raised a pair of binoculars, and scanned the river slowly. Drugs, Jack decided, driving on, remembering when they had all been not-so-simple children together.

An usher conducted him around the back of the groom's side and way down in front, next to an enormous rhododendron bush in full bloom and alive with bees, and probably right in the midst of Beryl's numerous aunts and cousins. But her mother was in Europe, and the aunts didn't know him.

A slender usher walked an enormous Connie Breene in a green tent dress down the aisle. She was at least three times the size of the skinny girl he had at least three times deftly relieved of her clothes in the back of her father's car. Suppose Tina, he thought. . . . In her sleeveless tent with the coy chiffon capelet veiling her upper arms, Connie slipped into her seat in the front row, and the guitarist segued incompetently from "And I Loved Her" to the wedding march from *Lohengrin*.

He turned to look for the bride, and behind him and across the aisle he saw Erica, caught her eye. She stared at him as if she were seeing a ghost. Didn't she *know* he was coming—wasn't it big news? Behind Erica sat Sybil, looking exactly as she had always looked: irked, as if people weren't doing what she wanted them to be doing. And behind Sybil sat what was probably Hugh Gardiner on the aisle next to what was undoubtedly Amy, who was next to what had to be Bo, for there was assuredly Tina (not burbed out and boojy at all, Beryl), but urbanely concentrating on a place high in the air where the stained-glass window would have been if they had been in a church instead of a tent. What did she see up there? he wondered. God? Was she soliciting God's help in not looking around for Jack Troy?

Hugh wasn't looking around for him either. In fact, Jack decided, Hugh Gardiner hadn't a clue in the world he was there. Maybe Hugh hadn't a clue in the world he had ever existed. Why had he come! It was going to be a disaster.

Hugh turned around, too, to look at the procession coming down the aisle. He had never seen such a sight in his life. He gaped. The girls were barefoot. Connie, of course, had been shod, and John Breene, too. But the bridesmaids and the bride and the groom were all barefoot! Hugh marveled. He had not only never seen such a thing before, he had never seen a female clergyperson before (barefoot or not, and she was), much less realized you could actually be married by one! He had never seen the father of a bride wear a white Nehru suit, or imagined that a bridegroom would turn up at his wedding in a white dress embroidered with white vines and flowers.

He had never heard homemade vows recited, never seen a barefoot bride with real daisies woven in her hair dance gravely at her vows with her barefoot groom, not realized the world had changed so much, this much, where weddings were concerned. He was way out of date!

He looked down at Amy, agog beside him, her lips parted,

her chest banging visibly under her thin pink dress, beneath the budding breasts she had thought at first were muscles from rowing on the river. Two months from being twelve. In seven years, he thought in despair, feeling for her hand beside him and squeezing it, in seven mere years she could be walking barefoot down some damned aisle. Did he have even seven years left of her? She squeezed his hand back, without taking her eyes off the proceedings, veritably enchanted by it all. He put his arm around her, his heart plunging at the thought of how much was going to happen to her in the next seven years, happen to him, for God's sake. He didn't want anything to happen. He wanted everything to stay just as it was.

He tried to concentrate on the wedding vows, but David for all he knew was promising to bake only whole-grained breads and Jenny was promising to keep her socket wrenches in order until death did them part. For all he knew. And then it was over, and all in white, all married, Jenny and David were romping up the white runner over the grass to the receiving line outside the tent. "It's all over, Amy," he said.

"Why is Mom crying?" Amy whispered.

"Everyone cries at weddings," Hugh said. "Come on."

He left by way of the rhododendron, and Tina remembered other deft exits he had made. His grandmother's backyard shared a picket fence with the parsonage on the corner of North Front Street and Church Street. After having lived in the rectory for nearly twelve years without anyone remotely interesting living next door in any direction, she had felt, when she discovered him on the other side of the fence one June morning, that she deserved exactly such a stroke of luck. She had been a good neighbor to Mrs. Thile for years, and now she was being re-warded with Mrs. Thile's grandson.

Mrs. Thile had been known to have a daughter and a grandson somewhere in the South, but they had never been known to visit her. The daughter, a Mona Troy, married a Captain Price in 1947 and went to live in an Army compound in Panama. She enrolled her son, who hated both the heat of Panama and Captain Price, in a military academy in Chattanooga. It was the son's idea to spend his first summer away from school with his mother's mother, whom he had never met. The Penneys, of course, had been apprised that he was coming. But still this had not prepared Tina Penney for actually seeing him, that first day.

It is axiomatic that almost any girl of eleven or twelve anywhere in America regards almost any boy anywhere near her age, particularly one new in town, as an opportunity for ro-mance. And for tall girls, the taller the boy, the more urgent that the opportunity be acted upon. For four years, since the third grade, as the increasingly tallest girl in the class, love and marriage had been seriously receding by inches before Tina Penney's eyes. The boys got shorter every year. Short boys were harder to take than short rations. Sybil Dye, who was also tall, entertained romantic plans for the future with a short, chubby boy named Beverley. It was Sybil's position that no matter how short he was he was acceptable. They grow, Sybil said. And then if you've laid the groundwork, they're all yours.

The morning after Jack Troy arrived, he walked out the back door of his grandmother's house and looked directly at the back door of Tina Penney's house, where she had just happened to come out on the stoop to fill the dog's dish. Hello, he said, from across the two backyards. That one is mine, all mine, she thought.

Love came upon her like a chemical change. She smiled, went in the house and braided her hair, and went to pay a call on Mrs. Thile and her grandson. Mrs. Penney, with the reflexive courtesy of a minister's wife, produced a Velveeta cheese box packed with homemade chocolate-chip cookies. Now, make sure you invite him to Sunday School tomorrow, she said.

Tina looked at Mrs. Penney as if she must take her for some kind of fool. She had already mapped out every Sunday morning for the whole summer, for the rest of his life, forever! —not to mention Bible School in July for two weeks.

He hated all Sunday Schools everywhere, and all teachers. They didn't teach you any of the things you needed to know.

It occurred to her to stop right there and ask him what exactly those things were he needed to know. But she had to argue the other point first. She wasn't a minister's daughter for nothing. Why don't you try thinking for yourself some time? he said, very old and bored. If God doesn't exist, who made us? He laughed. Maybe I'll tell you some time, he said.

She was very naive for her age, he said. Where he came from, girls of thirteen got married. And they had babies. That may be a southern custom, she said. It was certainly not one a northern girl would have in mind for herself. She asked him how old he was. I am going on thirteen, he said, in a lordly manner. *I* sounded like *Ah*. Do you think one paltry year makes such a difference? she said. One paltry year makes a big difference, he said. (He was thinking of Cora. He had dreamed of her on waking his first morning in Brewerton. He wanted a bicycle, so he could go and find her again in the town before Brewerton.) Especially when you've been more or less on your own for a long, long tahm, he said.

Tahm, she said to herself. A long, long *tahm.* She loved him. She had loved him, it seemed to her, for a long, long time already.

He finished the last cookie and wanted to move on. To meet the townsfolk.

The future was upon her! The townsfolk, she told him, would all be in church the next day. He would have plenty of time to meet them. Did his granny go? he wanted to know. He frowned when she told him that everybody went. I can see I'm going to have to get to know her a lot better, he said. And she could see that this was a habit of his, thinking out loud, giving all his strategies away in advance to anyone who bothered to listen to him.

But she had her own strategies. Boys his age had a way of banding together and ignoring girls her age. Besides, there were some boys he should avoid altogether. She told him about them. They hung out at the bowling alley and swam in the river at night and dropped rocks on trains from the trestle and sneaked up the back stairs of the movie theater into the loge and smoked and set people's dinghies and rowboats adrift on the river. He laughed. Those were the very ones he wanted to meet. He badgered her until she told him where to find them, in the park.

He borrowed her bike and tore down Front Street. They don't wear shorts, she thought sadly, watching him disappear from view under the arching oaks and maples. They won't go for his shorts. And she began to pace around the block in the broiling June sun, passing his house about once every quarter of an hour, knowing that somewhere, not very far away, he was in trouble.

An hour later, he returned, on foot, walking her bike with its fenders all dented. Drying mud stained his left sleeve and his khaki shorts and his bare legs. His cheek was bruised and muddy, and one of his laughing blue eyes was swollen shut. He had had a fight, but he didn't know who with and wouldn't say what it was about, except that it was partly about her dumb girl's bah-cycle. Is there a bah-cycle store in this little bitty town?

Did he have a fat chest and skinny legs that made him look like a pigeon? He didn't notice his legs, he said. That's because he was wearing long pants, she said. Boys your age don't wear shorts up here. It was Mickey Kolyrion, she said. He fights everybody. A fight was nothing, he said. Didn't she think he'd had fights before? It's something if you lose it, she said. I didn't lose a fight, he said. I lost a round.

"But why does everyone cry at weddings?" Amy said.

"They remember how nice their own was," she said, blowing her nose.

"Is he here?" Connie whispered, in the receiving line.

"It won't ruin my day if he is," Tina said.

"But will it ruin it if he isn't?"

"He's here, Connie," she said. "He was behind the big purple rhodo on the groom's side. Lovely wedding."

"Oh, loverly," Connie burbled. "Tell him to come and see me. I want to give him a big fat kiss."

"Good luck," Tina murmured to Jenny and David.

"Thank you Tina we love you" they said in one squeaky voice, without punctuation.

She laughed and moved down the line past the bridesmaids and ushers, all looking perfectly collegiately fresh, and somehow bored and decadent at the same time, as if they had all already gone to too many weddings, and this one was just a prelude to another nasty hangover. "Love your dresses," she murmured. "Love your hair."

"Love your little bare piggies," Hugh boomed ahead of her. "Never saw anything like it in my life."

"You've been acting like a foot fetishist all day," she said, out on the lawn. He plucked two glasses of champagne from the tray of a passing waitress. He handed her one. Beyond him, farther down on the lawn, Jack Troy emerged from behind another rhododendron bush, this one lavender. A shudder jolted her frame. "What's the matter?" Hugh said. "Nothing," she said. The champagne sloshed in her glass onto her hand. He kissed her. "Here's to sensuous feet and wedding days," he said. "Don't you love 'em?"

She turned her back to the lavender rhododendron. "Some of them," she said.

"I'm heading for the terrace," Hugh said. "For a little politicking and a bird's-eye view of the whole scene. Coming?"

She stared at him blankly. "No," she said. "Or should I?"

"Do both," he said. "Visit around now. Drop up later."

"Yes," she said. (Don't go! Don't leave me here! she almost called out after him, panicked suddenly. I'll go with you. You stay with me.) She took a half-step after him and then stopped, almost mid-step.

He didn't see her again to speak to until it was time to go home. But from the terrace at the back of the house, where he held forth all afternoon on topics he loved with people he loved, he caught a glimpse now and then of her melon-colored hair and her blue sundress over the heads of the milling guests on the lawn. He even saw her talking to a man he didn't recognize. He didn't see first Erica, then Sybil, dash up to her and the man, or see them all float off together toward one of the green-and-white striped tables set up under the trees. But he did catch a glimpse once of the two of them, the man and Tina, Tina barefoot, holding her shoes in one hand and a champagne glass in the other, wander away together from the tables toward the river.

And now and then he saw Amy's collie chase an Irish setter over the lawn and Amy race after them in her pale pink party dress, her feet bare now, too, and he drank another glass of the best and the coldest champagne, and he was very happy. When he was asked where Tina was, which he frequently was, he said vaguely, "She's visiting down on the lawn. She'll be along any minute." He felt like taking off his shoes, too, like a bridegroom, and walking on the grass, but he didn't.

7

He braved the bees in the rhododendrons to avoid the receiving line. And pressing any of Connie's excess flesh. Besides, he wanted to be outside when they emerged from the tent. Wanted to see her first, see them together, without their seeing him see them.

He saw them: laugh, share a joke, clink their glasses, kiss on the lips. So, they were in that archaic mode of the happily married. Believed in the possibility of happy marriages. Probably didn't even know or want to know people with the other kind. Maybe didn't know there were other kinds, other modes for marriages, a lot more modern ones. They were satisfied with one another. Liked each other, it appeared, though they'd been married long enough to have had plenty of time not to, plenty of chances, plenty of precedents all around them. He shouldn't have come.

They separated. Hugh headed for the terrace. She hesitated a second, almost followed him. And didn't.

And that was how he knew the armor wasn't chinkless. She knew he was there, and wanted him to be, waiting for her somewhere on the lawn. Some tall self-consciousness in her bearing, her indecisive movement toward Hugh, then not toward Hugh, some message he was sure she knew she was sending and knew that he, somewhere on the lawn, was receiving, told him what she wanted him to do.

Given the reverse set of circumstances, Hugh looked like the kind of man who would have followed his wife away from trouble. But then, Tina, Jack Troy thought, Hugh is not us. We are we, with a long common history, which has not yet ended. And he set out toward her, across the lawn.

Sybil, standing at the top of the sloping lawn, saw from a different angle the same scene Hugh could have seen, if he had been looking, acted out down on the same long green lawn. She saw a man emerge from the rhododendrons, and recognized that he was Jack Troy. She had heard only last night he was coming, though the person who told her had whispered that Tina had known for a month.

She watched him head like a pointer across the lawn toward Tina. Look at him, she said to herself. Why is he here? What does he want? More happy happy love? And why does he want it? And what makes him think she will? And doesn't he know how much trouble it will be to make her want it? She is well defended, Jack Troy. She is girded with bad memories!

But there he went, in a beeline straight for her anyway. Very goal-oriented man, Jack Troy. If you want something, consider it yours. You want it? You got it.

But what is it he thinks Tina Penney can do for him now: clear the cloudy vistas of his middle age? And how did they cloud up, anyway, if he's so terrific at getting everything he wants? Ask him that, Tina.

Hugh is plucking two glasses of champagne from a passing tray, handing one to her, clinking glasses with her, kissing her. They were a happy couple. *Are* a happy couple. They've thought so, so has everyone else. But what will happen now, Hugh and Tina? What will Tina want now? Hugh still? She thinks so now. Look, she wants to follow him. Look at her start after him. But Jack Troy's too fast for her. There he goes. In for the kill. Don't give her a chance to think it over.

Hugh wants Tina. Sybil wants (would like to have— would take anytime he crooked his little finger at her) Hugh, if Hugh should perhaps ever become available and it should perhaps ever enter his mind to crook his little finger at her. But if Jack decides he does want Tina, and goes after her in his old inimitable, irresistible, powerhouse way, what then will Tina want? If Tina keeps on wanting Hugh, everything will stay as it is. But if Tina is not steadfast, if Tina wants Jack again, everything will shift. A little divorce here, Tina and Hugh. A little divorce there, Jack and Denise. And maybe even a little late-blooming, postmarital, possibly premarital, romance here: Hugh and Sybil. A slight dislocation everywhere. The earth under us will move to the left or the right a few feet, and we will all perhaps be standing in slightly different places with different people.

And there they are already, staring at each other like starved ones at a banquet. The moment they have imagined is being lived. The space between them they already have imagined closed is closing. She does not hate him after all. It is something else she is thinking of. Her bad memories are not sufficient. There is another set of memories demanding its day. Oh, no! The hell with this, Cold Pastoral. The hell with unheard melodies and more happy happy love, too. I'm going, Sybil decided, and she set out down the lawn toward them, also like a pointer toward its quarry. Going to get her, point her back to Hugh. For, to be realistic, Sybil, saving lives is what you were trained in and for, and the only thing you are or will be any good at at all. And Hugh, to be further realistic, wants and will ever want only her, not anyone else but. Not you, ever. And Sybil didn't think she could stand the look on that man's face if Tina took off with Jack Troy: couldn't stand the grief to Hugh-she-hankered-for.

8

"It is you, isn't it?" he said.

"Is it you?" she said, turning. She shielded her eyes from the sun. It didn't look like him, close up.

But she looked exactly the way he had thought she would: her flesh had made peace with her bones. In some indefinable accommodation among hair, skin, muscle, skeleton, she had settled into exactly the satisfying production a woman could be at thirty-nine.

From a distance, she had recognized him at the river's edge in the morning sun. But face to face in the afternoon glare she didn't. He looked . . . Mephistophelian, she thought. Something in his eyes she should be wary of.

She was almost at eye level with him. "Are you taller?" He looked down at her feet. High-heeled sandals.

She shook her head.

He had forgotten how black her lashes were. They lay against her pale skin like the kind in the see-through boxes on Beryl's dressing table.

His eyes were faded. Stressed, she thought, in surprise. Life had not been a bowl of cherries, after all. "I never thought I'd see you again," she said.

"I'm here," he said. And he was out of breath suddenly, as if he had run a long way to get there. "I came up last night."

"Oh?"

"I wanted to get my bearings. Visit the cemetery."

(Where was the woman he was supposed to be coming with?)

"It's changed," he said.

"What has?"

"The town."

"Urban renewal," she said. Her voice sounded thick.

"I came alone," he said.

"Oh."

"You always did ask a lot of questions," he said.

"I didn't ask it out loud."

"She got married."

"Oh!" she said. Behind him, she saw Sybil, heading toward them down the long lawn. And Erica, dressed in white, like one of the bridal party, heading toward them from another part of the lawn. "Married?" she said, confused.

He was staring at her. "A whirlwind courtship," he said. "Some old flame turned up."

She was what he thought he needed to make his life good again, she thought, without any surprise at all. Some old flame of his turning up just when he could use her.

He loosened his collar. His throat was constricted, his pulse racing, his breathing probably audible. It had happened the time he talked to her on the phone, too, as if a rare pulmonary disease afflicted him when he came into voice contact with her. "I saw your shop," he said. It sounded to him like an ineffectual gasp from some other larynx, not his own. He tried to control his breathing. "You've gone public. Your name practically in lights, right on Main Street."

"You didn't know I had an entrepreneurial soul."

"It's good to hear you laugh," he said. "And I don't for a minute believe your soul is entrepreneurial."

"I laugh a lot. And it is," she said.

"I think I'll go now," he said. "I don't really much like weddings."

"Go?" Her voice echoed in her ears.

"I just wanted to see how you looked," he said. "That's why I came. You look great."

"Erica's coming," she said. "Sybil, too." (That's why you came?)

"Should I stay, then?" he said, not taking his eyes off her.

"Of course," she said. But she shrugged, as if to say it didn't matter to her what he did.

He sighed. It mattered to her what he did.

Erica bore down on them over the lawn, way ahead of Sybil. "It is!" she cried. "I don't believe this. It is Jack Troy in the flesh. What are you doing in Brewerton? Why didn't anybody tell me you were coming?"

"Friend, once-removed, of the groom," he said. "I guess it wasn't big news. Hello, Erica."

"Is Denise with you?"

They had been at Smith together, he remembered. "We're separated," he said.

"Ah so!" she said.

Like an Oriental detective on the trail of a pearl snatcher. No one ever gave him the benefit of a doubt.

Erica looked at Tina. "Well," she said briskly. "Shall we commandeer a table, Tina? Before they're all gone? We've got twenty years to catch up on."

"Wait for Sybil," Tina said weakly. "Shall I get Hugh?"

"Didn't anybody ever leave Brewerton except me?" he said. "Look who's here."

Sybil arrived, out of breath, from her clip down the lawn. "Jack Troy. Back from the dead. I don't believe it."

"Hello, Sybil," he said.

No one answered her, even though they must have heard her. Shall I get Hugh? I guess I won't, she decided. Why would I want to do that? He heard her in her head decide it: I guess I won't. He looked at her. See, Tina, I was right. Hugh would have gone and gotten you, given the reverse situation.

"You look different," Sybil said. "Is that a perm, or did it grow in curly?"

"It grew in curly. Just naturally curly."

"You always did have all the luck," Sybil said. "Here from Houston for a few days?"

"It was Dallas. And no. I live in New York now."

"Oh?" Sybil said. "Oh!" she said again. She flushed, didn't look at Tina. Her informant had so unfully informed her.

"Well, *shall* we get a table?" Erica said. "Wake up, Tina. Come on all." She took Jack Troy's arm. "Tell me all about you," she said, dragging him off. "I want to hear every single thing."

From the end of the terrace opposite from where Hugh was, Mickey Kolyrion saw them all move across the lawn to a table under the trees. Sybil and Erica had appropriated him, one on either side of him. Tina sat apart from them, half with another couple who had joined the table, half not; half watching Jack Troy, half seeming not to. But you could see the embers were still smoldering, he thought. After all these years. He ran a finger under one of the thick gold chains he wore around his neck and glanced down the terrace at Hugh. It struck him that, from the way Hugh was talking and laughing, he didn't have a clue that Jack Troy was on the premises. Just a nasty coincidence, he decided. Life full of them lately. Though this one would have to be dealt with, somehow.

She sat apart, glad they had him surrounded. Were talking a mile a minute to him, as if they thought they could keep him from wanting to talk to her. It was helpful to have a chance to regard him unregarded by him, to be able to see, without him seeing her see it, the face she remembered emerge from the face time had rendered. And as she watched him, it was helpful also to feel a certain cold objectivity she had taught herself to take toward him a long time ago return and affect what she perceived, feel even the old ill will she had practiced so well ooze up out of her memory again.

Yes, Mephistophelian, she decided a second time. Something diabolic and fatal in his cheerfulness, his old familiar joviality making Erica and Sybil already double up with laughter at some rueful, self-deprecating story he was telling to disarm them. Life in Dallas with Denise, and so on. She wouldn't let him make her laugh. She would remember:

He had arrived all innocently in her twelve-year-old present, innocent that a place had already been prepared for him in her future—whether by fate, by biological instinct, or by the potent action of adolescent imagination, it didn't matter. Whatever had arranged it, it was arranged.

She had had him all to herself only for that first day, that Saturday morning eating the chocolate-chip cookies on his grandmother's front porch, and then again in the late afternoon of the same day, when in clean clothes, he came up on her front porch and asked her to walk uptown with him to show him the sights. (Her mother's eyes filled with tears when she saw his black eye. Kind Mrs. Penney felt a natural sympathy for the virtually motherless boy anyway, whose history she had come to know a little of over the years. Mrs. Thile had to tell her troubles to someone. And the Reverend Mr. Penney had to tell his to someone.) They went for their walk that day, but he found other girls the next day. News of him traveled in the night like thirsty vines after water. There were, just a few blocks away, man-hungry eighth-grade girls whose existence she of course had known in her heart of hearts there was never any possibility of keeping from him.

Nevertheless, she tried.

This is the church. This is the library. This is the post office. This is the elementary school where I go. That's my homeroom up there on the third floor. See those windows there just above the flagpole? He didn't need to know a whole lot of what she was telling him, he said. Where's the high school?

This is the other church. And that one over there is where the Catholics go. This is the bakery. That's the colored section down there. This is the Y. That down there's the ferry slip. He wanted to take a ride on the ferry. But she wasn't allowed. He yawned. He wanted to know where the movie house was. And if there was a pool hall. And then he wanted to go into the East End Diner for a cup of coffee. That wasn't allowed either. What, he said crossly. There's just one diner in this little bitty town and you ain't allowed to go in *to* it? There were two luncheonettes, a tearoom, and two ice-cream parlors in the little bitty town of Brewerton, she told him. Not to mention a very nice hotel with a dining room, and two restaurants with table-cloths. I'm going in, he said. They sell beer in there, she said. So much the better, he said. He started for the door. You wouldn't dare. He smiled. See y'all.

She waited outside, fuming. How could anyone not see he was heading straight for trouble! After a while he came saunter-ing back out. You'll be eatin' in there before long, he an-nounced. I'm takin' you. It's a real fine place. Grits and gravy are served with all the main dishes, if you ask for them. Do you know we didn't have grits this morning? My granny never cooked them in her life. What are grits? she said. He didn't know what they were exactly. But they were white and tasty and they went with everything. Are they potatoes? Are they rice? No, they're grits. His granny was going with them. The two of them needed an education in southern style if they didn't know grits.

That place is a colored place, she blurted out. Your grand-mother would never go in there.

What? he said. There were whites in there.

But colored too?

Yes.

Well, then.

Oh, he said. So it's not all that different from the South. If people practiced what they preached it would be, she said. Your daddy's a preacher, isn't he? My father practices what he preaches, she said. It's because of the beer that I can't go in. That was the day he told her about the Ku Klux Klan and the Jim Crow laws in Tennessee and Willie and how Willie's family lived; he became so melancholy as he talked that it wasn't hard to guess some kind of segregation had also been practiced against him.

On the way home, she detoured him around the block where the eighth-grade girls lived, but it didn't do any good. They saw him in church the next morning. Overnight he had negotiated the Sunday-morning question with his grandmother: Church he would attend, Sunday School he would not. His grandmother, like Tina, had understood in a flash of instinct what she was up against with this boy she had never met before. But this didn't mean they didn't have plans for him, nevertheless, Mrs. Thile and Tina. And it didn't mean they weren't grateful for any slight movement of their plans in a forward direction. It just meant it was true Rome wasn't built in a day.

Tina prayed when she saw him walk down the aisle that first Sunday morning that her father would preach such an eloquent sermon as would make Jack Troy fall hopelessly in love with her. And this prayer was not completely inefficacious. The Reverend Mr. Penney's false teeth clicked twice toward the end, when he got excited over how the rain fell on the just and the unjust alike. But Jack Troy didn't even notice the teeth, and after it was over he said, now, I liked that sermon. It's the kind you're not apt to hear down South. Down South, they tell you that nice things happen to nice people. I think your daddy's got it figured out the way it really is. Nice things happen to bad people.

She rejoiced then in the power of prayer, but after that, most of her prayers regarding Jack Troy seemed to bear out what her father had taught her: that all prayers are answered, but some are answered yes, some are answered no, and some are answered wait.

The next day, she raced home from school. Where is he? she asked Mrs. Thile. Mrs. Thile wanted to know that herself. He sauntered along two hours later, all sweetened up on Meredith Satterslee's mother's peanut brittle. It was sickening to see how fast he worked, moving through the female population of Brewerton's eighth grade. His plan of action was to meet everyone and to get everyone to think he was the best thing since D day.

After Meredith, there was Debby, and after Debby there was Sally, and after her Meredith and Debby again and others, until the eighth-grade girls were reduced to a pack of hags, wrangling over which one of them he liked best. He moved on to the ninth grade.

She had to be satisfied with what he gave her, which was more than and different from and better than what he gave anyone else. She knew that, even at twelve. From the beginning, he trusted her, told her things about himself on the porch in the summer dusk—when the other girls were dreaming of him, the mysterious stranger in town for the summer, making their own plans for him on their own porches, or in their lighted bedrooms, dreamily brushing their hair to shine for him—things he never told another human soul. Perhaps she wasn't totally human to him, still too young at twelve to be totally human, yet he entrusted his soul to her from that first summer on, as if she had been appointed the earthly guardian of it, like some reflecting twin of his, or at least like some reliable and trustworthy sister.

And he resisted her, too, as if it were a matter of survival. You are the pain-in-the-butt type of girl, he told her.

What other type is there?

There are southern girls. Who like being nice to a boy.

I'm nice.

No, you're not. You're always trying to make me toe the line.

Toeing the line is what you have to do a lot of in life, she said. It's good to learn how when you're young.

What it would be good for you to learn, he said, is I toe my line, not your line. Okay?

Maybe.

Good. We'll go places then, you and me. He pulled her braid gently.

You and I, she said.

You are the type of girl who isn't satisfied till a person is perfect, he said. Why?

Why not? she said.

He laughed. She gave him a sense of the wonderful possibilities of life. He was full of plans and agendas for his life. He had goals he wanted her to hear. He was going to graduate from military school, go to Yale, collect expensive things, work on Wall Street, and marry and stay married to the same person for his whole life, and have three children.

It was fine with her. She could fit right in. But what do you mean, collect expensive things? she said.

From arrowheads to tinfoil, from tinfoil to marbles. Next year he would trade up from marbles to coins. He knew someone with a coin collection he might like to part with. Then on to stamps or Egyptian scarabs. It didn't matter what it was, as long as it was something you could sell or trade to somebody else.

She thought collections were things you saved to hand on. For some people, he said. But for me, a collection is only a way to get a better collection. And that's how to get rich.

Oh, rich, she said carelessly. She couldn't imagine it herself.

You should, he said. Because if you trade up, if you always pay more than you can afford, and if you always buy what's good, so somebody else will someday buy it from you, you'll *get* rich.

What if you buy something bad by mistake?

You get rid of it, fast.

She considered this. Who told you about it?

My mother.

Is she rich?

He laughed. No.

Why do you want to get rich anyway? She knew from the Bible the problems rich men had.

Because, he said, to make up for not having a rich daddy, he had to make his own fortune, or else marry a woman with one. He looked at her.

She flushed.

He smiled. You don't have a rich daddy, do you?

No.

Well, see?

I suppose you think you're going to marry me, she dared, half-choking on her nerve. He gave her a sense of the wonderful possibilities of life, too.

I suppose, I suppose you think so, too.

She turned her eyes on him, brilliant, dazzled eyes, full of . . . love!

And then he began to laugh, and he laughed his head off, at the way he had brought her to this foolish pitch.

I suppose I don't, she said, jumping up.

She could hear him still chortling on the porch, all the way through his grandmother's garden to the parsonage.

He had a very special collection. It was what had gotten him started on the idea of collecting, when he was ten. He showed it to her in his bedroom, hundreds and hundreds of little Civil War soldiers, boxes and boxes of them, a whole trunkful, given to him on his tenth birthday by his mother. They had been his father's. His mother had saved them for him until he was old enough to appreciate them. The soldiers were one collection he would never sell. Even though his mother hadn't asked him not to.

What's your mother like?

Oh, he said, she's not like other people's mothers. She's unique.

To be unique became in that instant Tina Penney's design. Unique to Jack Troy.

She listened to his ideas and all his plans with infinite

attention, because she wanted him not to be disappointed in them.

Yet his optimism worried her. Life, she was sure, even at twelve, was not going to be as easy to pass through as he believed. He didn't seem to understand what she knew: that trouble lay in store for everybody in life. Nobody went through it unscathed. If you liked the idea that the rain fell on the just and the unjust alike, how could you not prepare yourself for it?

You talk just like a little old lady, he said.

Someday we will be old.

You don't have to start practicing now. You're only twelve.

Oh . . . bother!

Oh, pshaw, he said. Oh, fiddlesticks.

Oh, shut up, she said. She could hear him laughing his head off behind her as she stalked home.

They discovered at the end of that first summer that they had the same birthday. He had known there was something special about her, this tall, strong, bossy northern girl. We were conceived on exactly the same night, one year apart, he said.

The word *conceived* sent a shiver of adult interest through her body. She imagined that act of love as if it were unique in their mothers' lives and believed it was no coincidence, but an indication of some shared fate, that common day of creation.

Their eyes met for an instant over the table. She averted hers.

Not going to be easy, he thought.

The first summer had passed so quickly that it was over

before he realized he had not done the thing in New York he had meant to do: have his lead soldiers appraised by the dealer on Madison Avenue. He left them at his grandmother's house when he went back to Chattanooga, with instructions to Tina that if his grandmother should die, or the house catch fire, it was the trunk in his bedroom that she must see was removed to her house for safekeeping.

She promised. And in his grandmother's kitchen, which smelled of fresh cake, he put his hands on her shoulders and kissed her seriously on the mouth, where not even her mother had ever kissed her. He said, I'll be back next summer. Hear?

She nodded, too sad to speak.

And he was gone.

She wept afterward so inconsolably and for so long that her mother finally flew into her room and said sharply, Stop this carrying on this minute.

The second summer, they took four shoe boxes of lead soldiers to New York. He had a train schedule and the address of the dealer in military miniatures. Mrs. Penney and Mrs. Thile believed they were going on their bikes for the day to a public swimming pool in the next town. Between them, they had sixteen dollars.

Instead of a towel and her bathing suit, she packed a dress and her pocketbook in her swim bag and changed in the ladies' room at the railroad station.

On the train, they sat opposite each other, he riding backward, the boxes on the seats beside them, and stared out the window at the passing scene, all leafy greenness and safe little white houses flashing by. (The train made him think of Cora and her voluptuous face inclining toward him. He liked to think that if he could ever find her again they would perform the full act of love together.)

At Weehawken, they set the boxes down in the sun on the wooden pier and waited silently for the ferry. There were twenty or thirty other people waiting also. He felt that everyone was looking at them, as if they were escaped inmates of an orphan asylum.

The bus driver let them out at the corner where they could get the Madison Avenue bus uptown. They found two seats in the back of the bus, and they read every doorway all the way uptown for the number they were looking for.

The shop was dim and deserted, except for the owner, who looked up at them when they entered. Yes? he said.

Sir, Jack said briskly. They placed the shoe boxes on the glass counter. Beneath the glass was a diorama of the Battle of Waterloo. I have a collection of military miniatures I want to have appraised, he said.

French? British?

American, sir.

The war?

Yes, sir.

The man looked at him curiously. I meant: which war? he said.

The Civil War, sir.

Union?

Confederate and Union. Sir.

Let's see what you have.

He opened the first box. Infantry here, he said. Confederate. In all, forty-eight pieces. Two officers, a bugler, a rifleman, and troops.

The dealer lifted the corner of the top piece of batting. Johillco, he said, sniffing.

What? Jack said. Inert and suddenly unprepossessing in a way they had never seemed before, the four dozen figures lay in their several layers of dingy cotton wool.

Johillco. The manufacturer. Next box?

Artillery, Jack said, uncertainly, opening the next box. Union and Confederate. Thirty-three pieces. Mounted officer horses, limbers, guns with commanders and crews.

Yes, said the dealer, lifting a tiny officer to the light and squinting at it. Next?

Jack opened the third box. Cavalry here, he said. Confederate. Officer, bugler, standard-bearer, troops, and horses. The dealer glanced cursorily at the contents of the third box and passed on to the fourth. In this one? he said.

In the fourth box were infantry, Union, four dozen pieces. Firing from kneeling and standing positions. Crawling, charging, running, walking, they were the most animated among the four boxes, his best, Jack thought. But now, under the eye of the specialist, they too lay still and dull in the dingy wool.

Provenance?

Sir?

Where did you get them?

Jack flushed. They were my father's, he said. I brought only these. I have a whole trunkful.

Accessories?

No, Jack said, uncertainly.

Well, the man said, with a helpless flutter of his hands. I'd like to help you, but you see, you have no connoisseur pieces. A terrible silence fell on the little shop. A terrible revelation had been made. Nothing unique. Just the run of the mill, the man went on, as if the stricken faces of children were something he was used to. Are you brother and sister? he said, then, more kindly.

Yes, Jack said.

She moved closer to him at the counter.

Well, children, here's the thing, the man said. The ideal in miniatures of any type is originality and versimilitude. Make it look real, that's the challenge. It takes a bit of doing. But that's what people pay for. What you have here, unfortunately (and he tapped the first three boxes with a gold pencil that he withdrew from an inner pocket), are British (tap), pre-World I (tap), hollow tin (tap), made by Hanks (tap), and fully modeled (tap). But . . . prepainted.

But . . . old, Tina said. Aren't they antiques?

Old? the dealer said vaguely. Well, as things go, perhaps. But age is less important than authenticity. (He pronounced it *authenteeceetay*.) Vivaceetay of expression. Naturalness of movement. That's the essence. You can get this in two ways. Take the bought pieces apart and remake them. Cut off their heads. Cut off their limbs. Resolder them to make them more natural looking. More animated. Change them. Pose them. Create. Take off their paint. Repaint them. Create, you see, that's the idea. Create a new realeetay. A new versimilitude. A new authenteeceetay.

And? Jack said.

And?

You said there were two ways.

Well, the other way is, you know, the connoisseur way, the man said. Have them made to your order. By experts. Then you know you have the best. Something unique. That's what I deal in.

In the silence of the shop, the dealer touched the tip of his tiny waxed moustache and twiddled it to a fine point. Your Union infantry, he said, trying to give them something, but even so, knowing that what they wanted was not his to give. It was bought unpainted and painted by someone. The original owner, or another. Who knows? But you see, he did it wrong. You have to paint the figure white first, which he did—a very thin coat of titanium white. And when it's dry, you have to file off any blisters with a little emery cloth. But look here, look at the blisters. He didn't even try. He was in a hurry. He didn't bother to smooth out the blisters. (He picked up a tiny charging soldier.) Look at the cracks in his tunic. He used a drying agent to speed the process, but he used too much of it. The paint contracted and cracked. You have to be very careful. If you want the best. He replaced the soldier on the batting, next to a blistered horse.

The children stared at the devalued treasures.

And, the dealer said, whoever did it should have used a mat varnish. Really. They're too shiny. Much too.

Thank you, Jack said. He put the lids on the boxes and began tying them up again.

That's right, the dealer said. That's the spirit. Keep them. Don't downgrade them. Have fun with them. Parade them! Maneuver them! Display them. Don't sell them. Create backgrounds for them. Get your accessories.

No, Jack said. I'll just put them away. I'm a little too old to play with toy soldiers.

Grown men play with them. It's a lifelong hobby. All over

the world, men play with them. They're not toys. Toys! They're history! They're our heroes. All we've got. They're our realeetay! There's a book, *Little Wars* by H.G. Wells. It tells you how.

I think I know all about little wars, Jack said. Thank you for your time. Sir.

(There are lots of kinds of wars, dear boy, his mother had told him. Winning them is what you want to do.)

The dealer's nature was to be very particular and very precise. He came around from behind the counter to open the door for them. He was kind, but he was particular. He had to mention, for their own good, one last thing. If you buy this sort of thing yourself, now or in the future, he said, do keep them in the original boxes? Fetches a higher price, you know.

Thank you very much, Tina said.

Damn him to hell, Jack said, at the bus stop.

Your father?

Yes.

But what about her? she thought to herself.

They boarded the downtown bus when it came and rode it to 42nd Street. There they transferred to a crosstown bus and rode west through Times Square to the river in the hot, hot sun. They ate their lunches on the bow deck of the ferry. He had mashed beans on white bread, prune plums, and Oreo cookies. She had Velveeta cheese on white bread, celery sticks, and a warm banana. He went inside when they were finished and got water for them, ice-cold water from the cooler in little white cone cups that made him think of Cora again.

Why, children, very old Mrs. Thile said, rising shakily from her rocking chair in the dim dining room at the back of the house. All the shades and curtains in the house were drawn against the sun, the rooms dim and cool. You're all dressed up! Where have you been?

We've been home for hours, Granny. Didn't you hear us? Playing soldiers on the porch? We spoke to you.

Why, no, I didn't, she said. You went out in those clothes? I didn't hear a thing. I don't remember atall talking to you. I must have cotton wool in these old ears today. Or in my head. You look so hot and fussed. Whatever possessed you to get all dressed up to ride to the pool?

We'll be right down, he said, heading up the stairs. Soon as we put the soldiers away.

They replaced the shoe boxes in the steamer trunk. She flopped facedown on his bed, hot and exhausted, and he lay beside her. After a while, he felt her body heave. He put his hand on the small of her back. Don't, he said.

She kicked her legs in rage. It doesn't matter, she said fiercely. It doesn't.

Well, it really does, he said. But, anyway. Her braids were coming loose, and he unbraided them and combed her hair out with his fingers, let it fall around her face, still buried in his chenille bedspread. I'm not even sure any more if he really is dead, he said softly. But I know one thing about him I didn't know before today: He made more than one mistake in his life. So, I'll keep them, to remind me.

She rolled over on her back. Her face was hot and wet and red and very fierce. You're not a mistake, she said.

He smoothed her damp hair back from her hot forehead. He felt far more than one year her senior. He set his face in her warm, damp hair. Will you marry me someday anyway? he whispered in her ear. She nodded. No other possibility was even imaginable. He kissed her on the mouth, and after a while they fell asleep.

When Mrs. Thile climbed the stairs later and discovered them in the deep connubial peace and ease of their slumber on the double bed in the dim, shaded room, his face in her damp hair, his arm over her waist, his leg thrown over one of her long tan legs, with the blond hairs of summer glistening on the shins, she uttered a small horrified cry that woke them up.

He looked at her from across the table. She looked back at him, hearing his grandmother's little scream in her own head. He looked at his watch. "Do you mind if we talk, Sybil? It's getting late."

"No!" cried Sybil. "Tell me about your work."

I meant with *her,* he thought hopelessly.

9

It was just about the time he first arrived in Brewerton that she and Sybil Dye began to be best friends. There was an excess of time in those days for girls of twelve to spend on friendship. On their porches, or lying across their beds, or on their way to and from school, the two girls dwelt for hours on their futures, planning their lives, basing their plans not on what they read in the magazines Mrs. Dye subscribed to, but on what they knew it was really going to be like.

Both of the Dyes were artists. Mrs. Dye designed costumes for paper dolls. She wore peasant dresses and hoop earrings and sat on a high-legged chair in front of a drafting board, the floor around her littered with colored papers, scraps of fabrics, and rejected sketches crumpled and thrown down in aesthetic rage.

Her tools were pens with slender nibs, scissors with flashing blades, paint boxes of watercolors. A glass of murky water was always at her elbow, and brushes nearby in a cut-glass vase. Sometimes, she got a job illustrating a children's book, and sometimes she had a sewing book to do, or dress patterns for *McCall's* or *Simplicity,* and the girls would come in after school to preview the new fashions: batwing sleeves, gored skirts, bow bodices. Mrs. Dye sketched them scornfully on her board, painted them in with deft strokes, then tacked them on the wall to dry while she started another. She was always working. Always sketching the styles she often grimly said she would never have time to make for herself, much less have money to buy.

Mr. Dye went to New York to do his artwork. It was no secret that this daily trip was a distasteful interruption in his life, made necessary by economic considerations. No one in his family had ever worked before. His father had once been considering it, but just about that time, the income tax was introduced, rendering the idea of employment impractical. Besides, Mr. Dye's father pointed out, if he had to be at the office at nine and didn't get back uptown until six, there wasn't any time in the day left for doing anything else. Mr. Dye had to work, but his real work took place on weekends on a small stool in fields or along roadsides, an easel and his paints at his right hand. He wore a woolen beret in the winter and a flat smart boater in the warm weather.

Mr. Dye arrived home from the train station at precisely the same moment every evening. He kissed Mrs. Dye and Sybil when he walked in, and whisked up a pitcher of martinis. The martini always enlivened Mrs. Dye, whose pretty, papery employment took such a heavy toll of her spirits. She began to laugh the minute the pitcher appeared in the living room. They were a happy couple, very much in love, Tina thought. But Sybil disapproved of them and disagreed that they were happy.

Tina was sometimes invited to stay for supper. She marveled at the seemingly effortless way this meal appeared at the Dyes' house. At a certain moment, Mrs. Dye would rise from her merry conversation with Mr. Dye and disappear into the kitchen. A few minutes later, the family would be called to the dining room.

Mrs. Dye seemed to be unacquainted with Mrs. Penney's notion that each meal should contain a representative of the seven basic food groups. Mrs. Dye had her dinner down to a chop or a bird and a green or a yellow vegetable and a boiled potato or a tablespoon or two of rice—followed by a small salad that throughout the meal stood, already dressed, on salad plates on the sideboard, waiting for the moment of its consumption, as if Mrs. Dye would not have the stamina or the wits to dress it at the last moment. Bread and butter were strangers to the Dye table, and the protein component was on its own. Ice water was the children's beverage, summer or winter.

But though it was so frugal, Mr. and Mrs. Dye consumed their evening meal slowly and elegantly, with every sign of enjoyment and satisfaction, and with a polite conversation during it that had the qualities of a ritual. His turn, her turn, an occasional invitation to the children to offer their opinion, a resolution, his turn again, and so on. On the table were candles, real lace-trimmed linen place mats and napkins (so old they were full of holes), individual salt dishes and tiny spoons, and wine in crystal glasses for Mr. and Mrs. Dye. The dinner plates were of a size to dwarf even a meal of substance. With éclat, as if it were a magnificent homemade seven-layer cake, the salad was sometimes followed by dessert: Jell-O or chocolate pudding, or a sliver of Dundee's pound cake.

Mr. Dye read the newspaper afterward, while out in the kitchen, Mrs. Dye, humming and whistling and polishing off the last of the wine, washed the dishes. She didn't bother to dry them, as Mrs. Penney most surely did, but left them to drain and dry by themselves. According to Sybil, she didn't always hum and whistle either. Sybil sometimes found her weeping in the gloomy kitchen, hanging over the sink in despair.

Sybil liked to eat at Tina's house, where meals began with prayer and homemade soup and ran to juicy roasts surrounded by potatoes, two vegetables, gravy, side dishes of fruit, homemade biscuits, frothy milk, and buttery pies and cakes, or bread puddings redolent with spices.

One night when Sybil was eating there, and Jack Troy, too, Mickey Kolyrion fell out of a tree outside the dining room window, where he sometimes climbed to watch the Penneys eat. They all rushed to the window to look at him, stunned on the ground under a large leafy maple limb. Mrs. Penney phoned for the doctor; she could see a shard of white bone protruding from his forearm.

He came every summer for years. But a card with a Panamanian stamp at Christmas was all there ever was of him between the summers, until he stopped going to Panama for Christmas and began spending it in Brewerton.

His annual departures crushed her. But then the memory of him receded gently in her consciousness, hibernating in the back of her mind as the winter bore on to spring, emerging by the time she could count the days till he appeared again: taller, handsomer, ever more cheerful, ever more certainly the object of her affections, and ever more elusive.

One summer evening, Mr. Dye, who hardly ever expressed an opinion verging on the judgmental, happened to catch a glimpse of Jack Troy flying down the Dyes' hill on his bike, standing on the pedals, his hands behind his head, laughing all the way. That boy is not going to get the last laugh in this life, I'm afraid, Mr. Dye said. Oh, she had cried in her heart. Others see it, too. Why won't he listen to me?

Mrs. Penney recommended when he came back the third summer that they not play in each other's bedrooms any more. They were too old for that, thirteen and fourteen, going on fourteen and fifteen.

That was the summer he cajoled his grandmother to let him activate the big Chrysler that had belonged to his grandfather and that had been up on blocks in the garage for years, since his grandfather died. He knew how to drive, but he didn't tell Mrs. Thile that. She agreed to let him try to start the car, only because she believed he wouldn't have the slightest idea how to. Before she knew it, he had jacked up the front, removed the block from under the axle, jacked up the back, removed the block from under the back axle, put gas in the tank, started the car on the first try, and found a girl with a driver's license. The girl let him do the driving.

Tina watched them, followed their movements, spied on them, wished the girl instant tragedy, all imaginable misfortune. But she seemed immune to any kind of bad luck at all.

[82]

Then one day, Mrs. Thile, out marketing, happened to glance up from the peaches in the grocer's front window just in time to see what looked like her grandson drive by in what looked like Mr. Thile's Chrysler. She left the peaches right in the scale and called a taxi to come get her. Jack confessed that he knew how to drive; in the South, everyone knew at thirteen. He promised he would never do it again, of course, except in the driveway, and Mrs. Thile believed him again. But she was hard of hearing, and she never heard him at night release the clutch and let the car slip backward into the street and down the hill and around the corner, where he turned on the headlights, started up the engine, and drove off into the dark.

Yet, the last week, he forgot all about the girl with the driver's license and spent every evening at the parsonage. They played Monopoly by kerosene lamp till way past midnight on the screened front porch, sometimes with Sybil and Mr. Penney, and sometimes alone, unbearably aware, both of them, of the separation coming, the long, long winter.

He wanted to get up and sit beside her. But Sybil and Erica were describing to him a recent tragedy in Wandsley, the town where Cora had gotten off the train in such a hurry. And he remembered Wandsley. Every summer he would get on his bike in the first week, and ride to Wandsley, half-wanting to find Cora, half-afraid he would. He imagined she worked in a hospital, bustling about in a white dress and nurse's cap, with a tray of thermometers and ice packs and pills, sometimes firmly closing the door of a private room and advancing toward the bed of an unsuspecting patient with that dark, serious look in her eye.

[83]

He had found the Wandsley hospital by following a speeding ambulance, but Cora did not appear at the emergency entrance to greet it.

And he remembered how, under the grape arbor in his grandmother's side yard, he had one day kissed Tina in the same serious way that Cora had kissed him, intently placing his stamp on her, then opening and exploring the territory he had claimed, knowing that this was one of the most excellent experiences life had to offer, and one he did indeed have a gift for, as Cora had said. She kissed him back with a proficient and even masterly dedication that amazed them both, considering that she had never tried it before. Intent as he was on his own pleasure in kissing her, he was also intently conscious of her solemn delight in being kissed and on kissing him back, and on smelling him and tasting him and nuzzling his face with her face. He could still remember how their skin in the summer after a day at the town pool tasted of sun and chlorine and sweat and steamy wet cement drying in the sun. And how joy stirred their beings when they went home from such a day and kissed. Impulses transmitted themselves between their bodies like electric shocks. Their mouths seemed to be molded for each other. The long, long spans of their concentration jibed. Their excited interest in each other made kissing blissfully compelling. And then, just when it began to be clear how much more there was to do, it was time for him to leave for Chattanooga. Don't ever do this, he commanded, with anyone but me. Their clothing was soaked with sweat. Their hair and skin was as wet as if they had been swimming. Their eyes swam in sweat. He lay flat on top of her on the prickly horsehair couch in the hot, dark, humid parlor of his grandmother's house. Above them, his grandmother

[84]

napped in the heat of deepest August. Hear? he said fiercely. She burst into hot, stormy sobs.

She blotted her face with a cocktail napkin and remembered how, the next summer, he appeared to have forgotten all about the wonderful transporting kissing they had shared, and took up with Marion Heard, Clarice Heard's sister. For spite, Tina acquired Eddy Bonner, whose life was rendered instantly lovely by her unsought presence in it. One night at the movies with Eddy, Jack Troy saw her. He accosted her in the lobby during the intermission. Who is he? None of your business, she said coolly. He took her by the arm. Tell me who he is. He squeezed her arm till she cried out in pain. No! Tell me. It's my business. It's not. It is. He maneuvered her backward against the wall. Let go of me! she cried.

People began to stare at them. The manager dashed toward them across the red-carpeted lobby. What's all this? What's going on here? Never you mind, Jack said, not even glancing at him. Let me go! she said through her teeth, trying to free her arm. Unhand this girl! the manager said fiercely. I'll find out, he said. Who could it be, in this two-bit town? He flung her arm down. You idiot, she said. Go! he shouted. Moron! she said. She fled up the long carpeted ramp to her seat beside Eddy Bonner. Go! he shouted after her. Out! the manager ordered. Stop this or out! Sir! Jack said, practically saluting.

He went back to his seat, yanked Marion Heard out of hers, and moved up to sit directly behind Tina and Eddy Bonner, who stealthily put his arm around Tina about halfway to the end. Jack, wearing cordovans, deftly raised his foot as if to cross his legs, and got Eddy a direct hit on the funny bone.

Eddy nearly wept, it hurt so. Sorry 'bout that, Jack said.

He appeared at the front door the next morning. I want to talk to you, he said. What about? she said, behind the screen. He opened the screen door and stepped into the hall. She turned her back on him and walked upstairs. He followed her. Jack, said Mrs. Penney sharply. He stopped on the stairs and looked down at Mrs. Penney in the hall. She shook her head just once. Why? She shook her head again. I just want to talk to her. Talk to Marion Heard! she shouted from up in her room. She slammed her door. I will then! he shouted back. She opened the door. You do anyway. And more than that, too! She slammed the door again. A little plaster fell from the ceiling in the hallway onto Mrs. Penney's hair. Horrors! Mrs. Penney said, dusting off her head, this is quite enough. Jack!

Ma'am!

You heard me.

Yes! Ma'am! But why?

There is no why or wherefore to it, Mrs. Penney said firmly. But Mr. Penney and I both agree that you should have many friends, both of you. And so does your granny. You're too young to get so very . . . possessive . . . of someone of the opposite . . . sex. Mrs. Penney's fair skin reddened at the mention of the word. He explained that he was leaving in a week. Departures do not really matter very much, Mrs. Penney said. You have gone before, and no doubt you will be back.

He turned on his heel and left the house. That night he climbed the chestnut tree next to the house and stepped softly onto the roof outside Tina's bedroom window. She was sitting next to the window in her nightgown, waiting for him in the pitch-black night. I love you, he whispered through the screen, tasting oxidized metal. Tina, I love you. Don't go out with anyone else. But *you* do, she whispered, her face so close to his that she could feel the warmth of it through the screen. I won't again, I promise. You promise too? She nodded in the dark. You're mine, he whispered into her mouth. Don't you know that? There's no one else. I love you, she whispered back. Then let me in, he whispered. No. Yes. I can't. I want to lie next to you. No. When? *When? When?*

On his last night, he took her to a movie, and afterward drove out into the country to the edge of a cliff above the river, and parked the car in the moonlight, and took her into his arms, and laid her down on the seat, smelling her face, her hair, skimming his dry lips over hers, whispering to her to take her blouse off, her bra, all her clothes. He told her about ovulation. She was stunned that nature had provided this special convenience to the race. And skeptical. But by the overhead light in the car, he showed her the book where he had discovered it, the little bell-shaped curves, the unsafe days and the safe days. She stared at them. She turned the book over and over and read the title page and the jacket copy. The book was written by a doctor. Please, he begged, turning out the light. I want to be next to you. Nothing between. He plucked at her clothes as if they were so many annoying leaves or burrs sticking to her. Take this off. Take it off. We won't do anything. Just be next to each other. No! she said, suddenly coming to. Yes! No! You will, one of these days, he said grimly. Fully clothed, they kissed to the fullest extent the circumstances allowed, and in the morning her mouth felt like a new mouth, with a mind of its own, full of desires and memories.

She pressed the damp cocktail napkin to her face again to cool it. She felt breathless and weak, pressed her fingers to the pulse at her wrist. Her nostrils dilated. She looked at him across the table. The old face, the one she remembered, flickered momentarily, eerily familiar, then disappeared again into the new. Twenty years and two lives apart. His brown hair, streaked with gray, had grown in curly. She picked up a paper plate embossed with silver wedding bells and fanned her throat. Nice, she thought. Becoming to you, Jack. But you are as nothing to me in my present sober contented life. As nothing! As the merest shadow of a shelf of bad memories a mile long! Hear it? He glanced at her. He heard it.

He had lived in Dallas for twelve years. His skin seemed permanently tanned from it. His blue eyes were faded from the Texan sun. Or from life getting to him. She wanted not to care which. The sun, she thought. Or why would he be laughing, telling Dallas jokes, in his expensive Dallas shirt that matched his eyes? A breeze caught his silk tie. The hand he raised to press it down was tan and leathery. The band was playing "Hello, Young Lovers." He looked across the table at her again. "You still haven't told me how you are," he said, suddenly getting up in the middle of a long story of Sybil's and coming around the table to sit beside her.

Right *next* to me, she thought wildly, moving her chair back from the table in a panic. Get away from me, you!

"So?" he said.

"Did you break your nose?" she said. He had an extra bump on the bridge of it. She couldn't think of anything else to say.

He touched it. "Someone did it for me. A long time ago. How *are* you?"

She tried to memorize the new face so she could remember it when he was gone. "As compared to last week? Or twenty years ago?"

"Let's start with twenty years ago."

But she remembered the summer when indignation, prudery, fear, nothing was an acceptable defense. He arrived in June, and it was like a first meeting, a new beginning. What made you get so beautiful? he asked her, staring at her. She hadn't noticed the change herself, it had been so gradual. She looked straight at him. You're still mine, aren't you? he said. Are you mine? she asked. Yes. Good, she said. That's settled, then, he said.

And with his usual forthrightness, his devastating quickness, his hyperconsciousness of time passing, passing fast, he told her how he was going to marry her, dizzyingly began treating her as if they were married already. A new courtly possessiveness was the tone he took. He loved her madly. It was his joy to say so, to give himself to her with an abandon that truly alarmed her, it was so intense, so singleminded!

She had a summer job at the drugstore. He worked for the County, cutting roadside weeds. He came by the drugstore at five, dark and handsome and intense and rank with field dust and sweat, and drove her home. And clean and soap-smelling, he came back again after supper to escort her around the dark country roads under the stars in his grandfather's Chrysler. He described how it would be: safe; wonderful; close; perfect. She resisted. No. He persisted. No. He insisted, fiercely determined. No! No! Jack, stop, stop!

I love you. I want you. You have to. In proof of his will, in defense of his desperation, he took all his clothes off one night, methodically, swiftly, fiercely, stripped himself before her eyes. Look. Look at me. Touch me.

No!

"Tina?"

"Vastly improved."

"You look . . . exactly the way I thought you would." he said.

"I'm happy. It's one of the improvements."

Why didn't you follow Hugh, then? Why didn't you go get him? Why are you looking at me like that, if you're so happy?

The breeze took his tie up in the air again. He swatted at it.

She closed her eyes. Had made him get dressed again, that time. But she knew her days were numbered.

The air by the beginning of August was heavy with the fragrance of cut fields and damp woods and roses, the scream of katydids and locusts, and the deep nocturnal hush in between. All the summer sounds and fragrances were on his side, and all the words, too: He loved her, only her. He would all his life. He would till he died. He was almost impossible to resist! But it was 1953. Girls had to resist, if they knew what was good for them. He parked on the brink of a quarry forty feet deep, with water as green in the daylight as motor oil, kissing her with a talent certain to have undone the Virgin Mary herself. Please! No! I have to. I'll die if I don't. Is it, would it be, have you . . . ever? No, he answered. And his answer was truthful, depending on which of her half-questions he had chosen to answer.

She resisted as long as she could. When she knew she couldn't any longer was when he told her, in final exasperation, to fish or cut bait. She had been cutting bait for five years. Besides, he had managed to uncover so much of her that one night they were both suddenly naked in the deep private country darkness, and there was no longer any use pretending she wasn't in fact his to do with as he wanted, and as she wanted.

Ah, but it was lovely, actually lovely, to be so close to the one you loved so dearly. Lovely! The proximity of him naked, the heat of him, the smell, the sounds he made in his passion were lovelier to her than she could have imagined. She gave herself up to it completely. Ah! she cried, when he did. His at last. He hers. It was, without a reservation, the happiest, sweetest, most harmonious, contented time of her life. Of his, too, he murmured, lying beside her in hay or on pine needles, ferns, moss, bracken, sand, grass. She always believed everything he said.

She raised her arms to lift her damp hair off her neck. Like a basin in the sun, the river valley town held the summer heat. Her dress was wet with sweat across her midriff. He looked at her. She lowered her arms. Remember, she thought, all day remember how he can't tolerate one's joy in him, in being one with him. Remember how it cools him when he understands how deep love can be, how very deep and driven and entangling. Remember that he likes simplicity, edges of things, clean lines, edge of the quarry, edge of a cliff over the river, edge of the woods in a clearing. Edge of her life. He had been driving other girls to the same edges for two summers, he told her, toward the end of that August. I wasn't the first? No, he said. What gave you that idea? You told me so. He shook his head, as if he didn't remember. He had met someone. Love at first sight it was. They could still be friends, of course. They would always be friends.

She didn't believe him, that there was someone else. But a few nights later, beyond the garden of the parsonage where she sat alone on a bench in the dark, staring dully at the curtains of his room, waiting for him to look out and see her and come back to her, a girl bare to the waist walked up to the window and looked briefly down into the garden. He appeared behind her and lowered the shade, his buttocks white behind the dark screen.

His chest when she had first lain on it had been as smooth as the inside of her arm. But in the gap between the buttons on his blue shirt, she could see now that it no longer was. She looked instead at his nose and tried to imagine the marriage that put hair on a man's chest. "Tell me about Denise," she said weakly. She slipped out of her shoes to cool her feet on the grass beneath the table.

He touched the bump on his nose. "I like to think it was an accident," he said. "We hadn't been married very long at all."

"Some wives break their husbands' noses accidentally, I guess," she said.

"It's not only noses she breaks," he said.

She almost laughed.

He looked at her. "Do you want to walk?" he said.

She looked right through him.

When dawn had begun to break, she was still sitting there on the garden bench, covered on every exposed part of her body with mosquito bites. She rose and walked to the house and up to her room, where she undressed herself and put on her night-gown and lay on her bed, like a corpse. Her mother found her there some hours later. She was removed to the guest room, which had an electric fan in the window, and remained there for several days. Her mother sponged her body with witch hazel every few hours, and in the belief that an infestation of insects had invaded it, had the bedroom of her only child fumigated.

He went back to Tennessee for his senior year at the military academy without seeing her.

There were undoubtedly some Presbyterian ministers' daughters in America in that era who could have risen above this experience, cursed him for a harebrained tomcat, and gone on with their lives. But she wasn't one of them. She spent the year sitting quietly in chairs, with her hands folded in her lap, when she wasn't in school. In school, she took notes with her hands, as if she cared about what her teachers were saying.

"Just down by the river?" he said.

She looked beyond him to the river. It seemed as good a place as any to say what it seemed like a good time to say. She picked up her shoes and her champagne glass, and walked ahead of him over the cool green grass to a wooden bench by the seawall.

She sat on the bench and stared out at the river, waiting.

"Tina," he began.

A chain of heavy-laden barges plowed up the river to Albany.

He came to Brewerton that Christmas, truly remorseful, and she forgave him. To show he was sincere, he gave her, as a sign of his contrition and a pledge of his devotion, his collection of lead soldiers. Mrs. Penney stood bemused in the downstairs hall, watching him go up and down the stairs, conveying the shoe boxes to her daughter's bedroom, as if the house were his to come and go in.

In his house, they made love in his bedroom. His grandmother was so deaf by then, the Chinese army could have gone up and down the back stairs without her hearing anything. But the week after Christmas, at a dance, he met someone's houseguest, a girl from Connecticut with an alliterative name. He went to visit Bobbie Bingham for the New Year's weekend in Darien.

She didn't see him again until the summer, when he came as usual, and when he was remorseful again, and when she forgave him as usual. But the same thing happened. Before the summer was half over, he had fallen in love again. She conceived a violent hatred for this girl, prayed for her death by any means, fire, a boating accident. When the girl broke her back from a misdive off a high board, she thought, Thank you.

He wrote to her from New Haven in the fall to express his remorse. She forgave him, naturally, and they went on as they had, that Thanksgiving and that Christmas, and everything seemed perfectly fine. This time, she believed, it would stick. She was happy, he was happy. She tried not to seem happy, because she knew how it unnerved him to be responsible for her joy. Nevertheless, she smiled all the time. That summer he went to Maine to work in a logging camp, and he must have met someone and fallen in love, because he only wrote to her once, the whole summer.

It was 1956.

In New Haven, against all college regulations, Jack Troy and Tina Penney made inventive and sweaty and lengthy and repeated love to each other every weekend. During one of these sessions, something utterly terrifying happened. She began to feel herself slip away from him and from herself. I'm going, she cried. I'm leaving. I'm going. Oh, oh, oh, oh, oh, oh! You're coming. You came, dummy, he said, laughing. Was that it? she cried, really crying, tears of love and joy. Oh, Jack. Oh, Jack. He laughed and held her. She was flushed and weak, her chest, her throat, her face and even her ears were bright pink and mottled. I love you, he whispered. Oh! Oh! Let's do it again, she cried, her strength returning.

Occasionally, they got out of bed and went to a movie. They saw *East of Eden* three times, *The Man with the Golden Arm* twice, and *The Rose Tattoo* once. In March, the Penneys, somewhat reluctantly, announced their daughter's engagement.

After the wedding, they planned they would live in New Haven until he graduated, and then move to New York, where she would go to design school and he to work on Wall Street. The Penneys wanted them to wait until she had graduated from Vassar to marry, but they didn't want to wait, and the Penneys were afraid to insist, for fear that he would lose the self-control they presumed he had and persuade her to . . . well, it was better to let them marry, if that was the direction things were taking.

In 1956 it was reported that in an average year, 1,732 Americans accidentally drowned. Clarice Heard drowned in April of 1956, but it wasn't an accident.

That year, Mickey Kolyrion worked briefly on or near Wall Street, selling uranium stocks out of a loft a few blocks from the Stock Exchange. His boss and the other brains behind this operation were indicted, tried, found guilty, and sent to Leavenworth. But Mickey was only a small-fry. Nobody even tried to indict him. He was also not indicted for the drowning death of Clarice Heard, because he had a perfect alibi (Mickey's brother Frank swore they were playing pinochle in the Kolyrions' cellar that night), and because there was no evidence but a tire tread, no motive (she wasn't pregnant), and no witnesses who came forth.

In the late winter of 1956, Mrs. Thile began to die in earnest, and Jack and Tina, who were planning to marry in June, began to meet on the weekends in Brewerton, he from New Haven, she from Poughkeepsie, to be with Mrs. Thile and to relieve the nurses. There were nurses around the clock.

One week in April—it was Spring vacation—it got freakishly hot. The thermometer read 96 on the front porch. Not a breath of air stirred. People went swimming in the river, it was so awfully hot. Tina went next door to Jack's house to take a fan to the day nurse. Jack was out, she thought. But she heard something in his room. She opened the door. He was sitting in his armchair. The day nurse was kneeling on the floor in front of him.

It was a confusing scene, because the nurse's dress, starched and white, was sitting in the other armchair, with her white shoes with her white stockings tucked into them on the floor directly beneath the skirt of her dress. But the nurse's hands were on Jack's knees, which were bare, and the nurse herself (Cora, of course) was wearing nothing at all.

She didn't go back to Vassar to finish her third year, but moved to New York, to a residential hotel for women, and got a job as an elevator operator in a Fifth Avenue department store. In later years, she was vague about which one, Bergdorf's, Bendel's, Bonwit's, or Best's. It was a job of up and down and door closing and door opening—a job and a period in her life in which external reality uncannily mirrored interior reality. Hordes of brides and debutantes and bridesmaids and college girls—some of whom she knew, though since they didn't so much as glance at her, there wasn't any need to speak to—poured back and forth past her, rode up and down with her, all day long, and she cared not. At night, she sat in a chair in her small room staring out the window, knowing it was her real job to restore herself to herself first with silence and facts, and finally with a fine, purging rage in which she threw everything movable in her room at its walls.

"Tina!"

She looked at him. Her face in the sun speckling down through the trees suddenly looked tired and older. Memories passed over it like scudding clouds dulling a sunny day. She looked away to avoid his seeing what was in her eyes, and he leaned forward to read her expression. "What are you remembering?" he said, remembering himself that year in America's life, and that particular month, when every person with any tenderness at all in his or her heart was moved to consider the past and to forgive and start over again. That year and that month, they had somehow found each other again. They drove to Washington together and stood all night in line at the rotunda, with the fallen leaves of the Capitol plane trees around their feet, to view the catafalque, and they decided, in line, to marry, even though he was married to Denise at the time, and even though Hugh Gardiner was waiting in New York for her to decide whether to marry him or not.

"*What* are you remembering?" he said again.

Edges of things. Porches, fences, brinks, verges, backs of buses and trains, margins, beaches, tides, the stern of a ferry. Banks, a lighted window, the tops of stairs, thresholds, rim of a ravine, woods beginning, sidewalks and curbs. A quarry, chasms, gaps, vistas. Edges.

"Everything you're forgetting," she said with a sudden wild fling of her arm that brushed her champagne glass off the bench and onto the cement seawall, where it shattered on the stone in a silence they hadn't noticed.

They sat staring at it, and then he knelt to pick up the pieces. "You would have to do that just between sets," he said.

Up the lawn, on the terrace far away, she saw Hugh, tiny and distant and oblivious, talking and laughing, and she saw someone else, at the other end of the terrace, looking down at them through field glasses. Mickey Kolyrion.

He set the pieces under the bench and sat beside her again and touched her arm.

"*Don't* touch me!" she said.

"Don't you remember any of the good things?"

Her eyes could have withered a green lawn.

"There were lots," he said. "Don't be like this, Tina."

"I never should have come here," she said bitterly. "I don't want to remember any of it." She stood.

She was barefoot, and sweating like a runner, he noticed. Her dress was damp and rumpled and sticking to her, her breasts outlined through the fabric, her face shining and dark. "You're attracting attention, I think," he said. "Sit down again."

Flushed and rumpled, she looked, he thought wonderingly, as if she'd been made love to with all her clothes on.

"Damn you, Jack," she said, sitting again. She had nothing to say that he wanted to hear. And no time to say what she wanted him to hear. Instead, "They're leaving soon," she said, "the bride and groom. . . ." She plucked the front of her damp dress away from her body, lifted her long damp hair off her neck again.

"I have to, too," he said.

"There's Amy," she said hopelessly.

He turned to stare at the young girl picking her way along the seawall under the willow branches. "She doesn't look like you," he said. There had to be time. He had to see her one more time again.

"She looks like her father," she said.

He stared at her daughter.

"They're rowing to it," she said.

"Rowing to what?"

"Their honeymoon. They're camping on Smith's Point for the rest of the summer."

"We made love there," he said. "That old gazebo, at the Greek Revival house. Don't you remember any of the good things?"

"I don't want to see you," she said. "I'm happy in my life."

His body gave off more heat than other bodies. She felt it rise from him, waft toward her. She closed her eyes.

Down on the beach, ushers were decorating the canoe with chains of daisies. Amy was helping to knot the stems.

In the distance, there was thunder again. A storm coming. "I have to go soon," he said again. He had promised his sons to see them. He was unsettled, uneasy as the weather.

"Rain's coming," she said fretfully.

"How old is she?" he said.

"Twelve. In August."

A month younger than Will and Otis. But taller. He turned to her again. "Good-bye then," he said desperately.

"Good-bye," she said. Her face looked as if she'd been kicked in the stomach.

"It should have been different," he said.

Hugh, on the terrace, happened to look up at about this time and see the man who had talked all afternoon to his wife bend toward her and kiss her swiftly on the cheek and leave without speaking to her or to anyone else, or even looking for anyone else to speak to, not even Connie, as if he had come for one reason only, to encounter Tina.

She sat as still as a statue after he was gone. But by the time Hugh, milling down the lawn with the crowd to see the bride and groom off in their garlanded canoe before the storm struck, got to where Tina had been sitting, she too was gone. Who was that man? Hugh wondered, vaguely aware that he should know.

He thought on the way home to ask. The night was heavy with the storm on its way, charged with catastrophe and the desired undesirable. In the dark, she touched the place on her face where Jack's mouth had been for one second.

"I love weddings," Amy sighed, in the back seat. "Wasn't Jenny beautiful, Mom?"

"All brides are beautiful," she said.

"I wanted this to be the most perfect day in my whole life," Amy said. "And it was."

"It wasn't in mine," Bo said.

"*Who* was it?" Hugh said again.

"Jack Troy."

"I saw you with him," Amy said dreamily. "He's handsome. He looks like Dan Rather, or Warren Beatty."

"Dan Rather doesn't look like Warren Beatty, so how could he?" Bo said.

"Shut up, Bo," Amy said. "They do look alike. Besides, where were you all day?"

"Fishing," Bo said.

"You don't fish at weddings," Amy said.

"I forgot he was coming," Hugh said. "That was Jack Troy?"

"When I get married," Amy said, "I'm going to have a wedding cake just like that, and my bridesmaidens are going to wear pale blue dresses with lavender hats and the maiden of honor will wear a lavender dress with a blue hat. With streamers. How will that be?"

"Lovely."

"Yucky," Bo said.

"But they will wear shoes. I don't think bare feet goes. Do you, Ma?"

"No," Tina said, in the dark. "I think shoes go."

"What will you wear?"

"Oh, something extravagant and gorgeous and aqua."

"Why was he here?"

"Friend of the groom." Once removed.

"Will you wear a white suit and give me away, Daddy?"

"Not on your life," Hugh said.

She laughed. "You will."

"I will," Bo said.

"Why didn't I recognize him?" Hugh said.

Why didn't I? she thought. "He's older," she said.

Amy grew very still in the back seat.

"You told me he was coming," Hugh said. But you didn't remind me, he thought. She had been jogging and dieting for a month. Heaven she is a woman, he had told her when she was finished getting dressed, loving the way she had made herself look. "Why didn't you remind me?"

"It wasn't important."

"I think it was," he said.

Amy heard him say it. There was probably no such thing as a perfect day, she glumly concluded.

They lay in bed staring at the ceiling in the dark. He took her hand.

"I thought it was all gone," she said dully. Her ears filled up with tears. She reached in the dark for the box of tissues on her night table.

"It's a momentary relapse," he said. "It will go away again." There was the Thirty Years War, but who ever heard of the Thirty Years Love? "Give it a week," he said. "I'm here. You can count on me."

She rolled toward him in the bed like a wave obliterating itself on a gentle beach.

He got out of bed after she was asleep and roamed into their sitting room and looked up the Keats ode again. But, why, why should unheard melodies be sweeter? he thought. Damn it, how could anything be sweeter than life on Stephen Street?

II

THE
DREAM

1

"It's a disease with him," Erica said. "He's given to women. The way some men are given to drink. Or to gambling."

They bounced along the dirt road to Smith's Point, Tina driving.

"Did he know you would be there? Did he call you before?"

He had no sense of propriety when it came to taking a woman he wanted. And she was the last to mind. Minded afterward. Never during. During, he was wonderfully focusing. Kept a girl very concentrated. Because he was. It was his gift.

"Did he?" Erica persisted.

"Yes," she said, steering around a puddle.

"Here we go again, then?"

It didn't matter whether the one he wanted belonged to someone else, or how many good reasons she might have for avoiding him. He took her anyway, if she was even slightly takable. Renunciation was not his style.

"Tina?"

"No!"

"Sure?"

"Yes."

"He's free."

"He's married."

"As good as free," Erica said. "And what about that Beryl that Connie says he's living with?"

"He's not, any more."

It had been a week. He hadn't called. She eased the car gently between the blackberry canes crowding the road.

"He hasn't changed, you know," Erica persisted. "You could see that, couldn't you?"

She had wanted to think he had. And that she had, too. At least enough to resist him when he would want her not to.

"It's all Darwinian," Erica said. "He will have adapted, not changed."

"Maybe that's what all of us do," she said. "He's survived."

"So far," Erica said.

"You were always so hard on him."

"And you were always so easy. You didn't give your friends the time of day when he came to town. Has he called you since?"

"But romantic love was our ideal, back then, not female friendship."

"And don't you think it still is?" Erica said.

They turned a bend in the road, driving slowly, because the road was rutted and bumpy. She laughed. "Not mine," she said.

"But has he?" Erica said.

"No."

Erica sighed. She had seen Jenny and David the day before, she said. "Speaking of romance. Cavorting in the cove. Skinny."

"It sounds as if you envied them."

"I did. Starting out fresh."

Tina poked the car slowly forward, clear of a ditch on the right. "I don't want to do that," she said, shuddering.

"Your tenses are showing already," Erica said. "See what I mean?"

"The wedding was a week ago. I'm still here. He hasn't called."

"He's waiting until your guard is down. So be careful. Your instinct to restore is a powerful one."

"It must be, if I've agreed to do this house," she said.

The Greek Revival house, a wreck, loomed ahead through the trees and brush. She stopped the car and they got out.

It was nearly a hundred and fifty years old and had been in the Smith family that long. The last resident Smith had died in it in 1969. It had stood empty ever since, except for a few years in the early 1970s when the heirs of the last Miss Smith had used it for a summer or two, then absentmindedly seemed to forget they owned it. Since then its deterioration had been nearly violent. The stone porch floors were crumbling and weed-ridden, and the columns holding up the porch roof were split from top to bottom. A few shutters hung askew at the windows. The rest leaned against the front of the house, as if exhausted and hopeless.

As her lawyer, Hugh had advised Erica from the start not to touch it with a ten-foot pole. It was not worth trying to save; he succinctly tried to demonstrate by plunging a broomstick into beams, floorboards, gutters, a raccoon's nest in the attic.

The two-story Ionic-columned portico in the center was flanked by two low hip-roofed wings decorated with slender Ionic pilasters. But the north wing had come loose from the central core of the house and listed alarmingly toward the beach. "Not to worry," Erica said. "What comes down can go up again. Look at that handsome cornice. Regardez that dentelle molding, that one-of-a-kind entablature. You don't see work of that kind every day. Do you realize those columns are individual tree trunks?"

"And filled with dry rot."

"Spoilsport. What's a little dry rot?"

Erica consulted a building engineer, who agreed with Hugh. The river, he pointed out, had undermined the foundations, which is why the north wing had departed from the center core. He thrust the same broomstick between the wing and its former connection and banged it back and forth from north to south, and Erica said, well, why not just jack it back in place and squeeze it together and bolt it nice and tight?

"And redirect the river?" Tina inquired.

"No," Erica said. "Just move the house back twenty feet."

"And dig a whole new cellar?"

"Why not?"

"And pour new footings?"

"Yes."

"But the engineer said the sill is rotted."

"The sill?" Erica said. "What is it to fix a little old sill?"

"It's not a little old sill, Erica. It's not a little old window-sill, or a little old doorsill. It's the *sill!* The main beam that goes under the perimeter of the whole bloody structure. The beam that rests on the foundation that supports the house. The termites have got it."

"If we can go to the moon," Erica said. "After all, we are smarter than termites." All it would take, she said again, would be to get it back on its pins and bolt it together, then jack it up on piles to repair the rotted joists and sills, and move it to a new foundation back from the river.

"And fix the squirrel holes in the roof, and the rotting clapboards, and reinforce the arches on the river side?"

"And replace the beams in the basement and the broken windows and the leaders and gutters and shutters."

"And do over the plumbing and the wiring and the kitchen?"

"And then find out what the original colors and wallpapers were, and start the fun part."

"But will we still be friends when the fun part is over?"

Still, she felt drawn to do it. The national style for sixty years. The temple style, Jefferson called it: a fitting expression of the ideals of the Republic. Yet, though born out of a sense of pride in civic and political virtue, no two were alike. Each one was imagined privately, each one an expression of a private ideal as well as a public one.

She stared up at it, a Greek temple in Brewerton, N.Y., complete with shutters, six-over-six windows, a captain's walk, a carriage house, and a gazebo. Ionic orders in an American woods on the banks of an American river. Why?

A rotting wooden carving ornamented the roofline. What

was it? It looked like nothing she had ever seen in any book she'd read or looked into on the style. A funny decorative doodad that didn't strike any bells. And then she recalled a Greek Revival mansion somewhere, a whaling captain's house in Nantucket, maybe, with an ornamental carving around the roof of stylized harpoon and blubber spade. And she remembered that the original owner of Erica's house, Elihu Smith, had owned the town's cotton mill. Which had become a woolen mill, and then a knitting mill, and then had finally knuckled under to polyesters and been abandoned. She had organized a campaign to save the building, and it had been saved. It was now a sail factory. And a dim recollection returned to her of the same design embossed on the walls in what had been Elihu's office. "I think it's a needle," she said. "A needle and a hook from a Jacquard drawloom."

"What is?" Erica said.

"That thing. Around the roof. Doesn't it look like a needle?"

Erica squinted up at it in the sun. "It could be. Yes, it is a needle, eye and all," she said. "See, you have an affinity for this house. You were made to do it."

She had already acknowledged to herself an affinity for it, its influence drawing her, but beyond that something more was drawing her, more than the pleasure of restoring it—another instinct, as if it were the very desuetude of the house that was contacting something inside of her that wanted to respond to it. A desire for disorder, when it was order she had so carefully established in her life? She felt uneasy as they waded toward it through fragile hip-high grasses.

The rotting ceiling boards of the porch sagged above

them. The clapboards, butt-joined to give the illusion of stone, were rotted, windows broken and boarded up, gutters hanging precariously from the eaves.

Yet standing on Elihu Smith's porch, dwarfed by his fluted walnut columns, she could look back out over his ruined gardens to the wrecked summerhouse his grandson had built and the straggling trellises and arbors of his great-grandson and the ruined carriage house, a mass of bare-bones lumber way down the point, and imagine it as it had been and how it could be again. And she could imagine him, too, arriving in America to make his fortune. Serious, hopeful, idealistic, leaving home and everything familiar to start over, make a new life in the new world.

And actually making it, too, in spite of all that must have thwarted him. Choosing a site for his mill. And then a site for his mansion, and paying the builder for it in cash, $4,000 in 1830. She had found the deed recorded in the county records. And wanting Greek Revival because it said what he wanted to say with his new house: something serious and hopeful, something even perhaps a little touched. The western part of the state, burned over in waves of religious revivals, Joseph Smith territory, territory of ecstatic, impossible visions, high hopes, and violent faiths, was dotted with it. Ancient Greece with a twist of Jefferson, an attic under a temple roof, rocking chairs behind Ionic orders. It made some utopian, democratic, touched, idealistic American declaration that was irresistible to her.

Possibility, perhaps, she thought. An architectural expression of a philosophical concept. Did her orderly life rule out the possibility of possibility?

Erica unlocked the door and they went into the spacious

entrance hall, the stairs growing up out of it like the branches of a tree, dividing, its arms extending left and right into the upstairs hall. The needle-and-hook motif was embossed on the ceiling and again around the walls of the rooms he had built to declare his faith in possibility. And in the rotted lintels over the windows, there was a suggestion of where it had first started; in the first lintel over the first Doric hut, Emerson had written. The tradition of possibility crumbling here into decay truly awesome.

She moved through the plaster and rubble-filled hall across the parlor and out onto the colonnaded porch on the river side, letting the spirit of the house overtake her, letting herself begin to imagine how to save it, how to know it well enough to begin to.

"Could it be just like it was again?" Erica wondered, beside her. "Exactly the way the Smiths had it, on the inside?"

"The house?" she said, starting.

"What else?" Erica said, staring at her.

She wandered away from Erica, off the porch onto the overgrown lawn. The smell of the warm grass, the sound of the waves lapping on the beach below, the sandpipers scurrying, the salt tide on the air, the wide ruffled water where she had swum with him. . . . A startled tern tried to distract her from its nest in the grass, and a beetle scurried over a flat rock. She crushed it with her foot, as if to crush the idea that scurried through her mind, a species of the disorderly she should want to resist. "It could be," she said vaguely, Erica beside her again, persisting. But suppose they hadn't gotten it right. Who would want to repeat it?

They really might have done it all wrong, she thought, in

Mrs. Smith's parlor. Might have stumbled around it in the light of Argand lamps, tripping over the splayed legs of "Grecian" chairs from Sears Roebuck (so wonderfully classical), might have sat on a horsehair Empire couch, staring at braided hair ornaments and wax flowers under bells and matching mercury-glass vases on the mantel. And back to that, why a mantel in the first place? Did Greek temples have furnaces and fireplaces, hearths, chimneys, flues, tinderboxes, and fire tools? It was all innovation and possibility. "No point in doing it the way the Smiths had it," she said.

Even though it was possible to know almost exactly how they did have it. There was plenty to go on. Most of the contents had been sold at auction, but she had seen some of the furniture, and there were descriptions. Even a few odd nine-teenth-century pieces nobody had wanted to go to the trouble of moving remained. There were hints and clues to go on in the debris in every room, and an album of interiors, watercolor drawings, found in the attic. An inventory of the contents made when Elihu died even existed, as well as a draft in his own hand of a letter to his mother in England describing the new house to her and its first furnishings.

She could construct a catalog of objects from these sources, expand it from contemporary inventories and period catalogs. She could photograph the rooms, make scaled elevations of every wall, re-create the past as they had lived it, note every hook and nail and screw hole, check around every door and window for evidence of curtain fixtures, steam paper off walls till she got back to the original layer. She could prepare sketches of the rooms on graph paper, place on it scale models of the furnishings, play with bits of colored pasteboard until the rooms came alive, think how they would have lived, what odds and ends and knickknacks they would have had.

But why? Suppose all the research led to was the conclusion that the Smiths could have done it better if they'd only known how?

"What, then?" Erica said.

"A new thing," she said, uneasily. "Have it like it was on the outside. That's not hard. But have it like it should have been on the inside." Have the history of it, the idealistic prototypes for it, the appearance of it, the idiosyncratic, touched American-ness of it, and have the designed interior coherence that educated hindsight allowed.

And even have something else, while she was at it: a sublimation in the dream for having other things the way she might once have wanted them. But don't let Erica know that.

"Have it all, you're saying?" Erica said.

Almost all, she thought. She pulled a long spear of timothy out of the dry grasses on the ruined lawn.

"Will it work?"

"In theory."

"But in effect?"

She imagined it, the symmetry, the balance, the harmony. The perfection of something hard to perfect. The jewel colors, the windows chastely festooned. Columns, space, classic space and classic forms. A fitting expression of a certain idea. She bit down on the timothy between her teeth. "Why the hell not?" she said.

2

A mile north of where they stood on the Point, Mickey Kolyrion's cruiser, engines thrumming, propellers churning, left its berth at the Brewerton boatyard and headed down the river toward New York. Past the Statue of Liberty, it would travel through the Narrows into the Sound and on out to the Atlantic, where it would be docked by his captain (a cousin on his mother's side) in a bay behind a rented mansion on the ocean in East Hampton.

He was alone on the bridge. In a stateroom below, Jeanne dozed under the influence of Dramamine. Jeanne was not a good sailor. His crew (all cousins and distant cousins) was swabbing decks and polishing brass and coiling lines and doing the other nautical chores that crews were supposed to do, and that he had sent them to a power-squadron course to learn to do.

Through his binoculars, he saw the two women on the Point. He waved. Erica waved back. Tina stared at him under her hand raised against the sun.

"If it's true about him," Erica said, "why do they let him prowl the earth the way he does?"

The yacht moved downriver purposefully and fast, its wake racing back toward them. "It's one of the minor drawbacks of a democracy," Tina said. "You just can't clap your undesirables in the slammer. There has to be a certain amount of legal ado."

"I heard Hugh was making some."

"A little. About Clarice."

"But who cares about poor old Clarice now?" Erica said. "What about the other?"

We know more than we used to, and there is more to know, she thought. We have to do things we never did before. Look at things and see a shape that wasn't there before. Life is more hazardous than it was. New kinds of danger bubble up around the edges of ordinary life and trickle down among us, establishing themselves as ordinary dangers. But they aren't. In the old days, anyone might expect to know over the course of a lifetime, by sight or name at least, a murderer, an arsonist, an embezzler. Every small town had such, the way every village had its idiot and its gambling man and its adulterous choir singer. Now it's come to be that anyone might just as easily know a drug runner, or a mass murderer, or a terrorist. Someone we sat next to in the third grade will build a nuclear bomb in his garage and threaten to explode it, and we won't be all that surprised to learn it on the evening news. Life is more hazardous than it was.

"Tina?"

Are we helpless? Are we stupid, that we've let it happen? she thought.

"He's very careful," she said. "He likes his freedom." Born free, he was going to stay free, no matter who paid. Exercised his right to it as if it were inalienable, constitutionally guaranteed to him to move to any frontier that opened, drugs one he didn't see any reason to pass up.

"How careful can he be if he's doing it right in Brewerton?"

"Is he? In that building?"

"That's what I've heard."

"You invited him to your party."

"Everyone does. I don't want to end up in the quarry," Erica said.

They turned away.

He had wanted them to watch him out of sight. To be disdained, especially on his incredibly outstanding yacht, filled him with helpless wrath.

Two months ago, it never would have happened. As recently as that, his reputation had been intact, the old rumors about Clarice ancient gossip no one took seriously, his image in town at best good old boy, at worst an upstart. He didn't mind that. That was America, wasn't it? He was friends with the mayor and the presidents of both banks. They had the priests to dinner on Easter Sunday. He supported the arts council and a dozen other causes. He had been to college, had a year of law school. He hobnobbed with the town council, the Protestant clergy, even the librarians. He was a member of the Chamber of Commerce. He hadn't made a false move in twenty years that anyone knew about.

He slumped in his chair in the shade of the bridge. Yet everything was crumbling. He owed Fulgencio, beyond what he owed Raul, $3.5 million. It should be nothing to Fulgencio. But he wanted it anyway, the whole thing, every penny.

He had never met Fulgencio, never even spoken to him on the phone. Fulgencio did not speak on the phone, Raul said. Others spoke for him. Fulgencio had many phone numbers, all of which were changed every few weeks. Fulgencio seldom left his house in Miami either, but conducted all his business through his sons and nephews and cousins, his wife, his nieces, and the spouses of all these faithful relations.

He stared at the river, rushing by like his world rushing to destruction. But the whole country was rushing to hell, and no one saw it. The Fourth of July and everyone partying, congratulating themselves on two hundred years of freedom, and the immigrants pouring in like it was 1850 and you needed Chinese coolies to build the railroads. He felt little hate balls forming in his head, popping and bursting. The pumps were running out of gas. The country was in hock to the Arabs. Illegal Mexicans and Cubans and Indians and Orientals were making out like bandits in the welfare lines. And the cement heads in Washington were banging their secretaries on their desks and saluting the flag and climbing poles and parading up and down Main Street like there was no tomorrow. They were assassinating U.S. diplomats in Beirut and planning coast-to-coast mass naturalizations to celebrate two hundred years of mismanagement, and trying to throw a net over him for something that thousands of others were getting away with.

Fulgencio had twelve boats and a plane, the boats for the marijuana, the plane for the coke and the cash. Coke in, cash out. The coke was little. The cash was big. Almost as bulky as a ton of grain: $300 million—nearly a million a day. In fifty- and hundred-dollar bills, the logistics of it, the deployment, was a daily headache. But at least they didn't ask questions in Bahamanian banks. Just emptied the suitcases and totted up the books.

Fulgencio kept careful books. Yet as entrepreneurs in the trade went, he was a nobody. What was $300 million a year in relation to an industry that grossed $30 billion, and that was probably only the half of it? One percent. And he, MK, owed one percent of that one percent, one one-thousandth of Ful- gencio's market, and Fulgencio cared!

But Fulgencio was a tidy man, Raul kept saying. Thrifty and close. It was well known of him that he was not one to shrug off bad debts.

When Fulgencio did leave the house, it was as a creditor visiting his debtors. He traveled in a black stretch Mercedes, Raul said, with a driver and two bodyguards, all of whom wore guns—one under the coat and one strapped to the ankle. Mickey did not wish to be favored with a visit from Fulgencio. With luck, a visit would not be necessary.

He had made mistakes before. But he had always been lucky. From the beginning, he had had good luck in his career, even when he was in the Army, just starting his life.

The idea behind going into the Army in the first place, his father said, was not because Uncle Sam wanted you. What Uncle Sam wanted had nothing to do with it. It was because you wanted Uncle Sam. Uncle Sam could teach you something to use when you got out. Uncle gave you the goods to get the goodies.

He was trained in supplies. He understood supplies almost instinctively. They arrived. They had to be disbursed. For everything that passed through the disburser's hands, a percentage could be removed and sold on the side. That in a nutshell was supplies: supplies generated supplies. He got so used to this idea that if he didn't get his percentage off the top every twenty-four hours, he felt as if the Army had cheated him out of his due that day and was morally obliged to make it up to him the next day. He had nearly $10,000 put away by the time he was honorably discharged.

He felt sick. His stomach churned and rolled like the water the yacht plowed through. He closed his eyes, lay his head back on the headrest. He had bought suits, a topcoat, good shoes. He had bought an expensive fedora and a brand-new car. A big blue De Soto with automatic transmission and power steering and overdrive. It cost him $3,700, and he paid cash for it.

That was more than his father had paid for the house they lived in, he, his father and mother, and Frank. And the car was almost as big as the house. He had hated that house, hated the sight of his new car parked next to it. He wanted to see it parked in the driveway of another kind of house in another kind of neighborhood. It had been his idea of respectability, then, to live in a ranch house with shutters with cutouts in them and a lawn out front with evergreens on it.

After his discharge from the Army, he got a job in the liquor store in Brewerton, Burd's. While at Burd's, he met Clarice Heard at a dance at the Y. A fatal meeting. If only he hadn't gone to the Y that night! A chance meeting, a little thing like asking a girl to dance could change your life forever. If only you could know things like that at the time. Twenty years later, and he still hadn't heard the end of it.

What attracted him to Clarice was her blond hair—he liked blonds, Jeanne was a blond—her fuzzy pink sweater set, and the way she kept looking at him over the shoulder of the boy she was dancing with. She wore also a gray flannel skirt, white socks, and penny loafers. Her blond hair was in a pageboy that swung all in a piece, as if it were a wig, when she danced. He asked her to dance. (First mistake.) She pressed herself against him without any encouragement on his part. Do you want to leave? he asked her. (Second mistake.) He didn't need to ask twice. He took her to the quarry. She was loose, but she wouldn't go all the way because it wasn't a real date. Besides, she had to be home within a few minutes of the time the dance was supposed to end. Her father kept close tabs on her. He got her home on time and made a real date.

He didn't stay long at Burd's. Didn't like the retail business. One day a cousin he had forgotten he had came in to buy a bottle of Four Roses. Another piece of luck.

Mickey had nieces and nephews and cousins and aunts and uncles coming out of his ears. His mother was one of twelve children, all of whom lived in or near Brewerton, and all of whom had a minimum of four children. One sister had twelve. Two brothers had ten apiece, and so on. When he was a kid in Brewerton, Mickey had, on his mother's side alone, sixty-two first cousins. There were also some twenty-odd Kolyrion cousins scattered around. Some of these cousins had children Mickey's age. Some of his first cousins once removed he had never even met; there were so many of them nobody could keep

[123]

track of them. Some of his uncles and aunts he hadn't seen in years. And some of his relatives had done very well for themselves. He remembered now how the day that his cousin had come into Burd's it had occurred to him to make a list of his relatives, with plus signs beside the names of those who had done well and minus signs beside the rest. When he quit Burd's, he took with him twenty-four bottles of Four Roses and decided to visit twenty-four of the ones with the plusses.

He had luck. His mother's oldest sister's oldest daughter was married to an expansive, cheerful man named John Huffman, who with his partner, John Johansson, had formed a construction company and was building a vast housing development out in the sticks. It just so happened they were looking for someone they could trust to keep track of . . . supplies. Who better than a first cousin trained by the U.S. Government as a supply officer?

They took Mickey to see the land they were clearing. From the knoll where they stood looking down into the broad valley to be transformed into ticky-tacky, Mickey counted nine pieces of earth-moving equipment. How full of possibilities were woods, he thought.

Outdoor work, but well paid. Well paid it was. In February, when he started, the woods, hundreds of acres of them, were not bare and brown in his eyes, but abloom with big yellow bulldozers, Caterpillars, back hoes, and so on and so forth. It was no skin off his cousin's husband's teeth when one of them mysteriously vanished in the night. In fact, it was in the nature of the work they did that no one noticed the disappearance for several days. Weird, but not to worry, John Huffman said. He leased them, and the company that owned them had them insured. Nobody lost, except the insurance company, but who cared about them?

It was amazing how much earth-moving equipment brought on the black market. The Israelis had an insatiable demand for it and paid near-new prices for just about anything you could get them. Of course, after he got started he didn't confine himself to Huffman and Johansson. The demand was too great; the Huffman and Johansson supplies too limited. There were other developments in other woods. His bank account grew by leaps and bounds, even though he had to split everything fifty-fifty with his friend the tractor-trailer owner.

He had been working for Huffman and Johansson only a week when he met John Johansson's daughter Jeanne, blond, beautiful, and very good, pure as a nun. He fell in love with her. She was eighteen, ready to graduate from high school, and already employed after school as a secretary at the light-and-power company, with a guarantee after graduation of sixty dollars a week to start and a discount on all appliances.

And then Clarice Heard told him she was pregnant. She expected him to marry her, of course. He had, of course, promised he would, if anything happened.

It was just incredible how hysterical an unmarried girl could get, back in 1956, about a pregnancy. Clarice was as cool as a cucumber, till her period was late. Then she changed, turned into a veritable tigress, as if she were fighting for her life! Mickey could still sweat to remember the terrible scenes, the sobbing, the crying, the begging, the noise, the confusion! But he was not going to throw away his future on Clarice Heard.

He tried accusing her of not knowing whose it was. But she took such a fit at this that he had to back off.

[125]

He pondered it and pondered it, and all the while Clarice was whimpering and begging and calling him up and telling him she had thrown up that morning, her mother was going to get suspicious, it was going to start to show, reminding him of his promise to marry her. And all the while he was getting crazier and crazier about Jeanne, who he couldn't get to first base with. Nothing of Jeanne between collarbone and knees could be touched by human hands.

There was only one practical way out of the mess. The essential goal was to avoid being trapped. He told Clarice he would marry her. Don't call me for a few days, he said. I'll call you when I get it all worked out. When will that be? she asked. When? When? When? She didn't want to go to college. She wanted to get married. Soon, he said, sweating. (He makes me so happy, so happy. Did she write that in her diary? She had told him about the diary she kept, and how she told it everything.)

It was the middle of April. A freak heat wave descended on the Northeast. People had to throw off their winter blankets and nightclothes and take the storm windows down, so they could catch a breath of air and get to sleep at night. It was humid and sticky, like the dog days of midsummer. The temperature reached 96.

He called her at around suppertime one night during this week. (Third and final mistake.) Everything's ready, he told her. He had a plan. Everything was going to be all right. Are we getting married? she whispered into the phone. Yes. But don't tell anyone. And wear your bathing suit. In case. Don't tell a soul. Sneak out after they go to bed. In case what? she said. In case we get caught. We can say we were just going swimming.

It was the hottest night of the spell, especially hot in the river valley towns, so hot that people went to bed much later than usual. Mickey's own bedroom, which he shared with his brother Frank, was as hot as the back of a bus. He waited for her at the corner. She had her bathing suit on under her blouse and shorts. And a dress, slip, underwear, hosiery, shoes, gloves, a hat, and a nightgown in a small suitcase. He suggested they take a dip before they drove to Elkton, Maryland, where they could be married without a blood test or a license.

They did an autopsy on the body when they found it. Guess what. Clarice wasn't pregnant. So where did that leave him? In luck again. No motive. If they had found her diary, they might have found a motive. But they didn't.

As it turned out now, twenty years later, her sister, Marion, had taken the diary, and to protect Clarice from the hideous stigma of impurity, which was more heinous than having been murdered because of it, concealed it among her own belongings. What did it say about him, that diary? What ancient trick did Clarice confess to in it?

Two years ago, the information she had burning a hole in her conscience, Marion Heard, living in a trailer park in Florida, composed a letter to the district attorney in Brewerton County, and told him what she had and what she suspected. But this man was lackadaisical, and he failed to act on the letter. It was left to Hugh Gardiner, when he decided to run for the job of D.A., to learn of it through the legal fraternity's grapevine. It was just the kind of case guaranteed to wake the slumbering electorate.

Through his own dense and tangled grapevine, with its shoots and tendrils in every law office and police station and courthouse in the county, Mickey had also heard about Marion's letter. And he had tried to find Marion. But she had already moved, no forwarding address.

Still, Hugh Gardiner was very thorough. He liked to win. And he almost never didn't win. But neither did Mickey almost never not win. Mickey had a second cousin working in Hugh's office. Gloria kept him posted on Hugh's so-far futile attempts to find Marion and the diary. When he found it, Gloria was to relieve him of it before he had a chance to photocopy it.

Afterward, he told his brother what he had done, and Frank agreed to swear the two of them had played pinochle in the cellar the whole night. Frank was believed. And Mickey never even went before a grand jury. Jack Troy and Tina Penney, who had actually seen him leaving the quarry that night, both left town before there was even any talk of calling a grand jury together. And it wasn't known in 1956 that tire treads were as incriminating as fingerprints or dental records. Interest fizzled out. He married Jeanne. Frank married Doreen. And life went on in its ordinary way.

Until now. Now the net. Just when he had made up his mind to get out before he was dealt out. Three years was about one year too long already.

From time to time, he raised his binoculars to view a passing boat or a particular mansion on the Palisades or to give the horizon a quick scan in a 180-degree arc, as if he were in some invisible conning tower, scanning for an enemy. But for the most part, he stared straight ahead, brooding.

The yacht was moving through the broad, majestic section of the river between the cloisters and the Palisades, and he thought of Doreen when he looked at the cloisters. Doreen had recently gotten religion and wanted Frank, according to Frank, to make a clean breast of things. Cold panic was engendered in Mickey by this. He knew what insane things religion could make a person do. Doreen went to her new church four or five times a week, every week. Doreen didn't believe in luck. Doreen believed in the wrath of God.

Huffman and Johansson went broke about a year after he and Jeanne were married, but luck was with him then, and he had a job within a week on Wall Street. He enrolled at City College at night, because Jeanne wanted him to.

He had to start at the bottom at his job, but even there the profits were nothing to sneeze at. He got to do the widows; the other apprentice got the G.I.s. The really brilliant thing about that operation was how the minds behind it got their hands on legitimate mailing lists, and how they sent out the literature beforehand, so all you had to do was a little soft sell. A couple of years later, the big fish, the organizers of the boiler room and their mysterious backers, all went to Leavenworth for their tricks, while the small-fry like Mickey quietly drifted away into other dark streams.

Wall Street had more to offer in the '60s than bilking gullible widows. With Frank, Mickey bought a foundering science company. About the only assets it had were a desk and a telephone and some stationery and some certificates. But that was enough. He flew to Chicago (his very first airplane flight, Northwest Orient Airlines; he didn't like heights), and got it listed on the Chicago exchange. Then he flew back to New York to trade it. He and Frank opened accounts under twenty different aliases at brokerage houses all over town. Placed orders everywhere, buy orders for the struggling but dynamic little science company, and sell orders for their blue-chip stocks.

Didn't have to hand over the blue-chip certificates for three days. And in those three days, stock in his go-go little science company was in big demand. After the bidding for Compu-Sci went as high as he figured it would, he sold his 300,000 shares of it, which he had bought for a dollar a share, and which through his puff had surged to five, bought back all his blue chips, and watched Compu-Sci go down, down, down. He never got caught. And anyway, he hadn't done anything that wasn't legal. And he had had expenses. He had advertised heavily in newspapers and over the radio, and he had had a direct-mail and a telephone campaign in advance, and all that had cost him close to a $100,000 right there.

Yes, he was lucky. In some part of his mind, he even believed that God answered Jeanne's prayers for his success for some mysterious reasons of His own. In other words, although Jeanne did not speak to him very often, he believed she spoke for him.

He made a little money in a credit-card scam in the late '60s, and a lot with another science company that he rode up in the early '70s. But drugs was the all-time best moneymaker, though it wasn't easy to break into, if you weren't from south of the border.

It all started out as a legitimate import-export business. Jeanne had found out about the credit-card scam and threatened to leave him unless he cleaned up his act. She meant it. Credit cards were almost as sacred to Jeanne as her rosary beads. So he bought the old ice and coal company building, had new and very classy letterheads printed up and a Telex machine installed, and he started Impex.

It was all aboveboard, and it was doing well. Until his

main trading partner in Korea went belly up. He lost a fortune, the whole ball of wax. Had to pledge his house to the bank. He was barely making enough to put food on the table. Naturally, he had to recoup.

Fortunately, he had met Raul in the somewhat flaky world of imports and exports. And Raul got him in with Fulgencio. It was a question of supplies. The treasury had to be replenished, one way or another. They began to distribute for Fulgencio on a very small scale at first. Just enough to build up Fulgencio's trust and establish their credit. And then enough to get his house back from the bank. And then enough to reactivate Impex and start to live well enough again to generate the deference without which life was hardly worth living. And then enough to get themselves the particular territory in the city that they wanted. And a dealer to run it.

And then, he and Raul made what in retrospect had probably been a mistake. They bought a boat of their own, just at the time everyone was switching to coke. For coke you needed a plane. And there they were with a boat. Still, it wasn't hard times. The country wasn't exactly switching en masse. Marijuana was still in demand. But there were nasty rumors that smart-ass hippie farmers were hybridizing their own. Two hundred and fifty dollars an ounce for she-weed retail, and a decent plant could produce two big pounds of bootiful boo buds. Developed in Hawaii. Maui Wowie. He never touched the stuff himself. Never get high on what you supply. Loyal to booze. You knew what it did to you.

As he rehearsed his history for himself, trying to find in it a route to his exit from it, his eyes scanned the Manhattan shore and skyline. Passing the Village, he brought naked male sunbathers into focus on the piers and lingered on them till they were too far away to see. Due east, on the other side of the island, was the building condemned and sealed by the city, but unsealed by Raul, where their dealer dealt. The building had been free. The boat not. Still, setbacks and all, they did all right. Until one fine night, when it turned out the boat wasn't as seaworthy as it was cracked up to be by the fisherman they bought it from, and fully loaded, sank off the Florida keys. They owed Fulgencio for the cargo. Everything was done on credit in the business.

Go the class way, Mickey decided. (Another little mistake.) So they bought a second boat, a new one, custom made, cost $250,000 because of the radar scanner and the night-vision scope. Fulgencio put up the money. Fulgencio had faith! You see, Jeanne. He trusts me. Jeanne, of course, thought Fulgencio was financing the shrimp and chicken business.

The real class way, as he looked back on it, would have been coke. So small, so neat, so easily transported. So lucrative. They could have bought a plane instead of a boat, hired a pilot. (He couldn't stand heights himself, ever since falling out of a tree once and breaking his arm.) They could have gotten their very own village, all growing and processing just for them. But Raul wanted to stick with pot. They chartered a shrimp boat after the first boat sank, took it down from New Orleans, waited offshore one dark night for a flotilla of canoes to paddle the stuff out to them. And thanked God for the Colombian Coast Guard all around them, poised to shoot the sharks and barracuda that made the warm South American waters so uninviting. They didn't do that again.

They were doing fine with the new boat. Even though

they had to have four of them in on it, Raul and a friend, and Mickey and Frank. And even though it cost them $50,000 a night for the two men who off-loaded the bales. But Jeanne either neglected to speak for him one week, or Something Else Happened, because one night the new boat met up with the U.S. Coast Guard, which seized it. They never saw it or its cargo again. But it wasn't traced to them either, because it was registered under aliases.

And then someone from Fulgencio's organization phoned one night, late, to remind him of what they owed as a group and of what he, Mickey, personally owed. Mickey had felt a cold dread seize him that night, a sick churning in the pit of his stomach. Help me, he prayed.

And then out of the blue, another call. Fulgencio was offering to lend him some more, to get started again. See, God was on Mickey's side!

This time, the four sat down together and got logical. Florida was too far away. Besides, it was getting too risky. U.S. warships had joined the Coast Guard in the Gulf. The government was panicking. You had to go as far east as Bermuda to stay clear of them. Why couldn't they get a nice innocent-looking yacht and arrange for a freighter to meet them fifty miles off the Hamptons? It was a highly original idea. In 1976, it had never been tried before.

They put a consortium together. Leased this very palatial place in East Hampton, $20,000 for the season, so magnificent it made his house in Brewerton look like poor folks. And they planned. The planning was crucial. Detail was all. He was being supermeticulous. He had to be.

He was taking Jeanne to see the house for the first time.

And in the fall, when everything was ready, the first big M.J. transaction in northern waters would take place, MK's very own brain child. If everything went according to plan, he would be able to pay off Fulgencio, buy Jack Troy, buy Doreen and Frank, buy Marion Heard, and buy the Attorney General himself to get Hugh Gardiner off his case. And retire.

He began to sweat as they turned into the choppy waters of the Narrows. He always broke out into a sweat just before he was about to be seasick.

3

Jack Troy stared out the window of his office. He was unhappy. A tiny silver plane straddled the space between the twin buildings of the World Trade Center, whose monolithic slabs obstructed his former view of the harbor and the Statue of Liberty the way Denise was obstructing other vistas of his freedom. Denise would not divorce him. That was slab A. And Denise would not sell their art collection so he could afford to divorce her. That was slab B. The buildings hovered. The plane disappeared, a transient connection only between the things that stalled him. In the privacy of his office, he smote his forehead and groaned his wife's name out loud.

On his desk console, the private number known only to his family lighted up. It was as if Denise had heard him speak her name. He did not want to talk to her this morning. He had given his secretary instructions to intercept the calls on 5305. After a moment, the lighted square went dark. He looked at his watch. It had to have been Denise. Mona would still be sleeping at ten of ten. And the boys were in French class, vying for a spot in the *Guinness Book of World Records* for number of times having failed French 1.

He gazed out the window and frowned. Another tiny jet crossed the tiny strip of airspace the twin slabs still allowed him. He was not at all happy.

He reread the article in front of him. The *Times* reported that the New York art season had just come to an official climax with sales of American folk paintings at the major auction houses that had stunned even the most jaded observers of what otherwise sane people would pay for a work of art. (Or made them look uneasily at their European masters and enviously at the naive portraits of anonymous American limners.) If Jack Troy had had his way, the Troy collection of nineteenth-century American folk art would have gone on the block, too. But the Troy Collection still belonged to the Troys. Where Denise was involved, he got his way a lot less often than he liked to think he did.

To make matters worse, in her eagle-eyed monitoring of trends in the fickle art world, Denise had begun to observe a phenomenon that made Jack's heart sink. Auction prices for restored American paintings were coming in consistently lower than prices for unrestored paintings.

From the beginning, he had insisted on restoring every piece they bought as nearly as possible to its original condition, whereas Denise had argued for merely cleaning the grime away and leaving the effects of time to be seen. He had prevailed. And even though she now tactfully suggested that the trend was a passing one and would be forgotten, Jack was alarmed. He wanted to sell. Trends had a way of becoming unbreachable standards! Besides, Bicentennial fever had driven prices up, and he was afraid of a post-Bicentennial deflation. His instinct was to jingle off the collection while the jingling was good. Liquidity was what he wanted, not a second-rate collection to decorate Denise's many walls.

Ninety blocks north of him, Denise was also staring out of a window. Though Beryl was the first woman Jack had ever moved out to live with, Beryl was not the first woman Jack had thought he was in love with, since marrying. But Denise had ridden them all out, and she had had no reason to believe she would not ride Beryl out. Beryl would one day vaporize, like those before her, and like those no doubt to follow her, and Jack would return. But Beryl had been gone for a month now. And where was Jack?

The first time she had learned of an infidelity of his, Denise, with the hard edge of a copy of *National Geographic,* had, among other spontaneous acts of fury, cracked him smartly on the nose. The permanent bump this had raised still gave her a satisfying sense of justice every time she noticed it. He had tried to hit her back, swinging wildly with one arm, while he held his extremely painful nose with the other. But she had ducked, and he had stayed, bump and all. Traded off bump for grind, as it were. The marriage the grind. But what one worth its salt wasn't? Denise said. They all required work. Negotiation, deals, compromises, bargains, trade-offs. This was the stuff of marriage, and second nature to Denise. She actually relished their long-drawn-out grapple toward what she told him would be harmony, and she secretly hoped they would not find it too soon. For where would the fun be, if the struggle ended?

Among other things Denise had decided were best, besides one intact marriage, two children, and a collection of American folk art, were two parents. Jack's illegitimacy had bothered her from the start. Marry a bastard? Not what she had in mind for herself.

When confronted with an obstacle, Denise's mind operated like a piece of earth-moving equipment. In 1959, it had seemed inappropriate to her that the last name she was going to take as her own and go through life with was in fact her future mother-in-law's mother's maiden name. She thought it would be best for all concerned if Jack's mother and father married. But he's dead, Jack had pointed out. Did you ever see the death certificate? Denise replied.

Jack knew that Mona was capable of telling a little white lie now and then to cover her tracks, and he didn't doubt that Denise, if his father was alive and single, and if she marshaled her prodigious energies in the service of her goal, could find him and even engineer such a ceremony. But he immediately disabused Denise of any idea she might have of his then changing his name. Jack Troy he was, and Jack Troy he would stay. So what was the point of going to all the trouble? In any of the real ways these things mattered, he was legitimate, a legitimate self-made man. It didn't matter that his mother and father had never been married to each other. It didn't matter!

Nothing ventured, nothing gained was Denise's outlook. And she never moved on two obstacles simultaneously anyway.

First things first. She had a long talk with Mona, explained her objections, outlined her objectives, brushed lightly on the delicate matter of Mona's upkeep. By 1959, Mona had been divorced from Captain Price for three or four years; the alimony was woefully small; she had learned to hate Panama with a passion. New York was where she wanted to be. It could perhaps be arranged, Denise murmured. Jack was doing very well. Mona sweetly revealed the name of the long-lost father from Chattanooga and hinted that she might indeed have exaggerated, though only for Jack's sake, when she told him his father was dead. Denise took it from there.

There was something quite awesome about Denise, actually: her fashion model's looks, her ash-blond bangs and pageboy, the elan with which she could toss an $8,000 fur coat over her husky shoulders just to go to the supermarket. Her efficiency, her thoroughness, the dauntless execution of her visions: they were all quite affecting to observe.

She was good at research, for instance. She had been a history major at Smith. When they began collecting art, she turned her research skills easily to the art world, researched each piece as they bought it, documented it, traced its provenance, authenticated it as well as it could be authenticated, and then published an article about it. Which had, of course, her very calculated effect of enhancing its value. It was nothing short of astonishing the way she had singlehandedly used her research techniques to increase the collection's value. Simply thrilling, too, the way she got the idea of offering to lend this piece or that to a museum, which she had made a point of ascertaining beforehand lacked an example of what she had. And once, she arranged to send the whole collection on tour through the

South. For this feat, she wrote the exhibition catalog and a flock of articles about the collection that appeared in magazines all over the country. The Troy Collection of nineteenth-century American folk art had been invited as far north as Wilmington.

When applying her research skills to locating Jack's father, it was also just amazing how after only one day in the New York Public Library poring over the social notes in the Chattanooga papers, she ascertained that one Colonel Harrison Bringhurst had retired from the Army in 1954, at age sixty, and moved to Hendersonville, North Carolina.

Her wedding was only two months away at the time, probably not long enough to bring about the result she was after, but she wrote to him anyway.

After a silence of many weeks, which Denise sympathetically could well imagine was one of consternation, a reply came. Dear Miss May, he wrote. He did indeed travel to New York on occasion, but always in the company of his wife of forty years. He, of course, would very much like to meet her and her fiancé, whose mother he had known during the Depression, but his wife was poorly, etc., and such a trip at this time would put an undue strain on her.

Denise understood perfectly! She and her fiancé were planning a post-honeymoon trip to the Great Smokies, she replied in a sweet note. (They weren't, but one could quickly be arranged.) Perhaps a meeting at their hotel, not far from Hendersonville, in Asheville, home of Thomas Wolfe, could also be arranged?

She was well Denise Troy by that time, and she had to be content with the maiden name of her mother-in-law's mother, but she had accomplished with relatively little effort what no one else in Jack Troy's life had ever even imagined doing: she had produced a father, at least informally, for a man she believed had always wanted one.

Thus it was that at the age of twenty-four, Jack Troy shook his sixty-five-year-old parent's hand for the first time on the veranda of an inn in Asheville, North Carolina. He had, childishly, counted on at least a physical resemblance, since he did not take after his mother in his looks. But his father was long-boned and wiry and fair-skinned. And Jack was of average height, and stocky, and dark. The colonel's eyes were a sparky, yellow-flecked Presbyterian sort of green, and Jack's were that shade of blue that, when they first met, had made Denise think of the Aegean.

What does a father say to a son he had never seen before? The colonel and his son awkwardly exchanged a little surface information, as any two strangers meeting on a hotel porch in a southern resort might, and then they turned and walked down the long veranda together, away from Denise, who tactfully departed for a stroll in the gardens. The colonel told his son how it had happened. Jack listened intently, curiously. Of course, he wanted to know. And of course, he did not hold it against the man. He understood the complications of a man's life, the temptations. These things happened. But he listened as much for nuance as for fact. Did he have a conscience? Did he have feelings? Did he have remorse? Was he a kind man? Was he good? Jack wanted him to have been good.

It had happened in the fall of 1934, the colonel began. His young wife, an asthmatic from childhood, had gone to stay with her family in Arizona for a few months. The damp smoky autumns in Tennessee were hard on her lungs. He was very lonely. He met Mona Thile at a card party at her cousin's house. Cousin Edna, he said. Cousin Edna's husband and the colonel were boyhood friends. Do you remember Cousin Edna? Jack had tried for so many years to forget her that he almost had. Still, yes, he said, vaguely, so as not to interrupt the story. He did remember her, if he searched. He did, a little. The man brushed his hand over his eyes as if to brush away a memory. I hardly know how it all happened, he murmured, his accent soft and southern. It happened so fast, so sudden. I never understood how I could have done what I did. She was only eighteen. I was forty. It was all my fault, believe me. I had been the soul of honor up to then. But she was a bewitchin' girl. Lovely.

Jack did believe him. He could see what a good man he really was, what an honorable man, though not, he suspected, an overly intelligent one. He must have gotten his own brains from Mona.

His wife came home for Christmas, much improved, the colonel said, and with the glad news that she was expecting a child, their second. Mona came to him within the week to tell him that she, too, was pregnant. What could he do? Two women in that condition, and he was married to one of them. And had one child besides. And his career in the Army to think of. And the Depression.

He sent money to Mona for twelve years, until she married. Jack wondered if he was supposed to thank him for this support, which he could imagine must have been a deprivation, on a captain's salary, in the Depression. He did thank him, and the colonel said, I don't deserve any thanks. I deserved to be horsewhipped and I wasn't. I got away scot-free. Your mother bore the whole brunt. How is she? She's well, Jack said. Please

[142]

remember me to her, his father said, bowing a little, in his courtly old-fashioned way. Ah've never forgotten her, believe me. Jack inquired politely about the three half-sisters he learned he had, and he thought he could see by the way the man looked at him that the daughters were fine, but that he was looking at his only son, and yet at no relation at all.

But Jack didn't care about the man's feelings. He had his own to deal with. He was what he was because of a card party, for God's sake. He thought wistfully of Mona, and he thought of how he would have preferred to have heard the story from her, rather than from a stranger.

Diffidently, his father asked him if he still had the collection of lead soldiers he had given Jack's mother for him. Oh, yes, Jack said. I've never parted with it. (Except for that once, when he had given it to Tina to show his love for her.) When he acquired it, at the auctioning of a deceased friend's estate, the colonel went on, it was said to be the finest, most complete collection of Civil War miniatures in the South. Someday, it would be worth a small fortune. Jack made a mental note to himself to look into this when he got back to New York. He doubted that it was true. He remembered all too well the humiliating disillusionment delivered only ten years before by the dealer on Madison Avenue.

The colonel went on and on about the little soldiers and how he himself had recently made collecting them a hobby, and Jack remembered Mrs. Penney, standing bemused in the downstairs hall under the ceiling fixture with the orange hand-painted Chinese figures on it, as he went up and down the stairs with the boxes, depositing them in Tina's bedroom to prove to her that he loved her, more than all the tin soldiers in the world.

Box after box he carried to her room, as if the house were his to go up and down in as he pleased, as if she were his to give anything to he pleased, expect anything of in return. I still have them, he said. The colonel looked gratified, as if this much of him at least had been accorded some recognition. And then something jogged Jack's memory. You say you bought them from a friend's estate? he said. They weren't yours? You didn't paint them yourself? Oh, no, the colonel said. I'm anything but artistic.

Funny, Jack thought afterward, how you assume something all your life and then find out you were mistaken.

Denise was more than satisfied with her work. It went very well, she said. Very well indeed. And when she dies, he'll marry Mona yet, you'll see. But who the hell cares, Denise? he said. You do, she said. I don't, you idiot, he said. I don't need some decrepit old soldier to make me feel authentic. It's universal to search for the father, Denise said serenely. It's at the root of all your problems that you don't have one. You're no different from the millions of men who need to know who they came from. It's a basic human instinct.

Leonardo da Vinci, Denise! Erasmus, Denise! Alexander Hamilton, John J. Audubon. . . . He could go on and on. Kings! Presidents! You don't have to be legitimate to be real. It doesn't matter if you're a bastard. It matters, Denise said. And you're not a king or a president. I am a president, he said. And I am rich. And I am good. In bed, she said, sweetheart. In other ways, he said fiercely. You're good enough for me, she said. That may not be good enough for me, he said. I want a divorce. No, she said. Marriage is best.

Uptown, Denise dialed his private number a second time.

She gave him a certain license; he gave her a certain leverage. She loved it! Right now, their collection was her fulcrum. She was not going to sell it, or divide it. She was not going to get a divorce. She wanted him just where she had him, in a nonliquid position, tied to her by nonincome-producing investments, jointly owned, and appreciating very nicely.

For Denise, the collection was not only at the heart of their stormy marriage, it was in fact its heart. From the first piece they had bought together in 1964—an early nineteenth-century portrait of solemn little twin boys in sailor suits, purchased just after the birth of their own twin boys—the impulse behind it had been the recording of all their happy occasions. (It was only years later, when they had a chance to acquire "View of the Almshouse and Lunatic Asylum of Bucks County, Pa.," that Jack decided the collection was nicely enough rounded out.)

That he did not attach the same importance to the events and milestones commemorated in the collection did not diminish Denise's enthusiasm for keeping him in wedlock and their paintings on their own walls. Denise's angle on him was that he would never be more content than he had seemed to be with her (and he had seemed to be, even if he now denied it). She believed he had been rendered permanently hungry for something no one had thought to give him, until she had thought of it. Further, though she knew her incessant psychologizing made him want to deck her, she had recently hinted to him that this deprivation in his life may have been what caused him to insist on restoring the paintings. Did you think, she suggested hesitantly, that by restoring the originals you could restore some condition lacking in your own origins?

In his office, he smote his head one more time. It was true he had insisted on restoring the paintings. But had he insisted for the wrong reasons? Or had he insisted because he believed it was the right thing to do? Or had he insisted simply for the irresistible pleasure of opposing her?

When he was very drunk, or very lonely, Jack sometimes wondered if he was drawn to strong-willed women like Denise so that he could satisfy some inner need to struggle against them. He never lingered long on this thought. For if it was so that he needed to struggle against them, why was it so? And if he needed to do it, how could he expect not to need to? And if it was so, did he also take pleasure in winning the struggle, in humiliating them, and replacing them, to start a new struggle with someone else? Moreover, if it was so, it had to be said it was also debilitating, expensive, and painful, and therefore dumb. It must not be so, then, he would conclude. It was a coincidence, a pattern without significance, a dim niggling idea not worth broaching to the light of discussion.

Extension 5305 lit up again. He did not want to speak to her today. This was the day and the very hour, eleven o'clock, that he had decided to call Tina. He had given himself two weeks to calm down from the agitation produced in him by seeing her again at the wedding. He had been in a state of turbulence ever since the wedding, of incessant inner turmoil and breathlessness and erotic anticipation. She had not made it crystal clear to him that day that she never wanted to hear from him again. And with each day since, it had in fact seemed to him that she had made it less and less clear, to the point where it now seemed to him that she had wanted to make it clear that she did want to hear from him again.

His phone console uttered a short, discreet beep. The disembodied voice of his secretary pursued the beep. "Your wife," she said.

He picked up the receiver.

"Jack," Denise said. "I called you earlier. Why didn't you answer? Your stepmother died."

He burst out laughing. Denise was truly splendid. She did insist on calling the colonel's wife his stepmother.

"What are you laughing about?"

"You," he said.

"It's your father's wife. Aren't you interested?"

Interested? He was sorry to hear it, of course. The man was very old now. Eighty-two. But he had three daughters. "Shall we send flowers?"

"It was three weeks ago," she said. "I think a sweet letter would be appropriate. I'll write it. You can add a note on Saturday."

"How do you happen to know these things?"

"What things?"

"That she died."

"One of your sisters wrote to me. We're in touch. Even if you're not."

Denise and her little zingers. He sighed. "How are the boys?"

"They miss you. They need you. I caught them smoking again. They're only twelve. It'll be pot next. They need a father, Jack!"

"They have a father."

"Not at home."

"This is no good, Denise," he said.

"I know," she said. "Darling."

"We have to come to terms. I want to sell the collection."

"I want to come to terms," she said soothingly. "We will. We shall."

"I want a divorce, Denise!"

"No, Jack. That's the last thing. Please. Let's try one more time."

He sighed.

"We'll talk about it on Saturday, dear," she said. "When you come for them. Did you see the article in the *Times* today?"

"That's why I want to sell it, Denise. Divorce or not, damn it! And don't call me dear."

But she had already hung up, with what sounded like a little sob.

4

At the sound of her voice, he felt as if his windpipe had closed off. "This is Jack Troy," he gasped. "I couldn't wait any longer to hear what their going-away clothes were."

A wave of heat flooded her body, almost knocking her out. But she took hold, rose in the next instant, despite all her resolutions not to, to the bait of his playfulness. "Their bathing suits, of course," she said. "And we all lit little candles and floated them on the river."

"How picturesque."

"Until a barge passed. The wake washed them out."

"How unpicturesque. But they beat the rain?" His heart thumped tumultuously. He could hardly hear his own words over the roar of blood in his ears.

"But they miscalculated the tide," he heard her say. "And an oar got away. He had to punt her over."

He liked that. Came to. Got control of himself. "That's a switch," he said. "Bucking the tide instead of. . . ."

"I'm sure he got to that, too," she said, just as suddenly getting control over her own self. No good old days, she meant. No disarming her with old Jack-think. This was to be new Tina-think.

He had meant to be merely frolicsome, no good old days so soon. A decent interval was imperative. He had to begin again slowly, if he was to get anywhere at all with her. But how? He had forgotten how! "Tina!" he said. He wanted to see her, hold her, lie down with her somewhere, their faces together so he could whisper to her what he wanted again.

Don't say my name! she thought. Don't get so familiar with me. It's been twenty years.

"Tina?"

"What?"

"Just," he said, helplessly, "just, can I call you again sometime?"

"What about?"

"Just to talk."

"Why can't you talk now?"

"I can't," he said.

"What do you want to talk about?"

"Should the U.S. sell arms to Kenya and Zaire?"

"No," she said.

"I want to rectify things. Between us."

"They are rectified," she said. "We did talk."

But not enough. He thought of all the years ahead, without her. Not enough. An almost unbearable prospect, now that he had seen her again. He had to get her back. He used to know exactly how. "Carter or Ford?" he said.

"Carter. I really don't want to do this," she said.

"Angola? Lebanon? *Viking I*? There are a thousand neutral topics. Will *Viking I* reach Mars?"

"Yes," she said.

"You will? I can?"

"No, *it* will. *Viking I*."

"See how easy it is. Once you get started."

"Jack."

"Mickey Kolyrion called me last week," he said.

"Oh?" she said. "What did he want?"

"I didn't speak to him. I was in Chicago. When did he get out of jail?"

"He never went in."

"Why not?"

"He wasn't indicted. There wasn't enough evidence. And no apparent motive."

"Wasn't she pregnant?"

"No."

"But, still, didn't everyone think he did it?"

"He did do it," she said. "That's not good enough."

"Didn't we see him one night at the quarry?" he said. "At around that time?" He recalled a note Clarice had written him just before it happened. Pink paper black poodles. He'd come across it only a few months ago, packing to leave Dallas.

"We saw him the night he did it," she said.

She had a thing about dates. How did she know? Because

[151]

it was the Saturday night before his grandmother died, of course.

That wonderful week. He was sorry he'd asked.

April 1956. His senior year. They were engaged. The nurses on twenty-four-hour duty. He had forgotten the chronology, but not the images: Cora's white shoes under the chair in his room, her white stockings tucked one in each shoe, her starched white dress laid on the chair like a nurse in effigy. His grandmother across the hall dying. The quarry for making love with Tina, because there was no privacy in the house with the three shifts of nurses. And one of them that hot spring-vacation week a substitute. Cora, of course. Surprised Cora. Eight years later. Remember me? I always looked for you, he said. I looked for you every summer. You turned out just the way I thought you would, she said. Then, he naked in the chair. The door opening. Cora's head like an explosive in his hands. Oh, get up, he had said. She set the fan down. Get dressed, she said in a deadly quiet voice. And then the hyacinths wrecked on the kitchen floor when he went down to find her, the dirt and clay fragments and the blue blooms all smashed to bits.

The collection of lead soldiers was left out on the porch that night. And he was left in the house with his dying grandmother and the three shifts of nurses, one of whom was no longer Cora. Tina has gone, Mrs. Penney said, three days later. You have disappointed all of us, Jack. For the last time, we hope.

They wouldn't tell him where she had gone. Finally, he had gotten it out of someone, Sybil maybe. The Barbizon. He went to find her. There was no way to get past the dragons at the desk. He lay in wait for her outside. She ran back inside when she saw him. The next time he accosted her she was cooler. Opened her purse and showed him a sharp little dagger. For you, she said. If you don't leave me alone.

She had read the coroner's report, over Hugh's shoulder. Worked it out. Hadn't ever put it together until Hugh got a copy of that faded report, twenty years after the fact.

He remembered the taste of blood and mud in his mouth, the fingernails raking down his cheek, his first day in Brewerton. Mickey was a dirty fighter, scratched and kicked like a girl. "How did he do it?"

"Took a rock and slammed her head with it against the quarry wall and held her under till she drowned."

"Nice. But why, if she wasn't pregnant?"

"Hugh thinks she told him she was, so he'd marry her." Hugh? he wondered.

"She kept a diary. It's missing. Hugh's trying to find it."

He had driven past them in the dark woods, speeding as much as the rutted dirt lane would allow. His hair was wet. He wore no shirt. He caught sight of their parked car as he passed, turned his head sharply and looked straight at them, looking out of the windshield straight back at him. "It's good of Hugh," he said, envying Hugh his long moral fury, his lawyer's long reach.

"He's doing it for votes," she said. "He wants to run for district attorney next year."

Not moral fury at all, then. And so she wasn't impressed. He had forgotten how small the hoops were that one had to jump through to please her. Still, one jumped, he thought. The way one climbed a hill, because it was there. He had responded to that power of hers all his life. And resisted it. Walked back down the hill. Left it standing there. "What business is he in?"

"Import-export. He says."

"You don't think so?"

"He's into a lot of things. Very fluid. Gets into any new thing that comes along."

"The pioneer type."

"You might say."

Crime, too, had its shifting, evolving frontiers, its pioneers and its squatters, and its settlers. He remembered the van loading or unloading behind the ice and coal company building.

"He's a pillar of Brewerton," she said. "Chums with all the town fathers."

"Does he do dope?"

"It's rumored."

"Why doesn't someone do something? Why doesn't Hugh?"

"Would you?"

His old loathing for Mickey rose in his throat. Nice way to get back. "I'd be tempted," he said.

"Squeal? How un-American."

He laughed. "Let's talk again?"

She stared at the sketch over her desk of the front elevation of the house on Smith's Point, balanced, symmetrical, harmonious, floating on a pale blue wash. "Maybe someday," she said.

"Some hot summer's day, then," he said.

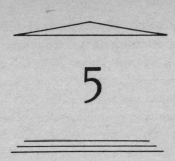

5

The next day wasn't hot, but he called her anyway, and the next day was even less hot, and he called her again. "Don't call so often," she said crossly. So he skipped a day. But he called the next day, and the day after that, and she didn't say it again.

It turned hot. It was 96 in the shade on Wall Street. When he called she opened the window next to her desk to feel the sun burning down on her arm, the same sun that broiled Wall Street.

She went away for a week. He felt bereft. But he began to call again as soon as she returned, and he knew she wanted him to. After that, if he missed a day, he felt as if he had missed something he vitally needed: a session in a lifelong dialogue he had to resume.

He wanted to tell her everything, about himself, about Denise, the boys, his work. He wanted to hear about her, her children, her life, her work, Hugh. "Why is Hugh running for office? What does he want to be when he grows up?"

"Hugh did grow up," she said. After Hugh got to be D.A., he wanted to be a state senator, traveling between Brewerton and Albany, representing his people. Hugh was patriotic, and patriarchal, too. (She kept Hugh between them, a paragon of manly virtue he had to dodge around and try not to bump into.)

"Why not a U.S. senator? Why not think big?"

"He likes to live here. Likes things the way they are."

"Denise grew up, too," he said glumly. "Denise likes being a wife." (His wife.)

So do I, she thought in despair. Liked being Hugh's wife. Wanted to go on being it, if it killed her.

Do you sail? Do you play tennis?, he asked. Who are your friends? What did you do today? What are you doing tomorrow? He confined himself to the neutral present, the past too charged, the future possibly too sweet. Yet he longed for that sweetness, primed her with adumbrations of it by planting himself in her daily life like a husband. How was your day? What did you do? How are Amy and Bo?

His patience with domestic trivia surprised her. He was used to a wife, domesticated in some way she had not foreseen he ever could be. What did the dentist say? How did your peach torte turn out? She saw his own former domesticity unfolding for her in the questions he asked, envied Denise the banality of married life with him.

"Why did Erica get divorced?" he asked. "Why didn't Sybil marry? Does she like girls?"

"No, she likes Hugh."

(Good, good, he thought. Hugh and Sybil. He wouldn't want to leave Hugh and Amy and Bo all alone, without her, when he took her. Sybil would make a good stepmother.) "Are you happy, Tina?"

"Yes," she said.

"Do you love Hugh?"

"Yes."

"I'm glad," he said sorrowfully. "I love him, too."

She began to dream at night of a beast, a gigantic termite, getting into the cellar and consuming the joists and beams of the house while her family slept. She woke from it, night after night, in a sweat. And one night in the dream, she went into the cellar to confront it and oust it, but it rose from its meal and grinned at her. Not a termite but a goat—in mythology, a symbol of lust, she recalled the next day.

Do you love me? he wanted to ask. "Will you see me someday?" he slipped in when she wasn't expecting it. At his end of the phone, he tried to picture her. But all he could conjure up was the way she had looked at the wedding in the blue cotton sundress, rumpled as if she had made love in it, her breasts outlined in the thin fabric. Her breasts, which he was the first human being ever to have laid eyes, or hands, on. Her belly, popped from pregnancy? He wanted to see for himself, lay his head on it, bury his face in it, thought of her long silky legs, her feet, whiter than her legs, from playing tennis or jogging with shoes on in the sun.

"No," she said. She felt safe only as long as he stayed at the other end of a long telephone line, as long as she remembered to keep him there. Yet she liked her new relation with him, she thought, roughing out scale plans for the rooms in the house on Smith's Point. It made her feel light, physically light to speak with him, as if a heavy weight that had been on her for a long time had been lifted.

"I'm glad you're happy," he said.

He made her laugh, as if he were launched upon a program to obliterate every bit of the ill will between them, because he had to obliterate it before he could go on to the next stage of what he had in mind. Still, she knew that the more she let herself laugh, the less chance there was of making him remember the thing she wanted him to remember, the connection she wanted him to make, the thing lodged inside her that was not funny and that she wanted to pluck out of herself and lay before him to look at: 1963. Not a very good year. He was good at avoiding it.

"But are you *really* happy?" he asked.

She lay awake at night, grieved to know he wasn't. Wanted him to be, felt indignant that he wasn't. She could have wept in sheer frustration. *Loved* him, she whispered to herself. Because he was so ignorant of why he was so alone.

Loved *him?* she railed scornfully in dry-eyed rage the next day, furiously sketching room plans for Erica, scraping paint chips and bits of wallpaper from the walls of the house, reading old inventories, studying period photographs, cutting colored pasteboard to scale, raising hate again like a sturdy wall to protect her from him.

He loved her, he said one day, and he knew how to be in love better than anyone did. It was a special talent. He moved delicately, but he had a goal. That she was it only fascinated her the more. Like a snake before a snake charmer, she rose from her jar to meet him, sure she could recoil at will, so long as she didn't see him, but kept him piping and charming from afar.

Nevertheless, she listened for the phone to ring like a dog trained to a bell. But as the summer passed, the possibility of rendering up to him her long accounting of grievances against him became ever more remote. Like the pain of childbirth, the memory of the pain associated with their history dissipated. By September, she had entered a new phase in her relations with him, a place he had deftly steered her toward. Accountings were beside the point in this pleasant place; debts and trespasses against her, if and when they were ever finally mentioned between them, could be spoken of there only ruefully, like faded emblems of a relation that had been, she had always known, too intense for him to bear.

"Rosie wants to meet you," he said one day.

Rosie was the only really friendly thing Denise had ever done for him, he said. "To make up for not wanting any more kids. Denise thinks four is the best size for an American family."

"Did you want more?"

"Yes," he said. "How about you?"

Over the phone she could feel him measuring her hips with his eyes. "No, thanks."

"Thirty-nine isn't too old."

"I'd be forty," she said. "Tell me about Rosie."

"They'd be great kids," he said.

"Rosie," she said.

Well, Denise gave him Rosie, way back in Dallas. Denise believed every American family should have a beautiful dog to bound in the autumn leaves with, to guard the hearth of a winter's eve. The trouble was, Denise didn't know that dogs didn't know they were supposed to be decorative. And the other trouble was, he got fonder of Rosie than he was of Denise. And the more he loved Rosie, the less Denise loved Rosie. But no matter how Denise carried on about dog hair and germs and Rosie's toenails clicking over the polished floors in the night and waking her, and Rosie's nocturnal snuffling keeping her awake, Rosie was Jack's dog, and Rosie slept on the floor next to Jack's side of the bed. Jack sometimes reached down and tenderly stroked Rosie's silky hair in the wee hours, and Rosie sometimes stood in a surfeit of devotion in the middle of the night and licked his face while he slept. They were in love, Jack and Rosie. He couldn't bear to leave her behind when they moved away from Dallas. He couldn't stand parting with anything as beautiful as Rosie, anything with such a soul as Rosie's.

Since an Irish setter, especially one brought up with Rosie's advantages, was not suited to New York apartment living, and since he wouldn't consider leaving her behind in Texas, Jack solved the problem by finding a family in the country, near New York, who would board her on a long-term basis. It was, of course, a euphemism for *keep her for good,* but then Jack had euphemisms for a lot of things. Besides, he had unlimited visiting privileges and he sometimes used them. He went to see her at least once a month, sometimes with the twins. The only reason he kept a car in the city, he said, was so he could visit Rosie. (Whisper sweet nothings in her long flossy ears, take her off to some private place where he could roll with her on the ground, tell his troubles to her, bury his face in her long warm neck. She knew when he was sad, grew sad and excited, too, when he crushed her in his arms, when some deep loneliness inside him imparted itself to Rosie. Rosie, Rosie! What's wrong with me, Rosie? What will make me right again? Poor Rosie, all she could do was whimper and nose at him with her soft, wet nose and paw anxiously at his chest.)

Never never *see* him, she thought strenuously. *Never meet Rosie.*

"The '60s," he said one day. "What did you do in the '60s?"

"Between Fifth and Madison? Or between '60 and '70?"

He considered. It was a trick question. He had encountered her between Fifth and Madison in the Sixties in '63. He sighed. He didn't want to explore 1963. " '60 and '70," he said. "Did you get involved? Protest? March?"

"We adopted Bo," she said.

"Bo is adopted?"

"Yes."

"But . . . but! Why?" He was stunned.

"Because he was there."

"But, is Amy yours?"

"They're both *ours,*" she said.

"But. . . ." He had a heart-thumping hope that Hugh was sterile, impotent, a eunuch, a castrato in the Thomas Jefferson wig and frock coat she'd told him he'd worn on a Bicentennial float. "But. . . ."

"Bo is a Chippewa Indian," she said, devastating him again. She hardly ever volunteered any information, made him ask what he wanted to know. It was how she learned what was important to him. By what he asked. By what he didn't. "Half Chippewa. Half white."

He tried to imagine what else he didn't know about her.

[161]

I *love* you, he wanted to tell her. I *love* you for adopting Bo.

She felt it coming at her over the phone. Didn't want him to love her. Didn't want him in her life any longer. Go now. This is enough. You know enough now. I did it for other reasons. Not why you think. Good-bye, she should say. But she didn't. She wanted him to know more. To know everything. To stay forever.

"And after Bo?"

After Bo she tried to save Brewerton, she said, or maybe it was the other way around.

"Brewerton tried to save you?"

"No, first came Brewerton. Then came Bo. There was an orphanage, actually. Do you remember it? That big brick factory on Cavalry Road?"

He remembered it, and she told him how Bo was one of the orphans in it and that there weren't many orphans in the late '60s. At least white ones. There was a dearth of white ones. Lots of black ones, though, and mixed ones, and handicapped and retarded ones. Bo wasn't handicapped, but he'd had to be detoxified at birth. His mother a junkie. Nobody wanted him because of it. He screamed for a year, and who knew if his brain would be mush.

Anyway, it was the Great Society. Only it didn't quite percolate down to Brewerton, or if it did, Brewerton folk didn't quite buy the message. They didn't mind white orphans in their midst, but they didn't dig black ones, or halfbreed ones, or damaged ones, or Puerto Rican ones. The idea was to close the orphanage and send the orphans back to the city, where they came from. To make a long story short, Bo made it, but the orphanage didn't.

"Where did the other kids go?"

"They were . . . dispersed. To other orphanages. The building stood empty. Nobody had any money to do anything with it. Vandals got at it. There was supposed to be this big war on poverty, and here was this perfectly sound brick building deteriorating before your eyes."

"So you formed a committee."

"And we went to workshops, learned how to apply for grants. Wrote letters. Went to Washington. Made pests of ourselves with our congressmen. But it worked. Brewerton got a piece of the pie. The building was saved, for senior housing." Her father lived in it now, she said.

And that was only the beginning. A big blast of federal money cleaned up the center of town. Urban redevelopment was all the rage. Low-income housing and a community center were built. Then private money began to trickle in. They cleaned up the waterfront, built a marina. Then the tourists came. The boat people, as opposed to the Boat People. There was suddenly money for everything. Low-interest loans for residential renovations. Merchants got practically free money for modernization. Everybody got into the act. Main Street got a face-lift. Brewerton got into the twentieth century. An electronics company moved into the old brewery on Hinckel Street. The hospital put on a new wing. The town was literally reborn. Everybody made out.

"Except the orphans."

"Except the orphans."

"So you did march."

"In that way, I guess."

"It was a good way."

"Self-serving, too." She started the ball rolling. But it kept rolling back to her, covered with opportunities. Hugh bought low. She got into the preservation end of it. Researched the buildings. Restored them. He sold high. And got in on all the legal turns, too. "How about you?"

He had concentrated on making the family fortune, he said. Let Denise discharge the Troy family social-guilt quotient, what there was of it. (He wanted to see her. Wanted to finish with this phone stage. Wanted to undress her and get into a bed with her and explore her, find out what else she cared for!) Denise was into busing, he remembered. "We had a few eggs thrown at the house, our mailbox bisected with a tire iron. Denise loved it. Opposition incites her."

"And did Dallas integrate?"

"Officially."

"And unofficially?"

"Plus ça change."

"I wonder if any of it changed anything," she said.

It changed things he hadn't thought could change. The big party started. Drugs arrived. The dream changed. An unanticipated morning broke. It filled him with sadness. The country gave him the jitters, he whispered.

It made her teeth chatter, she whispered back into the phone, as if it were subversive to admit it. One great big mindless carnival, everyone partying. . . .

"It was TV," he said.

"And the war."

"TV showed the war. The drugs. Spread the word."

"The kids got the word."

"I hate it sometimes, don't you? Having them?"

"Hate *them* sometimes," he said. "The enemy. Unreachable, unteachable. Their own rules."

"But the victims, too. Walking into it, innocent." She thought of his two, walking into it without him.

"Do you know when life begins?"

"When the dog dies and the kids leave home."

"You heard it."

"Everybody has."

Let's begin! he wanted to say. "It's making Denise crazy," he said instead. "She tries to keep it at bay. But she can't any longer. It's too vast. They don't want to listen to what they need to hear."

"Can't you go back to her? Kids need two of you to get through it."

"No," he said desperately. "It's too late for that." Didn't she see they were what he had to go back to? They had recaptured, she should see it by now, what it had been his intention to recapture—that bond of children cast together with no adult privy to what linked them; children conspiring toward a vision of an ideal world. He wasn't going to give it up now. I want *you,* he wanted to say. I want us all to live together in a big white house in a little green town. I want it to be the way it should have been.

"Make me laugh," she said.

"*Happy Days* attracts almost fifty percent of the TV-viewing audience in its time period."

"Not funny."

"Johnny Roselli was found floating in an oil drum off the Florida coast."

"Not at all funny."

"There's going to be a new TV show about a bionic dog."

"Positively not funny."

"Nothing's funny anymore," he said.

"I want to see you," he said one day, and his voice was so low and so commanding that it made her feel menaced.

"No."

"Yes."

"No, really."

"Won't you?"

She looked out the window of her office.

"Tina?"

"I'll think about it."

"Jack?"

"What?"

"Are you there?"

"Yes. I'm letting you think about it."

"Silly."

"Just a few hours. Just an hour and a half. Divide ninety minutes into twenty years. It amortizes out to about a second a day. Who could object to that?"

"Hugh could," she said. "And it's thirteen years. Don't you remember 1963, Jack?"

"He wouldn't."

"Yes, he would. And don't you?"

"Yes," he said. "How could I forget it? Will you?"

"Maybe," she said. "Maybe, someday."

"Good," he said.

What do you remember about it? she wanted to say.

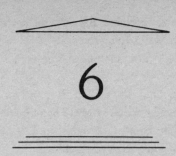

6

"How can you entertain for one minute the idea of seeing him?" Sybil said. "After all the trouble he caused you."

"I'm only entertaining it," she said. "I'm not embracing it."

"Your language," Sybil murmured.

"You never liked him," she said.

"To paraphrase Will Rogers," Sybil said, "I never met any man I liked." Except for Hugh, she thought despairingly. Had at first sight. It was easy to explain her own case, but Tina's? "How did it happen," she asked, "that he got into your life in the first place? What was there about him?"

He thought life was going to be marvelous. She had to warn him. He was alone, shooting through life like a comet to nowhere. She saw it as her mission to set him into orbit. "To paraphrase Edward Gibbon," she said, "I saw and loved. I was eleven."

"Then don't see him now," Sybil said. "You're thirty-nine."

"Yes," she said. "You're right. Thank you." It was inexplicable. "It makes me happy," she whispered. "Just talking to him on the phone. I don't have to see him."

"That's right," Sybil said. "And if talking to him makes you happy, then don't do that either. Tell him to vamoose."

"Yes."

"You're strong. You can do it."

"No," she said. "I'm weak. My moral fiber is frayed. I think he could have me just for the asking. He thinks I'm strong. He won't ask. He doesn't know how I've decayed."

"Beware," Sybil said.

She drove, stayed out on the road, looking for ideas, she said, houses, furniture, colors, fabrics, hardware. But it was to stay away from him, to not be there when he called. He was getting too close, gaining on her. Never call again, she should have said. Shouldn't you be minding the Dow Jones? she said, instead. When can I see you? You can't.

She saw, instead, hundreds of columned, pedimented houses. Came upon whole towns of them, in all degrees of upkeep and decay, from Pennsylvania to Vermont, from Brewerton to Chautauqua to towns called Homer and Cincinnatus and Ithaca—and Troy. As an expression of the ideals of ancient Greece and the death of the Colonial idea, the architecture was appropriate and logical. It was as an expression of possibility, neither inappropriate nor illogical, that it preyed on her mind. She lured them, Hugh and Amy and Bo, on weekends to far places. For ideas, she said, in Tully, Cicero, Corinth, Delphi. For time, she should have said. Time to listen to her conversations with him replay themselves in her head, time to decide if she would let herself . . . go.

To consider passion engendered it. Hugh was the unwitting beneficiary. Happy happy love! he thought, holding her body flushed and damp and weak. She loves me!

She kept driving, over country roads to photograph moldings and friezes, and architraves, capitals and cornices. And stayed on Smith's Point when she wasn't on the road, no phone, peeled wallpaper, hand-steamed it off the walls, fifteen layers of it, a layer at a time; on her hands and knees checked the stairs for signs of carpets and carpet rods; checked the walls for gas brackets; found a rat's nest in the wall and bits of ancient fabric; sent chips of paint out for analysis; held a magnifying glass to cornices and mantels and doors, looking for minute traces of paper and paint.

Hugh waited for her to return from her restless excursions, watched her stand and stare out of windows when she was at home, knew by the crumpled tissues he found in the bed that she wept softly to herself in the dead of night, knew the passion was not for him, knew she was trying to stick. Stick, he willed. He dreaded her distant gaze, her listening for something only she could hear, commanded it to go away, bury itself again, leave them in peace.

"Where have you been?" he cried, when he finally found her in.

"Working," she said. She had been as far as the Berkshires and back in a day, staying away from him. (Are you avoiding me? Yes. You can't forever. I don't want to forever.)

"I had another call today," he said. "From Mickey Kolyrion."

"What did he want?"

"To see me."

"He'll want something from you." He had driven out onto the Point one day, looking for her, Erica had told her. Had left his name twice on her answering machine.

"What will he want?"

"A favor he'll pay for."

"He's coming tomorrow."

"Go out of town."

"Will you go with me?"

"No."

He laughed.

"Do you know what his name means in Greek?"

"No."

"A *kollirion* is a shrike."

"What's a shrike?"

"A large bird native to North America. It looks as if it wears a black eye mask, and it has a sharp, hooked bill and a puffed chest, just like Mickey, and it's called by another name: butcher-bird. The butcher-bird impales its victims on thorns in order to be able to take its time consuming them."

"You make me laugh," he said. "So earnest. How do you know?"

"I looked it up in a Greek dictionary. Did you make love to Clarice Heard?"

"No."

[170]

She never knew whether to believe him or not.

"Now will you see me?"

"No."

"Who did I not have to have made love to in order for you to see me?"

(Everyone but me, she doesn't say. Because he has a horror of one-minded devotion. They had had a crucial conversation once:

What exactly do you want from me?

Presence. Your total all-thereness, all-hereness, all-mineness.

Perfect love.

Yes.

To walk on water.

No. No miracles. Just to love me. To be faithful to *me*. Only me.

Like swords he had to dodge around and slip under and get away from. You make things so hard, he said. Tiny hoops he had to try to jump through.

But that's how you like things, she said. Besides, why should fidelity be so hard?)

"Tina?"

"What?"

"*Will* you see me?"

"No," she said.

He sent flowers on their birthday, September 24. Hand-delivered in a yellow cab from Manhattan. So they couldn't be attributed, he probably thought. But miniature yellow lilies, edged in velvety black? Not at all Brewerton, Jack.

She tried to think of what to say if Hugh should ask who

sent them. Hugh was not particularly observant. She hoped he might not notice them. But he did, the minute he walked in.

"The flowers?" she said, despite a whole day to think of a plausible answer. She could have attributed them to Sybil, or Erica. Erica sometimes sent flowers on a person's birthday.

He bent to sniff the yellow lilies. "Who?"

"I don't know," she said.

He stared at her. "You don't know?"

"There was no card." (The card, with its moss green velvet ribbon, under the cloth on her bedside table: Felicitations. Le Votre.)

"Well, that's odd," he said. "Did you call Posey's?"

"I meant to. I forgot. I'll call tomorrow."

"Forgot?" he said. "I'll call. How *are* you, anyway?"

She almost diverted him from calling Posey's by telling him in great detail exactly how she was, and inquiring into all the details of how he was, and telling him how Amy and Bo were, and the dog and the cat.

"And how's your father?" he asked. "And by the way, where is he?"

She stared at him. "I forgot to call him."

"Forgot? What's wrong with you? Isn't he coming tonight?"

"No."

"On your birthday? He's not coming for dinner? What are we having, anyway?"

She had daydreamed all day, drawing pictures in her mind of rooms she invented to live in with him. "I forgot about dinner," she said.

"Well, damn it," he said. "What *is* wrong with you?"

Hugh went out for a pizza and a Carvel cake, and picked up her father, and called Posey's before he left, but they had no record of an FTD order or of any delivery to 28 Stephen Street. "Well, where the hell did they come from, then?" he wondered out loud.

They played Scrabble after the pizza, Hugh and Amy and Bo and the Reverend Mr. Penney, with Tina looking on. And when Amy's first seven letters spelled lad yurt, Tina quickly said "try dual" before Hugh could notice adultery, minus an e. (Adultery, Jack, no matter how discreetly and delicately it might be conducted, she must say to him, no matter how inevitable and logical it might seem, how divinely passionate, rapturous, appointed, and transporting it promises to be, diminishes in subtle, perhaps irrevocable ways the quality of a marital relation being conducted in good faith. She had always taken little stock in the many compelling reports, both fictional and factual, to the contrary.)

She went to bed while Hugh was out walking the dog. He probably never would have given the mystery another thought if he hadn't wandered into the study when he got back, where she had moved the flowers to be out of sight/out of mind, and seen the splash of yellow in the dark. It made him recall suddenly the yellow black-checkered cab he had noticed that morning turning down Main Street. A New York cab, arriving in Brewerton, with no passenger in the back seat? He stared at the city-style arrangement that had come in the city-style taxi for a long time, and then he went upstairs, where she was in bed, reading, and he said, "Did Jack Troy send those flowers?"

She looked up at him, standing over her like the highly percipient prosecuting attorney he was. "Yes," she said.

"Your birthday. How sweet. How did he remember?"

"It's his, too."

She looked defenseless in her pink cotton gown with the thin straps lying loose on her pale shoulders. Yet he felt like hitting her, and he believed that if he did he would be dealt with leniently by judge and jury. "And did you send him flowers?"

She lowered her eyes. "No."

"How often does he call?"

She shook her head.

"How often?"

She shook her head again.

"His nature, you know, is that of a bird dog."

She looked away from him.

"That's a dog whose instinct is to flush birds from their protection. When applied to a man, it's a. . . ."

"I know what it is," she said. She moved down under the covers. After a while, he got into bed beside her. He turned out the light and groped for her hand. "Why won't you ever listen to anything against him?" he said. "It's not as if he has some congenital defect that makes him a bastard against his wishes."

She took her hand back.

"There's something ruthless in him when it comes to women," he said in the dark. "He doesn't really like them."

She stared at the ceiling.

"He's got an old claim on you," he said. "If he exercises it, don't expect me to be pleased."

What Hugh remembered about 1963 was getting out of the Navy and going straight to Wall Street, where the father of his law-school roommate had a job waiting for him in his law office. After he had hung his uniforms in the attic of the house in Scarsdale where he had grown up, and hung his ceremonial sword over the fireplace in his bedroom, and checked in at the office, he set about looking for a girl to love. He was invited by a Navy friend to a cocktail party at the Boat Club in Brewerton, where he met Sybil Dye and Tina Penney.

Sybil was doing her residency in psychiatry in New York. This didn't surprise Hugh, that Sybil was going to be a psychiatrist. She seemed a little odd. Her mother had killed herself, he learned later. Dressed in dark clothes, Mrs. Dye had lain down one February evening in front of the commuter train bearing Mr. Dye home from the city. To Hugh that seemed as good a reason as any to become a psychiatrist. After the party, he didn't call Sybil, though he had spent most of the party talking to her and watching Tina over her shoulder. He called Tina.

He went to see her. He knew when he saw her apartment and read an article about a house she had designed and filled with low birch furniture, and hanging ferns in clay pots, that this girl, the inventor of those pleasing rooms where life couldn't help but be full of charm and ease and cheer, was the girl for him. But whenever he called her, she was usually busy. So he called Sybil, who was also busy, but not too busy to see him for coffee in the doctors' cafeteria, where he liked to talk to her about Tina Penney, and where she began to fall in love with him, because he didn't mind drinking coffee as weak as milky tea in the wee hours of the morning in the breaks of her rounds.

But Hugh didn't respond to Sybil's love. He kept after Tina, called her again and again, until he found a night she wasn't busy, and every time he saw her face-to-face a light went on in his head, and he thought, this is the person I will marry.

But Tina was not so quick to come to the same idea. She was doing fine on her own. Didn't need a man. So Hugh went often to see Sybil over coffee cups, and seek her opinions and advice, and Sybil was falling in love with Hugh all the while that Hugh was falling in love with Tina, taking her to movies and Shakespeare in the Park and East Side restaurants and discotheques. When Hugh finally told Tina he had fallen in love with her, Tina said, I've fallen in like with you. And she did like him. They made love, he trying to make her love him, and she trying to decide if she could trust him.

What she wasn't sure about was his will to have everything perfect. *Would a man like that throw you to the dogs if you missed a beat?* she wondered.

He planned to ask her to marry him at Christmas, and he went to Tiffany's and strolled around the counters looking at the diamond rings and the platinum wedding bands. But toward the beginning of November, she began to avoid him, at least during the week, though she still saw him on the weekends. So he asked her, are you seeing someone else during the week? (Do we have a future? he meant.) An old boyfriend, she said. She thought he had changed, this old boyfriend. But he hadn't. So Hugh bought the rings, and they were married before Christmas. She was pregnant.

He missed her. He had been in the habit of seeing her during the day, passing her car in his car, dropping into her shop for a cup of coffee, walking down Main Street with her for a sandwich at lunchtime, stopping by the house to see if she was working at home. But she was never at home during the day anymore, and seldom in her shop. He was lonely. Where did she go when she went? She had the time and opportunity to go anywhere, do anything, with anyone. She came easily by swatches and paint chips. Had whole drawersful of them. Didn't have to drive to Massachusetts for them. But he trusted her. He trusted her to remember 1963.

He began dropping in on her father more often. "Jack Troy was here," he said one day, over a cup of tea in the lounge of the senior housing. "He was up here in June, for Jenny Breene's wedding."

"Eh?" said the old man, startled out of his thoughts.

"Jack Troy," Hugh said. "He was up here."

"Is he still alive?" Mr. Penney said. "I would have thought someone would have put a round or two in him by this time."

"A nice vicarly turn of phrase," Hugh said.

"Eh?" the old man called out again.

"I said, he's alive," Hugh called back, over the table.

"Jack Troy is the only bastard I ever knew," the old man announced.

"You're lucky," Hugh said.

"What's that?"

"I said you're lucky. I've known more than one."

"I mean a real one," Mr. Penney said. "His mother had him without benefit of clergy."

"What?" Hugh said. "I didn't know that."

"You didn't, eh? Tina never told you?" Mr. Penney chuckled to himself.

Always true to him in her fashion, Hugh thought despairingly. So he did have a congenital defect, after all. "Are you sure she knows?"

"Oh, yes, she knows. He told her himself. The summer he found out."

Hugh stared into his tea.

"And if I were you, Hugh," Mr. Penney added, "I wouldn't let the son of a bitch within a mile of her. She never had any sense where he was concerned. Except the sense not to marry him. She had her wits about her that time."

Hugh fell silent, thinking of how in 1963 she would have married him, except that he was married to someone else at the time. And his wife got pregnant.

Mr. Penney fell silent, too, remembering Jack Troy, the son of Mona Thile, who called herself Mrs. Troy, but whose last name was actually the maiden name of her mother, Florence Thile. Mrs. Thile knew who should have married her daughter, if he hadn't already been married.

Mr. and Mrs. Penney had become acquainted, long before Jack Troy arrived to live with his grandmother, with the sorry details of his parentage. The Penneys would naturally have preferred that their only child marry someone with more regular origins, but it had been clear to them from the time he was twelve and she was eleven that there would never be anyone else for her but him.

Far more of a concern to the Penneys than his illegitimacy was his character. It wasn't that Jack was dishonest or venal. He was in fact upright and honest and fair, though too cheerful by far. It was rather that he didn't seem to have it in him to be good to their daughter, in the way that Mr. Penney, say, was good to Mrs. Penney. He seemed not to have what the Penneys thought of as the milk of human kindness in his veins. They had pointed this out to Tina on those occasions when something he did made their fears rise up in their hearts, but it only made her fierce and angry to hear him maligned. She saw his character not as lacking something, but rather as having an extra something —a drop too much of self-protection, perhaps—that made him harder and colder than he needed to be. She had faith that he would one day warm, soften, melt for her, and become tender and accommodating and joyful, like her father. She had understood from the beginning that a person with such a start in life as he had had would naturally be wary of closeness, would naturally want to thrust away those he loved, to protect himself from what love could wreak.

Mrs. Penney died about a year after the engagement was broken. She didn't live to see Tina married to Hugh Gardiner. The Reverend Mr. Penney not only survived his daughter's ruined dreams and his beloved wife's death, but he was blessed to live to see the happy day of his daughter's marriage to Hugh. Though he was pastor emeritus by that time, he had performed the ceremony himself. "If you're ever worried about a thing, Hugh," he said, starting up from his reveries, "pray. It works. Works like a charm sometimes."

"Yes, sir," Hugh said. "I always do, when I get in trouble."

"It doesn't hurt when you're not in trouble, either," the old man said. He was eighty-six, and he prayed on and off most of the day, every day. His homeliest thoughts and wishes were prayers of sorts. "Hugh?" he said, as he noticed Hugh getting up to leave. "What does a woman do today when faced with a situation like this?"

How does he know it's a situation already? Hugh wondered. He hadn't said it was. "Some of them stick, and some of them split," he said.

"Oh dear, oh dear," Mr. Penney muttered. "Then what will we do?"

"Maybe it will all blow over," Hugh said glumly, more than he had meant to say.

"Well, if it hasn't by this time. . . ." the old man said.

He hardly ever prayed for himself anymore. He had been forgiven long ago for his sins. He prayed nowadays intercessionary prayers, for the world, for peace, for starving children and drug addicts and national leaders and clean rivers and family life, for nuclear disarmament, and farmers and the Middle East and sanity at large. But he prayed, after Hugh left, aware of it as a prayer of petition very much on his own behalf, that Jack Troy wouldn't want his daughter again.

7

But Jack Troy did want her again. Though once he was finally sitting opposite her, flowers between them, knives and forks (hers pointing at him, his pointing at her), lying like accusations or weapons between them, he could not see how his hopes could be advanced. Seeing him face-to-face again had revived all the memories he had tried to make her forget. Months of ground-work all gone to hell, he thought.

He leaned across the table toward her, so he could see into her eyes, feel with his own eyes the texture of her skin and hair, the bones in her face, the crisp made-up edges of her lips. Time and nature had organized her features and flesh into an effect, a late, lush blaze of forty. But all he could read in the cool gray eyes was: dislike and distrust. All his work, gone for nothing!

She could tolerate him only on the phone, at a distance. Face-to-face she saw something in his face that stirred a residual fear of him in hers.

She ordered a Bloody Mary, without the vodka. Wanted to keep her wits about her, she was telling him. Wanted to remember everything he said, or didn't say, in case there was never another time.

There likely never would be, he thought, judging by the cool, awful way she looked at him. He ordered the same, also without vodka, to tell her in the same sign language she was using that he was ready now to do things her way, ready to be hers on her terms. He wanted to be hers, lay awake at night planning, figuring what he was worth, estimating in stocks and bonds and co-ops and cash and chattels and collections how much it would cost to unmarry Denise and marry Tina. But it was all academic, unless she stopped looking at him as if he were Hitler.

She ordered crabmeat salad; he ordered the same, again to tell her in sign those things he found the climate too cool to say. She understood what he was doing, telling her she could have him now, on her terms. He was ready to do what she wanted. But she looked at him and thought, with what seemed to her like a wonderful liberating clarity, that she didn't want him at all. On any terms.

By the time the coffee came, the meeting had to be classified a disaster. "All right," he said desperately. "1963. I think of it all the time."

She settled back against the banquette.

He had seen the same article about her that Hugh had seen, only he saw it about four months after Hugh saw it. Denise pointed it out to him, in the waiting room of a doctor they were consulting.

He flew to New York as soon as he could, found her address in the phone book, followed her to work in the morning, accosted her at noon outside an antique dealer's on Madison Avenue. It was late October or early November. He saw her coming down the block toward him in a brown tweed suit with a fur collar, her pale hair short and curled. It had been four years since their last meeting. She staggered sideways into a parking meter, dropped her shopping bag of swatches on the sidewalk. He picked it up, took her arm and steered her into the bar at the Carlyle.

He went back to Dallas at the end of the week, but he was in New York again the following week. I want to marry you, he said. Marry *me?* she said. You're married. That doesn't matter. I don't love her. I love you. We have no children. I don't want to marry you, she said. Think about it, he said. All it needs is for you to say yes. We should have been married seven years ago.

Things have changed in seven years, she said. Nothing has changed, he said. You think it over. I'll be back next week. I want you. (He had to go home to Denise for the weekend.) Want me? she said. Do you think I'm one of your collectibles? Think! Think what it could be. Just think, he said.

I have thought, she said. I'm thinking of someone else now. Rethink, he said. Imagine it.

He remembered the narrow bed they shared. Her hair, her beautiful golden body, the flush spreading up her throat like a wave up firm sand, a swift stain of passion. He came back the third week.

Will you? he asked. Maybe, she murmured, turning over to take him into her arms. That means yes, he said. Maybe, she said. Good, he said. Good, good, good.

They were lying in bed the next day, too, a Friday afternoon. It was her lunch hour. He was to leave for Dallas at four. The radio was on low. Duke Ellington. "Don't Get Around Much Any More."

In Dallas, a waiting eye squinted down upon the motorcade. The bulletin went through the room like a shot. Oh, no! the announcer cried. Oh, no! This is terrible! Robbed! they said. Oh, no no!

They dressed. They went out into the street. Storekeepers rushed to doorways; pedestrians clutched their hearts.

The whole nation, stolen from, wept. He canceled his flight to Dallas. Dallas? he said. Who would want to be there?

They sat in front of her television set. On Saturday morning she felt sick, and it crossed her mind that she couldn't be pregnant. She had an IUD. The next morning, Ruby shot Oswald in front of their very eyes. They could no longer stand their separation from the Capitol, any more than from each other. She was overcome with nausea at the idea, she thought, of giving him up again. They drove in a rented car to Washington and stood all night in a line at the Rotunda to file past the catafalque. He flew from Washington to Dallas, to tell Denise. She drove back to New York alone, to wait for his call. He didn't call for a week. Denise is pregnant, he said. I have to stay with her.

"What do you think?" she said, from the shadowed banquette.

"I should have left Denise, even if she was pregnant."

"I was too," she said. The case of the vanished intrauterine device. She had no idea how long it had been missing. Thought only of the two first weekends when he had gone back to Dallas and Denise, and she had wrathfully changed the sheets for Hugh Gardiner.

Something, some movement of his head, his hands, some sound he made, caused a threesome of waiters to stop in their work of flambéing a soufflé to look at them. He stared at her. "Why didn't you tell me?"

"What good would that have done?"

"I would have married you."

"Your father didn't marry Mona."

"You must despise me to say that," he said wonderingly. "I would have married you." He accented both pronouns.

She looked at him. "Ask," she said.

He stared at her again. "Is Amy mine?" With a random gesture of his hand he inadvertently knocked over the saltcellar.

"At the time," she said, "I didn't know."

"*Is* she?"

"You saw her," she said. "She looks like Hugh."

He picked up the cellar and set it down again.

(The Gardiner forehead, his mother's eyes, the Gardiner wrists, his dark straight hair, the long Gardiner legs. Hugh had studied her closely, had been persuaded long ago. No longer thought about it.)

"Did he know?"

"Yes."

"That it could have been mine?"

"Yes."

"You were unfaithful to me," he said.

"Don't make me laugh."

"You married him not knowing."

She looked at him.

"You should have told me."

She pushed her cup away. "I shouldn't have. Then or now. I'm sorry I did."

"Who gave women so much power over men, and why do they take so much pleasure in using it?" he said, half to himself.

"It's over and done with," she said. "I shouldn't have told you. I'm sorry."

"You're not sorry for the proper reason, then," he said. "You had no right not to have told me. You couldn't have known how I would react. You should have given me a chance. Let me in on the decision."

She thought of other chances he hadn't been given. Other ways he had been dismissed. "And what if it turned out to be Hugh's and looked like him?"

"I wouldn't have cared. Hugh didn't."

"You would have. And he would have too."

He shook his head.

"It was my decision to make," she said. "And Hugh's. You were married. Denise was pregnant. Why ruin her life?"

He gave a short laugh. "Denise is very resilient," he said. "And I wouldn't have cared."

"Boy twins?" she said. "You would have."

"The point," he said wearily, "is that you disregarded me."

"All right," she said. "I was wrong. But it wasn't yours."

"But you didn't know that. A human being was involved."

"Seven human beings were, as it turned out."

He shook his head. "You still don't understand."

"I do," she said. "You don't like being disregarded. Neither do I."

They walked out into the October sun on Third Avenue. His car was in a garage next to the restaurant. He gave his ticket to the attendant and stood, with his back to her, waiting for the car to come, almost forgetting she was there, alone in some world of his she had once been the only one to have entered. She touched his sleeve. "It wouldn't have worked anyway, you know," she said.

"It's as if I didn't exist." He shook his head.

The car came. He drove her up Third Avenue to an appointment she had at three. He double-parked on 61st Street under a plane tree whose leaves were already browned and curled. He turned off the ignition, turned to her in the front seat. "It wouldn't have worked," he said. "Because you were too strong for me. Didn't you see that? I drown in you. I had to resist you."

"I always understood that," she said. But she heard the present tense among the past. Drown. He still will. Nothing had changed.

They sat staring at each other. "It's not just me," she said. "You resist everyone."

He moved toward her.

"No," she said, the flat of her hand lightly against his chest to hold him away from her.

He moved her hand from his chest around to his side, where she felt the heat of his armpit and his ribs through his shirt. He put his mouth on her face, off center, somewhere between her eye and her nose and her ear.

She moved her mouth beneath his. He lifted her hair away from her shoulders and neck and brushed her lips with the tip of his tongue.

She moved her hand up under his arm, feeling his bulk, the heat and dampness of his armpit, the cotton of his shirt. His mouth smelled the same as it had the first time she had smelled and tasted it.

"We're going to be together in the end."

"If I believed that. . . ." she said.

"If you believed it, you wouldn't go home today."

"Don't call me any more!" she said.

Wasn't the enemy of romance supposed to be time? Hugh thought. They had had thirty years—time enough, Tina. Time should be on *his* side now. Family life required it—long horizontal planes of it. But both time and distance were obstinately on Jack Troy's side, obstacles fueling her yearning. He could see it in her wretched face.

The text on Sunday was from Romans. "Hold fast to what is good," the Reverend Raymond Auerbach read. From the attic, where she willed that order should take place, she held fast. Stayed there for a week, safe, she believed in a spurt of domesticity, from all threats to a loosening hold on what was good.

Below, the telephone rang and rang, but she went on separating clothes to give away from clothes to keep. Twice, he left his name on her answering machine, but she went on, through boxes of postcards and letters and playbills, found photos of him, of herself, in clothes she had forgotten, letters from him in a handwriting she thought she had forgotten. She read them, cruelly noticed his spelling, never good; noticed his gists and directions, always explanatory. When I see you again, I'll explain, he wrote. Until then, bare with me. She laughed out loud under the eaves.

She sniffed a gardenia corsage, brown and brittle, and remembered a dozen of them that over the years had perfumed the refrigerator in the parsonage, reminders of dancing cheek to cheek. How young they had been, how much in love, how badly showing it. She crushed the flowers in her hand to powder.

The side to the story she had made herself forget and he wanted her to remember came to light in the dim attic, nevertheless. It lay spread around her on the wooden floor in its unedited and unrevised fullness. She had rendered it in tabloid headlines, mocked it: Young Girl, Betrayed for Tenth Time by Incorrigible, Irresistible Childhood Sweetheart, Weds Solid Citizen—when what it required was what he had always had to make so many of: explanations. There was cause and effect, not just effect. An accounting was required for fidelity as well as infidelity, for reunion as well as separation, for passion, betrayal, despair, and desire, for abandon as well as abandonment.

She carried bric-a-brac and lamps from attic to garage, odds and ends of rugs and tables, linens, curtain rods, old window shades, enough to outfit a small cottage. "Leaving us?" Hugh teased, uncertainly. "Setting up house in the garage?" A van came and took it all away to Amy and Bo's school bazaar. She vacuumed the attic, tried on her wedding gown. It fit.

"Mother?" Amy gasped. "Is that you, mother?"

At the foot of the stairs, she lifted the veil.

"You're beautiful!" Amy breathed.

"I told you all brides were beautiful."

"Bo!" shouted Amy. "Bo! Come, see!"

"What's going on here?" Bo said. "Where are you *going*, Ma?"

At which Amy's brown eyes widened and narrowed: Tina could see the little wheels turning in her highly deductive Gardiner mind.

The phone rang. "I'll get that," Amy said.

"I'll get it," Tina said. She was reminded of the worried look on Bo's puckered little face when they adopted him. He was only six months old, but born worried, to worry.

She half-sprinted, half-glided ahead of Amy into the kitchen in her white peau de soie with bell-shaped skirt.

"Where have you been?"

"Busy."

"Don't you answer your phone?"

"I told you not to call."

"I thought you meant for a day or two. I didn't know you meant forever."

"I meant forever."

"Don't mean it," he said. "Where were you, anyway?"

"In the attic."

"For a whole week?"

"It took a whole week. I read your letters."

"Oh," he said. "Remembering the whole thing."

"Yes."

"Don't remember. Forget. Start over."

"If I forget, I may start over."

"That's what I want you to do," he said.

"That's what you want," she said.

"Tina," he said. "Don't you remember any of the good things, even now?"

"I'm beginning to," she said. "That's the trouble."

"Where will you be next week?" he said.

She wouldn't have told him if she hadn't wanted him to materialize in front of her in a corridor in the D & D Building. "Lunch," he said, late one rainy morning at the end of the week that she had waited, aching, all through, for him to appear. He took her firmly by the arm and steered her into a descending elevator.

"Yes, yes," she said, starving.

They had a sandwich and tea in a coffee shop on the corner and wandered afterward into specialty fabric and wallpaper shops, like man and wife, he thought, or client and decorator, or . . . lovers at loose ends.

"Do we look like client and decorator?"

"Maybe."

"Or like lovers?"

"Illicit ones," she said, touching silk twill for Erica's bedroom someday.

"Why would illicit lovers be wasting time in a fabric store at three in the afternoon?"

"Why would licit ones?"

"Because licit ones would have a place to go at night."

She turned away, tried to imagine that ordinary, impossible luxury.

Beside her on an Empire couch in an antique shop, he said, "How can we arrange it?"

"We can't."

"I want to."

She looked at him.

"Well?"

"I've been thinking," she said.

"Of it?"

"Yes."

"What about it?"

She looked away.

"That it would be . . . bliss?" he said.

"Yes."

"Even appropriate?"

"Yes."

"A friendly, forgiving sort of thing. Entirely in order? Entirely logical?"

"Entirely predictable?"

"Can we?"

"No," she said. She bought the couch for Erica, checked it off on a long list, had it sent to storage.

"It's going to be," he said. "Somehow. You're not going to get away from me this time."

"You were the one who always got away," she said.

"I can't stop thinking about it," he said, another day, in another shop. "Can you?"

She shook her head.

"How it would be," he said.

"How would it be?"

"Wonderful."

"Don't follow me any more," she said.

"Do you mean it?"

"Yes."

He didn't call for a week. She thought he never would again. A second week came and went, like a week of death. A third week passed. She was getting used to the idea.

Renunciation was no fun. It had never been his style. Twelve lots of Empire furniture were advertised. He saw the notice in the *Times*.

He found her on her hands and knees examining the construction of a pale gray-painted country bed. He climbed on the bed and lay down, hummed Brahms' "Lullaby" loudly.

"You!"

"Good morning."

"What are you doing up there?"

"Come on up. There's plenty of room."

"Get down!"

"It bounces," he said.

"Somebody will bounce you."

He sat up, swung his legs over the side, and rubbed his eyes. "You always were a spoilsport," he said, yawning.

She bought the bed and another like it, and two mahogany Empire chests.

"Why did you come?" she said. "After three weeks?"

"I had to. Can I come again tomorrow?"

"I'm not coming here tomorrow."

"Where are you going?"

She shook her head.

"Can I call you?"

She turned her back on him, opened a drawer in a nightstand. A great weariness overtook her to think that someone existed in the world with the power to make her consider giving up her world.

"Tina?"

She slammed the drawer shut.

"You don't want me to?"

"I don't want you to mess up my life," she said.

"Just to know you're there. That's all."

She looked at him.

"Friends," he said. "That's all I want to be."

She remembered the day he arrived in Brewerton, twelve years old, full of hope and ambition, wanting everyone to be his friend. "All right," she said.

"Let's walk," he said, taking her arm.

They walked like robbed tourists in a foreign city, no place to go, no roof over their heads, no bed to lie in, and all the while walking more and more dangerously close to his roof, his bed. He skirted her away from it at the last minute, though desperate to go into it.

"Here!" he said, looking up at a sign, seizing her arm. "In here."

"No."

"Yes. Just to hold you. I have to."

"No!"

She went home, tottering and faint, stared hopelessly at Amy and Bo next to Hugh on the couch, Hugh reading aloud to them from a book of Chippewa legends.

What would they do without her? How would they get along? If she died, they would have to; they would manage somehow. But it would be like dying to leave them. And for him? Him! She detested *him,* appearing out of nowhere to turn her upside down. She wandered through the house, clutching her arms, found her camera, ran downstairs and took a picture of them, racked her brain for answers, civilized solutions, alternatives, how to have everything without giving up anything.

"Is bigamy a crime?" Amy asked.

"Yes."

"Why?"

She couldn't think of the reason, couldn't imagine a reasonable one. "I don't know," she said, staring at her daughter with the suspicious Gardiner mind. It seemed as if a person ought to be able to have two spouses at once, if a person wanted to. It seems so to me, she imagined him saying. Why don't we?

Oh, forget bigamy, she said out loud in the attic. Forget moral training, common sense. Just do it. Get it over with. It was practically a rite, practically a right, these days!

But with him, her with him, it was far more than a rite, or right; it was a risk of risks—a mad dash across a slack rope over a deep chasm. Her feet cramped up to think of it, so that she cried out in pain in the dead of one awful sleepless night and woke Hugh.

"What are you doing up there?" Hugh said, finding her one day high on a ladder in the tower room on the third floor. "Cleaning," she said grimly. "This house used to sparkle."

"You make it sparkle just by being in it," he said. "Come have lunch with me."

"Oh, Hugh!" she said.

Leaves shot around the corners of the house as if blown from cannons. She went through more boxes, sorting, organizing, throwing out.

He accosted her in front of Bloomingdale's.

"Shouldn't you be checking out the industrial average?" she said. "Doing something other than following middle-aged housewives around? Go to work."

"I can't work, when I know you're wandering around town."

"I am not wandering. I'm working."

"Have a cup of tea with me. It's teatime." He steered her into a place, his hand on her arm like a command she wouldn't resist if she knew what was good for her.

She showed him photographs of those people he was threatening. She had begun to carry them around with her like talismans against his influence. He was cut by them, by the sweetness of the family life she tendered him, the safety of children being read to by their father, the security his own children were being deprived of. He handed the photos back to her, appalled to think he was going to break it all up. But he was. It was only a matter of time. He was proceeding slowly but steadily. She was weakening. All he had to do was expose just the right nerve to make her take the plunge.

"Love me!" he commanded, another day.

"I want you to go," she said. "Go away, out of my life again, please."

"I'll do anything you want," he said. "This time it's what you want."

But he just kept right on doing what he wanted, and they both wanted him to.

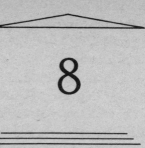

8

Though it was November, David and Jenny—six months married—still had not left the Point, but lived in a tree house they had built. Some of David's friends lived with them, or beneath them, under the tree in a tent. They all rode mopeds and dirt bikes. All summer, leaping vehicles, poised in midair, had appeared to Tina at unexpected moments through the trees.

Jack wanted to see Erica's house. They set a date to meet there on a day when no workmen were scheduled. But she felt uneasy as she drove to meet him, as if his incursion onto her home territory brought her closer to the edge she felt drawn to and hadn't yet decided to step out on. She could imagine it, and imagine leaping off it, too. And she could imagine him turning away, just as she leaped.

He was already there, with Rosie, standing knee-high in the rank weeds, gazing at the house. "This is it?" he said. "This is what you're trying to fix?"

"Hello, Rosie," she said. "Nice to meet you. This is it." Rosie leaped joyfully to contact her face, as if they had met before, romped in circles away through the tall grass. "Mr. Elihu Smith's dream house. Greek Revival, 1830. Do you like it?"

He tried to take it in. Up on jacks and dollies, it was ready to be moved back to a safe distance from the river and settled on piles over its new foundation pit, already dug. The former foundation lay in red sandstone heaps around the pit, awaiting reassembly. The former roof lay in a mountain of debris on the ground, waiting to be bulldozed into the gaping pit of the original cellar, deep with black water seeping underground from the river. "This? This is what you're trying to do?" he said.

They walked up a plank to the porch through piles of lumber and plaster rubble. "It can be beautiful again," she said, "if it's done right."

"If you can do this right. . . ." he said.

"We did go to the moon," she said.

Putting it all back together again, he thought. The impossible possible.

The wings were secured. The new roof on. The load-bearing beams and joists replaced. "Structurally, it's almost there," she said. She knew what she was doing. The hardest part was over. Once it was settled on the new foundation, the work on the inside could start. Hard work, too, she said. At first she had thought the woodwork was cast plaster, but it was hand-

carved chestnut under thirty coats of paint. It would take another year.

They went in, crossed a threshold together, stood inside a
real house again. He passed his hand over his eyes, felt as if it
were their house they were in, and that they had been in it
before. There was a logic to it that he recognized, a symmetry
he remembered, or wanted to remember. He had never been in
a house so balanced and composed: a center hall through to the
river side, twin rooms left and right, a double staircase twining
embracingly like enfolding arms, bridging the hall above them,
doors facing doors, windows mirroring windows. "I like it," he
said. "I see why you do."

She didn't respond.

He looked at her. She moved ahead of him.

Through living space where men and women like themselves had lived and loved and quarreled and reconciled and died
and grieved and survived, too, they wandered, imagined living.
But melancholy for what had passed and gone kept them silent.
They climbed the stairs without speaking, looked at heaps of
fallen plaster, wandered into empty rooms, stared at hearths as
cold as stone. And in rooms where beds had creaked with
passion and children had been conceived and born and cradles
rocked, they remembered their own shared childhood, the four
children between them (between us! was that all it was? he
despaired), gazed out windows where five generations before
them had gazed at the river pressing and surging in its uncounta-
ble tides.

They touched each other's arms and turned away their
faces to keep their thoughts from showing.

"Let's go up," he said. Bleakly they climbed a shaky ladder

to the widow's walk, as if at the top of it all, out in the fresh air, he would find the answer to the question he had asked himself a thousand times: Where is what I started out to find so long ago, and why have I not yet found it?

In the cupola, he took her in his arms, and they held on to each other like drowning sailors. Repaired with new lumber, primed white, the cupola smelled solid and hopeful and gave him hope. "It's not too late," he whispered. "Is it?"

"I don't know."

"It's not," he said. Why was she here if it was? "Restore us," he said. "You know how."

She stared down at the pit filled with dark water.

Outside, they spread a blanket in the tall warm grass, where one cricket chirped and one bee still weakly droned. The river slapped placidly on the rocky sand beyond, so close he could almost taste it, and he remembered the summers he had tasted it, the summers of his youth, when he had been so sure he knew what life would hold for him, so in love with her, so determined not to need her.

He fed her lobster salad from a fork, and they drank wine out of plastic glasses. He lay on his back in the weak, warm sun and imagined buying the house from Erica and living in it with Tina and Will and Otis and Amy and Bo. "Tell me about it," he said, touching her hand, wanting her to lie beside him on the blanket.

She lay down, her face so close to his she could smell his skin. He closed his eyes and in his mind moved back into the house, over the rubble, to stand under a ceiling medallion of roses and oats, ripe, drooping, bursting.

She wanted to do it the way it could have been done to

start with, she said. And hadn't been. She had found a set of watercolor drawings in the attic. By Abigail Smith, age fourteen, dated 1852. Drawings of every room in the house, preserved in a maroon velvet portfolio in a box under the rafters. And they *had* gotten it all wrong, slat-back side chairs and stenciled mirrors mixed in with Queen Anne tables and Chippendale sofas.

"They used what they had," he said.

"Yes."

"But you want to start with an ideal."

"That coincides with the ideal of the period."

"And move toward a realization of it."

"That coincides with what will function now."

"Ideally pragmatic."

"Or pragmatically ideal. You make a new reality."

"A new realeetay," he said.

She smiled. "A new authenteeceetay. A new vivaceetay."

He stroked her cheek with the side of his finger. "Will it work when it's finished?"

"I think so. If not, why do it?"

"It will then," he said. "Don't you think we will, too?"

"The trouble is," she said, capturing his hand on her thigh, holding it there like a poultice to soothe her, "you can't know whether it will or not until you've gone and done it."

"Let's go and do it, then."

She looked at him.

"You're waiting for some *thing* to tell you we'll work," he said.

"Or that we won't."

"What is it?"

"Some sign you've changed. Or some sign that I can stand your not having changed."

"You're hard," he said. "How about you changing? Give us a chance?"

Rosie tore past after a squirrel or a chipmunk, some distant scrambling in the fallen leaves only she could hear, and he lay back again beside her under the russet oak tree, used her shoulder as his cushion against the ground. She looked up into the black limbs of the tree fringed with dying leaves. Wanting it all restored, she thought despairingly. But to what? Suppose there had been nothing there to begin with, except a fantasy of harmony and union? Maybe the reality was a long sparring, a long vying for a prize that didn't exist. A pattern neither one of them could stop wanting to repeat.

Around the other side of the house they heard a car engine turn off and a heavy car door close.

They sat up, stared to see who would come around the corner of the house.

It was Mickey Kolyrion.

Jack shaded his eyes against the sun. Not long ago, Mickey had made an appointment to see him and canceled it at the last minute, had called twice since, talked hot tips, crude strategies for making money. He seemed to have a genius for smelling them out, dozens of schemes, all of which sounded infallible and indictable. Why was he here? He remembered Clarice's note, the black poodles on the pink paper: We're getting married!

He came toward them, adjusting his swimming trunks. His hair was wet, and he wore an open windbreaker over his graying chest. Around his neck he wore a heavy gold chain and crucifix. "Old Home Week," he said. "Having a picnic?"

"A private one," she said.

"Tell me," he said amiably, "what did I ever do, Tina, to deserve your special brand of bad manners?"

Scaring me, she thought. "What do you want?" she said.

"To say hello. To talk to Jack. Is there something wrong with that?"

"We were just about to leave," she said. She looked at her watch. It would be dark in an hour.

"She's been hostile to me for years," he said, speaking directly to Jack. "Last spring, she even pointed a gun at me." He laughed at the memory and held out his hand. "You're lookin' good. I would have known you anywhere, Jack. I saw you up here in June. From a distance. You didn't see me. It's been."

"It's been," Jack said, extending his hand without standing.

"I was out on the river. I saw you up on the widow's walk a little while ago," Mickey said. "From my boat. I hurried right in." He drew a card out of the front pocket of his windbreaker. "I promised you one," he said. "Remember? On the phone? When we talked?"

Jack took it. "Impex, Int., Ltd.," he read aloud.

"Chicken out. Shrimp in," Mickey said. "They love our poultry. We love their shellfish. Fourteen dollars a pound retail today for shrimp. Hard to believe, isn't it?"

"Yes," Jack said, looking at the heavy gold crucifix around his neck.

Mickey touched the crucifix. "If you're on God's side, God will be on your side. Right?"

[204]

"I don't know," Jack said. "Did God actually say that?"

"Something like it."

"How are you on God's side?" Tina asked.

He smiled. "Many ways."

"Such as?"

"He feeds the multitudes," Jack said.

Mickey smiled again. "Quick," he said. "You always were, Jack." But he hated him, for looking down on him, mocking him. Hated both of them. It was a legitimate taxpaying operation, even if it provided a cover for operations that weren't. And why shouldn't it? Whose teeth was it skin off? And what did they know about it, anyway? He despised them for being too good to pick up what lay there for the picking. For ignoring what it did no good to ignore. Was grass any different from ore or tin? It was given, by nature, for man to use. And besides, the little bit of it he handled was like a child's bucket of sand to the Mohave. And besides, besides, out of what he made on it, Jeanne managed to return enough to circulation to float an entire goddamned state all by herself. So why should Uncle Sam care? And why should they? And further besides, after two or three more runs, like the one last week off the Hamptons, he was quitting. He had wanted that one to be his last, but Raul desired to go a few more times. (All that nice square catch, Raul said. How can you pass it up?) So, be nice. He wanted a special favor from them. They could just be holding his fate in their four lily-white hands. His freedom could just possibly be at stake, "It's a legitimate business, Tina," he said mildly.

That flash, Jack thought. The gold, the signature wind-breaker and matching trunks, the heavy gold ID bracelet, the big gold pinkie ring with the one not-so-discreet diamond, the polished nails.

Mickey looked down at them on the blanket. They hadn't even stood for him! Little balls of rage formed and popped in his head. Common fornicators, he thought, and they looked down on him. He had seen them. From halfway across the river, he had seen them through his binoculars, holding onto each other up on the roof as if for dear life. He was hardly ever unfaithful to Jeanne, despite the fact that she submitted to him with distaste enough to make a dead man weep. But they had everything, and still they took more. The whole package, and then each other, just for the mere taking. But, still. The ice was thin. Be nice. "It's about going public," he said. "I mentioned it to you when I called. I'm still interested. I'd appreciate your advice."

"It's not my specialty," Jack said. He had explained that to him on the phone. "I'm a broker. You need an underwriter."

"You could help. Steer me in the right direction. You have the in's. And the instincts." He laughed. "You could sell anything. You sold a girl to me once. Remember? You sold Maureen Haggerty to me for twenty-five cents."

Jack flushed. "Maureen Haggerty? Did I? That was crass of me."

"But I always admired you for it," Mickey said. "A born businessman. I like that free-enterprise spirit."

"I probably needed twenty-five cents to take Tina to Hubert's," Jack said. "I don't remember it at all, really."

"She was pissed," Mickey said.

"Tina?"

"Maureen."

"I can't say I blame her. I hope it was a good deal for you anyway."

"It was a lousy deal," Mickey said. "She couldn't stand me."

Hasn't changed, never will, Jack could feel her thinking. Her face was expressionless. Thanks a lot, Mickey, I needed that. Or was she remembering Bo, born screaming for smack? His mother gone at sixteen to noddy land? A brief image flashed through Jack's head of himself doing a short turn as a stool pigeon, getting Mickey, catapulting himself right into her good graces, softening her. Would that do it? Six months, say, as the FBI's man on MK's soiled tracks? If people like us don't care, after all, who will. Get friendly with Mickey, then go to the DEA. Or go to them first, learn how to get friendly with him their way. Learn what they want to know. Give it to them. And silently slip away.

But did the Drug Enforcement Agency enforce drugs? Judges winked, banks laundered. Did the DEA deal?

"There's a rumor going around town that you're pushing dope," Tina said.

Mickey's color changed.

Jack relaxed. Never mind doing it for her or the DEA. Do it for himself, he thought, out of the purest motive of all: the revenge of Jack Troy/Bastard Boy. "Nobody pushes it," he said smoothly.

"That's right," Mickey said, surprised. "Nobody has to buy it, and nobody has to push it."

"It's what people want today," Jack said. "It's a question of supply and demand. They demand it. It is supplied. It's our new national leisure-time activity."

"It's not a legal one yet," she said.

"It's because of Impex," Mickey said. "Anything international today, and people's imaginations run away with them. It's an occupational hazard in the import business. What can you do?" He tried to imagine how she would look dead, which she would be if she screwed up his life. He wondered if she had her ridiculous little pistol with her. He had followed her at the end of the winter, just after he first heard about Hugh trying to reopen the Clarice case, to a barn way out in the country. He almost laughed to himself now, remembering her screaming and whirling around from her tripod, pulling this antique pearl-handled number out of her bag on him. And later he'd read in the paper some article she'd written about the "indigenous architecture" of Brewerton County—a falling-down cow barn, for Christ's sake.

Just press your thumbs on her throttle, he thought reasonably. Just break her moralistic little neck.

She shivered. Clouds covered the sun. His body, nearly naked under the open windbreaker, was repulsive, almost deformed in its disproportions—puffing chest and skinny hips that hardly held up his trunks, so that the dark hollows of his groin showed at the slipped waistband. Long spindly legs, hairy, threatening. She knew what he wanted.

He shifted uneasily, waiting. They must know he wanted only one thing from them. To forget that glimpse they'd had of him that night at the quarry. Though how could he ask for it? And what could he offer in return? Nobody did something for nothing. Yet he couldn't think of a thing they might want from him. Could think only of Clarice's sluggish white body floating on the dark green water.

Little bubbles of rage formed and popped inside his head again. His needs were not being met, by anybody, anywhere! He had walked in on Jeanne just the other day and startled her. Her hands leaping to cover her face, her mouth wide open, screaming at him as if he were Frankenstein's monster himself walking in on her.

Jack shivered, too. Never mind revenge either, he decided. With enough rope he'll hang himself. "We've got to go," he said. He looked up at the sky and then at his watch.

Mickey blinked. Dismissed? Like that? "Just like that?" he said. "You don't want to do something together?" He addressed Jack.

"Together, we might all be in court one of these days," Tina said. "If we're asked to testify against you."

Mickey reddened. What he saw when he looked at her was right in the middle of her forehead the kind of entrance hole made by a .22. "Then let's hope you're not asked," he said.

He turned and left. His Cadillac swung around in an angry circle in the grass and peeled off down the lane.

"Why did you do that?" Jack asked.

"What did you want me to do?" She felt trapped now, drawn by him, without wanting to be, into a triangle with Mickey Kolyrion that interlocked with the other triangles his reappearance in her life had involved her in, the past returning to complicate the present beyond her tolerance for complexity.

"Something's changed," he said.

"No. That's just it. Nothing has," she said. "This will never work, Jack. I want what I've always wanted. And you don't see what it is."

"I think I do," he said. "I think it's to have me the way

you want me. Maybe it's unreasonable to expect to have some-one else on your terms. Maybe you're the one who has to change."

She looked at him.

"Take a chance?" he said. "Forget the past? Take a flying leap?"

She stared out at the river, imagining him stepping aside at the last moment. "I can't," she said.

"I thought you were going to. Until he came."

"I almost thought I was, too."

"He has a way of bringing reality home?"

"Yes."

"I thought you wanted a new realeetay."

"I wanted . . . possibility."

"Well?"

She shook her head. "I don't think it exists, for us."

They packed up the picnic basket and folded the blanket and walked through the grass to their cars.

It was over? Not meant to be after all?

"Don't forget Rosie," she said.

He whistled for the dog. Whistling was difficult, the way his face felt.

Where was Rosie? He whistled again. Far away down the lane they heard a moped coming toward them. David and Jenny on one bike emerged from around the bend. "Are you looking for an Irish setter?" David said.

"Yes," Jack said, knowing already.

"She was hit by a car. She's down the lane a half a mile."

They followed the bike in Tina's car.

Blood was running from her side into the dirt of the road.

She convulsed just as they reached her, screamed in the low, dead grasses, gave one dreadful twitch from head to tail, and died.

"Everything I touch," she heard him say under his breath. "Why is it? Every damned thing I touch."

The dog's tongue lolled in the dirt. Saliva ran down it to make a little muck where it dripped. A long silky ear, mangled and bloody, fell untidily over her staring brown eye. He gazed at the wreckage. "Who did it?" he said.

She touched his sleeve. He shrugged off her touch angrily.

"All I saw was a car," David said. "A black Cadillac in a big hurry."

"It was Mickey Kolyrion," Jenny said.

He knelt beside her and put her tongue back in her mouth and closed her jaws and her eyelids. He straightened out the torn ear and arranged her broken legs in a more natural manner.

They went back to the house for a spade, and he dug a grave, fast and not very deep, and put her in it. She was very heavy, dead weight. He threw earth in on top of her. "Did he know she was mine?" he said, looking around at her.

She covered the earth with leaves.

"Did he?"

"Did he see you with her from his boat?"

He looked out at the water for a long moment, then walked on ahead of her, back to his car. That's it, he said to himself. That's it, then. That's it, Mickey.

She caught up with him at the car. "It's because I feel like Rosie," she said. "I'll run to you and you won't be there."

"I was there," he said. "Something intervened."

"Something always does."

"Something in us?"

"Yes."

"But you love me."

"Rosie loved you, too," she said.

9

It was the rainy season. Torrents battered the window of his room in the Sandpiper Motel, stopping without notice and starting up again with maddening unpredictability all through the long nights. The rain woke him from sleep. It was the only way he knew he slept. Otherwise, he would have sworn he only lay awake, in panic, wanting her, wanting a woman. His life without her was a long unnecessary mistake he had thought would be a simple thing to correct.

He had not planned to visit the Miami office until after the first of the year. They were not prepared for him in Miami. They had thought they had two more months to clean up their act, make more money than Dallas, L.A., Chicago, etc. They were the least profitable branch in the organization. He fired the manager the second day he was there. The man cried in front of him, begged for a second chance. "Clear out your desk," he said. "Today." The two salesmen dialed phones faster than they had ever dialed them before. The three secretaries instantly stopped chitchatting.

Coldly he interviewed replacement candidates for the manager's job, despising everyone he interviewed for wanting what he had to offer.

He fired one of the three chatting women, because she made the mistake of thinking she could sex him up. Her skirts were so short he could see the crotch of her underwear when she bent over. He despised her for thinking he was that weak. She called him a prick before she left. "That's right," he said.

He sat at her desk and did her work himself, and did it better and faster.

By the end of the second week he had found replacements, a woman so homely it made him swoon to look her in the face, and a prick just like himself to ride herd on the bunch of them.

His loathing for Miami was almost erotic, it was so consuming and complete. He stayed for two weeks to work, and then for a third, at first just because the city was so despicable to him that it mirrored something in himself he wanted to face but didn't know how. And then he stayed because he saw a girl whose looks he liked, sitting at a bar. Her name was Deedee. She moved into his room with him and his bourbon. He was drinking a quart a day.

The bubble-headed chatter of Deedee gave him time to remember something else he'd meant to do. Not related to heroism, patriotism, ideals, or Tina. Just a simple act of sweet revenge. He picked up the phone while she was waxing her underarms in the bathroom and asked the operator for the number of the DEA in Washington. An agent thanked him for calling and took the name of the motel and told him someone would be around to interview him. Jack didn't believe anyone would come. They probably got lots of crackpots calling. But he was glad he'd done it anyway.

Deedee showed him her armpits. She was twenty, and wonderfully gorgeous, and stupefyingly ignorant. Her conversation revolved around rock stars he'd never heard of, and actors, designers, and TV shows he'd also never heard of. She chewed gum. There was something about the way she did it that utterly fascinated him. It was so disfiguring to her wondrous loveliness, so degradingly sensual, it thrilled him. She also smoked or sucked on the balls of her fingers, or sang along with her tapes or the radio, the words of the songs like pieces of things rolling around on her tongue. She always had something in her luscious mouth, and often it was something of him. She could dwell on him for half an hour without coming up for air, dreamily feeding on him, like a large slug he had once watched ingest a whole cheese sandwich left in a school yard.

He was half-drunk most of the time, and he didn't remember a lot of it afterward. But he did remember that he did a lot of talking, too; told her the story of his life. She understood it had turned out to be a life he wanted now to change back to a direction it had once seemed to have. For him, it was a review of what he saw as the facts and what he saw as the fantasies, a separating of them, re-sorting and recording what he believed to be true about himself. He didn't want to be a bastard anymore, he told her. And had the fact produced the metaphor? Or would he have been one anyway? You don't seem like one to me, Deedee said. You haven't known me long enough, he said.

She lay on her back next to him while he talked, half-listening to him, while she really concentrated, he suspected, on her isometrics, or the imaginary bike she pedaled in the air, or some breathing exercise she could do for her muscle tone without appearing to be doing it. How do I look? was her biggest concern in life.

One of the criteria of a collection is that some of the objects in it be related to one another. About the only way Deedee could be related to almost any other woman he'd ever spent so much time at a stretch with was that she said to him once, the trouble with you is. . . . He laughed. Women always tried to tell him what the trouble with him was. I *do* like them, Dumb Dee, he almost said. My God, hadn't he been telling her for three days how much he liked them? He loved them. That was his problem in life: Love! Love made him feel real. Being seen through new eyes, telling a new version of his old story, these gave him new life, made him feel hallowed, authentic. He had love to spare. He was one of the lovingest men he knew.

"But don't they get sort of ticked, when they find out there's someone else?" Deedee said, popping a large seedless white grape into her mouth.

He poured himself a glass of bourbon. Don't even ask, he replied silently, and thought of Denise, the first time, sweeping down the long room like a skater down a rink, stopping him at the door, her anger rising around him like a play of flashing blades, outdoing any feat ever performed on ice before.

And that time at Yale, when Tina had found out about some little flirtation he was carrying on. She did one of those things everybody remembers forever. Got drunk. Filled the bathtub in the suite across the hall, and got into it fully clothed with a copy of his history term paper floating around her. Thank God it was only the carbon copy.

And then in Brewerton, the Cora time, Tina standing in front of him like an executioner. He had risen to his feet to face her, zipping his pants. That was Cora, he said of the woman who had fled. I didn't even recognize her at first. It was so long ago. Really I didn't. He couldn't look at Tina, couldn't bear her eyes, but sat back down on the edge of the chair again, beaten.

She stepped up to him and touched his bowed head, her hand settling with such a weight on his hair that he foresaw clumps of earth falling on his own coffin. I want you to know, she said. You are never going to do this to me again.

I know. I know.

And then the hyacinths smashed all over the kitchen.

"I don't blame her," Deedee said, nipping at a hangnail with her little white babyish teeth.

That night he had his dream again. From it he awoke as always, his heart racing, throat constricted with a sob. In the dream, he was holding onto the end of a long rope that dangled from a helicopter that had come to rescue him in a deep valley. But as the helicopter (or was it a monstrous bird? It changed form in the middle of the dream), rose over the chasm, the rope began to rubberize and lengthen, and he began to swing on the end of it in ever-wider arcs, until the rope was so long, and the helicopter-bird so high above him, and the arcs so extreme that he knew he would perish unless he chose a side of the chasm to be on, and then stayed on it.

Deedee. It made him smile, her name. It was perfect, a baby's name. She was like a baby herself, sucking and cooing and thinking with her baby's little brain. And once, her face grew wizened and serious, like a baby's face thinking, and she said to him, You really want something, you have to be ready to do anything to get it, you know? I know, sweetheart, he'd said.

She wasn't as dumb as he made out, actually. She could read and write and even compute. And she had some opinions. He had to admit there were certain archetypal myths fixed in that brain of hers to give her some insight into the world she moved in. Telling her, as she lay beside him, about Denise and a woman named Kate he had fallen in love with in the early years of his marriage, and a Terry and a Sara and a Blair and a Mona (she didn't realize at first that Mona was his mother!), telling her about Tina, Tina, popping up in his life again and again, he even had to admit that Deedee was probably sorry for him, for all the trouble all these women had put him to in his life, and for all the trouble he had put them to, without even understanding why.

Deedee *was* sorry for him. He was so ignorant. She knew he couldn't help himself. She had known other men like him. But she had too much tact to express her opinion to him. Besides, she wanted something from him in return for listening to him for a whole week.

"You should write a novel," she said one day. "It would make a great movie."

"Why else write a novel?" he said. "Deedee, I have been writing one, in my head, for twenty years. But there's one thing wrong with it."

"What?"

"There ain't no women in it."

"Well, put some in. It should be easy. For you."

"I can't," he said. "I just can't imagine them in it."

"It would be boring without any girls in it," Deedee said. "Are you afraid of women?"

And then Larry Holtzman from the DEA telephoned from the lobby.

Jack never bothered to answer that ridiculous question of Deedee's. He ceased his drunken babble, splashed water on his face, and sobered up just in time to open the door.

"What about her?" Larry said.

"In one ear and out the other," Jack said. Larry Holtzman wore a short-sleeved shirt with a tropical motif and khaki pants and running shoes without socks. He was not Jack's notion of a Fed. His eyeglasses were crooked, and his hair looked as if he'd arranged it with a currycomb. Jack liked him right away. You could trust a man who looked as if he'd lived all his life on Gilligan's Island.

Deedee did her nails in the bathroom, while Jack told Larry what he suspected about Mickey Kolyrion.

"Why are you doing this?" Larry said.

Jack felt drunk again. "To avenge Beauty," he said.

"Oh, yes?" Larry said. He wrote it down on a small pad he carried in his shirt pocket.

"Don't write it down," Jack said. "Do you have to write it down? It sounds stupid enough as it is."

"To avenge Beauty," Larry said, crossing it out, waiting.

"Because a reckoning is in order," Jack said. "A couple of old scores beg to be settled. And a new one, too."

Larry stared at Jack for a long while, as if he were trying to make out a figure at the back of a cave. "He is small-fry," he said. "But we would like to know his sources. Supposing you check out, and all, all you will be asked to do is a little entrapment. We will do everything else. It should be no sweat."

"For you or for me?"

"For you."

Jack smiled. He liked the idea of a little entrapment, as long as he didn't get caught in the trap. Larry assured him this would never happen.

When Deedee realized he would be leaving, she cried a little. Then she went out and bought a *Playboy* magazine and showed him the centerfold. "That's what I want to be," she said.

He considered the young lady who had so obligingly presented her private parts to the camera. "No reason you couldn't," he said. Unless they required a residency in gynecology. "You look as good as she does."

"But how?"

"How what?"

"How could I get to be it?"

"Well, how would I know?"

"Should I try to be a centerfold first, or should I try to be a bunny first and then get to be a centerfold?"

"I should think it would work either way," Jack said.

She ran her finger up the middle of his bare abdomen, over his chest and right into his mouth. "Can you find out for me?" she said in her little-baby voice.

He looked at her. She was smarter than he'd given her credit for. She ran her wet little finger back down again, lightly trailing down his sternum, over his navel and on down. "I think I know somebody," he groaned. "I'll call him."

"If he thinks I should be a bunny first," she whispered afterward, "I'd like to start out in the one in New Jersey."

He remembered a joke about New Jersey. A central intelligence governs the universe, except for certain parts of New Jersey. The Playboy Club was undoubtedly one of them. She made love to him again, and he wished he were drunk, one more time.

Afterward, he dialed a number out of his little address book and had a short conversation, and then dialed another number, and arranged an interview for her with a friend of a friend of a friend. "They'll fix you up," he said. Then he called Eastern and made two reservations to New York for the following day. "You're in the big time now, cute kid," he said. "Let's go down to dinner. How about it?"

"I knew you'd help me," she said. "You're sweet."

"I know," he said, kissing her lightly on her left nipple. "You're pretty sweet yourself."

"I'll make lots of money," she said dreamily.

"You will," he said. "Call me when you do." He gave her his card. "I'll make lots more for you."

All in all, he felt much better when he got back to New York. He was glad he'd gone. Glad he'd met Deedee, glad he'd never see her again, too, and he was glad he'd called the DEA. If he never did another thing to merit the good citizen of the year award, even if he never even voted again, at least he had done one small thing for mankind.

His apartment was still, and dim, and dusty. The last of Beryl's plants had died. He unpacked. His cleaning service didn't do laundry. His laundry service didn't do underwear. His underwear was bulging out of the hamper. Glumly, he took it to the basement and ran it through the machine.

"I suppose you want me to invite you for Thanksgiving dinner," Denise said when he called.

"Is it Thanksgiving already?" he said.

"What is wrong with you?" she said.

"Maybe I'm brain dead."

"I am furious with you," she said, "for not seeing us before you went on this extended trip. Do you realize we haven't seen you in three weeks?"

He sighed. "We're supposed to be getting a divorce, Denise. You don't have to invite me for Thanksgiving. I don't have to see you any more. I called you every day, didn't I?"

"You are not divorcing them," she said.

"You won't let me see them," he said.

"You may see them any time you like. But I will not have them staying overnight in your love nest."

"Denise," he said. "Beryl's been gone since June."

"Surely you've replaced her by this time," Denise said.

"Denise," he said softly.

"I don't want a divorce, darling," Denise said, also softly.

"Invite me for Thanksgiving dinner," he said. "I want to see my children. I wouldn't even mind seeing you again. How are you, anyway?" He was lonely.

"Your mother is here," Denise said. "And your father is on his way."

"My who?" he said.

"Your father."

"What *are* you talking about?"

"Mona and your father have been seeing each other," she said. "We are hoping they will get married."

"Mona and Colonel Bringhurst?"

"Don't call him that anymore," she said. "He's your father. He has been up here once already. He was disappointed not to see you. He's coming back tonight for the holidays. He's staying at the Pierre. They are devoted to each other. I have never seen anything like it. It's as if they never parted. He's quite youthful for his age."

"What have you been up to, Denise?"

"Arranging your legitimacy," she said. "Don't you think it's time?"

"I think it's obscene," he said. "Don't invite me to your turkey dinner. Why are you doing this to Mona?"

"I adore Mona as much as you do," she said. "That's why I want you to be here. It would cast a pall on things if you weren't. I do not want them to get the idea we are permanently estranged."

"Denise," he said.

"What?"

"We are permanently estranged. I want a divorce. I want to sell that collection and get a divorce."

"No," she said.

"I'm coming over there now. Be there," he said. "You be ready to talk. Be ready to look at those paintings through new eyes, Denise. You are going to see things my way for once and. . . ."

"I'll be ready," she said. Denise always hung up on him before he was finished.

[223]

He was there in an hour and to his surprise she *was* ready. He signed an agreement she had typed up in the interval, giving her the collection in return for a fifty-fifty split of the rest of their assets. "And you can have the boys," she said. What was he supposed to do with the boys? "Well, then, I'll keep them," she said sweetly. "The lawyers can work out the support. Happy Thanksgiving, Jack."

10

When he appeared in Jack's office, Mickey Kolyrion was accompanied by a small man in a dark overcoat. Jack had expected him to be alone. "This is Raul," Mickey said. He was Mickey and Frank's partner in Impex. Jack shook hands with both of them. Raul stood a little behind Mickey and listened carefully to what they were saying, only taking his hard little eyes off Jack Troy's face once to step over to the window and look twenty stories down into the street.

In the presence of Raul in his black coat and black fedora, Jack told them he was getting a divorce and suggested that he didn't like being diminished by half. He wanted to recoup.

Raul shifted a wad of gum in his mouth and kept his right hand inside his coat, like Napoleon or Al Capone.

"You need bucks," Mickey said meditatively. "Everything's fifty-fifty these days?"

"In a nutshell."

Mickey thought. Bucks were a question of supplies. You lost some. You replaced them. You put up some. They multiplied. "I heard about a franchise scheme," he said.

"Too complicated," Jack said. "Nothing long term."

"There's toxins," Mickey said. "Very lucrative. You have to get rid of them nice today. It's a problem of national scope. The oil companies are desperate. They don't care what you do with it. Just as long as they don't have to be involved."

"Isn't it a lot of paperwork?" Jack said.

"There's only one thing I know of with no paperwork," Mickey said.

Jack looked at him. It was going to be incredibly easy. Larry had said it would be.

"I don't believe this," Mickey said. "You?"

"Just a quick in and out." Talk return on investment, Larry said. Absolutely don't talk names or dates. They are always supersuspicious. The names and dates will come. We will discover them. "How much do I put up? And what's the return? And how fast do I see it?"

Mickey's eyes grew bright and interested, but wary. "You have to know someone."

"Don't you?" Jack said.

"What's in it for me?" Mickey said.

"What do you want?"

"Not to testify, if I'm indicted."

"It's no skin off my teeth," Jack said.

"But Tina, too," Mickey said. "You're a package."

[226]

"She'll go along."

"What makes you think so?"

"She doesn't really care about Clarice."

"She cares about dealing."

"She won't know about it."

Mickey looked perplexed. "Then how can you guarantee her?"

Jack looked at him. Appeal to his sense of what he lacks the most of, Larry had advised. Romance, he thought. Love. Loyalty. And devotion. All the good stuff. "She'll do it for me," Jack said. "If I ask her to."

Mickey swallowed. Jeanne did nothing for him. He looked almost persuaded.

"Didn't I see you at the Sandpiper Motel in Miami?" Raul said.

"Miami?" Mickey said.

Jack turned to look at Raul. He was aware that a stupid expression had overtaken his face. His bladder was suddenly uncomfortably full. "Sandpiper?" he said, thinking frantically. "I have an office in Miami. I was down there recently." He had had a drink at the bar with Larry. And he had also been in the Tropic Room with Deedee, their last night.

"Dancing," Raul said.

In that case, the Tropic Room.

"Dancing?" Mickey said. "With who?"

"A girl I met."

Mickey looked at him. "What about Tina?"

"You know the old saying. A wife is what you have when you're within forty miles of home."

"She's not your wife," Mickey said.

You might have to go for it, Larry said. They're never stupid.

"Why don't we all sit down," Jack said carefully. He sat at his desk, and Mickey sat in the chair opposite him. Raul sat on the windowsill.

"Let's go back to the beginning," Jack said. "It's 1956."

11

The New Testament lesson was from Romans again. "We rejoice in our sufferings knowing that suffering produces endurance, and endurance produces character, and character produces hope." Hugh could hope, and he had character, and he could endure, and he was suffering, but it was difficult to rejoice.

She had been irritable for weeks. She burned food, stared at the telephone, went down to the river at odd hours and stood looking out over the water, played certain records again and again. In the middle of dinner one night, she had suddenly clapped her hands to her face and jumped up from the table. Bo started after her. "Stay where you are," Hugh said sharply. "I only wanted to do the Heimlich maneuver," Bo said. Oh, God, Hugh prayed, make her remember, make her forget, oh shit!

make her remember and then make her forget. Make her stay with us.

Where were you all day, he had wanted to know, the day she forgot to pick up Amy and Bo after school, the day there was no dinner ready, the day she walked in at six o'clock, exhausted and nervous. She told him. Why? he said. To talk, she said. You don't have to worry, Hugh. It's over. Nothing has changed. Over? he said. Changed? I thought you learned a long time ago that nothing would ever change with him. I did, she said. I forgot it. I won't be seeing him again. Did you go to bed with him? No. I suppose he wanted you to. Or does he just want to be friends? You can't be friends with him, you know, he said. He doesn't waste his time on friendships with mere women. Don't be hard, she said. I told you not to think I'd be easy, he said. You can't have him for a friend. It won't stay as that. You'll want more. One meeting will lead to another. You'll want to be together all the time. That's what *love* is. When you love someone, you want to be with them, only with them. It's dangerous, Tina. It will make *love* start up again!

Oh! Stop it!

Love! Like a wild beast she had to keep locked up in a cage. If it once got out, it would get her!

Still, though she was as prickly as a boar brush, she was sticking. He held his breath, walked on eggs. Even though two weeks before Christmas—at *Madame Butterfly*—beside her in the warm tense darkness, he was aware that somewhere deep inside herself she was weeping. At the end of Cio-cio San's aria she threw her face into her hands. But then, so did many others in the audience rustle for tissue, blow noses. He nearly wept himself!

In the car on the way home, he took her hand in the dark, noticed with a start, when he lifted her hand to the light of a street lamp, that her nails were filed and shaped and polished with a clear varnish. Her face beside him in profile was radiant, too, a polish on it, for some reason, as if a storm had passed and she was clear again. Was she? he wondered. Or was she steadying herself, grooming for one?

Sometimes, he came upon her standing statue-still, listening to a voice no one but she could hear, a look on her face so intent, yet so distant, it chilled him to the bone. She was listening to *him*, wherever he was. Some telepathic message, telling her he had left New York, gone to some faraway place to think of her, was on his way back now, was back, was trying not to call her. . . . When she came out of these trancelike listenings, she had a hungry look on her face.

She sat beside him in firelight, Christmas coming, the house smelling of paste wax and bayberry candles, and she was young and soft and beautiful to him, her skin unlined, her waist and hips neat and small, her bosom full. He told her all this. It's the lighting, she said. Was Jack Troy the kind of man it was wise to reveal oneself to only in soft lights? Was she practicing?

And once, late, late at night, he woke to hear her radio on as low as it could be. Tina, he whispered. But she was asleep. He got out of bed and went around to her side to turn it off. "I'll Never Love This Way Again."

He shivered.

But he had his song, too. "Send in the Clowns." He played it on the tape deck in his car, everywhere he went. *I thought that you'd want what I want. Sorry, my dear.* It was only slightly better than listening to the news. Tales of infidelity were rampant in the news. American spouses were being egregiously unfaithful to one another. The papers, the TV, the radio, the latest novels, the latest nonfiction, the movies, Broadway, off-Broadway. His practice boomed on adulteries. Brewerton was a hotbed of divorce.

"Losing my timing. . . ."

"Yes, awful timing, awful timing," Sybil said, over coffee. "Thirty-nine's a bad age for a woman."

"She's forty," he said. "What should I do?"

"Sit tight. It has nothing to do with a lack in you."

"I can't believe it's happening to me," Hugh said. A disastrous chemistry. A fatal attachment. Where had he heard those phrases before? They kept running through his head. He felt helpless. A nonevent, a thing that hadn't happened, and maybe even wouldn't, was sweeping him out to sea. Send in the goddamn clowns!

And then at the last minute, miraculously, a change. Christmas, to his delightful surprise, was going to be as cheerful as it always had been. They were going to make it! She was happy again. She sang in the kitchen. She laughed. She hugged Amy and Bo for no reason. She even hugged him. They were going to make it! Mysterious packages arrived at the door. She spirited them away to places Amy and Bo knew about but wouldn't dream of looking in.

He breathed again. He was happy. He wanted to give a huge party to show how happy he was. They hand-delivered invitations for the day after Christmas. To their surprise, no one regretted. The whole world, sixty of their dearest friends, were going to celebrate with Hugh! They hired a bartender and two maids, and ordered a ham and a turkey, and she cheerfully whirred things in the blender for days, and Amy and Bo cut up vegetables and stamped out little sandwiches with cookie cutters, and Hugh hired a man to play the piano.

Mr. Penney arrived two hours early in his new red Christmas tie from Amy, and his new red Christmas socks from Bo. He was clean and pink and fresh, and what was left of his white hair was brushed to a gravity-defying tuft on top of his shiny pink head. They sat him down in his favorite chair by the fire. From there, he could see everyone come in. Didn't want to miss a soul. It might be his last Christmas on earth, after all, and he wanted to make the most of it. He was old, and it didn't disturb him to think that he could go at any minute. He was looking forward to going, to seeing Mrs. Penney again. In fact, the prospect overjoyed him at times. . . . After all these years. Amy and Bo set up a card table in front of him and taught him their new board games, and he beat Bo at Othello the second time around.

The house smelled of the juniper and cedar garlands that decorated the mantels and banisters; the fire crackled; the silver and glass gleamed. But Mr. Penney kept one eye on Tina. Something wrong with her, he decided. He watched her whirling through the rooms, deploying ashtrays and coasters and napkins and bowls of nuts and dips and vegetables and crackers. And it occurred to him that she was avoiding him.

She had been, he would say, for some months. She came to see him, of course, dropped in three or four times a week, but there was something evasive about her. Her visits too brisk and short for his liking. He had a good idea what was behind it.

She came and knelt beside his chair with a plate of little

sandwiches and gherkins for him and a glass of milk. "For you," she said. "Before they start coming." He searched her face. Beautiful and noncommittal, she smiled at him, her lashes black as ink against her fair skin. "Do you say your prayers any more?" he said.

"Why, Daddy!" she said.

"Well, do you?"

"On Sundays."

"Why only on Sundays?" he asked.

"I'm busy."

"It doesn't take any time at all," he said mildly. "Just a sentence or two. Just a little contact. It gives you strength."

"I don't need any extra strength. Or any divine intervention either," she said. "I'm doing just fine."

His only child, he thought in despair. He would be leaving her soon! He had thought Hugh would always be there, by her. His heart swelled and thumped in his chest. "I worry," he said.

"Don't worry about me," she said fiercely. "And please don't pray for me."

She believed he had God's ear, and he did. "I do anyway," he said.

"Intercession is not in order," she said. "I'm doing just fine, Daddy. Really. Really."

His love for her beat in his veins. He hadn't much time. He didn't want the sour little gherkins. He didn't want to try to swallow a shrimp-salad sandwich. He wanted to talk to her. He. . . . The door bell rang. "It's starting," he said, dismayed. He was too late. He should have taken this up much sooner.

"Yes," she said. But instead of going to the front door to

let her guests in, she rushed off to the kitchen in the other direction and closed the swinging door behind her.

The pianist was playing "All the Things You Are," and everyone was pouring into the house at once in great puffs of cold air and goosedown coats, and new fluffy Christmas scarves and hats, and shiny boots and new mittens, and gusts of greetings and kisses and hugs, and the pianist segued into "I Wish You Love," and she put her hands over her ears and ran up the back stairs and locked herself in her bathroom.

The phone rang about ten minutes later, just as she was about to go downstairs again to face the music. "I'm in Brewerton," he said. "At Beimer's. Will you meet me?"

"Yes," she said.

"Right now?"

"Yes."

"I'll be at the corner," he said.

And the next thing Hugh or anyone else knew, she was disappearing out the back door in her fur coat and her tall new shiny boots.

12

He shut the door to the room he had taken at Beimer's. In the dark, moving toward him, she closed her eyes, drew in her breath, and opened her arms. They stood in the dark, touching. We have gone and done it, she thought. We are here now.

Patiently, they took in each other's presence: breath rising and falling, bones and flesh and heartbeats, a deep trembling in the veins under the layers of wool and cotton and silk. Beyond his face, over his shoulders, she became vaguely aware of yardage and deep colors, draperies of deep red and blue. Faint with panicked joy, she stepped backward against the door for support, pulling him with her. He reached behind her in the dark to lock the door, parted the opening of her coat, touched her, lightly at first, her midriff, her breasts, her waist, her back, her thighs; pulled her toward his thighs. She was shaking. "Is this for good?" he said.

She nodded.

He sighed. He thought of all the things she would never do again, because of him.

He took her coat off and hung it in the closet and followed her across the room in the dark to the bed. They lay down on it on their sides, tried to make out each other's faces in the light coming in through the draperies from the street. He touched her hair. "New."

She touched his face, laid her hand on his rib cage. Old, she thought. Old, old old love.

"I tried to stay away," he whispered.

"Where were you?"

He gripped her body, locked her to him. He moved his mouth over hers in a dry, tense, rough kiss, parted her lips, skimmed the tip of her tongue with his own.

"For so long?" she whispered. "Why were you gone so long?"

He told her about Larry Holtzman.

"You shouldn't have done that," she said, struck with uneasiness.

"I had to."

"Not for me," she said. "I wrote to you yesterday. You didn't do it for me, I hope. I would have come anyway."

"I did it for myself. And for Rosie," he said. "Did you really write to me?" He unbuttoned the top button of her blouse, and she loosened the knot of his tie.

In the dark warm room, they stripped quickly, tossing clothes in chairs, feeling tentatively under the sheets for limbs and joints—hands, arms, knees. He pulled her to him, her body warmer even than the air they quickly warmed beneath the covers, felt for signs of recognition, time, wear.

Her breasts were larger than he remembered, her abdomen softer, her hipbones sharper. He touched her cautiously, feeling his way around her in the dark. Her thighs were still as hard as bolts of smooth, warm silk. Her body, as if imprinted in his hands' memory, began to come back to him. The familiar smell of her breath, taste of her skin, light flatness of her fingers on his back, her inner thighs locking his ribs, her hips rising, opening, her body feeling its way back to its own accommodation with his, adjusting to memory, weight, procedure.

"Don't go away," he whispered fiercely, his mouth on hers again.

"I never did. You did."

"I never will again."

"I love you."

"You are me," he said.

She moved to meet him. "Now," she said.

His head jerked up to the ceiling, as if he had heard some urgent command. His sweat fell on her face. "There," he said.

She pulled the blanket up over them, and fell asleep against the pulse throbbing in his throat.

When the phone rang, she knew it would be Hugh.

"I knew you'd be there. I knew you were with him," he said. " 'More happy happy love.' Is that it?"

"Hugh," she said.

"Come home."

"I can't."

"Yes, you can. It's not too late."

"No, Hugh. It is."

"You have to," he said. "You can't not. It's not decent. You can't just walk out. We were having a party. We were having a life, Tina. We have to talk."

"Hugh!"

"Don't you care?" he said. "About us? About Amy and Bo?"

"Yes, I care."

"Come home, then."

She stared at her reflection in the mirror over the low chest of drawers opposite the bed.

Behind her, he put his hands on her naked shoulders. "Don't," he whispered.

"I have to," she said wildly.

"No."

"Tina!" Hugh said.

"I'll be there in the morning," she said wearily.

"No," Jack said.

"I *have* to."

"He'll make you change your mind."

"He won't," she said. "I had made up my mind before you called. I told you I wrote to you."

He sighed. They lay down again in the warm bed. He drew the covers up over them. "Good," he said.

He drove her to Stephen Street in the morning. She went around the house and in by the back door. Hugh was alone in the kitchen. He opened the door for her. He was wearing the

[239]

same clothes he had been wearing at the party. "You haven't been to bed," she said.

"No."

She started putting away the platters and bowls washed and left on the drainboard.

"Tina."

"You're going to hate me," she said. "But I'm going."

"Why?" he said. "Why with him? Of all people?"

"Who else would I ever have left you for?" she said wearily.

"What are you going to tell Amy and Bo? What about your father?"

"Oh, please," she said. "Don't be hard."

"Hard!"

"I love him, Hugh. I'll have to tell them that."

"It's so inconsistent of you," he said. "How can you work at restoring other people's houses and take a sledgehammer to your own?"

"But that's it," she said.

"What's it?"

He was her house. In her life before they were. It had its own kind of consistency.

"How can you restore something that may never have been there in the first place?"

"It was," she said.

"What if it wasn't?"

"Then I'll have to take my lumps."

He looked at her. "Do you expect me to take you back, in that case?"

"No."

"Because I don't think I will," he said. "I have some pride."

She moved across the kitchen and put her arms around him.

"If you go through with it, I'm going to make it tough on you," he said. "You won't get Amy and Bo."

"I know," she said.

He buried his face in her hair. "It's my life," he whispered. His well-planned happy life.

"I know," she whispered. "It's going to be awful, I know."

They fixed breakfast together for Amy and Bo, and she looked out the front window and saw that Jack Troy was gone, and for a moment she almost believed he had changed his mind and gone away again for good and she would sit down and eat with them as if nothing had happened. But she couldn't eat, or even sit, only pace around the kitchen. Finally, the front doorbell rang, and he stood on the porch, red from the cold, hatless and determined. "Tina," he said, not looking at Amy or Bo, who stood in the hall behind her, "Let's go."

They will never forget this, she thought. This is how they'll always remember it. "Get your coats on, kids, and play outside for a while," she said.

"No," they said.

"Yes," Hugh said, appearing at her side. "We're going to have a discussion." They moved behind Tina for protection, but she kept her arms at her side, of no help to them, and Hugh caught them and turned them toward the back door. "Go outside, please," he said. He herded them into the kitchen and pushed their snow coats at them and their mittens and hats and boots, and when they were only half-dressed, he put them out the back door and locked it behind them. "It's cold out here," they shouted, angry and fearful, banging on the panes of the door.

"I'm not going to let you do this," Hugh said to Jack, ignoring them, and she knew by his face that not unstrained mercy but an eye for an eye was the philosophy that undergirded his lawyer's sense of justice.

Jack pulled her gently away from the window, where she stood staring out at them in the backyard of trampled snow. They stared back at the house, like human accusations, exerting pressure on her with the very fact of their existence. Amy lay across the horizontal ladder of the swing set, her chin on her folded arms, staring, and Bo leaned against one of the vertical ladders of the set, as if too stunned to stand on his own, and every once in a while he scooped up some snow and made a ball and threw it down again. "This is terrible!" she cried.

"I'm not forcing her to do it," Jack said. "She's free."

"She's not free at all," Hugh said. "She's my wife. You just can't walk in here and take my wife away."

"I didn't mean to, Hugh," he said. "It just happened that way."

"Let it unhappen then," Hugh said. "Go away. She'll recover."

"No," she said. "Let them in. I'm going, Hugh."

They were an ominous purplish-red color when they came in. Bo's mittens were frozen stiff and encrusted with little grey pellets of ice. They cried when they found her upstairs packing a suitcase. "What will happen to us?" they cried. "Where are we going to live? Who is he, anyway? Where did he come from? Who will cook? Who will drive us? What about our *family?*"

She tried to answer, but her answers were all absurd.

They handed her notes before she left. Mom, Bo wrote, what you say you are gonna do is a bad thing. It is not write to leave a family without a mother, I am sorry to tell you that its a mistake. Your son, Bo. Mother, Amy wrote, your just as bad as all those you talk about who leave there families flat for there own selfish reasons. I will never come to visit you as you say you want me to do and as for Mr. Troy I hate him. I plan to take charge in this house Daddy won't have to worry wear his next meal is coming from. Don't bother ansering. Your (former) daughter Amy Gardiner.

Someday, Amy and Bo, she wrote back, you will read a poem about the road not taken. The poet means that a life can be a good and right and full one, and yet at the same time, a person can believe it could have been good and right and full lived in another way. I have a chance to take a road I didn't take a long time ago, even though it hurts all of us very much for me to do it. I hope that someday, when the worst part of the hurt is over, you'll choose a road that brings you close to my new road, where there will always be a special place for you.

From the room where she finished packing, she heard Amy crumple the note and throw it on the floor.

"It's not the end of family life," she said to her. "It's the end of one kind of family life. There are different kinds. Different kinds of families."

"Bully!" Amy shouted. "Bully for us!"

"Tina," Hugh said, catching her by the arm in the front hall. "He'll leave you again. He hasn't changed."

"He might do that," she said. "But I've changed."

13

In the middle of a cold driving rain, they left for a Caribbean island. And in a house they rented, on a hill high above the sea, a house perfect in every respect, down even to the maid, competent and perfectly deaf and mute, they were happy. "I've never had the feeling before this," he whispered. "I never knew what it meant to feel 'happy.' I feel happy." "Don't say so. It might go away," she whispered. They talked in whispers, despite the deaf maid, as if not to call attention to themselves, as if the gods to whom their paradise belonged might banish them if they noticed their presence.

"Happy anyway," he whispered.

Unforgivably happy, she thought, and didn't care, beside him in the sun. Happiness unpardonably snatched, and she was glad, nevertheless. But I always thought of Hugh as my son, her father had said. You can, still. No, he said. When they say blood is thicker than water, this is what they mean. I have to see everything through your eyes. You're my daughter. But he needs you more than I do, she wanted to say. See through his eyes. Did he mistreat you all these years? he asked stiffly. No! He was good to me! But why, then? Tell me why? It's what I wanted, she said. Nothing else mattered as much.

She lay beside him on the bed, next to the open windows, beyond which: a straw hat in the sun on a chair, a bowl of warm-skinned melons, blue sky, mountains split by deep ravines. Pink stucco, white cement, vines of magenta bougainvillea, two small brown children slipping hand in hand through a wall of blossoms invisibly parted, slipping as silently as fish into the shallow end of the pool. They came every day, hand in hand, to slip into the blue water, lie together on the submerged steps, to cup small handfuls of water on each other's bare brown shoulders, and slip away again through the wall of pink and orange bloom. She assumed they were the maid's children.

It was like all their old summers together, he whispered. But it was different, summer in winter this time, fragrant and warm in a pink villa overlooking the flat shimmering sea, clouds of honeysuckle and bougainvillea tumbling up walls and spilling down roofs, endless blue skies. And winter and the other life only hours away. So fragile, she thought. All so fragile.

"How did we do it?" he whispered. "How did it happen, anyway?"

"We got the chance, and we took it."

He kissed her.

"You, of all people in the world. Me with you, after all this time."

"Of all people in the world," he whispered, his mouth so close to hers he could deposit the words on her lips, "I love you best. Do you know that?"

"Yes," she whispered, turning over on him, lowering the word into his mouth. "Yes! Yes, yes, love." Filled with the inexplicable sadness of happiness, seeing in every passing hour adumbrations of its transience, she held him in her arms. "I'm so happy, so happy," he whispered. "What *is* it?"

"It's getting what you wanted when you were fourteen when you're forty-one."

"That fits," he sighed.

She was struck that she had never seen him happy before, only in states of mind peripheral to happiness: cheerfulness, confidence, optimism. Not this unguarded serenity so foreign to him as to contain in it, she half-knew already, its own reasons for disappearing. Sad, she cried to herself. She was so sad. So very very sad. Like a pit, it stuck in her craw, her sad happiness.

Across the space between their lounge chairs, she stroked his hand, traced the long scar across the back of it with her index finger. They analyzed all their scars, their bodies historic documents of stress and trial, pain and years; noted corns and calluses and graying hair and loosening skin and declining muscles and unyielding fat. Life half-over, and they had only just begun.

It was time, she thought drowsily, time to begin. In the shade of an almond tree, whose brown scratchy leaves the gardener swept up each morning and yet whose branches were always abundantly full of gleaming flossy green new leaves, she let herself float finally into a state of undefended contentment;

let go, or told herself she had, of the image in her mind of Hugh and Amy and Bo and her father, waiting, hoping. Perfectly in love, she thought. One last chance and we took it. It would never have come again. They had done the only thing to do, and they were ready at last to do whatever they imagined could be done.

He imagined it first, whispered it to her, to create life with her. It was not only imaginable, it was irresistible and inevitable. Later, they would even believe they could remember which warm clamorous night it must have been, though the nights were all like one another. The southern stars were so low they seemed to hang just above the dark garden. Pariah dogs barked in the black hills; the night air was loud all around them with tree frogs and innumerable strumming insects. Their sunburned bodies tingled on the cool sheets, and outside, beyond the bed, bats and swallows swooped gracefully across the pool. All the nights were the same. But they remembered one night more clearly than other nights, one coming together sweeter and more urgent than the others. That will be it, he murmured into her ear, his face in her damp hair, and they fell asleep. And when she woke, she felt sure it had been it, that she was one hour pregnant. She touched his body under the sheet he had pulled up over them, and he woke and turned to her and touched hers.

"We'll be sixty when she's twenty."

"And a hundred and twenty when she's eighty. Is it a she?"

"Yes."

"Good," he whispered.

But was it a thing to have done? she thought with utmost clarity one morning, on waking. Was it at all the thing to have done in a moment of unthinking rapture? Was unthinking rapture a mode indicated by their time, their age, their place, their history? Was thinking unrapture perhaps more appropriate?

"Not at all," he said. "We will make a very fine family. And next year we'll add to it, to make it an even number."

Still, she slept lightly after that, listening for the twenty-three nights that remained to them, to the fertilized egg traveling to her uterus, to the sounds of it implanting itself on her uterine wall, to the new blood vessels forming around it, to pituitary hormones rushing to her adrenals, to her milk glands swelling, to the skin darkening around her areolas, to the estrogen gathering in her stomach, to herself retching one morning.

The past is not indicative, he said. And the future will be pluperfect. But for her the present suddenly had the potential for getting tense. He didn't like ties that bound. She hadn't planned to marry him. She had made the one mistake the gods had wanted her to make. She could almost hear them laughing.

"Do you know," he said, one day. "Life isn't short, after all. It's long. Long enough for three or four lives."

"Which one is this?"

"This is the third. They come in twenty-year cycles. The first twenty we were together."

"More or less."

"The second twenty we weren't."

"That's for sure."

"The third twenty we will be."

"And the last twenty?"

"You mean the last twenty twenty. We're going to live forever and be together the whole time."

"I wish."

"Believe," he said.

She played with the fine white sand.

"What shall we name her?" he said, one day.

"What do you want?"

"Claire?"

"Light?"

"Yes."

"Let there be? . . ."

"Yes."

But while he thought in terms of new beginnings and light, the images taking shape in her mind as their month together waned were already becoming ones of endings. Shall I have an abortion? she asked him. Wouldn't that be better? No! he said. We're getting married! We're getting married, Tina! But I don't want to, she said. Don't be silly, he said.

The Caribbean sunset came with the swiftness and predictability of an eclipse. At the moment of the sun's disappearance, bats dived crazily over the pool, and lizards fled from chaise to chaise across the tiled patio to nighttime safe places, and she shivered, as if a certain shadow had poised itself at the edge of her life. Maybe I should, she said. I'm too old. No, he said fiercely, gripping her arm. Don't even think it.

One night, just before they left, she dreamed of the little brown-skinned boy and girl who slipped through the parted flowers every day to dabble silently and smilingly in the shallow water of the pool, and in the dream a tiny flicker of boredom, or annoyance, crossed the boy's pretty face and darkened his brown eyes, and he placed a hand gently on the girl's smooth dark head and held her under the water until she floated silently away from him, face down across the pool.

14

Hugh was there when she drove into the driveway on Stephen Street, opened the back door for her, as if she were coming in from work, or the supermarket. She felt as if she were, knew by his face how it was for him that she wasn't. He looked at the suitcase she was carrying. She handed it to him. "It's empty," he said.

"I came for some things I need," she said. "I told you that, Hugh."

"I can't believe you mean to go through with this," he said. "Isn't three months enough of an experiment?"

He followed her up to the attic and sat near her on a broken chair while she went through her trunks, taking what she needed, trying to recall which box or garment bag her maternity clothes from Amy were in, wondering if she could pack them, too, without his recognizing them. She would not tell him today, not the way he looked.

She found the trunk with the maternity clothes. Most of them were summer things. Amy had been born in August.

Hugh tried to remember her wearing the clothes she looked at. One red dress was so familiar he could almost see her in it, at a summer wedding. Weddings, he thought with a sickening sinking in his stomach. "You won't reconsider?"

"No, Hugh."

"For an interlude?" he said. "You've left us for good, your family, because of an interlude?"

"An interlude?"

"An affair. A romance. A middle-aged romance, for God's sake!"

"Hugh," she said, "Would it make it any easier for you if I made you hate me?"

"I could never hate you. I love you."

"I'm going to have a baby," she said. "These are my maternity clothes from Amy."

Stupidly, he stared at her, at her stomach, flat and apparently innocent. "When?" he said.

"In October."

He was too staggered to count the months. "Were you, before you? . . ."

"No."

"On purpose, are you?"

"Yes."

"You're not even married to him."

"I'm not going to marry him," she said.

"Why not?"

She shook her head.

"What about it? What name will it have?"

"I don't know," she said. "Legally, it would have my name, wouldn't it?"

"Legally, it would have my name," he said coldly.

They looked at each other.

"You're too old to have a baby."

"I was tested. It's okay." She looked at him. "It's a girl."

"You disgust me," he said.

"Hugh," she said. "It's not your fault. You were always good to me."

"So much for gratitude then," he said. "Not the strongest foundation for marriage, apparently."

"I didn't marry you out of gratitude."

"Why did you?"

"Because you were good. Because I loved you."

"When did I stop being good? When did you stop loving me? Am I evil now? Do you hate me now? You're leaving me because of an interlude, for God's sake?"

"Don't keep calling it that," she said. "You have to start thinking of yourself as the interlude. He was there first."

"Fuck Jack Troy!" he shouted. He picked up an ice-hockey stick of Bo's and cracked it in two on a rafter, and hurled the jagged pieces at the brick chimney at the end of the cavernous attic. "So much for justice," he said.

III

THE
MORNING

1

It was cold and damp for May. In winter running garb, an orange windbreaker over a mismatched warm-up suit and shirts of various vintages, red knit cap down over his ears, Larry Holtzman jogged in the gray drizzle up and down the block past Raul's building on Central Park South. The Cadillac had gone into the garage underneath an hour before. Finally, Raul's beat-up Honda wagon emerged. Raul on his rounds. A dealer's work was never done.

Larry jogged to his own beat-up VW double-parked up the block, and moved out into the traffic after Raul and his driver, five cars ahead in the traffic heading east.

At Second Avenue the wagon turned south, downtown. Larry took off his knit cap and put on a pair of sunglasses. Twice before, they had turned off Second and gone into the Queens Midtown Tunnel without signaling, and he had lost them both times, because of a light. But at the tunnel they kept on going, downtown to the East Village house. Where did they go when they went through the tunnel? He had to find out.

They were telling no secrets, Raul and Mickey. Relieved Jack Troy of $50,000 in cold (DEA) cash for a part of the action. No info in return. Except that it was coming in by sea in June. June what? What sea? Jack asked. Don't ask, Mickey said. Don't, Larry said. Just absorb. And remember. So Jack remembered: the panel truck loading or unloading late at night in the back of the Kolyrion Bros. building in Brewerton. And Larry took it from there. The van's plate, the van's route, the license number of Raul's Cadillac (driver double-parked downstairs at Jack's office while the two of them went up and got the money). Larry in a taxi followed the Cadillac from Wall Street up the West Side right to Central Park South, Raul's Manhattan domicile. He discovered the condemned building they had taken over on East 11th Street. So from somewhere (a stash in the Hamptons?), in the van to the building in Brewerton. Where it was cut up, cleaned, and packaged. (The trash was full of sweepings.) From there in the van to the garage under the Central Park South building. From there in busy Raul's Honda to the East Village, where it was dealt. And out into the wide world with it.

Larry had been following Raul for weeks, driving everything from his mother's Buick to a rented Toyota to his girlfriend's Pinto to his own fifteen-year-old VW to a friend's Thunderbird, in as many different outfits and pairs of glasses. Inadvertently he had discovered Raul's private operation on

East 7th Street, the one MK probably didn't know about, while he was at it.

Raul's driver drove past the house to make sure the preteen spotters were spotting, even in the rain; and the two guys on the roof in place, too. He would drive once around the block before unloading. Then onward and upward, counting, depositing, testing, weighing, measuring, making calls, making drops. All in a day's work. Sunday no exception.

Other roofs were manned for other operations. The street as busy as always, even in the rain. Doleful plainclothes cops around, dressed as joggers, bums, beats, heads. Larry flowed on past. He wasn't interested in the outgoing end.

He drove across Manhattan in the rain to West 11th Street, to the house Jack and Tina had moved into. Narrow, of white stone, with a pointed roofline and columns, it reminded him through the scaffolding of a church.

Jack laughed and showed him a sketch of the way it would look when it was finished. It still looked to Larry like a church. All it needed was a steeple. "Let's put a steeple on, for Larry," Jack said. But she was not amused. Something wrong, Larry saw right away.

They showed him around inside. It looked fine to him, the way it was. "You should see where I live," he said. He would have left everything the way it was, just put on another coat of paint.

Jack laughed again. There were twenty coats of paint already, and under them, on the fireplaces, hand-carved acorns, chestnuts, leaves, berries, flowers. Pilasters, woodwork, moldings, cornices decorated with carved roses and sheaves of grain.

Even caryatids (ladies in togas) carved into pillars holding up the rooms. It would take six men working six weeks to strip it all.

The kitchen was on the ground floor. Up a flight were the living and dining rooms. Their bedroom and a room for the baby, when it was born, were on the third, and on the top floor were rooms for their other children, when they came to visit. "If they ever do," Jack said, suddenly gloomy.

Larry looked at her. She looked away, as if it were his fault. Rain pelted against the windows. Outside, the scaffolding, wet and shiny, seemed to be holding the house up. Fragile, he thought. It's all very delicate here.

They ate in the kitchen, at a table next to the sliding glass doors. They laughed when he said he had never had eggs Benedict before, and he laughed, too, and said they had probably never had an egg cream, and they all laughed. But there was a tension in the air, something between them, or between them and him, that hung like a web in the air.

Rain fell on the ivied garden enclosed by old brick walls. He asked about the bush that looked like a menorah trained to grow against the back brick wall. "Quince," she said. "Espaliered." She gave a little shudder.

"You don't like it?"

"No," she said.

He didn't want to ask her why. She looked sick.

The tension heightened when he showed them his newest DEA-issued listening device. And how it worked. Or was supposed to. "It transmits, too," he said.

"Why does it squawk?" she said.

"It must be the rain," he said.

"What if he finds out, Larry?" she said.

So that was it, he thought. Nerves. "I'm careful," he said. "Not to worry. It'll all be over in a month."

They walked him out to the front gate after lunch. The rain had stopped, though the skies were still low and gray. A heavy iron fence separated another little garden of ivy and myrtle from the front sidewalk. The spikes of the fence were smothered by another thorny quince bush, this one overgrown and dense. She imagined Mickey in his car crushing her and Claire inside of her against the fence, impaling her on the iron spikes, leaving her for dead in the dense thorned bushes.

Jack laughed. "He's not going to have a clue in the world who did it."

"He's not stupid," she said.

"Larry Holtzman's not stupid either," he said.

"Larry Holtzman lives with his mother and wears a safety pin in his eyeglasses. And his fancy transmitter squawks."

"There's nothing to link us to him. Or him to the agency. He's very careful."

"He came here. That's a link. He goes to your office."

"He was there twice. If they had any suspicions, we wouldn't be standing here chatting about it."

"All they have to do is get the suspicion," she said.

He laughed. "Let's go in and steam wallpaper," he said. "I want this place looking great for Claire."

"Why couldn't you have just made an anonymous call?"

"Nothing will go wrong," he said. But he felt it, too, the presence in their new life of something from the past that he had either reintroduced to it, or perhaps not eliminated from it to begin with. Some reason between them to struggle. Some hurdle they couldn't clear. Whatever, it was there, affecting what it was he thought he'd hoped for. Maybe he didn't, after all, hope for it.

They camped in the living room. Buckets of plaster and lathe moved on pulleys down the scaffolding. Whole walls went down it, whole rooms, new doors and windows and tubs and toilets and sinks went up it. He thought of it as buckets of money moving up and down the outside of a house he sometimes couldn't remember why he had wanted to buy. She went out every day to look for fabric and wallpaper and paint to match the old colors she scalpeled and scraped off the walls. But she progressed at a snail's pace, her body heavy with a program of its own.

"I love you," he said. "But when did you get so slow? And when are we getting married?"

"I'm hurrying," she said.

But not to get married. Their marrying, she believed, as sure a blow to their future as machine-gun fire or a jar full of gasoline through the front windows. The five doors to love are Desire, Prayer, Service, Kissing, and Doing, whereby Love perishes, she read to herself from a collection of the writings of the troubadours. She copied the words out and kept them near her to sustain her in her intention, not yet fully assimilated by him, not to pass from kissing to doing, her strategy to keep him undone and desirous. Off-center. Free, in some way he imagined it was possible to be. But Denise ruined it. Said to him, when he was there one weekend picking up the boys, when are you ever going to get married? Mona thinks she must want to go back to her husband. Don't be dumb, Denise, he said.

Still, he went back to 11th Street and regarded her, lying

on a mat in the unfurnished living room between piles of plastery dropcloths, doing her birth exercises. She got up and kissed him, absentmindedly, he thought, and wandered downstairs to the kitchen to stir something on the stove, pliéed soberly at the sink, scraping and slicing vegetables, riding his daughter up and down, up and down, in her womb. She was maddeningly vague, it seemed to him, temporizing, planning (he was suddenly sure Denise was right) to get back at him now for all the times he had left her, by leaving him. He accused her of it.

"Silly," she said calmly, her body Claire's elevator, up and down, up and down, in front of the stove. "I actually prefer being your lover. It's sexier."

"It all goes back to Cora," he said hopelessly. "You've never gotten over that."

"It doesn't go back to Cora," she said.

"What then? Who?"

"You'll tell me. When you're ready to."

"Just set a date," he said "I'm ready now."

She touched his mouth with one finger, kissed him. "Why don't we not?"

"She'll be illegitimate!"

"I like it like this," she said vaguely.

"Don't you know how insufferably patronizing you are when you pretend you know what's good for me?"

"Don't you know how incredibly obtuse you are when you pretend I don't?"

"Presumptuous twit. Dog in the manger."

"Sticks and stones," she said.

"Come on," he said one day.

[263]

"I will."

"When?"

"When you're ready."

"What am I, a cake?"

"My sugar cake," she said, kissing him. "Ravish me while my sauce simmers."

"You're disgustingly regressive."

"I know."

"You're supposed to ravish me. It's 1977."

"I know. Some other time."

"Why was the Baptist minister against sex standing up?"

"It leads to dancing?"

"You heard it."

She kissed him, raised her skirt. "Let's dance."

"Stop it," he said. "You're too fat. And be serious. Suppose I died. You're a woman with no status. No position."

"I'm your concubine. That's a position."

"An unfit concubine."

"How so?"

"A proper one doesn't go off in the middle of everything to have a baby. That's what wives do."

"I'll be back," she said. "I love you."

"Don't love you. Hate you."

"Think why," she said.

"You're going to leave me, that's why. You're going to take your revenge on me, now that you've got me where you want me."

"I will not leave you," she said. "And where is it you think I want you, anyway?"

"Everybody leaves me," he said.

"Name one."

He couldn't.

"Only one?"

He couldn't!

"You're not ready to," she said.

"Oh, for Christ's sake, a goddamned pie again."

"Yes, my pie, my sweetness, my sugar tart." She enfolded him like beaten egg whites in her arms, held him, kissed him, and then set him aside, like egg whites, calmly going on with her dinner preparations, the baby they had made getting larger every day, and her hips so narrow it had nowhere to go but straight out in front of her, like the bow of a frail ship they were sailing.

At the end of May, Larry in carpenter's overalls and baseball cap, driving a rented Chevy pickup truck, followed two of Mickey Kolyrion's cousins from Brewerton to Central Park South, where one of them got out and the other drove on, with Larry behind him, over the 59th Street Bridge to the Island. He stayed well behind for miles at a time, then speeded up and passed him, keeping him in the rearview mirror, then let him pass, trusting to dumb luck that he would catch up with him down the line and be led to the house in East Hampton. Which he was, although he lost him at the last, because he was gawking at the mansions set on the dunes in confident opulence, the likes of which he had never even imagined.

He spotted the van again and parked in a lane near one of the houses, and on foot that night followed the sounds of a party from the house where they all were to the boats, Mickey's and four smaller ones. He went aboard Mickey's boat after they had all gone to bed and left the little new-model DEA listening device taped under the instrument panel.

"What about my $50,000?" Jack demanded.

"Something went wrong," Mickey Kolyrion said. "Don't get excited. We're going for it again."

"Don't get excited?" Jack said. "Where the fuck do you think I got that fifty grand?"

"Please. Don't put any ideas in his head," Larry said, pained. "We want them to go again. We want to stay alive, too. Don't we?"

Jack laughed. He was almost enjoying the whole thing.

Larry was in despair. Getting the $50,000 out of the DEA had been like prying gold out of a lockjaw. The most they usually allocated for a direct payment on an account was a measly $4,000. But they had made an exception, finally rendered greedy themselves by the novelty, and the scope, of it. Twelve dealers that Larry knew of for sure were involved, and maybe more. A Colombian trawler with a false name arriving fifty miles off the Hamptons and off-loading by night in the middle of the ocean right off East Hampton. It was irresistible. They would be so many sitting ducks when they arrived on the beach. The DEA gave him the money, a spotter plane, and twenty agents waiting behind the dunes, ready to bust them in the sand. And their newest device. Which squawked at the wrong time and blew the whole operation.

They'll go again, you'll see, Jack said. Don't sweat the program.

And he was right. Mickey Kolyrion called within a week to say they were going again. In November.

By land or by sea? Jack asked.
Don't ask, Mickey said.
Jack laughed.

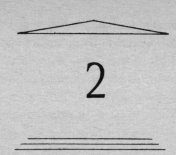

2

In his Impex office, Mickey Kolyrion brooded over his balance sheets, trying to determine whether or not his long, slow passage into the grasp of his creditors, Raul and family, and Fulgencio and family, was an irreversible one.

A year ago, he had been confident that, given East Hampton, and all other things being equal, he would be able to make good on his debts in a year. But other things had been not only not equal but also not predictable.

And now Gloria had reported that Hugh had found the diary, and she had found a KOLYRION, FRANK, folder in Hugh's files.

For any act of unbrotherly love likely to limit his freedom of movement, Frank Kolyrion did not, in Mickey's opinion, or

Raul's either, deserve to live. But before arranging for fratricide, Mickey had decided to try to undo some of the damage by relieving Hugh of the diary. Without it, any testimony Frank might give could be attributed to sibling rivalry or sour grapes or presenile dementia.

Once the diary was in his possession, Mickey's second order of business, as he saw it, was to conduct his life for a time so as not to attract the attention of any other law-enforcement agencies. To this end, he wanted to cancel the meeting with the freighter off the Hamptons, scheduled for November.

The offshore meeting in May had been a disaster. They had had the boats all loaded, loaded so full they would have run aground at low tide, when a Coast Guard plane appeared in the sky, and a squawk, a frenzied squawk came over his radio. He jettisoned the whole cargo and gave the other boats the signal to jettison, too. Now, he wasn't even sure it was the Coast Guard. All he knew was he didn't throttle up and cruise back to East Hampton rich as a king, but sat in the water watching all those nice big bales float away and slowly sink beneath the waves of the Atlantic. That was the trouble with pot. It was so goddamned bulky. His whole fortune! All his nice square catch! Gone to the bottom of the ocean. And Fulgencio onshore with his hand out. And then he discovered, just by chance, a week later, the little thing the size of a quarter taped under his instrument panel.

Who put it there? Raul wanted to know. Frank? Mickey didn't know. Frank had been unpredictable ever since the day about a year ago when up his driveway, very nicely, very neatly, walked two black ladies and a little black girl. All starched and clean and shining with salvation. Jehovahs, Jeanne whispered. Would you believe, he said to Raul, six months later Doreen was a Jehovah. And was after Frank to become one?

Never mind about that. We just want to find out who put it there, Raul said.

We? Mickey said fearfully.

Fulgencio, Raul said.

Though the business was so lucrative it made your mind swivel, Fulgencio was not one to let a dollar that was rightfully his go unaccounted for. For a Latino, Fulgencio did not have your typical mañana outlook. Fulgencio had the character of a pharmacist in an impoverished mountain town in Basque country. Every gram counted, and every gram would be accounted for. Raul was owed a large sum of money by Mickey; and Fulgencio, on whose favor Raul's future well-being depended, was owed an even larger sum by Mickey, not to mention the sum Fulgencio was owed by Raul. Raul was right. All of these debts could be repaid only if November stayed on.

Raul was this very minute on his way to Mickey's house to drive Mickey to a meeting with Fulgencio at a Playboy Club somewhere out in the New Jersey sticks. Fulgencio had heard the story that others had also heard that an indictment was about to be brought against Mickey Kolyrion for an old misdeed. Fulgencio wanted to know more about this. Fulgencio liked to be in possession of all the facts before he acted.

"Acted?" Mickey said.

"Acts," Raul said. Raul was wearing a white silk suit and a navy-blue silk shirt with a white silk tie.

"Do you know anything about last night?" Mickey said.

"What about last night?"

Jeanne had gone to the city to shop. He was supposed to meet her train at 8:20. He was early. Because if you were a second late, Jeanne might not look at you for days, let alone speak to you. When he got to the station and stepped out of his car to go to the platform, a man parked in a long black Cadillac in the shadows under a streetlight that might have been shot out with a gun even moments before (there was glass all over the parking lot beneath the light) walked toward him. Someone else, behind the man, also got out of the Cadillac and stood by the car with his hand inside his coat. Mickey hesitated. He didn't even attempt to get back into his car. He waited. When the man got to within ten feet of him, he stopped walking and stood with his hands in his pockets, his feet firmly planted under him. Even though it was only the middle of September, he wore a suede coat with a collar of beaver, which augmented his barreled, threatening chest. The parking lot suddenly began to get busy. Wives were arriving to pick up husbands. He could hear the train. He made a move toward the platform. Stay, the man said.

He had to be there when she got off the train. She insisted on it. Who are you? he said.

Headlights swung around the lot. The man looked at him steadily. The gates went down. Red lights flashed. Bells dinged. The train arrived in a noisy commotion. Cars started up. No one paid any attention to them off in a corner of the lot. He should be there, looking for Jeanne. She liked to be met right at the steps of the car as she alighted.

Do you see him over there? the man said.

Yes.

You owe a friend of his a lot of money. He doesn't want

you idling your time away in Sing Sing. Is there a murder rap against you?

No, Mickey said.

Make sure of it, the man said. He signaled to the other man. As Mickey watched, the second man walked up to a small maple tree and with the side of his hand chopped a sizable branch off it. Get the picture? the first man said.

Yes, Mickey said.

Jeanne was angry, standing all alone on the station platform. Why are you late, she said. He wanted to kiss her temple. He needed to touch someone. He wanted to be held, loved. She deflected her face. He kissed air. He followed her to the car. He wanted to lie down and die.

The Cadillac with the other man in the back seat tailgated him out of the parking lot and over the bridge, almost nudging him over the river. Once off the bridge, it sped around him and stopped short ahead of him. Jeanne screamed. The Cadillac peeled away, leaving him alone on the dark road, bordered by a stone wall and a brambled hedge. I hate you, Jeanne screamed. I hate you I hate you I hate you.

"Somebody's doing me," he said.

"Who?" Raul said.

Mickey traced and retraced the bottom line on the little balance sheet he had drawn up on his doodling pad in the car. On one side, at the bottom, in the credits column, was Jack Troy's name. For a shot at $500,000, Jack Troy had put up $50,000 in cash and agreed to forget he'd seen Mickey the night Clarice drowned. On the debit side, Mickey made a little check mark next to the sum of $450,000, the amount by which his own take was reduced by this arrangement.

"There's a missing link somewhere," he said.

"I don't know anything about last night," Raul said.

They drove silently over many connecting highways through the dark New Jersey countryside.

Fulgencio was already waiting at the table. "Is it your brother?" Fulgencio said to Mickey.

"It could be," Mickey said. "But I just don't know."

"Who else could it be?" Fulgencio said.

Raul lit a cigar. His cigars were Cuban. He drove to Montreal to get them. He was staring at a waitress waiting on a table two away from theirs. He had seen that big luscious mouth somewhere before.

"I want to talk to your brother," Fulgencio said.

"He has a bodyguard," Mickey said.

"Buy the bodyguard," Fulgencio said.

Raul kept on staring and thinking. When Raul thought, his thinking was so intense it could almost be smelled, like the cigar smoldering between his fingers. "Where have I seen that one before?" he asked.

"What one?" Mickey said.

Raul pointed his cigar at the waitress in her little black bunny suit. "The one with the tits and the big mouth."

Mickey Kolyrion turned to look at Deedee. "I never saw her before," he said.

"I saw her," Raul said. "She was the one I saw with Jack Troy in Miami last year," he said. He never forgot a face, or tits. Not like those.

"Jack Troy?" Mickey said, staring at her.

"He must like them like that," Raul said. "Do you remember the other one?"

"What other one?" Mickey said.

"The one in his office," Raul said. "The other one with the tits."

"Who is Jack Troy?" Fulgencio said.

"An investor," Mickey said. He knew exactly who Raul meant. She had been leaning over his shoulder, the day they walked into Jack's office unannounced to tell him about the May fiasco, her head so close to his that her hair was brushing his face. When she stood up, Mickey began to remember dozens of Dolly Parton jokes. Aren't they marvelous, Jack said, when she walked out. That was my new PR girl.

What's PR? Raul said.

Pulchritude to be reconnoitered, Jack said dreamily.

What? Raul said.

Public Relations, Jack said.

It wouldn't be hard to find out her name. All he had to do was call Troy, Troy & Troy and ask to speak to the new PR girl. "I'll take care of everything," Mickey said. "The bodyguard and the girl."

"What girl?" Raul said.

Mickey stared at him. "The one in the fucking office. What one were we talking about?"

"Don't you think any more?" Raul said. "The one from Miami."

Mickey flushed. "Well, that one, too," he said. "Call her over."

"Not tonight," Raul said. "Just find out who she is tonight. Call her later."

"Who is she?" Fulgencio said.

"Maybe she's the missing link," Raul said.

3

He had never been inside Hugh's Gardiner's office, but he knew the backyard of the building it was in, and all the backyards of the buildings on the block. He had run through them, after someone, or with someone after him, more times than he could remember, dodging ash cans and sagging clotheslines and barking dogs and chicken coops and pigeon houses. These were all replaced now, the broken cement and the cinders and the sumac trees and the dirty pigeons, with myrtle and pachysandra and bricks in patterns and flowering trees encircled in redwood benches and a private mews of law offices, dark and deserted at midnight. This transformation seemed to him as natural as his own from the boy he had been to this man who did what it was necessary to do to survive. Put a new face on things. Just like the town had. Allow the future to exist.

With a glass-cutting knife, he made a neat square in the sliding glass door big enough for his hand and reached in and unlocked the door. He slipped inside and closed and locked the door behind him. He wore thin gloves, a fully loaded small .25-caliber Browning automatic inside his jacket, and a small .45, also with a full clip in the magazine, strapped to his ankle. This was uncomfortable. He had bony legs and ankles and the heavy metal hurt his lower shin. But he had learned from Raul to wear the second gun when he was doing anything dangerous. Raul never went anywhere without it any more. Trouble is everywhere, Raul said. Today, everywhere.

He picked his way across the room and into the next office by the slim beam of his flashlight. When he was beyond the door to that room, in an inner office with no windows, he lit his way into the room where the safe was.

The combination Gloria had given him, which she had discovered neatly taped on the inside of the secretary's desk, worked. The little white leatherette diary with the fake brass lock was right up front on the middle shelf. He put it into his breast pocket and looked around for the filing cabinets. It hadn't taken Gloria any time at all to learn where the key was kept, and the key worked, just the way she said it would, a bit on the sticky side. And a thin file, brand new, labeled KOLYRION, FRANK, was just where she had said it would be. He opened it and looked inside. Some scribbled notes. A bill for a conference last spring. (Last spring already, he thought.) And behind it in the cabinet, also just where Gloria said it would be, was the thin old file, browning and fragile, labeled KOLYRION-THILE, that she had discovered in the room where the dead files were kept, and had slipped in here for him to take a look at. So old it must date from the original partners' day, he thought. He put the KOLYRION, FRANK, file back, but took the other one. Hugh would never miss it. Probably didn't even know it existed. And there were two letters in it he wanted to read at his leisure. He returned the key to its place and left by the front door.

In his study on Cliff Avenue, he spent what was left of the night reading and rereading the diary and the two letters in the old file.

He tried to recall Clarice. She was a blurry figure in his mind, four or five years younger than he was. He hadn't known her in high school. She had been a friend of Jack Troy's, apparently. Jack Troy made a number of appearances in her diary. Mickey read them over and over again, trying to figure out how he could use them. You never knew when a certain bit of information might come in handy. Engaged to Tina in 1956, but friendly with Marion and Clarice Heard. Especially Marion. How friendly was not perfectly clear.

The next morning he took the diary out of the safe and reread one more time the last entry, which was perfectly clear: *Mickey just called. Everything's going to be all right! We're getting married! I'm meeting him tonight. I left a note at Jack's house to tell him, in case I don't see him again before.* Before was underlined. Mickey stared at it, the last word Clarice had ever written. Why would she have left a note for Jack Troy? he wondered. He should think about Jack Troy more . . . creatively. He had been thinking creatively when he got Jack's P.R. girl Heather on the team. And he should call Heather soon, too, to find out how Jack Troy was reconnoitering her pulchritude. Find out what she had found out.

Deedee at the Playboy Club had been no help at all. Claimed she didn't even recognize his name.

The phone beside him rang, making him jump a little. "Your brother was just in," Gloria whispered. "What's a deposition?"

"Is that son of a bitch going to give one?"

"Friday morning," she said.

He was stunned. He believed he had made it crystal clear to Frank what would happen to him if he didn't back off. He felt sick. Everything was leaking! The dike was leaking in a hundred places at once. It was like trying to hold water in your hands to hold all the pieces together, call off this dog, call off that dog. It was like trying to shovel sand against the tide. "Thanks, Gloria," he said wearily. "You do good work."

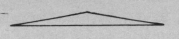

4

In mid-September, around the time the news of Frank Koly-rion's disappearance occupied the front page of the Brewerton *Record* and even made an inside column in *The New York Times* and a slot on the Channel 5 "Ten O'clock News," the Reverend Mr. Penney's intestines became blocked and had to be operated on. To be near him, Tina moved into Beimer's Motel.

Jack felt abandoned. He remembered the time Mona had moved and forgotten to give her new address to his school. She had an unlisted number, and he had had an appendectomy, all by himself. The doctors and nurses were there, weren't they, Mona said, when the school finally caught up with her. You mustn't exaggerate. Weren't you just showered with attention? Everyone felt sorry for me, he said. Well, don't feel sorry for yourself, she said. No one likes a crybaby.

"Where are you?" Heather said, when he called her.

"In Chicago and alone," he said.

As if alone is a place, too, she thought. He wanted to have lunch with her when he got back.

He felt almost as if she had been daring him to ask her. They went, several times in a row, to the same place. They were beginning to be smiled at by the waiters. Lovers? Getting to know you? It was hard to keep his mind on what she was saying, she was so attractive, her face so mobile and intelligent, her stories so funny, her. . . .

Stop! he thought. He wanted to be good. He didn't want to start up all over again.

Tina called to tell him about Frank Kolyrion. Mickey had another perfect alibi. He had been in the Berkshires at the summer home of the mayor of Brewerton. Won't you come home, he begged. I miss you. I can't, she said. I think my father's dying.

By the time he called Heather back, she had made plans to go away for the weekend.

And then, at the office, Deedee called. Dumb Dee. Of course he remembered her. Somebody was at the Playboy Club who knew you, she said. I didn't like them. So I told them I didn't remember you. They wanted to know all about you.

Good girl, Deedee. Smart of you! Fast thinking. Thanks, my dear. Let me invest all your Bunny money for you. No commission, ever.

He called Larry. "And you said in one ear, out the other," Larry said. "What does she know?"

"Nothing," he said. "I told her they were from the IRS."

"What *did* she know?" Larry said.

"What do you want me to *do?*" he said. He had only meant to take a little long-overdue retribution, not lob a hand grenade toward his own life.

In the evenings, all alone, all week, he walked.

Heather was always busy in the evenings. Heather, he groaned in his heart, her luscious form in a dark red dress appearing before his eyes every time he closed them for a second. So firm, so fully packed, so like an unopened jar of Damson plums she was. He felt drawn to her, falling toward her like a mist to earth, wanted to tell her so, was put off only by the tiny fear she wouldn't believe him, or care, or expect or want anything from him anyway. There were enough men in her life. She wouldn't need him. But she liked him, better than some of the men who were in it. He made her laugh. He loved to make her throw her head back at lunch and laugh out loud, laugh so he could see the trembling of her uvula and the gleam of all her nice, white teeth.

He walked, fantasized love scenes with her, and battle scenes. He was afraid of her and afraid of Tina's detecting her. Tina had radar for other women. Afraid of her? Nonsense, he told himself. They were not enemies, he and Heather. They were friends! There were no battle lines drawn between them. Where did he get the feeling that she was after him, after something he had that she was determined to draw out of him! What could she know about him that he had not told her, or let her see for herself? He was making something out of nothing. Still, he had dreamed of her, and in the dream she turned into a siren—a large birdlike creature with the head of a woman. After him.

He jogged. Thought of himself as preparing himself for an

encounter—with Heather. Of going into training for it. He ate frugally. For lunch on Saturday, he arranged a quartered tomato and a few slices of cheese on his plate, meditatively drank a glass of skim milk, polished an apple. He walked that night, lonely; inhaled deeply of the autumn air, girding himself against the in-dwelling power he sensed in Heather to steal something from him. But what? What was there to fear? I'm beginning to care for you, you know, she said, in a low, strange voice. He slipped on wet leaves and fell, all his weight on his right elbow, sat there on the sidewalk on Perry Street for a moment to gather his sense. (No one noticed him.) She had done it. Heather. He had been thinking of her when it happened. She was after him. A little blood oozed through his sleeve. He rolled up the sleeve to look. By the streetlamp he could see the torn flap of bloody skin. It hurt.

Sunday morning it hurt even more, and he walked around with the arm hanging limply and uselessly close to his side. He took care not to bend his elbow. It felt diminished, as if his arm were gone, an empty sleeve hanging there, where an arm had once been, full of the power of making love, making money.

He was sick of himself. He was neglecting his business. Screwing up again. Forgetting Tina. He wanted *her!* He wanted to commit fideleetay! But he hadn't had any training for it. How could he do it if he didn't know how?

All alone! he thought. Denise had hauled Will and Otis off to Concord and Lexington. Mona and the colonel were on their honeymoon in England. Tina was still married to Hugh. Everything was unsettled!

He called Larry to find out if Frank Kolyrion had turned up. He hadn't. Larry was on tenterhooks, hoping it wasn't going to affect November. "There could be even more boats involved than I thought," he said. "Think of it!"

"I didn't know you cared so much," Jack said.

"I like to make busts," Larry said. "I want a clean America." He wanted to see the country return to its original ideals. He wanted to see the work ethic reinvigorated. He wanted honesty, trust, honor, hope, value for value, integrity. He wanted, in short, to make a tiny dent in the coast-to-coast mountain of shit the country was sinking under.

"I couldn't have put it better myself," Jack said. "Have you been drinking?"

"No," Larry said.

"Would you like to tie one on this evening?"

"Sure," Larry said.

"Come on over," Jack said. "I've already started."

He drank bourbon. Larry drank bourbon and Tab. Jack was already tight. But even sober he could get pleased by the idea of the FBI stepping out from behind the dunes, herding them, all handcuffed, onto a bus for the ride to the East Hampton slammer. He smiled.

Larry told him how it was going to be in a few years, with coke catching on. "Housewives will be selling. Businessmen, lawyers, doctors, cops, judges, teachers. The figures are irresistible. A rank amateur can make $300,000 on a $500 investment. Who is strong enough?"

"We are," Jack said. "We will overcome. Have another drink."

"We won't," Larry said, holding out his glass. "It's a losing battle already. Their planes are better than ours. Their boats are better. Their radios are better. Their surveillance is better. The tonnage per year is going to triple every year. The whole middle class will be either selling it or buying it. A kilo costs $50,000. Retail it grosses for ten times that. Eighth-graders will be pooling their allowances to deal it. Nuns will be doing it. They'll justify it, too. Use the profits to feed the poor. Why not? It's a natural. Can't miss."

Jack tried to imagine the sums generated. What was it used for. What did it buy, those unaccounted-for billions?

"The market is expanding by quantum leaps. In five years, everyone will be doing it every day, twice a day. Snorting will be like brushing your teeth."

"Do you ever do it?" Jack said.

"Coke's coming," Larry said, gazing straight down into his glass. "Coming. Coming. Transforming whole economies out there already. A whole new way to earn hard currency, and more of it than they've ever dreamed of, has suddenly emerged. Governments don't stand a chance. In soft countries. Which is most of them."

"And hard countries? Us?"

"Think of it," he said. "How can you have a viable government without a viable banking system? And how can you have that when an invisible one with ten times the assets and none of the expenses exists alongside it?"

Jack swirled the bourbon in his glass.

"There are lawful foreign-exchange earnings," Larry said thickly, swirling his. "And unlawful. And the unlawful are ten times the size of the lawful these days. That's just a rough estimate. Do you know what that means?"

"Terrorism?"

"Right. Terrorists get launched and kept aloft. On the humongous profits of the drug trade."

Imagine Albanian guns in return for Golden Crescent dope. Or Cuban guns in return for Colombian. Who cares who he trades with, left wing, right wing, East, West. They're ending up, and that's what matters, trained on the West, both the guns and the dope. The latter afflicting a tidily increasing annual percentage of capitalists from senators and sports stars to judges and sweet Chippewa maidens. A befogged America fails to comprehend. Noddy land temporizes. And before ye know it, Johnny, drug-free fanaticals clean up the fallen West their way.

Larry looked at him over the rim of his glass, which Jack noticed he was holding between his teeth. "They're vertically integrated," he said, without taking the glass out of his mouth. "They plant it, water it, hoe it, pick it, dry it, refine it, and ship it."

"Quite," Jack said.

"No more maize," Larry said, adding a little bourbon to his mixture. "No more rice and beans. The cash crop of choice is cocoa."

"What are the poor folk eating?"

"Weight Watchers frozen dinners. Easy come, easy go."

"Where will it end? Who will blow the whistle?"

"The government can't afford to. And the banks won't. They know a golden goose."

The legitimate banks facilitating the traffic. If you can't fight it, join it. A shadow banking system existing alongside the visible one. So, cooperate. Share the goodies. Untaxed, untaxable billions, merrily circulating. "Do you ever?" Jack said again. He poured bourbon over the last of his melting cubes. The ice in the bucket on the table between them had changed states. He was too drunk to forage for more in the kitchen.

Larry closed his eyes, rested his head against the back of the couch where he sat, opposite Jack's couch, in the gathering dusk. "It's greed," he said. "Twelve friends can make a million bucks a week. So much money comes in so fast they can't count it. It cuts off the circulation in their fingers. They get these little telltale calluses. So they weigh it instead, by denomination. And they never get caught. The government can't keep up with the numbers."

"*Do* you?"

Larry sighed. "No," he said. "I am very straight. I believe in the social contract. I believe in the law. I believe in good faith. That's why I like to bust them. For the sheer pleasure of enforcing the law of the land. That's how I get high. I'm not even used to drinking."

"I am," Jack said. He was getting very drunk, in fact. He had started early in the day.

"I don't like booze," Larry said. "I don't like dope. I don't like anything. Except busting dealers. I like to see scum where it belongs. Don't you? Isn't that why you called us?" He was getting tired; he put his feet up on the couch.

"I called because of my dog," Jack said, from the other couch, across the darkening room. "He killed my damned dog."

"You said it was because of Beauty," Larry said.

"My dog was Beauty," Jack said. "Other things, too." Like unconditional love. Like never asking a thing in return, except her daily dish of Alpo.

"I'm not quibbling," Larry said. "It sounds reasonable. You have to go with Dog. Right?"

"Right," Jack said. "Dog was there. Then she wasn't there. What do you think happened?"

"Carelessness set in," Larry said. "It will. It will slip in through any crack. So you decide. You go with Dog, or you go against Dog. You have to go one way or the other. Be careful. Mind the store. Dog is man's best friend. Right?"

"Right again," Jack said. Was it carelessness? Or callousness? Or simple vengeance? Or was it disregard? He couldn't stand disregard.

"Right?" Larry said again.

"Right," Jack said.

"Right," Larry said. "I'm for Dog. That's why I do it. Dog needs man."

"Everything boils down to it," Jack said in the dusk. He was too drunk to get up and turn on a light. "That dog was a good, good dog. Stuck by me, thick and thin. No dog like that dog." Loved him sans reason, sans reserve.

"Right," Larry said. "My best friend was dealing smack, senior year. Got behind in his payments. They dropped him off a roof in the South Bronx."

Jack lit a cigarette. "So that's why you do it."

"Right," Larry said. He didn't know whether he was pouring Tab in his bourbon or bourbon in his Tab. "Stupid. Right?"

"Right."

Larry was holding the rim of his glass in his teeth again. "Like some dogdamned do-gooding white knight. But I do it."

"*God* damned," Jack corrected him.

"Is dog God or is God dog?" Larry said.

"Whichever, help is needed."

"That's why we're in there, right?" Larry said. "Isn't that why we're in there, pal?"

"In that range of things," Jack said. He noticed that Larry's head had moved from the back of the couch to the arm and that his feet were up on the other arm. Jack hadn't thought he expected an answer. He had given one anyway. He put his own head down on the arm of his couch and put his feet up on the other arm. "Good night," he said, into the dark room.

5

On Monday morning, he drove to Brewerton and walked into Hugh's office building.

The receptionist flushed when he gave his name, announced it in a loaded voice over the intercom. A girl appeared at the door and asked him if he had an appointment.

"No."

"Is he expecting you?"

"No."

The girl looked confused and turned to the receptionist for advice, but the receptionist went on typing, not allowing her eyes to be engaged. I'm his goddamned wife's goddamned lover, goddamn it, he wanted to say. "I'm a friend," he said. "Just tell him I'm here. He'll see me."

"You can, Gloria," said the receptionist, without looking up from her typewriter.

Gloria disappeared through the door again. The receptionist looked at him covertly from under her long bangs.

How could Gloria seem never to have heard the name? Hugh thought bitterly. The whole town knew his wife had run off with one Jack Troy. She announced it with double question marks and a screwed-up face. Not the brightest girl he'd ever employed.

He had almost been expecting him to show up, wishing he would. When a man takes off with another man's wife, there should be some contact between them afterward, some chance for accountings, or explanations, apologies, insults, blows. Some connection, if only a chance to refuse to shake his hand. Some chance to salvage a shred of pride. He had just barely restrained himself from appearing unannounced in Jack Troy's office. He had gotten as far as the sidewalk in front of the building one winter's day and turned around and went home, only because he knew it wouldn't make any difference.

He swiveled in his chair to gaze out into the garden through the sliding glass door behind him. "Tell him to come in," he said, though his mind was suddenly a blank. The speeches that had churned in it for the first few months had vanished, now when he could have used them. What would he say? What should he say? That he hurt? That he wanted some recompense? That he wanted to hurt *them?* That they had robbed him of his children, of the family he had wrought, of his pride, of his lost paradise? Tell him that it really had been a kind of dumb happy paradise when she was in it? Tell him that rage had filled his life for months like a flow tide a cave, rushing in and out of his days in horrible cycles of remembrance and forgetfulness? That he was filled with horror that he was forgetting, already? That not even a year had gone by, and he was forgetting the first pain, even forgetting her, when she had been the one detail of his life that had once held it all together? Damn him! he thought. We owned property together. We made flesh together. We were friends. We trusted each other. If women like her could walk out on all that, civilization was in bad shape. The anger bubbled inside of him like milk boiling up the side of a pan.

The door opened. He swiveled around in his chair and stood, out of sheer reflex. But he kept his hand at his side, wouldn't offer it first. He was larger than Jack Troy, and he was four years older. But Jack Troy, he thought with a shock, looked older. His face in the morning light that poured in the windows was older than it had been at Christmas, anxious, tired, leathery, and his hair was grayer.

"Hello, Hugh," Jack said, walking toward Hugh with his hand out. Hugh had never refused to shake a man's hand before, so he reached out over his desk and shook his wife's lover's hand. But he couldn't bring himself to offer him a chair, or ease any of his discomfort.

Why would she leave such a man? Jack wondered, disoriented and nervous. Here was Hugh, a tall, good American, an affluent, healthy male U.S. citizen, a man. The father of her children. Kind, honest, true, and generous. Nice. Never hurt a flea. Why would she leave him? Why would any woman leave such a man? Or did he have some hidden defect that justified her in exchanging him?

Hugh stirred restlessly, shifted his weight, moved from

behind the desk, so he wouldn't look cut off at the knees. And Jack remembered that in fact she hadn't "exchanged" him, that she was still married to him, and not in any hurry to change the *status quo*. "Hugh," he said painfully. "I'm here to talk about the divorce."

"My . . . divorce," Hugh stammered. "Mine? Ours?"

"Yes," Jack said.

Hugh flushed. "What about it?" It was his only hope, Tina's indifference to remarrying, that it would blow over and that she would call him someday and say she wanted to come back to him. Denise had called him a month ago, to say she, too, and Jack's mother as well, believed this would happen.

"I want to marry her," Jack said.

Hugh's misery deepened. "I didn't think she wa- . . . wa-. . . ." (Wanted to marry you, he was going to say. But she did want to marry him. She only wanted to make him think she didn't, so he could feel free to stay. Anyone could see that.)

"Didn't think she wanted to marry me?" Jack said glumly. "Yes."

"Well, she does," he said. "She just needs a little encouragement."

"Well, for God's sake! Don't ask me," Hugh said. "Don't ask me to help you marry her. She's my wife. My wife! I want her to stay married to me."

"We're going to have a baby in a month. It won't be legitimate."

"Well," Hugh said. "Like father, like daughter."

Zapped. By Mr. Nice Guy himself. "How long would it take?" he said. "The fastest way."

Hugh's instinct for the punitive rose in his throat, almost

choking him. Though he had successfully represented thieves and rapists and cold-blooded murderers, he didn't like to see anyone getting away with any offenses against civilized society. Adultery. Home wrecking, etcetera. They were as bad as the other. "It depends on if there are any fights over property and custody," he said stiffly.

"There won't be."

"Did she say that?"

"We know you'll be fair about property. And she wants Amy and Bo. But not till they want her."

"She said this?" Hugh persisted.

"She thinks it."

"I'll have to hear it from her to believe it."

What would he take in exchange for her? Jack wondered, almost idly. And then it came to him what he had that Hugh might want.

Hugh was staring at him, thinking *1948*. You came here in 1948. And you changed my life's course that day. Everything was laid down from that time forth, and no one knew. But, then, what did anybody know in 1948? How did anyone know society would develop a fault line sometime not too long afterward? Everything got out of whack, somewhere along the line. Anything goes now. Nothing fits right any more. Nothing is like we thought it would always be. One side shrank. It was like the woolen sweater of Amy's he had tried to wash for her the other day. The buttons no longer matched up with the button holes.

"Hugh," Jack said. "I do love her."

Hugh stared past him out the window at the dogwood tree. As if saying it proved it, he thought. The leaves were already beginning to be tinged with red. In a month they would fall. What is a proof of love anyway? he wondered.

"I have something you might be interested in," Jack said. "It has to do with Clarice."

"Clarice is a dead issue," Hugh said. "They stole the evidence out of the safe. A diary. The day after I found it. I hadn't even had a chance to photocopy it. Then we had his brother set to give a deposition, and his damned brother disappeared. He's probably floating out in the river somewhere."

Jack wondered how Mickey knew within a day of Hugh's finding it that he had found it. The secretary? He felt sorry for him, losing his wife and his case, too, and maybe even the D.A.'s job in the bargain. "Did you get a chance to read it before it disappeared?"

"Oh, yes," Hugh said wryly. "You were in it. Good friend of hers?"

"Let's walk," Jack said. "Down by the river."

As if we're old buddies? Hugh thought. "What's wrong with here?" he said.

"I don't care for your secretary."

Hugh took his binoculars from the bookshelf and, as if they *were* old friends, left the office with him and walked down the street to the river.

A breeze kicked the river into whitecaps out in the channel and whipped their ties over their shoulders. Hugh stared out at the river through the binoculars, thinking what in the hell am I doing here with him, anyway?

"Do you know I collect?" Jack said.

"Art?"

"Yes. And other things."

"No," Hugh said. "I don't know much about you."

"Clarice wrote to me," he said.

Hugh shivered in the wind, scanning the river. "Wrote to you?" The tide was coming in.

"I still have it," Jack said.

Still have what? Hugh wondered, and then he remembered the last entry in the diary. He turned to stare at Jack. "The note she wrote you the day he killed her?"

"I have a correspondence trunk," Jack said.

But as Hugh had turned his head, something bobbing in on the tide had caught his eye, and he turned back to pick it up in the glasses.

"All personal correspondence from 1945 to 1975," Jack said. "Filed chronologically. I brought it up to date before we moved up from Dallas. I remember seeing it."

"My God, I don't believe this," Hugh said. "Do you see that? Take these. Out there."

"Believe what?" Jack said.

Hugh handed him the heavy glasses. He looked through them to where Hugh was pointing, out in the river.

"What does it look like to you?" Hugh said.

"Dead man's float. Dead man in red shirt."

"Frank Kolyrion was wearing a red shirt the night he disappeared," Hugh said. "Let's go get him."

"Us?" Jack said.

"There's a rowboat right down there. Let's go."

"Dressed like this?"

"Let's *go!*"

"Why don't we just call the Coast Guard, or the police, or the swim team?"

"No, no no," Hugh said. "The current's very strong here. We could lose him. We can row. It's not far."

"You can row," Jack said. "You're the fucking Navy man."

They jumped down off the seawall and took off their jackets and ties, and their shoes and socks, and rolled up their pants, and dragged somebody's aluminum rowboat down to the water. "Where's your trunk?" Hugh grunted, hauling on the oars against the tide.

"In storage. Starboard oar. In upper Manhattan." He felt happy, suddenly, exhilarated at being out on the water. On a mission, playing cops and robbers with Hugh. "Do you know I haven't been in a rowboat in twenty-five years? And before that, only a few times, on a lake near Chattanooga?"

But Hugh didn't want to know his rowing history. "Is it dated?" he said.

"I don't remember."

"Is it postmarked?"

"No. She left it at the house."

"Still, it's something. What did it say?"

"That she was meeting him that night. Port oar. I think she thought they were going to elope."

"Why the hell didn't you produce it at the time?"

"That's a terrible question," Jack said. "I really can't answer it. At the time, I guess, nobody knew she was dead for three days. Then Tina and I broke up. Port oar. Then my grandmother died on me. Tina left town. I was making funeral arrangements, and by the time I heard she was dead and he was a suspect, I suppose I'd forgotten I had it. It was only a little note."

"Catch hold of him," Hugh said, looking over his shoulder. "Grab his foot. Why didn't you tell me this six months ago?"

"It didn't strike me till just now."

"Maybe you just wanted to wait till the last minute," Hugh said.

"The clincher that enables the prosecutor to stun the court?" Jack grabbed Frank Kolyrion's foot.

"The hero that queers things for everybody else," Hugh said. "Are you really that egocentric?"

"Truthfully," Jack said, "I assumed you were in perfect control."

I don't like you, Hugh thought clearly. I don't. I really don't.

"How are we going to get him into the boat?"

"We're not. Slip a line through his belt and tow him. This is all rather beautiful, isn't it? Working out fine, after all. How can I get it?"

"I'll send it to you."

"No. I'll go back with you to get it."

"Back water," Jack said. The foot slipped through his fingers. "Starboard oar. Where did you learn to row?"

"Don't mention it to anyone. Don't tell them at the storage place." Hugh back-watered.

"I have to tell them, so they can get the trunk out for me."

"Isn't it in a cage? Just tell them you want to visit the cage." The boat went full circle.

"Mickey's not clairvoyant. *Port* oar."

"He has the diary. She mentioned in it that she'd written

to you. It could occur to him that you still have the letter. Does he know you're a saver?"

"Collector. Back water again. Not that I know of. I can reach." He caught the khaki material of the pants leg and pulled the body alongside the boat. "He's all bloated," he said. "How can I pass the line through? Hold the boat still!"

"Just hang onto his leg," Hugh said. He turned the boat around and Jack leaned out over the stern, hanging onto pants fabric while Hugh laboriously rowed to shore. "Somebody called the police," Hugh said, looking over his shoulder. "Here comes the putter."

The police launch skimmed over the water to them and relieved them of Frank Kolyrion.

"The fish ate his face, but it's Frank," Jack heard someone say, when they turned the body over on the beach.

Jack felt sick, then. It was all getting out of control. Why had he done it? Or why not just have spelled it out in words cut out of newspapers, pasted up with gloved hands, sneaked into a post-office box some dark night? And why had he now complicated everything by bringing up Clarice's note? Was it that important to get Tina? Or Mickey?

They dried their feet with their socks and dressed and walked back up the hill.

"It was good you came," Hugh said grudgingly. "I wouldn't have walked down there by myself."

"Someone else would have seen him."

"I liked the personal participation," Hugh said.

"I did, too," he said. But he wasn't so sure anymore. "Do me a favor, Hugh," he said, when they reached his car. "Keep my name out of the paper about it?"

Hugh looked at him. "Might start Mickey wondering?"

About more than one thing, Jack thought. He nodded.

"And, of course, you want me to move ahead, too, on the . . . other?"

"Yes."

"Swapping my wife for a letter," Hugh said.

"It's not a swap."

"It's not much of one," said Hugh, remembering Tina. "But it does smack of a swap."

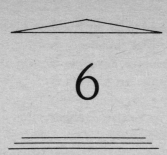

6

A week after Hugh flew to Port au Prince and divorced Tina, before they had a chance to get married, and about three weeks before she was supposed to be, Claire was born. She was so tiny that her bottom when he picked her up naked the first time fit into the palm of his hand with room to spare. Is she so small because we're so old? Jack wondered. He was terrified of what he had done: made a human being, and with Tina, and at their age.

We did it, he thought. We went and did it. Tina! You got me. Right where you want me. After all these years. How did you?

He wanted to run away now. She was right. She was always right. He doesn't want to belong to her, to them. To anyone. He wanted to go. Be free. Live his own life his own way. Run, he thought in panic.

On the other hand, he was enamored of his daughter, stood smitten and adoring, watching her sleep, a tiny blip of humanity, grown from a tiny combination of genetic materials, lying in the center of a crib mattress that seemed unnecessarily enormous. She cried and woke, fed voraciously with her eyes shut, her tiny parody of a hand splaying itself like a miniature emblem of indisputable ownership on Tina's swollen breast, while Tina, exhausted, dozed in the chair, her strength sapped by this living thing they had so rashly made.

He rushed out of the house when he couldn't stand it any longer to take long walks in the night, wishing someone were with him to validate his panic. Someone. Heather!

She was familiar with the signs: a beatific look, a scattered attention, a withdrawing. The tie was tied, the circle drawn about him, the center the thing to be avoided now. A marriage license not necessary after all. All it took was love to make him run. She had received the same wordless messages before. He tried to live his life on levels, as if in secret subterranean caverns. But she had divining forks for all of them. She smelled patchouli, the heavy middle note in a perfume she had once liked, remembered the children in the pool at the villa in St. Croix.

He didn't.

"The little boy and girl who came every day to swim?"

"No," he said.

"The maid's children?"

"No."

Was it just a dream? Had she imagined them? She held the baby to her, smelling its soft, clean head.

They had a nurse at first, but the nurse had had another case lined up, a cesarean, and left after a week. Left them like novice sailors adrift in an appalling sea of infant paraphernalia. They looked at each other when the door shut upon her and thought, Now what?

"We're on our own," he said glumly. Wan and tired, she agreed. They were on their own. Mr. Troy and Mrs. Gardiner and Baby Claire. "Do you think Mona might come?" he wondered out loud.

She laughed.

They couldn't keep a cleaning woman because the house was in such disarray from the construction work going on on every floor that no one would stay for more than a day. They came once and never returned. No cleaning service would take it on either, once they came to see it. "We'll manage," she said.

But he wasn't so sure. He felt swamped and bedeviled by all manner of things he had to try to manage. Denise imperturbably made claims on him as if she were still Number One wife, the mother of his real children, Claire only an insensate blob that Tina could manage, an afterthought of a child, one to consider far in the future, not now. Now Denise needed him in the management of his real children, required daily phone consultations on their education, their social life, their health, their wardrobes, their need for skis and a winter vacation. And he had to answer, too, needs they had that they left Denise ignorant of, or that he merely understood they had without their even understanding it. They called him at the office and at home with endless questions to answer, arguments to settle, decisions to make. Even Mona consulted him on this or that, her investments, mostly. And then there was the colonel. He had to give him some time, too. After all, it was his father, wasn't it? And Amy and Bo. Try to make them like him, even a little bit. And Hugh. He tried to give Hugh a friendly call from time to time, but Hugh was cold. Hugh didn't want to be on the team. Hugh was a bit of a sore loser, Jack decided.

And even Tina needed him more than he had expected her to, and her needs were so immediate, so visceral, so human: a breast infection one night, so painful, so urgent, she wept and sweat and cried for him to do something, while Claire screamed to be fed. He had to run out in the wee hours of the city night to find an open drugstore, where he could buy a breast pump and the antibiotics she needed, and formula for Claire to tide her over till the clogged milk could flow again.

And that was only the domestic side of things! There was the business side, with him trying to keep a hundred clients calm in a bear market and six office managers on their sixty toes, secretaries pacified, clerks clerking. In the maelstrom, in the fierce juggling of time and attention that was his life, there was one calm, clear thing that offered him no trouble at all, that made no demands at all:

Heather.

Tina stood at the long windows of the house when he was gone, watching the street for a black Cadillac prowling, imagining random violences, the past returning to butcher the future.

On her way through the iron fence one day, she saw a black Cadillac appear suddenly from around the corner of the street. The two men in the front seat looked at her, their eyes impaling her on the spikes of the fence, crushing her against the thorny quince. The car double-parked up the street, and one of the men got out and went into an apartment building. The license plate was not Mickey Kolyrion's. She felt too vulnerable to stay out, and turned around and dragged the carriage back up the front steps and into the foyer. I'm afraid, she told him. Don't be, he said. What could happen? What if he finds out? He won't, he said. By the first week in November he'll be had.

He wandered all over the Village, and one night he took a cab uptown and wandered around in the east Sixties looking for Heather, who walked her dog at ten, he knew. He couldn't find her. "This is Jack Troy," he said, calling her from a pay phone.

"Well, hello," she said, as if she had been expecting him.

She had long dark hair, long silky bangs, and cheeks like apples. He stood back and looked at her, admired her as if she were a work of art. Her long-sleeved, high-necked red silk blouse had expensive tucking at the shoulders that made the fabric fall like caresses over her arms and shoulders and breasts. She wore black, well-made slacks and fancy flat black slippers decorated with bits of glittering, colored glass. The toes curled up like gondolas. He held out the flowers he had bought on the street, a bunch of red roses and a bunch of white.

"Two!"

"I couldn't decide. Anyway, I love you. So, have two."

She laughed, as if he were a stand-up comic, he thought, despairing of ever making her take him seriously.

He followed her when she went into the kitchen to put the flowers in water. Because she was wearing flat slippers, she seemed smaller than he had realized. He liked small, neat women. He put his arms around her at the sink, buried his face in her long fragrant hair, turned her toward him. She resisted for just a second, then let herself be held. "I want to make love to you," he whispered into her hair.

She laughed.

"Stop laughing, damn it. I mean it."

She unwound herself from his arms and neatly slipped, half-skipped, away from him. He caught her hand and drew her back to him and pulled her against him, kissed her, and again she resisted a little and then let herself go. "No," she said, disengaging. "Let's go talk."

He liked negotiating sessions; he always came out ahead. But her dog, a large white poodle, watched them suspiciously from the rug. They sat on the couch, her hands in his. He turned his back on the poodle and kissed her, wanted to ravish her, neutralize with sex the gobbling-up danger of her. She smelled good. He felt faint. "Make love?" he whispered.

"What about your roommate?"

"It was her idea," he said. "To be free."

"Strange."

"She is."

"*Her* idea?"

"Yes."

"Does she, too?"

"No."

"But you do?"

"This would be the first."

"How flattering. Your very first nonmarital adultery. Or is it my very first affair with a man who's having an affair?"

"Don't laugh. It's not an affair with her. It's like a marriage. I want you. I adore you."

She laughed again, traced his brow with a finger. *"Like* a marriage?" she said. "Who is that nerdlike fellow who comes to your office once in a while? The one with the pin in his eyeglasses."

"He's only been twice," Jack said. "Just a nerdlike fellow." He tried to kiss her neck. "Works for a messenger service."

"What do you talk about?"

"World affairs. He's a Ph.D. You'd like him."

She laughed.

It thrilled him, her laughing, her mouth open so you could see her big red juicy tonsils, her uvula, red and dancing. "Listen," he said. "What I want is, a nice old-fashioned honest-to-God affair—a *liaison dangereuse* with love letters, secret codes, rendezvous in the intimate French restaurants of your choice, afternoons in bed, midnight phone signals, and my toothbrush next to yours on certain stolen occasions. How about it?"

"My lover wouldn't like it."

"Does that matter?"

"I don't know. What would it be like?"

"It might depend on what he's like."

"A jealous brute. Black belt. Bites glass when he's provoked."

He laughed. Liked her. "I'm counting on it. Oh, I'm counting on it, Heather. Say you will."

"Tell me how it would be."

"I like Saturday afternoons."

"Like to reward yourself for a good week's work?"

He kissed her ear.

"Is infidelity an integral part of your life?"

"Probably."

"Have you ever wondered why?"

"No."

"You should."

"When are we? . . ."

"We're not," she said.

He was subverted. Dashed and disheartened. He had wanted her!

She hated having to cut him down, so vulnerable, so dumb. "I'm sorry," she said. "But I like being somebody's main squeeze. Don't like being one of even a teeny-tiny group."

"I'm inconsolable."

"I know. Ruined for life?"

"I'll get over it. You won't change your mind?"

She shook her head.

"I don't give up easily," he said.

"He's coming," she said.

"How do you know?"

"He always comes at eleven. It's five of."

"Oh," he said. "Sticky."

"Use the back door," she said. "I'll show you." She smoothed her clothing and her hair and led him through the apartment to the kitchen.

"What about the flowers?"

She smiled. "I always have flowers."

"Heather?"

"Go home," she said. "Be good to those who love you."

The house was dark. He let himself in. His keys shook. There was a dead feeling in the air. He turned on lights, went up the stairs, looking for signs that would lead him to her, blood, or scattered limbs or bits of scalp and hair. He found her on the second floor in the living room slumped in a chair like a clobbered ostrich, her long legs kicked out uselessly in front of her. He knelt beside her, his heart racing, the tissues of his mouth sticky and thick. Her eyes fluttered open. She looked at him as if he were a stranger. "You're all right?" he said.

She sat up and tried to look organized. "What time is it?"

He kissed her lightly on the forehead. "You were asleep. Quarter of twelve."

"Where were you?" She smelled patchouli, or imagined it.

He took her hand. Loves her. *Loves* her! "Out walking."

"Thinking?"

"Yes."

He had separated from her, she felt, like a capsule from the mother ship. "You were with someone?"

"No."

"I smell patchouli."

"What?"

"Something. In a perfume." She thought of the house on Smith's Point, nearly finished now, no longer an ephemeral watercolor trembling on a blue wash pinned to her wall, but a reality, about to be lived in again. And their house, trembling on the edge of dissolution. Built on sand? The conception faulty?

"I want it to work this time, Tina."

"It's not," she said.

"Why not?"

"You don't really want it to."

"I want you to marry me."

"That won't make any difference."

"What will?"

"Your seeing why you do this. Why you go."

"I'm here."

She shook her head.

"I saw a woman tonight," he said. "We talked about you. Us. That's all."

"Yes?" she said.

"What do you want me to do? Go?"

"For good?"

"Yes."

She sat very still in the shadowed chair. "I won't be the first to say that," she said, after a while.

"I won't either. We've come this far."

This far, but it's not far enough, she thought.

They went to bed and he lay in her arms, almost asleep, stirred once, kissed her cheek, tasted salt.

She felt his breath steadying on her throat, some perfect peace overtaking him, his conscience as clear as Claire's. He had perhaps gone as far as he could go. Holding out for more was her problem.

7

She diapered Claire and snapped her tiny, seven-week-old form into a clean sleeper and held her to her face for a moment to kiss her soft forehead. Claire, smelling of Castile and baby oil, executed a rudimentary knee bend and uttered an exultant crow. In pure joy she batted Tina's hair with her tiny fists. Tina laughed and pressed her mouth again against the baby's nearly hairless head and placed her on her stomach in the crib.

She turned out the light and leaving the door ajar went downstairs to the parlor floor. Jack was at his mother's birthday dinner at Denise's.

She looked at her watch. It was just six. He would be back before ten, he had said.

In the hallway, where he had set them up no sooner than they had moved into the house, on shelving installed by the previous owner and due soon to be removed, were his lead soldiers. She paused to look at them. South still squared off against North. His own life still a war he still didn't know what over. Troy my Waterloo, she said out loud. Will you be again? Will we fail? Have we already?

The sound of her own voice in the empty house emphasized her isolation. She felt uneasy and crossed the room to the uncurtained windows to look down into the empty street. The mother ship was on its way up from the Florida straits. The meeting only a few days away.

No one moved in the Sunday-evening street. No traffic passed. It was raining lightly. She drew a makeshift window covering, a sheet on a pole, across the window.

From the street, silhouetted by the light behind her, she appeared like a figure in a shadow play. It reminded him of the shadow play Erica Bowen and her daughters had acted out on Smith's Point what seemed like a hundred years ago.

He watched her, with her arms outstretched, guide the balky sheet across the glass, like a blind woman feeling her way cautiously out of an unfamiliar room.

He had no business with her, of course. Only with him, tonight. Heather had told him he was having dinner at his wife's apartment. At seven, she had said. It was just six. Sitting with Raul in a parked car on a side street from where they could see the house, yet not be seen from it, he waited for Jack to come out of the front door.

She shivered again and turned away from the window. The room was chilly, the house uninsulated. She was used to a house with storm windows and shades and draperies to keep out the drafts. The storm windows were ordered, but delayed. She threw a shawl over her shoulders. What furniture they were using was all herded to the center of the room. And to the confusing signs of the work in progress had been added all the signs of new baby in the house. A playpen in the corner, a stroller on the stair landing, a carriage in the foyer. A changing blanket spread on the couch, clean piled diapers, cotton balls, talcum, and a diaper pail, rattles and tiny garments to be folded on the low table next to the fireplace, a teddy bear from Heather Platnick standing up in its gift box, looking straight at her, the person most responsible for the mess. It will all get done, she kept telling him. A year from now it will be done. A year! Is a year so long? This one is, he said.

They didn't want it to fail, either one of them, but it would unless he. . . . Unless he what? Sybil asked when she came to see the baby. Unless he what?

Unless he changes.

Unless you do, Sybil said.

But I thought I had, she said.

You go with the flow, Sybil said. You have to go against it. Break the pattern.

A fire languished in the fireplace. She put a log on it and looked at her watch again. Only ten after six. She pulled a light armchair closer to the warmth and sat in it, staring into the yellow flames that sent flickering shadows dancing around the room. It's a question of language, Sybil said. You are failing, because you are not speaking the same language. Your language is a vocal one. Your spoken words mean what they seem to mean. His language is one of act and gesture. What he says he means is not what he does mean. What he does is what he means. What does he do?

He comes. He goes, she said. He comes back again. He goes again.

Right, Sybil said.

What, then?

For linguistic failures, Sybil said, there can be linguistic solutions.

What are they? Tell me. Tell me.

Speech, Sybil sighed, is not essential to the definition of an infinitely productive communication system. Speaking is only the expression of thought by signs invented for the purpose. He has invented a system of communication, signs for his deepest meanings, that are nonverbal ones. And he has persuaded you to participate in his system. Doesn't it weary you? To contemplate a future in which he comes and goes and you must go and come in response?

She stared into the firelight, thinking of the ants in Bo's ant farm, programmed to construct their endless eloquent tunnels to nowhere, and him, programmed to fulfill some endless eloquent journey to self-protection in a process of endlessly repeated advances and withdrawals, while she withdrew and advanced in a counterrhythm to complement it. Tunneling out of closeness toward freedom, and once out on the edge, free, burrowing back to closeness. But what else, she thought in despair. How else, but by not enclosing him, while at the same time providing enclosure when he wanted it? This is his language, Sybil said. Don't speak it.

I haven't married him.

Sybil laughed. What does that matter? Married or not,

you're his official adversary. For the time being. The appointed one for now, that he is appointed to struggle with, overcome, and replace, so that he can begin again.

But why?

Look at the effect, and you won't have to wonder why.

The effect?

How it makes *you* feel.

Expendable.

Yes.

She stared into the fire.

Persuade him to speak your language, Sybil said.

How?

Show him what he's doing.

Shouldn't he see it for himself?

Some people need help, Sybil said. It's unpardonable to keep silent when it's only a few plain words that are needed to point him in the right direction.

I think he should see it for himself, she said.

You are very stubborn, Sybil said.

A noise outside, down in the street, startled her. She tightened the shawl around her and went to the window to look out behind the sheet into the street again. But no one. She shivered. The drizzle had increased to a rain. Heather Platnick's teddy bear gazed at her from his shiny Saks Fifth Avenue box on the table. She crossed the room and flicked on the wall sconces to light the dark stairwell, turned up the thermostat a degree and returned to the fire, moved closer to it, and thought of her little antique revolver.

It had been, since they moved in, in the kitchen, in a

wicker basket on top of the refrigerator. She had brought it upstairs just a day ago. She opened the drawer of the table next to her and took it out and laid it on the table and stared at it gleaming in the low light. No help. No answer. Too late, she thought, tracing with one finger its elaborate Victorian scroll-work. Too late to imagine raising it to her temple. Or aiming it at him, either. It had ceased to be the abandoned woman's answer a century ago. Suicide was Victorian, and even murder anachronistic. Early- to mid-twentieth century the latest that murder was a viable response to infidelity. She was mid- to late-century, awash in other options.

Beside her on the floor, the phone rang. She started. Looked at her watch. Twenty past seven.

"Is Jack there?" a man's voice said.

"Who's this?"

He hung up. She stared at the dead receiver in her hand. A nasal voice. Someone with his hand over his nose. Her heart pounded, forcing blood like fire through her veins. Four days to go, and thirty FBI agents would stand up in the dune grass and arrest what Larry calculated now would be MK and twenty-one of his friends, stepping out of fourteen heavy-laden boats on the beach at East Hampton. And all for Jack Troy to get even.

A floorboard creaked. She froze, reached for the revolver. "Is that you, Jack?" Her voice quavered, hung like thistledown in the dead air of the big, bare room.

"All alone by the telephone, Tina?" said Mickey Kolyrion, from the hallway door.

She stood, clutching her shawl around her. She thought she heard herself scream.

"Sit down," he said cordially, from the doorway. "Don't scream. Nobody can hear you. Is your doorbell out of order?"

"How did you get in?"

He laughed. "Your door wasn't even double-locked. Move the chair over a little, away from that ridiculous weapon of yours. You have no idea, Tina, how dangerous those things are." He indicated by a wave of his own gun the direction he wanted her to move in. "Not thinking of doing away with yourself, I hope?"

She moved the chair with her foot, across the bare floor, keeping it between herself and him like a barricade, keeping the shawl tight around her. "He's not worth it," he said, lounging in the doorway. "You should know that by now, shouldn't you? Where is he, anyway? Did he tell you he was going to his mother's at seven? Did he go there?"

Six, he had told her. Drinks and dinner at Denise's at six. Home before ten. He had left at quarter of six.

Mickey Kolyrion moved out of the dark doorway of the landing into the dim room, lit only by the wall sconces and the flickering firelight and a table lamp in the corner. His shadow was thrown onto the sheet at the window as he crossed the room. "You should double lock your front door when you're alone," he said.

"What do you want?"

"To talk to you."

"What about?"

"I'm sure you imagine."

"No."

"Don't know the big news? Didn't read the *Times* today?"

They had slept late, gone back to bed after Claire's ten A.M.

[316]

feeding, slept till noon. He had read the sports and business sections. She had looked at the *Magazine*. She shook her head.

"Probably don't read the news sections on Sunday, anyway," he said. "You should have, today. Seems Jack passed a letter along to Hugh. An incriminating sort of letter. That wasn't nice of Jack. I thought we understood each other better than that."

"I don't know what you're talking about," she said faintly. Hugh, she thought. You threw me to the dogs. You did after all.

Mickey laughed. He took a clipping out of his jacket pocket and handed it to her.

She read it. "How do you know it was Jack? It doesn't say so."

"Who else could it have been?"

"It could have been anyone."

"She wrote to Jack. She mentioned she wrote to him in her diary. Hugh had the diary. Long enough to have read the last entry. Which in any case was the one he would have been most likely to read first."

"What would ever have made Hugh think it still existed?" she said. "Who keeps letters for twenty years?"

"That's right," he said. "Who does and who would have known it? And who would have told Hugh about it?"

She stared at him.

"If Jack was nice, the way I expected him to be nice, the way I've been nice to him, he would have told Hugh that letter went the way most such letters go in twenty years."

"I don't know what to say. There's a mistake." A dreadful mistake.

He laughed. "I hear you're still not married," he said. "Why don't you go back to Hugh where you belong while you still can?"

"Mickey," she said. "Don't stay here, please. There must be an explanation."

He laughed again. "Jack Troy has nearly sold you right down the river," he said. "He could have got me real pissed at you for this. But I'm going to spare you, Tina. Doing away with you would really muddy the waters." He took another paper out of his breast pocket. "Make yourself comfortable," he said. "This won't take long. And he won't be here for an hour or two. I'll be gone long before then." He sat, put his gun down on the table next to hers, both of them closer to him than to her. "I guess you don't know about Heather," he began.

She felt sick, under her shawl placed her hand on her abdomen to settle it. Her lips and mouth and throat were dry and tight.

"Do you?"

She shook her head.

"Well, I'll tell you all about them. And then after I tell you about Jack and Heather, I'll tell you something else I don't think you know. About Jack and me."

"You're revolting," she said. "Really, Mickey, you make me sick."

He laughed. "That's the idea," he said. "I want to make you good and sick. And I will. Heather's from Portland. A smart gal from Portland, Oregon. Heather Platnick. Russian extraction. I call her Plotnik. Get it?"

"No," she said.

"Heather is attractive," he said. "Late twenties, early thir-

[318]

ties, high cheekbones, Slavic type. Platnick/Plotnik. Good looking. Loose. Smart. She can do anything. And she will do anything. He met her right in his very own office. You've heard of her?"

She felt sicker and sicker. Heather, she thought. And so soon. "I don't want to know this," she said. "You've been an obscene little bully all your life." It was too bizarre to comprehend almost, to think she had known him all her life, that he had been there since her childhood like a lethal disease waiting to metastasize. In fact, that they both had been. He was right about that.

"I want you to know it," he said. "I owe Hugh something now. He'll take you back. I know he would."

"Oh, go," she said. "Get out. You're insane."

"I am sane," he said. "I didn't come here to make you mad. I came to tell you something that will make you want to go home, when you hear."

"He'll still make me testify," she said.

"Not with Jack gone. He won't make you do anything you don't want to do."

The phone on the floor beside her rang again. It was ten after eight. "Act natural," he said. He drew up close to her and put his ear so close to the receiver that she could smell his oily skin. It was Denise, calling to say that Jack had left without his umbrella and raincoat.

"Left?"

"He left forty minutes ago. He had a scene with his mother."

"With Mona?" Jack never had scenes with Mona.

"Isn't he there yet?"

"No."

"Have him call me."

"Denise?" she said, her voice a kind of gurgle in her throat.

Shut up, he said, with his elbow in her ribs.

"Is something the matter?"

"No," she said.

"Mona's crying," Denise said. "I have no idea what it's about. He's ruined the whole evening. Have him call me the minute he gets there, will you?"

"He left?" Mickey said. "At 7:30? Why isn't he here?" He got up and looked down into the street. Raul was standing under a streetlamp. Raul was supposed to stay in the car. They had waited outside for an hour and a half. Finally figured out that Jack Troy had read the news and taken off for the territory. Still, they could be wrong. And they wouldn't want to meet up with him now. Not here, with a witness around. Get back in the car, Raul. No action tonight. Not here. He picked up the phone and punched seven little squares with his forefinger. "Hello," he said.

"Hello," Heather said, from her bedroom phone.

"What's happening?"

"I have a guest. He just arrived."

It was 8:15. What had taken him so long to get there? "Right," he said.

He hung up. "There's no evidence, Tina," he said. "The diary's gone. My brother's gone. And Jack Troy is as good as gone. Go back to Hugh."

He left.

She went downstairs after him, and double-locked the front door, and propped a straight chair under the knob. Trembling, she went into the kitchen and dialed Larry Holtzman's number while she fumbled through the Manhattan directory for Platnick, Heather. Larry's line was busy, or off the hook. Heather's wasn't.

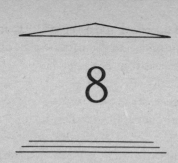

8

Drinks at six, Denise had said. Dinner at seven. In the taxi speeding up Park Avenue, Jack stared disconsolately at the dark glistening street slipping under the cab in the rain. He didn't want to be having his mother's birthday dinner at Denise's. It was a perverse mockery of the family life he wanted. His mother should be celebrating at his house. He should be married to Tina. The boys should be living under his roof. He wanted it to revolve around him, not around Denise, his family life. He wanted to have it going on around him as in all the animal kingdom and all the human kingdom it went on: male, female, and progeny, past generations, present and future, all the seven ages of man seen at once around the table, ancestors framed on the walls, silver feeding spoons and christening cups tarnishing on baize in the sideboard; the continuity felt: meaning, order, tradition, genetic pride, and the march of time as palpable as the mashed potatoes and roast beef.

From the hall between the elevator and his former front door, he could smell the beef roasting in the kitchen of his former fourteen-room apartment. Denise! he thought in a rage. First, she refused to divorce him, then she insisted on divorcing him, and now she was acting as if they'd never been divorced. He cursed aloud, and his swift flash of rage, unhabitual for him, drained the blood away from his heart, and he felt almost faint. He struck the doorbell with his fist. What a damned lot of trouble women had put him to in his life!

Somewhat to his surprise, as if she lived there, Mona answered the doorbell. But then he recalled that Mona actually did live there. Now that she and the colonel were married, her small apartment wasn't at all right for the kind of life she had in mind for their married selves. The colonel was so tall, he made her little place seem like a shoe box, she said; made her look like Alice down the rabbit hole in it, dwarfed everything. And so Denise had offered them the suite at one end of the apartment—bedroom, huge sitting room, and bath, with, as Denise laughingly put it, kitchen privileges: the cook cooked, and they ate. And Jack paid. They weren't going to stay forever, Mona had made clear. They were planning to summer in Asheville and buy a condo in Boca Raton once Mona sold her little shoe box, but Denise's place was perfect for the in-between times, when they wanted to be with the grandsons. The colonel didn't have any other grandsons. Only granddaughters.

"Darling! Come right in!" Mona said. "We've already started. Aren't we naughty?"

"Hello, Mona." He kissed her. Pretty lady, he thought wistfully. Very good perfume mingled with the aroma of very good gin. "You look . . . marvelous. Gorgeous. Love ya!"

"You, too," she said. "So handsome, lovey. So nice." She touched his face.

"Your hair. Your . . . face," he said. He stood back to survey her, as if they were lovers.

"I had a little help," she said, taking his raincoat and his umbrella.

"Oh?"

She laid a manicured finger lightly across his lips. "Shhh. In London. Just a stitch or two. Here and here." She showed him the two tiny scars above and behind her ears. "A stitch in time, . . ." she said gaily. "Mum's the word."

Mum's the word? he wondered. But who was it who didn't know? If the colonel paid. . . . But it was probably he himself who had paid, in a roundabout fashion. Denise was generous with Mona, and Denise had seen to it that he had been generous with Denise. So it was Denise who didn't know. He smiled. Vain Mona.

"Nature needs a little assist *de temps en temps.* When a girl gets to be . . . of an age."

"You're of no age," he said, and he smiled to himself again at *de temps en temps.* He had often wondered where she picked up her stock of apt little French phrases. Admiringly, he followed her through the foyer past his former dining room and into his former living room, appreciating her ash-blond hair swinging, her still-girlish figure in her soft green cashmere dress, her trim legs in the sheerest of sheer stockings, her exquisite green lizard shoes clicking over the parquet just ahead of him.

She could pass for a girl from the rear; full face for a woman of forty-five. He marveled at it. Only eighteen when he was born. He was forty-two. She was sixty. No one would mention it, of course.

In the living room, they all rose to greet him, the boys from the floor where they were playing Monopoly in front of the fire, Denise and his father from the side chairs where they waited for him to join them. He had the distinct impression that he was being led by his mother to what they all wanted him to see was the bosom of his rightful family.

He kissed Denise and shook hands with the colonel. He sat on a couch, and the boys, gangly and loose-jointed left their game to flop down on either side of him. They wanted contact with him, touched up against him, held his hands, rubbed their faces on his tweed jacket. They were almost girlishly affectionate and tender boys, loved him almost passionately. And he was filled with something like grief now, to be so near to what he once had had and had lost. Sometimes he wished, with no compunctions at all, that Denise would drop dead. Painlessly, of course. So he could have them back again under his roof.

"Well, now," said the colonel, rubbing his hands. "What will it be? We're one or two up on you, I must admit, this gloomy Sunday."

"Bourbon and water," Jack said.

"Mona, my love?"

"Another teenie-weenie for me," Mona said.

"Same for me," Denise said.

At the bar, the colonel poured the martinis into their glasses from a silver pitcher engraved with Jack's monogram. He poured Jack's bourbon, and one for himself, from a crystal decanter that had also once been Jack's to pour from. Jack felt immensely irked again.

"We were talking about you just this morning, son," the colonel said. (He blushed to call his son son, but Mona liked it, so he did it.)

Jack looked at him. The more he saw of him, the less he saw anything of himself in him. He made a nice appearance, of course. With his military bearing, he was even rather elegant, even at eighty. But it was not an appearance that rang filial chords in Jack's breast. He frowned at the colonel, as if trying to see a genetic connection between them. But there was nothing, nothing at all familiar in the tall, erect fellow who stood before him, proffering a glass. Jack took the glass from his father, whose eyebrows shot up at a unique angle, and whose chin had a prominent cleft in it, which might logically have been expected to appear in another generation, but hadn't, in his son or his grandsons.

"Jack!" Denise said sharply.

"About me?" he said, coming to.

"About the article in the *Times* this morning. Didn't you see it?"

"About me? In the *Times?*" He was occasionally quoted in the business section, sometimes mentioned as one of the (still) young Turks of Wall Street. "This morning?" He had only glanced at the business section.

"Not about you. About the murder trial. In Brewerton," Denise said. She picked up the *Times*. "Isn't Tina's husband Hugh Gardiner?"

"Ex-husband."

"Well, he's in here. It seems that someone named [she read

[326]

it out of the paper] Mickey Kolyrion killed someone named Clarice Heard in 1956 and got away with it till now. It's all here."

"What's his name?" Mona said. "Where was I this morning?"

"Did you say I was mentioned?" Jack said.

"Why would you be mentioned?" Denise said.

"You said you were talking about me."

"Just because of the connection, son," the colonel said softly.

"To Hugh Gardiner," Denise said. "Why would they mention you? It's all right here. Second section, page 47, bottom. Hugh Gardiner is running for district attorney on Tuesday. This ought to get him elected: 'Suspect Sought on Homicide Charge Twenty-one Years after Brutal Slaying.' "

But he blew it, Jack thought, in a daze. He blew it. And to get elected? A clean America would have to wait now, Larry. They would never risk meeting the freighter with murder in the air.

" 'The break in the case came,' " Denise went on reading, " 'when a note written by the deceased on the night she died came into the possession of the Brewerton law firm of Gardiner, Hollis, Cooper and King. The note establishes that Clarice Heard had arranged to meet the suspect on the evening of her death at the place where her battered body was found some days later. The case was never brought to trial, nor the suspect, Mickey Kolyrion, 43, indicted, because he was able to establish that he was elsewhere on the night in question. Further, there was no apparent motive. A diary kept by the deceased, which also recently surfaced, however, established not only a motive but also referred to the meeting arranged with the suspect on the night of her death. Soon after it was obtained, the diary disappeared from a safe in the offices of Gardiner, Hollis, Cooper and King. Mickey Kolyrion is wanted for questioning in connection with that disappearance, as well as with the slaying of his brother Frank Kolyrion last September 12.' "

Where do I go and how do I get there from here and do plastic surgeons work on Sundays and does anybody have a wig I can borrow, Jack thought. Holy Jesus, Hugh. How could you?

"Where was I?" Mona said again in a loud voice. "What's all this? Who's on trial? Mickey who? I didn't hear a thing about it."

"You were having your morning bathe, my love," the colonel said fondly. "We were quite fascinated by the story, Denise and I, weren't we, Denise? Given the connection, that is." He looked at Jack. "To the lawyer," he said.

Jack, stricken, gazed back stupidly at the colonel.

"Such a horrid tale," said Denise, shuddering. She handed the paper to Jack. He took it.

"What's their name again?" Mona demanded.

Jack looked at the article, ignoring Mona. When she drank, he had noticed before, she sometimes tended, after the second or third one, to get just a tiny bit too loud.

"What was it?" she said once more.

"Kolyrion," he said shortly.

"Oh," Mona said. "Well, well, well. Let me take a look at that." A little unsteadily she got up and walked over to Jack and peremptorily removed the paper from his hand. Mona hardly ever made peremptory movements. She was a poised, graceful person, who almost never forgot her manners. Even in his mortal panic, Jack couldn't help but notice the startled look that passed fleetingly over Denise's face when Mona swiped the paper out of his hand. He looked at the colonel to see if he had noticed any breach in Mona's decorum, but he was as oblivious to any current in the room as the boys were.

"Frank Kolyrion, forty-four, Mickey Kolyrion, forty-three," Mona murmured. "What do you know? Pigeon Kolyrion's sons."

Aviary images stirred in Jack's mind. Pigeon-breasted Pigeon Kolyrion. Butcher-bird, the shrike impaling its victim in a bramblebush. The siren he dreamed of after him. He looked at his mother. As far back as he could remember, she had never admitted to remembering anyone in Brewerton. The only person she knew in Brewerton was her own mother, and she hardly knew her, she once said. Didn't even go to her funeral.

"Would they be?" she said.

"How should we know?" Denise said loftily.

"Did you know them, Mona?" Otis said.

Mona pored over the article again.

Jack sat very still, waiting, as if for a perfectly formed thought to come and knock on the door of his boggled mind. "Why did they call him Pigeon?" he asked, his perfectly formed thought just one step away from utterance.

"He was shaped like one," she said. She gave a short laugh, like a vulgar hoot out of a dark woods.

He shivered. "Mickey Kolyrion is shaped like one, too," he said. "But his brother Frank wasn't."

"How do you know, Daddy?"

"I pulled him out of the river."

"Since when do you go around pulling bodies out of rivers?" Denise said.

"Was he dead, Dad?"

"Very."

"Well," Mona said. "One's good and dead, then, and the other's as good as dead. And good for Hugh Gardiner, I say."

Three sons, Jack thought. One dead, and two as good as.

"What did he look like?" Will said.

"Who?" Mona said.

"Pigeon?" Jack said.

"No! The dead one, Daddy!"

"Sort of like me," Jack said. "Come to think of it. Dark hair, curly, turning gray. About my height. But I couldn't see his face. The fish had eaten it."

"Oh, let's change the subject," said Denise.

"You brought it up, Mom," Otis said.

"What sort of man was he, Mona?" Jack said.

"Who?"

"Pigeon Kolyrion."

"A ladies' man," Mona said, shivering. "Quite the Romeo."

"Imagine! Knowing a murderer's father," Denise said. "Now that's America for you. Small town and all."

Small world and all, Jack thought. And out in it somewhere tonight was Mickey Kolyrion, looking for him. Hugh, how the hell could you?

"He helped himself to anything he pleased," Mona said. "As if he deserved it, just for living."

"Well, let's all have one more little drinkie," Denise said.

"And toast Hugh Gardiner. At least someone cares about justice in America."

"Why, my dear, what a perfectly brilliant idea," the colonel said, pouring a little more gin into the pitcher and stirring it vigorously.

He was always a beat late, Jack noticed, responding to the first in a series of remarks rather than to the last. But after all, he was an old, old man. Twenty years older than Mona.

"No one here wants to," said Mona, holding out her glass. "Let's talk about Christmas. Boys, what is Santa going to bring you?"

"A Trans Am," Otis said promptly.

"A Porsche," Will said.

"Electric guitars are far more likely," Denise said.

"Military miniatures make a fine gift for boys of your age," the colonel said. "They can get you started on a lifelong pursuit. Why, even on our honeymoon in England, it was our focus, wasn't it, my love? We saw all the regimental museums worth seeing. Magnificent dioramas of Julius Caesar landing in Britain, the Siege of Acre, the Charge of the Light Brigade, Waterloo, the Battle of the Somme, D day. A veritable feast. How many castles and museums did we visit, Mona, and what else did we see that was so interesting?"

Mona's eyes turned glassy. "The bookstores," she said.

"The trip of a lifetime," the colonel said joyfully. "We haunted the bookshops in London. Hunting for plates and prints and secondhand books. Literature on the miniatures of the Civil War. (Ours, of course, not theirs.) London is a gold mine of information about the subject. Why, I was even converted to the virtues of plastic in London. The details are finer. The visage, you know, can be so much more clearly delineated. A fidelity can be achieved, a fidelity that. . . ."

Jack stood. Colonel Bringhurst stopped mid-sentence and gazed at him. "Could we go to your . . . quarters for a moment, Mona?" Jack said. His voice sounded sharp, even to himself.

"My quarters!" she said. "You make me feel as if I'm back in the Army again, God forbid. And you interrupted, dear."

"It won't take long," he said.

"Now?"

"Yes."

"In the middle of cocktails?"

"Yes." He had to get it over, and get in touch with Larry, and get Tina and the baby, and get going. Checking out tonight. Won't everyone be surprised.

"Well, excuse us, Denise," she said.

"Well!" Denise said gaily. "Maybe it has something to do with what Santa might be bringing you, Mona."

Mona smiled.

"Let's go," he said. The famous Troy turn was about to be executed. In mid-life, he was going to get a new life. Larry had one all ready for him, in case anything happened. Larry couldn't have imagined Hugh in overkill would happen. "Leave your drink here," he said.

"Well, what could it be?" Mona twittered.

He followed her through the apartment to her suite, once his office-away-from-the-office. He closed the heavy door behind them. He couldn't remember the last time they had been alone together in a room.

"Okay," he said. "Be seated, Mona. And tell me all about 1934."

Mona looked faint. She reached out to hold onto the corner of his desk.

"You were seventeen, just out of high school. George Kolyrion was what . . . the same age? Older? Married? How old was he?"

"This is out of order," Mona said.

"Sit down, please," he said. "This is in order. It won't take long. I have about three questions. I want you to hurry." He pulled out his desk chair for her and sat on a swivel chair facing her. She flushed and sat.

"Why didn't he marry you?"

"I wouldn't marry him," she said haughtily. "He was beneath me."

"Beneath you? In your predicament? Were you really that proud, at seventeen?"

She pressed her lips together and nervously picked up a paperweight from his former desk. "He was already married," she said.

"Oh," he said. Marriage gives one commonplace ideas. He knew. He had even had a few himself while married. Romance, on the other hand, was so exalting. Love so splendid, vital, ennobling, enlightening. That transfiguring torment, that lacerating, searing high frenzy. He knew that well, too. And then it mysteriously dissipates. Why? She thought she loved him. She thought he loved her. He thought he loved her. And then she got pregnant. And then he got one of those commonplace ideas that marriage leads to. "Did you love him?" he said.

Her chin trembled. "Yes."

"He was? . . ." A dozen adjectives tied his tongue.

She began to cry. "Damn you," she said.

"Mona," he said.

"I couldn't help it," she said. "He wanted to stay with his wife. He had those boys."

"I know you couldn't," he said. "Don't ruin your makeup. Please. Please don't cry." He couldn't stand to see her cry.

"You're angry with me."

Why had it always been forbidden to be angry with her? "I'm not," he said. "I'm just trying to figure something out."

"What?"

"Something. Chronology. Character. Genes. Motives. Rationales. Reasons. Why people do what they do. Who I am. A lot of things. Shit! Hurry! I have a lot to do yet tonight."

"Tonight?" she said.

"Just talk," he said. "Hurry."

"I was helpless," she began. "What could I do? I knew as soon as it happened. I made the mistake of telling my mother. She sent me to Chattanooga. Just like that. I never forgave her. I detested the South. She sent me to stay with an elderly cousin of hers. Until I had it."

"It?"

"You."

"You're sure it was me?"

"I only ever had one."

"But the colonel? Where did he come in?"

"I met him no sooner than I was down there. My mother's cousin invited him for dinner and bridge. He was a relative on her husband's side. His wife was sick. I thought she might die. I took a chance on it."

"She wasn't sick enough to die?"

"No. She only had asthma. She recovered."

"And he was loyal?"

"Of course."

"And you told him the baby was his, and he believed you."

"Yes."

"Didn't your cousin? . . ."

"She didn't know about us. I never intended anyone to know about him. Or for him to know about anyone else."

"You were clever. And lucky. He supported you for thirteen years."

"And you."

"And me." He thought of the years of collusion, the deception of the colonel, of the colonel's wife, of Cousin Edna. The burden of guilt and debt laid on the colonel, the deprivations his wife had paid for without even knowing. "How much did he give you?"

"Not much. It was cheap as dirt to live in the South then."

"It was all relative. It was the Depression. He had three children of his own."

"He never dreamed you weren't his own. And he never grudged what he gave me. He sent it faithfully every month. He wanted nothing in return. I never saw him again. Besides," she said, "after a year, I worked."

"I don't remember."

"I was a doctor's receptionist. I made four dollars a week. He gave me two. It was plenty." She almost laughed.

"Where did we live?" (What did you do with me when you went to work? was what he meant. It wasn't relevant, perhaps, and there wasn't time. But a picture of a house was stuck in his mind's eye, had been all his life, and an image of himself at three or four standing in a room between two other rooms. A woman was standing in the door to the kitchen. Another woman was standing in the door to the parlor. He was in between. To survive, he must somehow have known, even then, he had to elude them both.)

She looked exasperated. "I moved a lot," she said. "You lived with Cousin Edna."

He had known that so well he had forgotten it, the way you sometimes forgot you were ever a child.

"He's a good man, Jack," she said. "I hope you don't tell him and ruin everything."

"A bit dense though, isn't he? Porch light out?"

"Don't be rude," she said. "And please don't disillusion him. Nothing could be gained. And so much lost."

"Morality as a profit-and-loss statement."

"It has nothing to do with morality," she said.

"Everything does," he said. "Except the weather."

"I'm not the first woman to have to tell a lie to live."

"You used a man."

"How many ways do you think there were for a woman to survive in 1934?"

"Oh, it's not that," he said, trying to identify for himself what in fact it really was, why he felt so empty and flat and dull. "It's not that at all. I don't blame you for that. I don't imagine there were many ways at all."

"What is it you blame me for?"

He searched his mind for the exact thing. Putting herself first. "A certain . . . disregard . . . I think I would call it," he said slowly. "The way you've simply . . . disregarded so many of us for so many years. Your mother. Him. His wife. Me. Denise. The boys, even. Had it all your way. Like Pigeon. You took what you wanted. Supplied your own grandsons with a phony grandfather. A sort of class-act hoodwinking. Quite impressive. But I do hold it against you. A lack of . . . grit. You know? As if no one counted but you?"

"Hoodwinking?" she said. "That's a nice word to use for your mother. And who's had more grit than I've had, all these years on my own?"

"Mother," he repeated after her. "The funny thing is, I've been trying and trying lately. But I can't seem to remember your. . . ."

"My what?"

"Your. . . ."

"Being there?"

"Yes."

"Being there wasn't one of my talents," she said. "Cousin Edna liked being there. I let her have you until you were ready for school."

They stood looking at each other for a long while in the quiet room. "Did you hate me?"

"I resented you," she said. "I was eighteen. Why should my life be ruined?"

"Cousin Edna didn't like me," he said. "She was always washing me." She made him take a nap every afternoon, and she made him go to bed at night at seven o'clock, even when the sun was shining.

"Cousin Edna was old and very strict," she said. "She died when you were about six. You came to live with me. The colonel sent us more money after that. Every month a money order would come. He was as generous as he could be, he assured me. And I believed him."

There was a knock on the study door. "Dinner, Dad," Will said. Jack looked at his watch. He had to call Larry. Get his new physiognomy. A moustache? Glasses? Blackface? Moles? Buckteeth and a big nose?

"When he left Chattanooga, he gave me those lead soldiers for you," she said. "I saved them for you, until you were old enough to appreciate them."

He nodded.

"I hope they're worth something. I could have kept them for myself, but I didn't. He said they'd be worth something someday."

"I've not looked into it," he said vaguely. "In a long while."

"You should. Because, I'm sorry, Jack. I owe you something. I do owe you."

"Oh," he said. "Don't worry about it." He almost laughed to think of it now. "Lots of other women have paid for it. You don't owe me a thing."

"You're disappointed in me, aren't you?"

He looked at her. "No."

"Angry?"

"I guess, maybe."

"Dinner's ready, Dad," Will said again, through the door.

"Don't be," she said.

"I'll get over it," he said. "But I have to go now. I have so much to do."

"Go?"

"I just want to . . . go," he said. "I have to make a call first." He felt anxious and uneasy. Where should he go? He dialed Larry's number from the phone on the desk. No answer.

He looked at his watch. 7:25. He would go to 11th Street. Get Tina and Claire and the car and go. Ask questions later. Plan the itinerary en route. "You don't happen to have a wig around the house, do you?"

"A wig! What *are* you talking about? Where are you going? Don't go, Jack. You'll ruin everything."

"Well, it won't be the first time," he said.

"Don't start feeling sorry for yourself."

"I'm not sorry for myself." He was sorry for Tina, mostly. "I think I'm ready," he said.

"Ready for what?"

He laughed. "Good-bye. Mother."

"For Denise, stay."

"For Denise?" He laughed again. "Poor Denise," he said. "She's stuck with you, isn't she? Stuck with you and the colonel and the whole sorry swindle."

"There's no need to be rude."

"I regret."

"You won't stay?"

"No."

"You're being a very poor sport," she said. "What *about* . . . Harrison?"

"Harrison? Oh, I'll play along," he said. "So he's a pinch hitter. What difference does it make now?"

"That's right," she said. "In the long run, every life has to be of its own making."

"You're right, Mona," he said. "You certainly are right about that."

He opened the door. Down the hall, Denise and the colonel stood, waiting nervously.

"I have to go," he said. He shook hands with the colonel and kissed Denise. "I have to go home."

"Home?" Denise said.

"I'll see you boys," he said, hugging them. "But not next weekend. I'll be in touch. Don't worry about me." It was like hugging brand-new children, the grandchildren of George Ko-lyrion. He would tell them himself someday. Take them there, even. If he lived. "I'm sorry about all this," he said. "I'm really sorry." He fled.

"He forgot his raincoat and his umbrella," Mona said, weeping.

"Home!" Denise said. "This is his home."

9

Down on the street, he checked his watch again under a street-lamp. It was half-past seven. He headed west through the driz-zle, looking for a cab. Madison Avenue was deserted. He turned east on 78th Street, toward Park, and hailed a lone cab heading downtown. He had to get Tina. Get Larry on the phone, and get out of town. Some sweet revenge, he thought. In a fright wig in lower Montana. Circling the drain over a childhood taunt and a dead dog.

She had visited him on the farm from time to time, always arriving unannounced in one car or another, with one gentle-man or another at the wheel. He remembered her thin dresses and her perfume and her red fingernails. Cousin Edna always left them alone together, which he wished she wouldn't do, because he was shy with her, very shy in front of her gentlemen friends. She called him Little Boy, as if she couldn't remember what his name was. When Cousin Edna died, he went to live with her in the city. She let him stay up as late as he liked. And they moved a lot. They moved every year or two. She taught him how to play cards, and when he was ten, she gave him the lead soldiers for Christmas. And she said, there was a big war once. The Civil War. I'm sure you've studied it. These little soldiers with the gray suits were on the side that lost. If you ever get in a war, make sure you're on the side that wins. And there are lots of different kinds of wars, Little Boy, she said, lifting his face, with one warm finger under his chin, to her beautiful face. Winning them is what you want to do. Understand?

The cab turned west on 14th Street. She would be waiting for him in the drafty, badly lit, unfurnished, unfinished house. Claire would be breathing peacefully in her crib, sucking her thumb, already callused and only seven weeks old. And the lead soldiers would be on the shelves in the hall, where he had set them up when they moved in.

He would give them away now, perhaps. Give them to Otis and Will, be done with the long-drawn-out resistance they must have meant to him. Done with his little wars. History was a matter of fact, not perspective or interpretation. The fact was: he was a northerner by parentage. His southern history had been given to him with one stroke of Mona's imagination, and abolished with one stroke of his own. What a waste, he thought, boxing with her shadow all these years without even knowing it. He felt a flash of anger again, like the one outside of Denise's apartment, waiting for the door to open. He had been getting them lately. Things dawning on him, perhaps. Very, very slowly. Getting brown around the edges. Finally. I *am* ready, he thought. To be angry with Mona. Only, somehow, it wasn't even going to be worth the trouble. There were too many other things to start to learn how to do.

He knocked on the plastic partition and told the driver to go south of Washington Square and across the Village on West 4th. He wanted to survey his block from the safety of the cab before getting out. If they weren't looking for him already, they would be before the night was out.

At the corner of West 4th and Perry he saw the Cadillac, Raul standing beside it in the light rain, smoking a cigar. He signaled to the driver to keep going on down the block. The cabby turned around to look at him, his foot on the brake. A red light two blocks ahead. "Just keep going," he said harshly, through the thick plastic. "Turn right at the light. For God's sake, *move.*" The cabby shrugged and drove on.

He shrank back into the shadows of the back seat. Raul, on the corner, was looking up at the front windows of the house on 11th Street, and in the windows on the parlor floor the shadow of a man fell on the sheet that was drawn across the windows.

Up 8th Avenue, near the Garden, he told the cabby to wait. He got out to call Larry from a bar. Still not answering. Where was he? Where should he go? He thought of Heather. He dialed her number. "I need a place to stay tonight," he said.

"I'm a good place," she said.

She was all in black, her long dark hair silky and shiny under the foyer light.

"Come into my parlor." She stood aside. He smelled her

perfume, heavy and pungent, put on fresh for him, followed her.

"Don't you have a coat?"

"I left it somewhere. Is your friend coming tonight?"

"He's not my friend any more."

"Good," he said. "I'll be your friend."

She smiled.

Beyond, in her bedroom, the phone rang. He looked at his watch. It was 8:10. He followed her again, stood in the doorway of her room. Safe for a night.

"I have a visitor," he heard her say in her silky, smoky voice. "He's just arrived."

She hung up the phone and sat for a moment on the edge of the bed. Then she stood and turned toward him.

She hadn't realized he was standing there, and her face, he saw right away, had been curiously altered by some knowledge she had received that he did not have. He's just arrived. A coincidence? he thought, in the doorway.

And then, as if by some telepathic communication, her knowledge imparted itself to him in a vivid mental picture of Mickey Kolyrion standing in the living room of the house on 11th Street, replacing the white phone in its cradle.

She walked toward him, smiling, her arms open to enfold him. "Now tell me all your troubles," she said. "Auntie Heather is here to listen."

Smothering unfreedom swept over him. He backed away from her. They had seen her in his office. Contacted her. (Who is that nerdlike fellow who visits you in your office?) "I have to go," he heard himself say, as if from another body. A slight hearing impairment from an old viral infection in his right ear seemed to have transmitted itself to his left.

"Go?" she mouthed.

"I have to," he heard himself say.

"You're wise then," she said. Or that's wise. He wasn't sure which.

"What?" he said.

"Wise?" she said.

To you. Bought and paid for.

"Where are you going?"

He shook his head. Somewhere far and safe.

"Use the service elevator," she said.

She led him through the apartment to the kitchen. "Short and not very sweet," she said.

"Next time," he said.

He rang for the service elevator.

She closed the door and locked it. He heard her slip the chain into place. Inside the apartment, he could hear the phone ringing again.

He ran down the fire stairs instead of waiting for the elevator and out the service door into an alleyway in back of the building. On Lexington, he caught a cab and went back downtown, because he couldn't think of where else to go. Ride around all night. Make calls from pay phones until he found out what he should do. Go to a hotel? As he reached the outskirts of the Village, he heard police sirens. Where the hell was Larry?

He couldn't go home. Even going in the back way, through his neighbor's iron gate, over the brick wall, in through the sliding glass kitchen doors. Even getting her antique revolver out of the straw basket on top of the refrigerator and surprising him, even armed he wasn't meant for it. She was right again. He wasn't meant for it.

Go, he thought, panicked.

Time to, now.

He gave the driver the address of the garage where he kept his car.

They would have to fend for themselves, Tina and Claire. He had done all he could. Done enough. Had to take care of himself once again. Keep on truckin', Jack. Through the Holland Tunnel to somewhere else.

To Washington, he thought. Find, somewhere inside one of the colonnaded, pedimented buildings where justice was done, Larry Holtzman's friends, who would tell him what to do, where to go until he was safe.

That's where Larry was all day, he knew suddenly. In Washington, fixing Hugh's screw-up. Or maybe in Brewerton, arranging for the D.A.'s office to retract the story. No evidence. Clarice's note mysteriously purloined. MK free and clear. So East Hampton could proceed. MK wouldn't dream he'd screw him in two places at once.

Around the corner, in front of his neighbor's house, the cab stopped for another light. It wasn't too late. He could still get out, climb the fence, make his way through the garden. No one was at home in his neighbor's house: dark except for the front porch light and a hall light inside.

Inside, the dog, a German shepherd, started up a low, furious bark.

He imagined setting his foot into the dense hedge of privet backing the iron fence, the brittle branches cracking and crashing under his weight as he tried to get a foothold on the horizontal bar of the fence. When his hands reached the iron finials, he would pull himself up, and the dog would go mad in the house, leaping and snarling at the windows like Cerberus guarding the gates of Hell itself.

He felt dizzy.

He imagined his foot finding the top horizontal, and then his other foot finding it, waffling unsteadily six feet in the air for a second, then jumping. His jacket, perhaps, would catch on the iron finial and rip. Six feet and a second later he would hit the wet ground, clearing the privet. He would pick himself up and run toward the brick wall at the back of the garden, which was also the side wall of his own garden, the invisible dog racing the length of the house alongside him, barking and snarling, his nails clicking over the bare floors.

His stomach churned.

The top floor of his own house would be dark. In Claire's room, on the third floor, a pale glimmer of reflected light would shine, as through a door left ajar, and on the parlor floor a streak of light would shine dimly through the blankets rigged up on the dining room windows to keep out the drafts. The ground floor would be dark. The iron rod would be thrown in place across the glass doors.

He would therefore have to carry a metal yard chair over to the scaffolding and climb up onto it and up the back of the house on the slippery wet planks and iron pipes to the parlor floor.

She would hear him call her name, come into view in the archway between parlor and dining room, listening, to be sure.

He would want to step down into the room through the window, put his arms around her, close a break in a circle with her, consolidate for good. But she would stand where she was,

[347]

her arms at her side, as if she had washed her hands of him one last time. Mickey had been there. He would have told her what he may always have known: A corresponding strain, she would have been told, a blood connection explaining finally all manner of screwings he was capable of. Shrikes of a feather.

The cab moved ahead.

In his own car, he drove through the dark, deserted streets of lower Manhattan, past warehouses and lofts and meat-packing houses to the tunnel. He drove cautiously, but steadily, through red lights. Carefully and surely. Going was the best thing he could do. In front of him through the wet windshield, the huge green exact-change signs loomed.

On the New Jersey side of the tunnel, he looked for the Statue of Liberty and made her out through the rain, majestic and eternal, off to his left in the harbor, her scale humanized by her distance from him.

She was rusting out, he had read. Twenty-five million to fix her up. But it was worth every penny. Every penny, Liberty.

Angela, he remembered, on the turnpike. Angela lived in Washington. He would call her. Stay with her for a night.

He phoned her from an Amoco station. "This is Jack Troy," he said. He hadn't talked to Angela in years.

"Jack Troy!" she cried, in her rich, playful voice. "On his way to see Angela, isn't he?"

But how did she know? How did Angela know he was on his way to see her?

Again he felt the smothery panic of unfreedom, got the psychic message, a network of pursuers out there, someone, maybe many, watching him, reporting his every move to every possible link in his chain of survival. "No," he said. "No, just calling to say hello, Angela. Good-bye, Angela."

He hung up and rushed across the brightly lit pump area to his car on the dark edge of the station. He drove on into the night.

Much later, somewhere off the turnpike, somewhere way off the beaten track, far out in the Maryland hills, somewhere where no one could possibly know where he was, he found a small, obscure motel, The Elk, and he went to bed and slept soundly.

Toward morning, he dreamed a wonderful dream of moving on beyond the hills where he slept, through the Cumberland Gap near the point where Kentucky and Virginia meet Tennessee.

In the dream, beyond the Gap, scene of many Civil War battles, he traveled to a great open plain, flat and perfectly unencumbered with hills or other obstacles. And upon this vast, seemingly endless plain, laid out in satisfying versimilitude of Lee's successful campaign at Bull Run, he discovered his own collection of military miniatures. He smiled in his dream, and beside them on the plain, on his side he lay to play with them, like a giant happy boy.

This dream was so satisfying that when he woke from it during the night, nearer dawn than midnight, he woke faintly smiling, refreshed and even contented. Safe and free, he thought. Safe and free.

He had an almost overwhelming urge to verify this, to get up and touch his reflection in a mirror. Instead, he lay where he was, listening to the rain falling fast, knowing when he fully woke that he wasn't either free or safe.

After a while, he dialed her number.

On 11th Street, too, the rain was falling fast, lashing against the windows, rinsing over the new roof and along the new gutters and down the copper leaders like spring torrents down a mountain.

She had moved Claire's crib into her room and had lain wide awake all night. She felt alert and attentive, yet not waiting as if for a calamity. She felt serene and decisive, free from calamity, and safe, after a long time.

By the streetlight coming through the curtainless windows, she could make out as the morning began to break the carved medallion in the center of the ceiling, a rosette repeated like a benediction on the foreheads of the caryatids guarding the four corners of the room.

Beside her, the phone began to ring. She picked it up.

She understood, she said, but she had to explain something, too.

He understood, he said, after he had heard her.

Gently, they replaced the receivers. He lay down again on the bed. He closed his eyes.

Outside, in the dawn, something had begun to go against the flow.